Praise for *Cities of Refuge*

"Standout . . . [*Cities of Refuge*] is a powerful depiction of the struggle to overcome adversity."

—*PUBLISHERS WEEKLY*, Starred Review

"[*Cities of Refuge*] is ambitious; a prototypical big book with deft touches of metafiction. The writing is marvelous, the omniscient narrator almost too wise . . . Helm's novel is sure to both delight and provoke."

—*BOOKLIST*

"Provocative, political and astonishingly well-written."

—*SHELF AWARENESS*

"*Cities of Refuge* has a Faulknerian commitment to diverse perspectives . . . think of *Cities of Refuge* as the Toronto cousin of contemporary New York novels by and about immigrants such as Colum McCann's *Let the Great World Spin*, Joseph O'Neill's *Netherland*, or Teju Cole's *Open City*. Welcome to our shores, Michael Helm, and apologies for the delay."

—*THE DAILY BEAST*

"A powerful and intricate novel about political guilt in contemporary times, intellectually astute and with crystalline writing. The book weaves together the clashes of culture, alongside that of a father and a daughter, to make large issues intimate and in the end heartbreaking."

—MICHAEL ONDAATJE

"*Cities of Refuge* is an unsettling and powerful novel that beautifully engages the complexities of memory, trauma, and history."

—DANA SPIOTTA

"The profound empathy with which Michael Helm imagines his characters into multidimensional life is only one of his many, great gifts. As *Cities of Refuge* demonstrates, he is also a spectacularly good storyteller and prose stylist with a range and nerve that set him apart from almost every other writer of his generation."

—BARBARA GOWDY, author of *Helpless*

"Michael Helm delivers us to the rarified and unsettling regions of the heart and mind, with winning results: he is a capable navigator, a superb craftsman, and *Cities of Refuge* is a humane and harrowing novel."

—PATRICK DEWITT, author of *The Sisters Brothers*

AFTER JAMES

Published by Tin House Books, Portland, Oregon and Brooklyn, New York

Distributed by W. W. Norton and Company.

Library of Congress Cataloging-in-Publication Data
Names: Helm, Michael, 1961- author.
Title: After James / by Michael Helm.
Description: First U.S. edition. | Portland, OR : Tin House Books, 2016.
Identifiers: LCCN 2016006738 (print) | LCCN 2016010391 (ebook) | ISBN
    9781941040416 (softcover : acid-free paper) | ISBN 9781941040423
Subjects: | GSAFD: Science fiction. | Mystery fiction. | Dystopias.
Classification: LCC PR9199.3.H44495 A69 2016 (print) | LCC
PR9199.3.H44495
    (ebook) | DDC 813/.54--dc23
LC record available at http://lccn.loc.gov/2016006738

First US edition 2016
Printed in the USA
Interior design by Diane Chonette
www.tinhouse.com

W. S. Merwin, excerpt from "The Dreamers" from *Migration: New and Selected Poems*. Copyright © 1973 by W. S. Merwin. Reprinted with the permission of The Permissions 40Company, Inc., on behalf of Copper Canyon Press, www.coppercanyonpress.org.

AFTER JAMES

MICHAEL HELM

 TIN HOUSE BOOKS / Portland, Oregon & Brooklyn, New York

For Alex

PART I

Alice After James

WHEN THE SUN BREACHED THE HILL THAT MORNING IT caught for the first time since October the narrow edge of the streambed exposed by a break in the trees. By midmorning the haze had burned off and the light made lenses in the ice that melted themselves beneath the surface. The stream began moving and as the thaw took hold in the leaves clotted on the bank and the mud farther along, the water ran into the shade of birch and maples and coaxed snow into motion as, unexampled in memory, the late-winter warmth became a baking heat all in a day, effecting weeks of return in just hours.

The dog kept to the bed, where the vapors were strongest, crazed into the firstness of things. He had come a long way and had organized the scents as they recurred along the route until a new one came on the air and he found himself moving into the leaves. He was at the source and digging before he understood that the form set into the ground was human. The discovery confused him and he backed off the shape and barked and continued barking until the smell sent him forward again in a wonderment half-full of forgetting, and when he followed up from the human hand along the arm and then uncovered the muddy head, the discovery was new again and he ran up out of the trees and stopped and circled back down, then came up a second time and a third. At some point he lowered onto his belly and looked for a long while in the direction of the humanform until a shortened whimper escaped him, the sound sending him to his feet barking again, hearing the strangeness of his sounding in the air of this new place. Again he took the route down the bank and up, barking the whole time, and he stood high now and was about to go back down when the shot tore through him and sent him over the bank and into the creekbed as if even dead he could regard the humanform yet again and again find it a great mystery uncovered but not dispelled.

That night the dog's body burned along with that of the human he'd found, and then burned again until its ashes were general with all else on the wind. They lifted on the heat and floated out under stars and over the country thawed and returning with a force beyond that of any since people first appeared. They drifted over the creek now run to a river, and a river run into the broken fields and roads and up into the lower slopes of hills, disturbing even the wet, heavy soil there and exposing shards of pottery and bone that hadn't breathed in centuries and were now carried by water to greater waters and replaced into other muds with other sediments over them. The ashes fell thinly on the currents in grayblack flakes without distinction, and the knowing that was the dog moved there too, running inland to the heart of the wild returned from its dream to its last waking.

1

SHE WOKE TO SOME NEW SLANT OF LIGHT. AT THE WINDOW she stood barefoot before her uncertain reflection, white pajama bottoms, red T-shirt. These woods she pretended to be hers were already transforming, with changes to follow in the ash and beech trees, the maples along the creek, the light fixed harder in the runneled bark of the black cherry and silvers in the sumacs on the hill. This was once the Carolinian zone, a fossilized designation. There were now wasps in the high arctic, a place with no native word for them.

The temperature had nosed above freezing at 7:33 and she thought, thirty-three Fahrenheit in the seventh day of my residency, still making links with numbers.

Crooner stood in profile at the door, looking at her sidelong, unwilling to ask directly. She let him out and he made it five feet before peeing, then put his nose down and followed it off through the heavy snow. There was some mistake in the grand design ever to have worked up creatures more complicated than dogs.

She went about her morning. Putting on her jeans and old running shoes, building the fire, bringing in more wood from the side of the house. Bread and tea while staring out the glass back wall, the light really was different today. Yesterday afternoon from this chair she'd seen a red fox trotting through the snow on the hill across the ravine and he had seemed to disappear in the depths of it but then emerged in stride a few feet along and she knew she had just lost him in the flat light. This morning she could see every contour, every drift, even in places the trace of his passage on the white.

She went back outside and dipped the bamboo pole into the cistern and drew it up. She'd need a water delivery in two or three days. She stocked the feeders and then stood at ten paces in the dying cold and waited for the first bird to light. It was often a finch or junco, then cardinals. There were still a few whose names she didn't know. Soon she'd give in to curiosity and consult her field guide but she liked the ones unknown to her. There were thousands of unknown creatures in the oceans. It was possible at a certain pitch of consciousness to feel the weight of these beings in the nightly draw of the earth through space. The force was likely exerted both ways, so that somewhere on the planet was an alien mind feeling her existence. Was it a bird? She didn't think so.

No birds yet this morning. There was something new on the air.

It was all new every day. That was the idea. She was off the map, somewhere north of Georgia, south of the Canadian Shield. She thought, three hard snows in the first week and good luck finding me through weather systems. She thought, don't even try.

There was real heat in the light now. The day was up.

The couple who owned this place, Stefan and Denise, the Dahls, had left post-it notes for her all around the house. Stefan's tended to be in the furnace room or fuse box—"don't run the dryer at the same time as the electric heater"—and were unsigned. Denise's showed up in unlikely places. The utensils drawer ("this tips, be careful D"), tucked into the linen stack ("these look the same but arent so dont bother trying to match D"), on the radio ("this dial isnt accurate, too low D"). She'd labeled the spices in the rack, as if her city-woman tenant wouldn't know them. Denise knew more or less nothing about her, they'd not even spoken by phone. One midmorning three weeks ago the Dahls posted their home with two pictures, and a half continent to the west Ali got out of bed, checked the new listings, and called them. Stefan answered. The arrangements were made within minutes. She directed him to her online bio at the Gilshey site but he asked no questions. She told him how she'd pay, when she'd arrive, that she had a car and a dog. He didn't even ask about the dog. They'd signed on for a year of mission work, the Dahls, and flew off to French West Africa two days before she drove down the long gravel driveway and emerged for a first live look at her hideaway. It was low, set into a small depression, against high maples. She looked right through it, through the front windows to the back ones, with the trees beyond interrupted briefly by the roofline. She saw the ravine behind the house and the hill rising up the other side of it. The arresting effect of seeing through obstruction held her for a time until Crooner shot across her field of vision and set her back into motion. As described, the key was under the T formed by two cherry logs beside the woodpile. Then she opened the door and was home.

This morning's note turned up in the phone book. The Dahls had dog-eared several yellow pages and circled listings. On the page for the water service, in the familiar hand, the note read, "look in the flour jar. important. D." The ceramic jar marked "flour" was empty but for a folded plastic sandwich bag with something inside it like a bundle of vanilla beans. She held the bag up and saw a key drive. It was all wrong, not just the drive in the bag and the bag in the jar, not just that it had obviously been hidden for her, but that the distance between the Dahls and her had been compromised. She could choose not to open the drive but that would involve pretending to ignore it. The thing was now a presence in her day and she would have to accept it before she could fold it away.

At the desk she set it down on the papers beside her laptop. Every passing day promised a future further removed from human meaning. She had been putting off the thought of consequences, of what happened when a person loaded her dog into a car and drove thousands of miles away from her life. You could put off almost anything, it turned out, with chores and long walks and new kinds of findings, the blue shades of snow in deep woods, the patterns of burn marks on lightning-split trees. Two mornings ago she'd come across a kill site covered in deer fur, and eighty feet away by a stream, the carcass. Spine and pelvis, the legs gnawed white to a few inches from the hooves, the pelt piled beside, and coyote prints all around. Her being there in the aftermath did not feel like an intrusion.

She'd had a week to settle, to prepare herself. Now it was time to see who she might be.

An open letter. She would send it to a whistleblower site.

She wrote that until days ago she worked at a branch of an unnamed pharmaceutical company in Vancouver. For years the goal had been a memory aid, but an unintended breakthrough led to work on a wholly new designer drug. She wrote about DNA molecules and the data won from an in-house brain booster whose market name she didn't use, but then worried she was being too technical and apologized and said it would all be there in the attachment for those who cared. But the idea, the way to think of it, this drug, was as a narcotic-free neuroenhancer of generative and lateral thought. A creativity pill.

She left the pharms race off the record, the millions in research failures, all trails cold, hypotheses busted. What mattered was much bigger. She was not a creative person herself but, and she almost skipped this part too, one cold November Monday in the lab, she'd been sitting at her station with a cup of green tea having gone straight to her bladder, when it came to her. She pictured a green, lucent fish, like a large *S* from an illuminated manuscript, swimming in an underground river. For a long time she just watched it, her eyes closed, until finally the dark river was the bloodstream. The fish-letter was a mystery, a certain long-tailed molecule not yet discovered, but she saw its chemical integrity and then remembered the colored synteny graph she'd seen weeks ago that depicted the genetic evolution of a virus. The graph had begun to appear in her thoughts and on the walls of her dreams, like a grid painting with fine, curving lines running through it. From the lines she could imagine and so begin to create the fish-letter.

It wouldn't have revealed itself to her, she decided not to write, if she hadn't had to pee, without that slight urgency, which had some-how also triggered the intuition that Carl, team leader for Neuropharmaceutical Research, was sleeping with her research assistant, whom he privately liked to refer to by her salary as "your low-midlevel Joannie." Ali herself had no romantic investments in the lab or outside of it, but the change in the air, Carl's sudden soft-eyed deference to a twenty-four-year-old, effected a kind of pole reversal that opened possibilities in her thoughts. Before the day ended she'd worked through the graphs of chemical compounds and the data on delivery systems and then mocked up a substance that over the weeks in the preclinical stage looked promising in toxicity measures and pharmacokinetic behavior. In time it took form as a rectangular yellow pill with beveled edges. She didn't include the company's name for the drug—Claritas .4—it would identify Gilshey (it would all come out in time, of course), and anyway it was the wrong name. The name that came to her was Alph. She designed the drug. It should have the name she gave it.

Five weeks ago she was sitting in her car, having pulled over to watch dozens of skaters on a great sunken pond, a scene out of Bruegel, when Carl called her cellphone. She hadn't answered his calls for days but something in the moment, the sheer joyfulness of the scene, seemed reliable as a counter to whatever he might say. But they let her down, that scene, those skaters. She should have been picturing the clinical trial test subjects. They were mostly students, self-described artists, screenplay writers, animators, a poet. All but one loved Alph (the love was not entered into the data), composing work faster and, in their view (not entered), better than they ever had, despite the limiting factors imposed by the controlled conditions of the early trials. Most subjects reported nothing that wouldn't pass oversight approval. Almost three-quarters of volunteers reported a "jump cut" feeling of having lost two or three seconds of time during composition. Many reported a sense of lucid dreaming while awake. The feeling was of some other agent authoring a part of their experience, their sense of self-command undermined by changing contexts, parallel realities. One described finishing his lab session, going to play tennis, and in the middle of a long rally seeing himself in a staged sword fight against dozens of foes, as if in an old swashbuckler movie. In the lab they called this the Daffy effect, in reference to the *Looney Tunes* segment in which Daffy and his world are repeatedly redrawn by the animator midstory.

It turned out that the Daffy effect could also be brought on without Alph, if your professional mission was betrayed. Emotional hurt erased any distinction between the objective and subjective. Her apartment, her miso soup, the very sound of her own voice, all were made strange. The person who had strung together the days, weeks, and years was suddenly exposed to an impossible truth, that she'd been misperceiving her world all along, and this truth, as far as it had been uncovered, meant she didn't really know herself.

The betrayal was Carl's. "You're on speakerphone, Ali." She watched a girl in black tights and white mittens cutting figures in the ice. "I'm here with Kalif Keady." Kalif was one of the company's lawyers. He explained her position and ended the call. Her position, simply put, was that she had to keep her mouth shut, whether she stayed with Gilshey or not. The company was supporting Carl's decision not to enter one other side effect into the data. He argued it didn't exist. She knew it did and, there in her house in the woods, put it down in words. A few weeks after the trial ended, Subject 11, the poet, who by all evidence came into the trial a well-adjusted, talented young man full of level enthusiasms, jumped off the Lions Gate Bridge. In the suicide note he sent to the qualified investigator who oversaw the trial, he described himself as newly awake. In full control. He said he was making a choice. Since beginning the trial he had been presented a kind of knowledge, "'a showing forth,' is what my grandma used to call it," he wrote. He said the drug had "torn the fabric of what we're wrong to call reality" and revealed something beyond that there were no words for, though he felt ever closer to finding the words the longer he stayed in the trial. After his first doses of Alph he'd begun to imagine the drug's maker, and to speculate about her and praise her in poems and prose he sent to the QI. They switched him off of the drug and gave him a placebo. The loss killed him.

Ali wrote it through, the events in order, conversations as she recalled them. She quoted Carl from the day when it seemed they'd made a breakthrough, "There's nothing that can't be imagined, nothing imagined that can't now be made real. What we're design-ing is an engine to accelerate the real." "In the end," Ali wrote, "the real accelerated toward Subject 11, rushing up in a sudden assertion, as is its nature."

She placed a call to the water service. There was no answer, no option to leave a message. It was past noon. In the front room, Crooner's bed. She opened the door and there, somehow, was another season, sun hot. She got into her boots and walked behind the house against a warm wind. At the bottom of the ravine a stream had formed and seemed to be gaining strength even as she watched it, a slurry of icy water and through-force. She walked clear around the house, looking for Crooner or his tracks, but the old tracks that had marked their passages of days ago had already melted, and when she came back around she saw that his prints from this morning had disappeared in the melt. She called his name. Every day she'd let him roam and he was sometimes gone for an hour or so. The snow tired him out, kept him from running too far, and covered the sorts of things that might get him in trouble—irresistible scents, decay. She headed up the approach and around the bend to the wetblack road. The ditches were filling with runoff. She called him again.

There was no sign of him or of anything. For a minute or more she looked out at the sky where it rose in the west above the road. The clouds were lined with white shelves foreshortened by a blackness massing above them. She saw far off a car coming her way, and heard it. As it took shape it became an SUV and it was really flying. She took two steps farther off the road and the SUV shot past and the driver, a woman in a headscarf, about her age, she guessed, turned and looked at Ali for a static moment with a face, though of a stranger, still somehow not itself.

She came down the road and set off to the east across the field where they walked at night. Crooner left trenches in the deeper snow in open fields, but now there were no trenches. He must have gone into the forest or down into the ravine. She veered left and passed into the turning woods where the light was weaker and moved along the edge of the creekbank where the snow thinned. Streams of melting water ran down the steepest falls. She called his name, stopped walking and listened, heard the water, called again. She kept walking and the place, now changing before her, was strange twice over. Her tracks were already dying into the general thaw, and she'd have to stay to the creek to find her way back. She walked at an angle out into the field to look for his passage but didn't find it, and turned and continued along the edge of the ravine.

Just past the point where she told herself to turn back she discovered a print, a single, canine step. But was it of coyote or Lab-shepherd cross? How could she not recognize her own dog's track? She squatted. Up close the shape was a little too large, maybe. How could it have kept its neat integrity in such a rapid melt? It would have to be fresh but she had seen nothing, and Crooner would have come if he'd heard her call. Then, ahead, she saw a clump of snow fall from a branch and form a crater pattern. She looked up and saw above her a branch, a break in the ridge of snow it held. The print was false, she decided, an accident, a trick of the brain's tendency to mistake nothing for something, related to the life-saving, god-imagining instinct called "agent detection." We mistake rocks for bears, but never bears for rocks. Returning to the house with the shadows angled differently she passed dozens of small, soft, doubtful depressions. Tracks or not, he must have come through here, she reasoned, and so he could find his way back by following the bank.

Just as she made it to the door she thought she heard something, a distant barking maybe, but the wind covered it. She waited to hear it again but there was nothing. She called for him once more, waited, and went inside.

In the study she opened the window a few inches and for the first time in her stay a warm wind gained the house. She was approaching the desk when she heard something else, like a great branch snapping far away. She listened. It was a wind of phantom sounds, as if the limb had broken years ago.

She had just been getting used to the place and its perfect winter solitude and now it was changing. Stefan had left a list of duties for each season—the spring ones ran for three tight pages—and she was likely to stay through the spring, maybe summer. She had committed to three months but could extend it to six. She would have to solve problems on her own, Stefan said, because he'd be out of reach, but if she wanted to stay longer she was simply to send another three months' rent electronically to their account and they'd get the message. The simple arrangement suited her needs, and she liked the thought of them, the Dahls and herself, at work on their respective missions.

On the desk were colored scans of the voxel-based morphometry and printouts of the test subjects' written statements. One believed that she could suddenly make connections she was not in the habit of making. Everything was more vivid. Prose seemed musical. Subtext showed through text. It became easy to distinguish the good from the less so, the great from the merely excellent. One wrote, "It's like I've been cured of a vision deficit." These were not false certainties. The subjects were not simply high and happy. Their feelings of well-being came not directly from Alph, but from the world to which their capacities were opened and they knew they'd be returning. When the drug wore off they lost their eye but retained the new love, as if joy and beauty existed apart from the person who felt it, apart from the physical brain.

She'd devoted her life to brains and compounds, delivery systems. For some time—a half hour? more?—she studied the scans until she sort of didn't see them, until they formed abstractions and she felt close to recovering the half knowing she'd felt that morning of discovery in the lab. When she looked up from the images the room seemed to float for an instant.

Here she was, at the end of a week without voices. She'd left her phone behind. She hadn't turned on the TV or radio or opened her email. She hadn't watched clips on the internet or checked the news headlines. Other than a few words to Crooner and the woman at the till in the grocery store in the small town twenty minutes away, she had spoken only once since arriving. Last night under a sliver of moon she had taken Crooner out on the snow and prepared for her monthly call from her father.

She was beginning to understand that difficult emotional problems and decisions could not always be worked through directly, that they were best put in mind and then left to roll around on their own while her attention was elsewhere, until some tilt of the skull dropped them into the right place. And so she'd walked. They crossed over the unmarked property lines, into the woods. She watched Crooner and tried to examine the quality of her attention. The dark obscured all particulars, it was just the dog and her, Ali, whoever, and shapes and the cold air, the slow treetops passing overhead. These days she received all things in their distinction. Walking through her hanging breath and an air textured with the general ridiculousness of wagging joy. When they came out into a sloping pasture the night sky resumed, the blackest she'd ever seen, with the brightest stars. It was a dull paradox that the blackest sky should best illuminate the night. The light was not distant—it was here, reaching her— but ancient beyond time, and the blackness ancient too. At some evolutionary moment the mind resolved to take the measure of all magnitudes. Most people described numbers out toward infinity as "astronomical," unsuspecting of the numbers inside themselves. There were more nucleotides in the genes in your jeans than there were stars in the galaxy, and a hundred billion neurons in the brain.

Crooner began to flag but couldn't stop bounding on. He seemed likely to run himself dead of exuberance. When she called to him he looked at her with a mask of ice on his mad face. Without a bribe he wouldn't come to her. She said "cookie" and watched him stunned for seconds in tortured ambivalence. She turned and a moment later he was on her flank, happy, near spent and half-composed, and they walked back through their tracks to the house.

She toweled him off, left the ice in his coat to melt. She put on dry pants and took her laptop to the chair by the woodstove, held

the machine in one hand and the iron poker in the other, disturbing the coals. She watched them for a long time before the call
arrived.

Her father came up on-screen as if conjured out of the reflected
firelight.

"Can you see me okay?" he asked. Where were the familiar book
spines? He was not in his study.

"You look good."

"I'm affecting calm. You send a note that you're disappearing,
no explanation, and then you disappear. And then your boss,
Carl, calls me, failing not to sound alarmed."

"I'm sorry. Sorry to you, not to him."

"Where the christ are you, Alice?"

He leaned forward into the camera with a face of mock anger
meant to denote the real thing. He used to avoid subjects not w
in rational terms. For this reason he had failed to understand Ali
or, especially, her sister, or to understand why he'd been unable to
reason them free of their most troubling emotions. Now that he
was getting old, he asked more direct questions.

She said she was off in the country, in the woods. She said things
at Gilshey went south and she went east.

"Okay, east. I'll write that down. Is this a love thing? Are you
with someone or is it just you and your dumb dog?"

"Just us."

"And your stolen goods. Carl said you've run off with company
goods. What goods? What do you do out there in cyberspace with
goods?"

"I'm a researcher. I haven't stopped working."

He switched on a desk lamp and his face flared briefly, then
settled into regions of sand and pitch.

"Where are you, Dad? That doesn't look like your place."

"I'm down the coast, with friends. We're going scuba diving tomorrow."

"I didn't know you dove. Dived."

"I don't. None of us do. A local kid's coming to teach us, take us out."

"But you're not even a good swimmer."

"It'll be all right. I'm with friends."

She couldn't picture the friends, let alone her father with an oxygen tank on his back.

"So you've found a new place to live out your convictions for a while," he said. "I understand that. Claire would understand it, too." Her sister sang and played piano and had spent years in ever-dissolving and re-forming bands. A few months ago she'd married a producer with a recording studio in his basement. "How long has it been since you've spoken to her?"

"Since you saw us." The Christmas rituals. They exchanged gifts, Claire found occasion to insult Ali's life, and Ali called her naive. Then another silent new year.

"You're envious of each other." In his often implied, never stated view, Ali wanted a good man and Claire wanted to have done something with her brain.

"And she's naive."

"Well, she's more than that now."

And so it arrived, as she had known it would, somehow. Not straight from her sister but through him. Ali had been waiting for years and now came the annunciation.

"When?"

"She's almost four months. That puts it late summer." Claire wouldn't have been able to tell her. She'd feel she was playing a cruel, winning card and didn't know how. A small, foreign part of her wouldn't want to play it.

"And she's good?"

"Yes, good. They're all good. It bothers me she didn't tell you." He raised his eyes above the screen, as if looking out a window. "The oddest sunset tonight."

"I had one, too." The sky had cleared in the late light. The colors in the west had seemed wrong, the wrong red holding in the rim.

"Are you okay?"

"Of course. I'm happy for her." She supposed she was happy for her, if not happy herself at the news. It was not so simple as being happy. And he was not, in fact, looking good. He was looking old, worn out by the turns in his fortunes, by his daughters, their opposing lives, their failure all but five days a year to appear to him in the flesh. She wanted to reach through the screen and clasp his shoulders. "Will you tell her you told me, please. I don't want her worrying about it."

"I will." His eyes flitted slightly to another window on-screen. He was looking at himself as he looked to her. "She adores you, you know. It's no fun to be disappointed in the object of your adoration."

"Are you disappointed, too?"

"I just want you to be happy. I look for signs of it."

They depended on one another, the three of them, for their disappointments. In that respect they really came through.

She felt the end of the call coming. This minute, this hour, this day, each month.

He rocked back slightly in the desk chair and reached up and brushed his earlobe with a finger and she saw, in the veins in his wrist curling around the tendons, a snake eating its tail. The gesture, touching his ear, was odd. She'd never seen it before or hadn't noticed. It was almost nothing, one of those nonthings that didn't normally register between the things that did. Ouroboros. The nonthings strung the world together.

"I've been having nightmares lately," he said. "I had a dream last night that the ceiling in my bedroom had eyes. They just opened and watched me as I slept."

In so many ways he was a little boy.

"No more spicy food for you, Dad. Scary dreams are the worst."

"No they're not. Sad dreams are the worst." He never used to admit sadness, the invisible given. She fended off another request for her whereabouts. "Are you inland?"

"Inland? Yes, why?"

"You can escape anywhere but it's safer inland than up the coast."

"I'm not escaping. I'm just going to ground for a while."

A note in her voice wavered, sounding not grounded at all, and she knew its expression would concern him, so she said things were okay. Everything was okay and more than okay. He received the news silently, then said it himself, "Okay," and assented to say good night, and she closed him away.

2

A BLUE JAY DROPPED TO THE FEEDER AND DISPERSED THE smaller birds, order asserted in a bright blue swoop. Ali drifted to the study, caught in a thought below her awareness. It was a few seconds before she realized her eyes had come to rest on the drive Denise had hidden for her. She'd forgotten about it but now the day made a space for it in her attentions. She supposed she could use the company, and opened the drive to find an audio file.

Hello, Alice. Stefan is away in town for the afternoon and I thought I'd use the quiet to say hello. I'm sorry we didn't talk on the phone. Now you'll be here in three days and we'll be gone. I hope you like our place, that it feels like home. I always thought it was funny how the same place could be home to different people.

Stefan's gone—I guess I said that already—and so I'm here doing what I shouldn't be, or what he thinks I shouldn't, and that's talking to you. Talking to you and you're not even here.

You're probably out on a highway somewhere right now and
here I am sitting where you maybe are, in the future, listening to me. The only thing that feels strange about all this is
that it doesn't feel strange and it should, don't you think?
Guess we get used to any old magical thing.

Somewhere under the voice's rhythm was another, running more
slowly, as if Denise breathed only while speaking, never in the
pauses, and the effect was a punctuation of small, loaded silences. As
Denise told the story of the house and how they'd come to own it,
Ali got up from the desk and let the voice run without listening to it.
She wondered vaguely about her future, then saw herself where she
was, amazed at where she'd landed. You spend years building small
armatures to fit around the life you believe you're living, and then
the supports are gone, blown clean away, and you have to learn the
motions all over again.

It was warm now in the living room. With barely an updraft, the
fire was dying. She closed the woodstove doors and shut off the
feed to smother the last flames. Out the window the line of towering black locusts had a sheen where the ice had melted, except near
the tops, where the bark was already dry. These creatures that lived
and died in the same spot of earth. Their thorny branches might
have made them remote, untouchable, somehow more beautiful,
but they were simply themselves, present to her if she paused over
them. Nothing was more or less than itself. No matter that selves
were immeasurable.

She sank into the green plush of what had become her favorite
armchair and took up yesterday's reading. She'd been researching
nineteenth-century experiments with mind-altering chemicals and
gases and ended up on a site devoted to the James brothers, William

and Henry, whom Ali knew almost nothing about. Beginning in 1870, William, the philosopher, had recorded his experiences with chloral hydrate, amyl nitrate, peyote. Here she might find an antecedent for her subjects' experiences with Alph. William claimed he could understand certain philosophers only when reading them under the influence of nitrous oxide. He described an "intense metaphysical illumination" during which "Truth lies open to the view in depth beneath depth of almost blinding evidence." The problem was that, on evidence of the jottings he'd made while high, many of his insights were nonsensical. "There are no differences but differences of degree between different degrees of difference and no difference." Ali's test subjects were more lucid and felt grounded in a heightened condition that was self-regulating and continuous with sober understanding. The pill's little trips held them steady.

William's interest in alternate mindstates extended to the supernatural. In one of his letters to the Society for Psychical Research in London he reported an evening with a medium who when entranced seemed able to render the names and details of dead family members. Having reasoned through the possibilities, he concluded that the medium possessed "supernatural powers." The letter was read aloud to the society by the other brother, Henry, a skeptic whose use for the supernatural was expended in writing fiction. The site contained a link to one of his short novels, *The Turn of the Screw*, which she'd printed off and read half through.

Now she found her place—how strange to read without Crooner at her feet—and resituated herself into the tale, a sort of ghost story. After another ten pages of what continued as it had seemed yesterday, a stylish but dated entertainment, she detected an interference in her reading. It originated somewhere other than the obvious—life upheaval, dead test subject, dog off the range—and searching for the source led her to a thought. She needed a focusing aid to hold her steady. She went to the bedroom and removed the sealed plastic bag from her suitcase. She lifted out a single pill, thirty milligrams. For her, Alph had always been numbers and graphs, measures and behaviors, nothing she'd actually experienced. In the kitchen she poured herself a small glass of orange juice and tried to gauge her mood. The objective view was that her motives were complicated, and yet she would use the excuse of a reading experiment to sample her drug and see what she would be availed to see.

The yellow rectangle against the lines of her palm. She brought her hand to her mouth and there, in the interval between feeling the pill on her tongue and taking a sip, she met doubt. In minutes it would dissolve to a single grain and yet she knew already that it would never wash out of her. It was as if the doubt, necessary to sharp perception, were in the pill itself. Had she engineered it into the drug? Did it hide by some greater design in the mastered arrangement of nucleotides? All her life doubt had been something to be abolished, an impediment to understanding. Now she wasn't so sure.

She waited for her body to begin the absorption and respond with its reported flush of recognition. What else could she expect? A numinous lifting she wasn't to trust, present too in the placebo results. The stronger effects were unbordered, without a clear onset. They fell under one name, one syllable. It took time for the substance to release, took time for it to run its course and subside, but the space between these times was described as "clockless." The drug brought a feeling of simultaneity, not tick or tock but both at once, sustained. It opened the mind to connections

otherwise obscured by temporal distances, by fading and forgetting. One of the subjects had written of "absolute presence."

A memory surfaced that retained the distraction, the private
commentary in her thoughts at the time. She saw Carl, a thin man
with a paunch, nearing fifty, leading her into the boardroom. Two
days before things went wrong. They took their usual seats at the
same end of the long conference table and he rolled the chair back
and put one hiking boot on the table. "The modern mind was
born six million years ago. It belonged to the common ancestor.
The next advances in self-awareness will turn our gaze out from
the self." Already writing promotionals, she thought. He'd chosen
a twenty-four-year-old because he didn't want to be challenged.
Ali would have been a better match. "Until now," he said, "time
was a narrow prison cell. All we've needed to escape it wasn't an
open door, but the slit of a window, an opening in perception.
True vision is now available to all of us. We just swallow it."

She told him to avoid the word "vision." It conjured clouds parting, eyes rolling up in the head. Based on their descriptions, the
test subjects, while conscious, never left the world as it was, hard
reality with its stuck doors and broken shoelaces and just enough
milk in the carton. The things they called "visions" simply turned
up. Some had no clear source, some were variations on the day.
Some were spatial, a map of connections, and others sequential,
with characters and causality. The fantasies could maintain themselves coherently for minutes or hours. It occurred to Ali to wonder
if their nature derived from the structure of the drug or the structure of pictures and stories, something in the air, ancient and popular, that everyone knew at a subconscious level.

To have the fantasy and the thought about it, all while beating
eggs or shaking a shampoo bottle, this was the new modern

consciousness. Alph generated faith, another word they couldn't use. "What if everyone was this aware, this open to beauty? Before now we all had a waking life and a dream life. Your little magic pill opens a third state of heightened possibility inside the real world, the one we're born into, where we really live and die." The note in his voice was conviction. She knew it then. He'd sampled the pill. The night before she left, she went to the lab and found the stash in his office. It was hers now. But then Alph had always been hers. He wouldn't easily get more until the next trial stage began. By then she'd have told her story and posted it online, though she'd keep the chemistry to herself, here in her fugitive hard drive.

She heard it on the roof, a rain had started, and now there it was through the window. Crooner hated rain. He'd be at the door within minutes.

She returned to the chair to see if the ghost story opened up differently. She read the rest of the pages with calm focus and the sense that, yes, she understood something rarely conveyed. The story seemed to confirm the existence of a thing not yet named, like an invisible planet postulated through math, the evidence of bending light, gravitational forces. Whatever the social worlds of late nineteenth-century Europe, Henry James understood them from the inside. Both the insider's report of them and the interior, psychological report. Both the mind of the times and the mind of the lone soul in time. And whether or not writing ghost stories suggested a belief in ghosts, he certainly understood the compulsion to believe, and that this compulsion could be connected to an experience of evil, a being or act of ungoverned appetites, isolated from empathy.

In the real world evil wasn't supernatural. And yet Alph brought to her the presence of something unseen. Not the apparition in the story, but the story itself, even after she had finished it and sat looking at the dead embers. The story had a ghostlike being of its own, and to the extent that she still felt close to this spirit, she could say it haunted her.

In the study her computer stood open. Only then did she remember Denise's audio file, which had finished playing with no one to hear it. She started it again, skipped ahead a couple of minutes. She thought the voice sounded different, a bit strained. Ali listened more closely and gathered as she could the part she'd missed. There was a woman named Irina, apparently a friend of Denise's. For mysterious reasons never explained, she'd needed to leave her home in Russia suddenly and ended up here, married to a neighbor.

I need to tell you about her. She was the sweetest woman, even despite everything that had happened to her. She must have known from the minute she came here that she was the unluckiest person in the world, and yet she'd come by every Tuesday and we'd sit here and talk, and she'd tell stories about growing up in Russia and there was never any sadness in her voice. She just accepted her life. At least at first.

Because we've traveled a bit in mission, Stefan and me, I told her about Mexico and Africa and Jordan, places she would never go, and somehow she thought I was interesting, though I'm not. I know I'm not an interesting person. I showed her pictures from all these places. She was so curious about them. I think it was because if she'd had a bit of luck she might have ended up in one of them herself. Or maybe she was pretending to be curious because she wanted to stay longer in our house so she wouldn't have to go back to hers.

I never asked her about luck.

But I did tell her what I thought of her husband, the very first time we met.

His name is Clayton Shoad. Clay Shoad. You don't want to have anything to do with him, Alice.

It's possible, when first hearing a name, to feel a space inside in the exact shape of the sound it makes. What Ali felt now wasn't dire portent exactly, that note was coming from Denise, but rather like, in Ali's experience, a surprise finding that makes sense the moment it appears. Some principle forever in effect, waiting to be discovered.

She listened. She came to understand that she'd done a disservice to Denise and Irina both by having skipped ahead, and her failing to listen to their stories wasn't to be excused, wherever her own mind was today, whatever the weather.

Pooled in her thoughts, feeling them without seeing them whole, she clicked back to the beginning—"Hello, Alice"— paying attention this time to everything being told to her.

Irina. 35. Cheboksary, Chuvashia, Russia. My preferred man should be affectionate and a friend, who can treat me with respect and to protect me in case of need. There is no place for suspicions. I don't smoke so prefer nonsmoker man.

Denise had named the website. The page on-screen showed a smiling, narrow-faced woman with thin, darkened lips, huge brown eyes, and badly dyed yellow hair. Behind her was a wood-paneled wall and a window with a prospect of what seemed to be a residential street in summer, a car roof in motion spilling open a bead of sunlight.

Taking all she could into account, Ali had to conclude that Denise was right. Irina had been unlucky. For evolutionary reasons in the development of the brain, failure to account for the factors that worked into what most people thought of as luck led to superstition, myth, religious thinking, false hopes. But you could eliminate the factors—adaptability, attractiveness, intelligence, community, education, genetic coding—only if you ignored the role of chance in the making of each of them. It was luck, good or bad, to be born in a certain time and place, looking and thinking a certain way. Ali imagined luck as a particle by-product of chance. She pictured vectors of contingencies, moving at high speed through each life, colliding when they intersected. Some things just came down to the wind on a given day. On learning Irina's story, many would say, there but for the grace of God go I, when they could as easily say, simply, there I go. Ali could feel her connection to Irina. They had both once been hopeful and in need of escape. They had both arrived here knowing no one. What else? Irina's Russian history wasn't known, but Ali could see it looming in her features, the darkness that belonged to a good soul under threat.

Irina had first appeared at the house on a hot July day. From the kitchen window Denise saw Shoad's brown pickup with its rust-red hood coming down the driveway and felt the pricks of fear in the soles of her feet. She was already calling Stefan's cell number when she saw through the windshield that it was a woman. She didn't finish the call. The woman stopped and stepped out of the truck. She was thin and foreign-looking, and right away Denise could see what had happened. She knows it came all at once because, later, when Irina told her the story of having come as a bride, Denise felt she already knew it, though until she'd seen the woman standing there by the truck, looking toward the house, the thought of Shoad buying a foreign bride was too cruel for her to have imagined. There was no car in the driveway so Irina must have wondered whether anyone was home. Then she leaned back into the truck and took something from the seat—it was a cake, Denise could see—and she started toward the house.

Denise met her at the door. They introduced themselves. Irina presented the cake.

"I am the wife of Clayton."

Denise didn't know what to say. The pause seemed to have trapped them both.

"I'm sorry. I didn't know he got married." She'd forgotten even to take the cake, but she took it now, and invited Irina in, and felt that in doing so she was making a passage for ill fate to enter her home.

She learned that Irina had been living there for almost three weeks, that this was the first time she'd left Shoad's place, and she'd done so when he was out on his tractor, and that she couldn't stay long or he'd realize she was gone.

Denise nodded. The women understood each other.

"I remember about the truck, how it was. When I go back, I put it same way."

Otherwise she would have to explain the truck, Denise thought, just as she herself would have to explain the cake. Stefan would question her, give her that look. He pretended Shoad was other than he was. She would transfer the cake to her own plate and wash the other and return it to Irina before she left.

"Do you know my husband, Clayton?"

Denise took in the woman's cheap wedding ring. It looked like it was made of a bent tin spoon handle and a bit of chipped quartz.

"We've known him. My husband, Stefan, and I know him, yes, but we don't see him much. We don't see him often."

"Will you tell me about him?"

"About Stefan?"

"No. Will you tell me about Clayton."

"Oh." Denise said they didn't know him well. "I don't think he has many friends."

Irina looked at her, deciding.

"My English is not so good, and there is no time. Tell me what you know, please."

Irina went missing on a Tuesday in mid-October. They had arranged to meet at the house at ten in the morning, their usual time, when Stefan was at work and Shoad drove his truck to town for his weekly food and supplies run. If she followed the creek Irina could walk to the Dahls' place in about forty minutes, which left her forty-five minutes before she had to return. Over the summer and fall Denise and Irina spent their time together every Tuesday talking about gardening, their husbands, the wide world, Jesus Christ, how hope could be maintained in these, the end times.

Only once did Irina appear other than on a Tuesday morning, though Stefan believed she had not appeared, that Denise had imagined the appearance, fooled by the night itself and the wind rushing through it. On the Sunday before she vanished, the Sunday after what would come to be their last Tuesday meeting, the last time Denise and Irina ever spoke to each other, Denise and Stefan were reading by the fireplace in their small living room when all at once the fire stood to its feet upon a sudden, powerful updraft, and Denise, who had been reading one of her favorite old British mystery books, found herself looking with horror at the flames that

were growing, twisting, not unlike a burning woman turning at
the waist, and then not a woman at all, but still something other
than flames, and she heard the huge sucking of wind, as if the
whole house were rising into a vortex. Then the house went dark
and the wind was gone, and the fire sat down in its usual place.

Stefan went for the flashlights and candles—outages were
common, they had their routines—but when he returned to the
living room he found that Denise hadn't moved. She was supposed
to be calling the power company. He asked what she was doing,
and she said, "There's something wrong out there." He went outside to collect firewood to heat the house through the night, and
she followed and walked around the property in the dark, without
a flashlight, and for no reason that she'd ever been able to explain.
The storm, if that's what it had been, had passed as suddenly as it
had arrived. The sky was full of stars. There was still a strong wind
up in the trees but she knew it was being pulled behind the storm,
and promised nothing in itself. She was halfway around the house
when she noticed the serpent—that's what she called it, the word
was there with the thing itself—and began walking toward it.
When she got to within about forty yards she stopped. The power
line running eastward was down and thrashing in the field, shooting sparks, arcing, striking the ground with its mouth, and Denise
had the urge to continue walking and to pick it up, to correct it
somehow, an act that she knew should kill her, and so she saw it,
too, as a serpent to take up in test of her faith, thinking this even
though she didn't agree with such practices, such readings of every
last word of Scripture as if the Lord Himself had no poetry in Him
when every book of both testaments was filled with it.

For a long time she stood watching the snake in its wheeling as
if tormented by the stars, she and the snake both, feeling the pull

to go closer. The line popped its speech and she was in the throat of it when she saw Irina, or the shape of her, standing, as the line strobed this way and that. Though never fully illuminated, even as the sparks flew upon her, the figure was there in the field as surely as was Denise herself, bent in on itself somehow, as if, impossibly, one side of it, from shoulder to waist, was crouching or broken. It looked like the figure in the fireplace, the burning woman. Denise had this impression in seconds, for when the line showered light on Irina again, she seemed only half there, floating, and then upon the next showering was gone, and Denise knew that she had been addressed.

When he got the story out of her Stefan tried to convince her that the vision was a mistake in perception. Denise said that whatever it was, it had not been an ordinary moment and shouldn't be explained as such. She refused to talk about it further.

At four thirty that morning, Stefan asleep, she got out of bed with the intention of driving to Shoad's farm, but Stefan had hidden the car keys. She put a log on the fire and returned to the cold bedroom. The firelight coming through the doorway made shadow planes like great silent herds moving to near extinction. He spoke without opening his eyes. "If something has happened to your friend, I don't want you going, and if it hasn't there's no need." When the flashing lights came into their room she was still awake. The power trucks had turned off the road. Men in hard hats were making their way across the field.

So you see he understood, did Stefan. It wasn't hard to attribute the understanding. Shoad had bought the farm eight years ago, and Stefan had visited him a few times. Denise had met him twice then, and though they didn't have much conversation she sensed there was something troubling about the way he kept to himself.

There was something inside him he didn't want others to see. Then he went to Europe and came back many months later, much changed, changed to his true self. He looked different, spoke differently, the halt and lurch of it. It was as if he'd fallen into an accent. Stefan tried to explain it away but she put into evidence the day Shoad entered the feedstore where he bought seeds and supplies, and behind the counter the old woman was watching a little TV she had propped on a stool. On the midday news a mass grave was being exhumed—the woman, who'd told her husband, who'd told the man at the butcher counter standing next to Denise, didn't say where the grave was—and Shoad stared fixed as if he'd never seen images on-screen before. Then he looked at the woman and she was "horror-struck," her word, because the set of Shoad's face was wrong, as if he were having some kind of vision or seizure. She would never forget that face, the woman had said, not for as long as she lived.

Stefan understood, yes, but his understanding wasn't the same as a certain kind of knowledge, the kind Denise gained that night and carried with her into the next days. The days themselves lost meaning. Tuesday was not Tuesday, the day Irina was expected, because Denise no longer expected her. She seemed in fact to be somehow outside of expectation, of a world of approaching events, as if resigned to them, even though in any other time in her life this feeling, a red certainty was how she described it, would have been fear, the most acute form of expectation. This was a terrible time, of heavy hours. Though he didn't say as much, Stefan wanted her to pretend the knowledge away. He himself had a limited ability to pretend, and he used it. But the knowledge Denise had been stricken with was bodily, and she knew it could not be expelled and that trying to do so would be not just folly but a turning away from her friend and from one of God's mysteries and so she held the red certainty, became its keeper. Nothing, not the doctor Stefan called in, not the medications, not the Scripture he read to her of Naomi's bitter sufferings relieved (Stefan not hearing how it only confirmed her as a chosen subject of the Lord), nothing could uncolor the knowledge.

He said it was blasphemy to call a spell a vision. He said it was not a communication but something stirred up by her nerves, and so she kept the next episode to herself. She was hanging sheets in the laundry room when it came upon her, brief but intense, and she let it play out. A cold fall day. She is running scared behind a naked woman in the creek, the water splashing their legs, and someone unseen is chasing them. Then there's just her, or rather she has become the other woman, Irina and not, and everything surrounding her now has a strange name. She is running without clothes or English words. Then she's falling into a hole or animal den and she's hurt and can't stand. She reaches as she can and covers herself with leaves and dead branches and tries not to breathe. The steps come near and pass by. The spell ends and she is standing at the fuse box with a black towel draped over her head.

What was between Denise and Stefan now would always be between them, she knew. She had no choice but to deceive her husband. He stayed with her at the house and worked from home, and took her to town when he ran errands. Her escape wasn't planned but rather enacted as if it had already been scripted by Another, and so when she found herself waiting in the car for him to emerge from the post office, and getting out and going around to the driver's side and starting away, she knew not to look in the rearview mirror, knew he wouldn't have come out of the building yet, and then she was out of town and on the highway. And the certainty and the fear cleaved as one, and for the first time in her life she understood that the trials endured in Scripture by Jonah and Job were not a way of putting modern human fate in perspective, or a way of seeing our own small troubles in dramatic stories, but were real. For the first time in the life of her faith she felt truly descended from Eve and from Noah's wife, and she drove with images flashing in her from her dreams of the previous night, which had fired into puzzling shapes and happenings so that all morning she felt more alone for not understanding them and having no Old Testament Daniel to interpret the dreams for her.

From the highway Denise saw the hard gray stem of smoke marking Shoad's hill and she covered the miles feeling directed, confirmed in her direction. She turned onto Shoad's property and started up the winding, wooded road, past the hand-drawn Private Do Not Enter sign, and the store-bought No Trespassing sign farther up, and came out at the clearing that held Shoad's house and outbuildings. She stopped the car between the house and the barn and sat looking at the clapboard building, weather-spackled green, with a few steps up to the front door, two large blind windows in front, and a simple, medium-pitched roof, not the peaked, terrible thing that was its truer form. The yard was orderly, dominated by the solid-looking barn. Shoad's truck, the one Irina had driven to the house, was nowhere. There were no cars or trucks at all. The only presence was the smoke coming from behind the barn.

She got out of the car and stood for a second in the silence with the door open and the keys in her hand, scenting something on the air she thought was time itself burning up, revealing a new character in the shadowless noon light. All moments in Scripture are eternal, the time of the resurrection and the time of the Lord's dying, and in the certainty of her righteousness she advanced on the house thinking that whatever would happen had already happened and the only choice before her was no choice but to act according to the examples handed down through the turning ages that began upon the first disobedience and expulsion. She climbed the steps and looked through the window in the door into a mudroom leading to a kitchen. Covering the floor as far as she could see, from the door to the cupboards under the counter, were the horns of animals, cow horns and deer antlers strewn and tangled in a small apocalypse. Shoad wanted no one stepping inside. The door was either locked or in some way composed into a trap and so she stepped back down and moved along the length of the house and around to a padlocked door, up the other side, barely able to see into the windows and then finding in each only dull yellow blinds admitting nothing. The whole place was the shape and dimension of the sickness of despair.

Somewhere in crossing the yard she opened herself to guidance and knew again what she had tried not to know since the highway. She headed for the pillar of smoke that somehow pointed to the ground even as it pointed skyward. When she came around the barn she did so without fear or with fear secured by her conviction and watching her so that Shoad would be equally there and not there regardless of what or whom she found, and she felt every living thing for miles, every leaf on every tree felt distinctly without falling to senselessness or the lie of words like *green*. And so she approached the forge as the lone human but not the lone soul and saw it in all its terrible design. The two propane tanks, the petroleum pipes, and the huge brick oven. When she was little she'd asked her father who made the forge and he said God made the forge in which He fashioned all things, but he himself made the forge beside the shed. He said you need a sheet of paper and five hundred pounds of brick.

Shoad's forge was bigger, a stack chimney on top, so that it looked like a small house, and she pictured herself and her father in their house placed in sight of the town and the church, a scene she'd painted once, sitting with their ball-peen copper bowls and spoons. You light the paper, throw it in, he said. Turn the valve. In time you'll have three thousand degrees standing there staring at you like something pulled up from hell on a chain. He had made her scared of the furnace, scared for her own good, but now she knew the early lesson was only so she'd remember it in this moment as she approached the forge and thought of Daniel's friends who were thrown into the furnace on Nebuchadnezzar's order but kept their faith and were saved by the archangel Michael.

There was a steel door the size and shape of a knight's shield. When she took hold of the lever handle she felt the heat on the back of her hand and she pushed the lever down and swung the door and let go of it so that the furnace yawned open and then seemed to wake upon the new air and the heat bolted and caught her and she felt it on the skin and the hairs of her arms and face and she stepped back.

In the mouth of the furnace something moved or seemed to in the heat-furled light. She narrowed her eyes against the burning and tried to make sense of the mouth and saw forms there or imagined them, a metal skid like a small bed frame, a torso of fire and ash, a wooden dummy dying in a garment factory blaze, and she saw stars and planets there, the low wet moon of autumn in transit, the stars now high-shouldered animals lifted from the disturbed breathing of the coals. And then it was only flame and ash and the smoke called up, and no more sense could be made of it. She looked at the pillar, open to revelation, but saw only the column of smoke rising inside itself and she thought of the visions that had come to her, in the fireplace, in the field, and she looked back down and there it was. Not in the forge but on the door. Melted to the bottom hinge, a blackened raised spot catching pins of light that she knew, was given to know, were cast by the quartz in the small tin setting of Irina's wedding ring.

She knew it but the light didn't hold. The pins of light were there for Denise but not for Stefan later when he went to the yard, still empty, the forge spilled out. His only evidence, her hands, burned and bandaged, the blood on the steering wheel of the car, and her report from the hospital bed. There was no ring, no rock on the hinge, no sign that anything had been chipped off. Whatever she had seen had disappeared, maybe when she'd taken hold of the door. He'd found nothing at the base but a spade with a charred handle. And though Denise knew he would lie to her, for her sake or for his, she believed him, and so came to understand that it was Irina who had shown her the melted ring, as if to communicate the end of her story. She had not wanted Denise to be hurt, of course, or to fill her heart with destruction. Stefan asked her if that was what happened, if she'd been trying to destroy the forge. But she hadn't. She'd only wanted to release the fire, by spade, by hand, and burn everything Shoad put his name to.

Yet though she believed Stefan, he doubted her. He arranged to have her kept in the hospital longer than necessary. She was "formed," they called it, and when the young woman doctor who seemed frightened of Denise reduced the painkillers, they put her on other medications. Over the next weeks Stefan and the doctors, there were three of them by then, tried to convince her not only that Shoad hadn't killed Irina but also that Irina never existed, or rather existed in Russia, and on the internet, but not there. At first Stefan had believed her stories of Irina and the visits, he told her, but on the night of the storm he began to have doubts. They said Denise's visions had crossed into her reality and confused it. As if she was the trouble, and it was only trouble they had to stand against. As if they didn't believe in evil.

3

NINE WEEKS INTO THE PHASE ONE TRIAL, THE QUALIFIED
investigator asked Ali to breakfast. They met at their usual place,
an old hotel with a view of runners and dogs along English Bay.
The trial updates were documented but Ali liked feeling close to
the human particularity unrecorded in the numbers and graphs.
They were not above swapping stories from their fields, she and
Anja Seding, and Anja was not above exaggerating hers for comic
effect. For a physician she was not especially circumspect or prone
to displays of excessive professional gravitas.

Anja announced that she had to "present a circumstance." One
of the trial subjects had begun sending her things.

"The subjects have my contact info through the clinic, and he's
started to email me his writings. Pages every day."

"He's a writer."

"According to his declaration he began the trial as a thirty-one-
year-old B-negative eco-activist and poet with no drug allergies or
history of mental illness."

"Hard enough being a poet, but to be a sane one."

"The point of interest being you're a recurring character in these things, poems, mini-essays, pages from what seems to be a novel. Or not you exactly but someone he calls 'Maker.'"

Ali had wondered at times who the subjects thought was behind the tests, the drugs, the money, who exactly was playing with and reading their blood. She did not want to be thought of. She tried to feel sheltered in the company name.

"Is this a known syndrome? Is he fixated?"

"He's likely not dangerous, Ali. It began he was just singing your praises. Then he speculated upon a life, what you think, personal history stuff. I repeat, not dangerous."

From what Anja and the research nurse had learned in their brief conversations with Subject 11, he was a full-time test subject, a so-called guinea pigger, who bussed around the country, getting paid to be injected, blood-drawn, electroded, cardio-tested, whatever the trial required. It used to be the tests were done on the local poor. Now the poor had organized. They mass-communicated about new trials and flocked here and there. Even if they declared what they'd already had done to them, you never really knew what hadn't been flushed from their systems.

"Does he know my name?"

"Well, you head out onto the internet, you find things."

"Maybe he's fixed on Carl."

"He's imagining a woman. That's part of the adoration."

"But he hasn't used my name."

"It feels like he's on the verge. He might be withholding it out of decorum."

"Or so you don't think he's dangerous when maybe he is."

They wouldn't have been there if a lot weren't hanging on Anja's reading of Subject 11, on her own reading of Anja. She tried to

remember what she knew of the woman's life. There was an unemployed husband, a scholar of Greek and Latin, or was it Roman
history? She'd forgotten, and their social-professional relationship
was well past the point where she could ask because she'd also forgotten his name.

"He calls the pill 'One True,' short for the One True God. Give
us our One True, spread it far and wide. He uses terms like 'New
Enlightenment,' capital *N* capital *E*."

"But not dangerous."

"It's half-ironical. He means it all but he's not, I don't think,
nuts. He's got a sense of humor. I'm just telling you this because
you should know. If you want I'll remove him from the trial."

"But, given his devotion, couldn't dropping him trigger real
trouble?"

"I doubt it, but a reasonable question."

They decided to switch him to a placebo and keep his numbers
off the final report. He would have lost his One True anyway when
the trial ended but better that he not feel singled out for the loss.

In the park along the bay a scene was unfolding. A car had stopped
by the pathway and a man in a dark suit and sunglasses emerged and
was watching the runners and dogs and mothers trotting with their
strollers. He stepped forward, in front of a running man in spandex
shorts, who stopped. They had a brief exchange. Ali got the sense
they were neither strangers nor friends. She found herself expecting
to see the man in the suit take a thick envelope out of his pocket and
hand it to the runner. The runner was failing to register the inevita-
bility of the envelope. His face read only exertion.

Any given moment was too complicated. How was it that time
itself did not just seize up?

"Subject 11. What's his name?"

Together they said, "Confidential."

"It's safer if you don't know. That way you can't follow any temptation to act. I act for you."

"He knows my name but I don't know his. I'm worried I'll be acted upon."

"Tricky position for us both."

Setting up blinds. It was what they did professionally. Now one might have been set for her, hidden somewhere in the current run of days. Ali had fed him into this state and now they were thinking of each other, she and Subject 11, each picturing the other, imagining a voice, getting it wrong. It wouldn't just go away, this wondering.

The time was 1:47.

On the old console radio she dialed through bands to find only dim warps in the static suggesting voices that in their failure to form were oddly beguiling. From nowhere came the memory of a resonance image she'd once seen on a med-sci site of the nameless, hollow space between an infant's ribs and lungs. The space was common to mammals. Ali imagined it holding abstract feelings and ideas. Secreted there between the bone and tissue, love, hope, goodness, evil.

Denise had said "evil." Within the span of a few hours Ali had encountered the word twice, in the Henry James story and now in Denise's. It was Denise whose presence she felt around her in traces. The woman had needed someone to believe her. She'd opened her soul to a stranger and yet Ali had trouble accepting what she'd been shown. She wanted some objective reading but had only Denise's handwritten notes and the audio file, which she returned to, at the desk, looking for clues. According to the file signature it had been created three days before Ali arrived and last revised on the same afternoon. The time between the making and final saving was less than forty minutes. She must have recorded it straight through. But the drive contained a second, much smaller file, created earlier. Ali assumed it contained operational data, but when she opened it she saw the audio meter appear again on-screen. The needle jumped as it picked up a very slow mechanical ticking and then a low fuzz emerged and she heard a voice, a distant voice, Denise, saying, "Hello, Alice. Stefan is away in town for the afternoon and I thought I'd use the quiet to say hello." It was a muted version of the first recording, as if someone in another room had secretly recorded Denise leaving her message for Ali. The theory made no sense. No, the time code told the story. The file was just an earlier attempt in which something had gone wrong with the recording, and Denise had forgotten to delete it. The voice broke off suddenly and the needle went dead.

In the new silence Ali had a sudden, sharp memory of sitting by the woodstove yesterday with Crooner at her feet. She could see the page she'd been reading in *The Turn of the Screw*, the very words on it. It was the scene in which the young governess is herself reading a novel—"I recollect in short that, though I was deeply interested in my author, I found myself, at the turn of a page and with his spell all scattered, looking straight up from him and hard at the door of my room"—and then, though this hadn't happened at the time, Ali was presented an inward vision that dropped before her, obscuring the remembered page, a vision of what she came to understand was Alph itself crossing the blood-brain barrier. The chemical appeared as small attenuating swirlings in the blood, like tornadoes whose tails bent toward the tissues and elongated into thin vessels that slipped into the cortex. The image lasted only a few seconds, but it was as certain as the remembered lines of text or the fur bunched into furrows on Crooner's curved neck. The vision was even more vivid than her present moment as she stood at the desk, the remembered words from the novel returning with more force than they'd had when she first read them.

She was two places at once, in two times at once. When the sensation abated she walked back to the kitchen and looked into the living area, half expecting to see herself there. In this stage of the drug's effect she was able to distinguish between an extreme vision and reality, but was the border between these states eroding? And was her present reality itself already compromised? She had no way of knowing.

Certainly she was experiencing slight jump cuts in time. Without seeming to have returned to it, she was at the desk, trying to record her thoughts. Her awareness of the missing transition complicated her notes. The possibilities for memory enhancement alone should have brought on an elated focus of concentration, but as she looked through what she'd written, it seemed disordered, random. There were lines on mRNA synthesis and transcription factors, others on interactions between brain substrates, circuit-specific regulation of discrete memories, the possibility of accelerated networks and dynamic methylation changes. Whatever knowledge she should have been able to access had been lost in a jumble of half-recalled data she'd studied on unrelated aspects of memory and waking visions. How could she explain the drug producing a vision of itself and its progress through her system?

She dropped her hands from the keyboard and let them fall to her sides. They had never felt so empty. She wanted to run them over Crooner's back and neck and for a second she could feel him beside her, breathing fast, afraid.

All connection to the outer world had disappeared by 3:11. The internet was dead. The landline was out. When the power died at 3:34 she put on her boots and went outside, behind the house to the ravine. Before seeing it, through the sound of the rain, she could hear that the stream was something greater now, and then there it was, the black surface turning dozens of catbacks and fluted shapes, seemingly hand-formed, breaking and overrunning the bend, flooding the small field on the east side of the property with mud and branches. The house was on low ground and if the water rose much farther or the new lake grew in her direction, she would be in trouble.

It was now possible that the day, the landscape, had changed enough to fool Crooner. He wasn't that bright to begin with. And neither was she, apparently—it had been stupid of her not to have gone online for the forecast. There would have been warnings. She pictured townspeople lining up for provisions or taking to the highways in advance of the occurrence, whatever it was. Was there a name for it, a sudden, obliterating thaw? The seasons had gone out of turn, there'd been a skip in time, some error in the vernal code. The instability was general. Denise held distorted, maybe hallucinatory, perceptions, but it was the murder, the events of the story that gave her away, not the story's telling. The telling was controlled. And though you didn't want the story to be true, her voice, intent with concern, made you want to believe her. Ali could still hear the voice inside the sound of the building stream, as if the water itself were striving to make human sense, or as if all sense were drowning. She listened until there was only the rain and the water sounding like a hard summer wind in the trees.

She called Crooner's name again, then again with full lung, and as if her voice itself had broken it, one of the trees in the ravine

began to move. As she looked down at the surge, a fifty-foot
maple slid upright into her view, a parallax shift that dizzied her
for a moment as if the earth were pitching beneath her rather than
beneath the tree, and then the bank gave way altogether and the
tree fell, twisting from its anchoring, into the stream. Immediately
a dam began to form and it seemed the water was intent on engi-
neering its ascent, eddying higher, then shoring the gaps with
whatever it carried, climbing to her, pulling itself up hand by
hand.

She found sometime later that she hadn't taken her eyes from the
rising water. She'd been thinking about this place, about what had
brought her here, and the way some people felt elected to their
misfortunes when their fates emerged slowly. She understood these
people now. She was not without empathy, but used to think that
there was no mechanism that could deliver one person's experience
and understanding into another's. Before reading the subjects'
statements about Alph she thought that when people said they
empathized they were just saying they felt sorry for someone, not
that they felt what the other was feeling. There was little scientific
evidence of selflessness. Even grieving death could be seen as self-
directed. There was a master design, that much she had always
known, but it had seemed disregarding of so paltry a thing as
human feeling. Now it was possible to believe in a clear, calm,
visionary emotion that connected you to others, maybe to the
planet itself. Without belief in true empathy, you would always be
utterly alone. Without belief, standing there, she would have been
in bigger trouble, without means, nearly cornered into prayer.

Could she trust the run of her thoughts? Her dog was lost and
the water was rising, and the day had turned into a dark anomaly.
Circumstances were, if anything, a bit too sobering.

Something was moving above her. Birds, dozens and dozens, mostly gulls, flying east in advance of the system. She turned and went through the back door, closed it, removed her boots, and saw on the windows facing her the underbellies of countless insects. She went across and looked closely at one larger than her thumb, with four membranous, spotted, transversely banded wings. It was out of season, out of place, blown in from somewhere far south.

She focused now on the bare maples in the distance waving at her in the wind, a rush in the dendrites. The ramified shape was there in an image from Denise's story, in the antlers tangled on the floor of Shoad's house. And there again in the lines on the insect's wings, though the wings were still, flakes of ice waiting for the warm breath of consciousness and motion. Waiting to wake inside a waking state. She looked at the wings and saw invisible planes, like the pane of glass between her and the insect. And there, across the window, in the crowded peripheries of her attention, insectile, came something brown, not on the glass but moving through the trees up the road. It emerged just as she'd imagined it, had been made to imagine it in Denise's story. It emerged from its turning, the brown pickup. Emerging as if Denise were rising inside her, as if their times had run together, looking out at the truck with the rust-red hood moving on the property, coming down the road. Carrying its lone soul.

4

IT ROLLED TO A STOP BEHIND HER CAR. THERE WAS BARELY time to register disbelief, and yet she felt it, and felt it pass into some coiled neurocircuitry. The truck with the rust-red hood was muddied halfway up the doors and on the windshield. She stood staring at the flat-front grille and knew something was about to happen to ruin all scale. Chance favors the prepared mind and the wipers smeared the mud across the glass. The driver was hard to make out but the shape in the seat was a man's. She stepped back from the window. The image of the self-consuming snake repeated throughout centuries and cultures and the wipers smeared the glass. It appeared in the Book of the Dead. Plato thought it depicted the first living thing. She would have expected the jolt of fear—it was fear, she must call it that—to have tossed words and learning beyond her reach, but Alph was holding them close. If anything she felt even stronger, more intricate connections between these things she'd read or knew in the bone. In Hindu folk myths the snake swallowing its tail was an image of creation calling itself into being and the wipers smeared the glass and stopped.

The driveway was in a moment of calm sun, fifty feet from the house, up a short slope. The door opened and the driver stepped out. The sight of him, his frame. He seemed apart, outlined more precisely than the things around him, and yet at this distance his face withheld precise features. He was white, very tall, maybe six and a half feet. She couldn't tell his age. His head cast shadows on itself. The brow was greatly pronounced and there were indentations around the eyes. He'd turned off the engine. He seemed to be looking above the house, past it, but she couldn't tell for sure. From where she stood it was maybe twenty steps to the front door, the unlocked door, but the door had a window and he'd see her there trying to lock it. If she had time she'd make a note of this behavior, the way Alph made her vulnerable to gothic anxieties loosed into the house by a madwoman's ghost story. Maybe the drug should be sold at multiplex concession counters. She could see the movie playing as she lived it, see herself in peril as the nervous laughter broke.

She waited for him to look away so she could move and then he did, he looked west to the hills and she crossed past the windows and door and went to the bedroom, though she didn't exactly know why. She stood at the wall, beside the open curtains. She told herself that standing there was reasonable—she was a woman alone, utterly vulnerable, without her useless dog, concealing herself from a man she'd been warned was dangerous. Dangerous to women. His name was Clayton Shoad. Either it was reasonable to go outside and greet him as a visitor, or it was reasonable to hide, even to find a weapon if she had one, though now that she'd left the kitchen she did not have one at hand, and could not quite surmount the absurdity, the desperation she felt at imagining possible weapons in bedside lamps or toothbrushes. What she did have was her wits—she was thinking clearly. Her imagination did not have the best of her, or rather, Alph had directed it groundward. She was imagining herself as clear-thinking, convincing herself she was able to control her actions rationally, standing there, distracted by her own standing still, as if to trigger a stoppage in time, just standing, afraid to look out the window.

She was trapped quite precisely, thinking fast to no sure end. What her father came to call his "conversion experience" he had first called an "anomalous event." It began as a storm of intense dreams occurring over nine nights. He was sure it was nine. The dreams were physically punishing but he was unable to wake from them until sunrise. By day he investigated the condition. He couldn't dismiss the possibility of sleep paralysis but saw it only as a symptom of the dreams' mysterious intensity. Ali first heard of them when he called her one morning at 6:15 to ask if she was okay. She'd just awoken when the phone rang. He said he'd just woken himself—they were both on Pacific time—and his dreams were still all around him. In the last one he'd been with her on a train platform somewhere and she was holding a woven bag. She kept making him promise that he'd take the bag if anything happened to her. He said that if he made the promise something *would* happen to her, but she said no, it would happen or it wouldn't, all he could affect was the fate of the bag and its contents. In the dream he seemed to know what was in the bag but not the words for it, though now, awake, he had no idea what it was. "But are you okay?" She said of course she was and turned the question back on him. She said he spent too much time with grisly details of the TV crime shows he watched every night and that she had to get ready for work. The truth was that the previous night she'd made a hard decision, that she would not become one of those single women who in their early thirties begin to view men only as delivery systems for sperm, that she would not become a desperate seeker of someone just as desperate to have children, and so that very likely, given her dating record, she would never have children. She'd made the decision calmly, she thought, but in one of her own dreams in the night she'd been unable to stop weeping. Now, standing beside the window, she heard his voice as he'd signed off that morning—"So little time to learn so much"—and it was as if they were thinking the same thing at the same moment. She needed him now and closed her eyes as if to petition for his protection and he came to her as a shape floating in a space without contour, motionless, looking out through glass.

One story rises inside another. The truck had come down the driveway and stopped and so, in arriving along the day's first predictable path, the knocking at the door had meaning. And it made sense that he would try the door, and open it, and then the meaning broke down as he stepped inside and said nothing, called nothing, and his absent voice seemed somehow to match the rust-red hood that didn't match the truck. She struggled against a powerful need to dispel the silence, to just say something, some unwise assertion of self. He was moving in the pause, either he was there or he wasn't. In straining to hear she availed herself fully, willing to receive the smallest, telling fragment of sound, an odor, some change in the air, until at last she understood that he was about to appear in the bedroom doorway, she could see three seconds into the future, and then it happened that his form came into view, not in the doorway but his shadow on the floor as he passed by outside the window and out of the frame, into the shadow of the wall she stood against.

She stayed there in a kind of shame, self-indulgent cowardice. After some time she made herself look. The truck blocked her car. Heat waves curled up from the red hood and the roof, distorting the light. The sky to the south behind the line of trees was yellowed in streaks, as if swept with an old corn broom, particles of earth, dense in the atmosphere. The world was laws and conditions. Stillness was a condition—how many women in how many places and times had come to this stillness?—and the laws could be described in models, in shapes and formulas, names and words, and laws were everything and knowing them didn't matter. Everyone arrived at a day when knowing didn't matter.

He appeared from the west side of the yard. Not just tall but large, with long strides through the mud and standing water, walking away at an angle, toward his truck. His hair in back was crudely cropped, maybe gray-blond. He wore dirty brass-colored overalls, a plaid shirt, muddied work boots. His hands were huge, they hung oddly, with the thumbs slightly turned in, barely swinging as he walked. As he approached the truck she stepped farther back into the room and crouched out of the direct windowlight. He went around to the tailgate and was partly obscured by the cab but she saw he was rolling his sleeves and she said to herself, oh well, oh well, he's not going away. From the truck bed he hauled out a heavy coil of rope and ducked his head and one arm through it and wore the rope across his shoulder and chest. He came around the side and reached again into the bed and lifted out a chainsaw. Then he started back the way he'd come, to the west side of the house, and now she saw his face. He was younger than she would have thought from Denise's story, though Denise had said nothing about age, maybe late thirties or forty, but the skin around his eyes was lined deeply, as if he'd been staring into the sun his whole life.

For a full minute she didn't move. Then she went across the hall to the back bedroom, where the Dahls stored their things behind a plastic sheet tacked to the ceiling. She lifted the draping and edged into the narrow aisle between stacks of boxes and along to the north-facing window. He stood at the edge of the ravine, facing the house. The chainsaw nodded from his chest where he'd latched it onto his gaping bib. He had looped the rope around a tree and tied it into a makeshift harness at his waist. He paid out the rope from a coil on his arm and it drew across the maple trunk as he lowered himself over the edge and dropped away.

She was conscious of the drama of it all. There he was, or had been. She'd seen him drop over the edge and thought that if he was harmless then it wouldn't matter that she show herself and so she should stay out of sight in case he was not harmless. But if he was not harmless then she wasn't safe even inside the house—he might already have suspected she was inside, and even if she locked the doors now, he had a chainsaw, after all. What he was doing in the ravine was either in aid of her or a misdirection to draw her out or to occupy him in work, loud work that she could hear from wherever he assumed she might have walked to, and so to lure her back to the house, predisposed to be thankful to the helpful neighbor and so to put his benevolence out in front of his appearance, or in case she'd heard of him by name, an arrangement he would have learned to seek out over the course of his life. From the ravine the saw coughed and then shot high and fierce, and the sound seemed to compress the light and the time in it. If he was the man Denise had described, if she believed Denise, then she should run while he was in the ravine in all that noise. But she didn't believe Denise, or rather she believed only bodily, adrenally, not in her brain. The mistake would be to trust the flight instinct. Even if Shoad was dangerous she should show herself and evince strength and fearlessness, and act in ways he wouldn't predict to keep him out of reach of his own triggers.

She was about to choose. The brain itself contained a means of foreknowledge—changes in the retrosplenial cortex predicted certain kinds of human errors by about thirty seconds. She thought, I need a live image of my default mode region. She thought, I need a knife.

In the laundry room she found a fishing knife in a sheath in the basket of tools sitting beside the clothes dryer. The note read, "for gardening, set inside for winter D" It was the only tool with a note attached. The blade was curved, flat silver, maybe six inches long, pointed at the tip. It was clean. She squeezed the grip and it did not belong in her hand. The blade closed into the sheath with a single clip that she left open. She undid her belt, pulled it out of the first loop, slipped the sheath on, refastened the belt, and tucked her shirt in so the knife was visible at her hip.

When she crossed through the kitchen she saw another note, in a small, uncertain script, next to the empty fruit platter.

The river will take this house. Clear out now.
Come east one mile.
Up the hill.

I found a dog is it your

C. Shoad

A bolt of breath and expended denial shot out of her and opened wider other fears. Crooner was safe but now the house was in danger. But could the creek really take the house? It didn't seem possible. Letter to letter the note was half-printed, half in a failing cursive. The lines were oddly narrow, the whole thing over-clipped, right to the last missing letter. It was written on the back of a print-out page from the James novel, which meant he'd come in as far as the chair by the woodstove and taken what he needed, the page and the pen she'd used to mark significant lines.

At the back door she again laced on her boots—they were walking boots, low on the ankle, not best for the heavy snow and now just as ill-suited to the mud and slush—and stepped out and walked toward the lip of the ravine and the loud saw thrumming the light. As she drew close to the rope she noticed that he'd positioned it over a small metal tap that was directing a steady drip of sap onto the base of the tree. She looked along the ridge and registered for the first time a dozen other tapped sugar maples, all bleeding out in the sudden heat. What she had thought from the house was one loop was in fact two, one drawn over and across another so the rope pinched itself into place, twice fixed. She thought back to the image of the man lowering himself, the coil on his arm, and could not square it with the mechanics of the system she was looking at. Had he come up and remade the rigging while she was finding the knife? The rope was taut, parallel to the ground, down the slope, and she stepped up and saw it whole to the end running into the harness around his body. His back was to her.

He had cut through the top sections of the fallen tree and thrown them onto a crib of branches he'd laid on the bank and was now bent low over the trunk, his feet in the heavy current. He tilted the tip of the blade upward slightly as he entered the thickest part of the log, drew it downward. At some point that he seemed to know precisely he brought the blade out and made a cut from underneath and just as the two cuts met he pulled the saw free and the part of the tree in the river shifted and was taken up by the waters and drawn away lengthways. He watched it as she did, as it was carried downstream, lodging again a hundred or so feet along, the flow coursing around and over it.

She watched the stream in hopes it would calm her. Alph was working against her now, telling her she'd made a mistake. Or maybe her brain was telling her to run and Alph was keeping her in place, feeding off dumb suspense.

He was no longer standing in water, the level had dropped already. He held the low-growling saw in one hand and twisted back to pull himself higher with the other. He looked to his footing as he stepped up once, then again, and stood staring at the rest of the downed tree. Some calculation absorbed him. He killed the saw and held it by one finger. He put his boot to the trunk and seemed to test its position. He looked upstream, then down. Then he took in the northern sky and above the sound of the water he called out,

"That won't buy much time."

He turned and looked up at her. Though she had seen the face, she now felt its address and it penetrated her breath and seemed to take up in the base of her spine. He turned away and stepped down to the new edge of the water and dipped the saw blade into it for several seconds, then lifted it and tested something in it with the side of his hand. He climbed back to the log, took a length of the slackening rope and tied it around the saw and hitched it over his shoulder, then used both hands to pull himself up the slope. He had murdered and burned his Russian wife or he had not. She moved back as he came closer, came up over the edge. He stood unhitching the rope from the saw and then pulling the line up out of the ravine, and when the rope went slack she knew things had gone off script and her father was diving amid sea creatures as he'd seen them in dreams but he was drifting farther, deeper, out of touch.

He stood before her, nodded, and said, "Clay Shoad." He shifted his eyes to the rope as he worked it. "You rent this place." A statement not a question.

She nodded yes.

"I knocked on the door."

She sensed he knew she'd been inside, and knew even now that she was going to lie about it.

"I was out. Looking for my dog. I saw your note. Is he okay?"

"He's all mud. I tied him outside."

He drew the rope through his hand as he coiled it. It must have burned in the palm.

"It was unusual for him to be gone so long."

"Nothing usual today." He tied the coil and looked down at the river. "It's already rising again. I should have cut smaller. Smaller section. Let it run off."

He spoke slowly. There was something in his vowels, a narrow shelf. She guessed he was a native English speaker but his parents were not. Some tongue of northern Europe in a region of his brain.

"Thank you for helping out."

He looked at her only briefly. His eyes paused at the knife on her hip, then slipped away.

"It's no help."

The angles of his jawline were taken up in his hands, the cocked thumbs. His face was offset by a nose pressed slightly sideways at the bridge. That he wouldn't look at her directly might be for his sake, she thought. A means of self-control. But it was only Denise who made her think this way. Normally she'd see this man as shy. She needed to get a read on him.

"You're in a bad spot," he said. He wasn't describing impressions but asserting truths. If she found herself in trouble with him, it would be the asserted truths and half-truths that drew her there. "Nothing to be done. Better clear out."

"I owe it to Denise and Stefan to stay. If you can bring Crooner back I'll wait it out with him."

"Not here. There's no electricity." He seemed to read her surprise, anticipate her question. "All along the road. No power, no phone. Won't be back for a long time."

He said the sky was getting bigger and she felt it was true, that he understood something and the way to say it belonged to a children's story, the sky's getting bigger, it's falling. He was a stater of facts, a maker of pronouncements. Then he said it again.

"It's getting bigger. From the west and south. A long ways off. It's the continent. There's no break in it." She couldn't see in his expression if something was building in him. "You're in a bad spot here." He looked to the lake forming again below them in the field. "The house will wash away."

"The water might go down."

"Too dangerous. You need a tow. Out to the highway. Your road's washing out. I have change."

Not "change." He'd said "chains," to tow her car to the highway. The mistake was small, odd, but she wasn't sure if it was his or her own. Something to pay attention to. Distinguishing between an *s* and a soft *g* engaged twenty-two sites in the brain.

"Well. That's kind of you. But I feel a duty to the Dahls."

"The house can't be saved."

He was overstating the danger. He liked to shock. She said it was just a rising creek. Not even a river, really. If the water reached the house, of course she'd leave.

"There's a river. It bends half a mile from here. Soon the water won't make the curve. Then it's straight for you. It will show up there"—he pointed to a crotch in the hills across the ravine—"and there." He pointed to the ridge just west of the house. "I opened the stream to make more time. Now it's closed." Without moving he seemed to set himself more squarely. "We need to leave. Go pack your things."

For the flint of a second his mouth tightened slightly, unreadable, a faint half smile or not. Then he nodded once in a short, sure movement and walked off. She felt calmer now than when he'd arrived. She had not panicked, she had seen what to do. She detected an interference in her reasoning—Denise was there in the works, telling her to run—but suppressed the thought. Denise had seen evil, but real evil was of the world, not of murder stories, pretended horrors. He'd not hesitated when she'd mentioned the Dahls by name.

From behind the house she watched him through the bank of back windows, through the front ones. He started his truck, turned it around in three movements, and positioned its rear bumper in front of her car. He took the chains from his truck bed and crouched between the vehicles. Of course she would not run, though yes, whether she ran or left with this man, the terms of her leaving would not be entirely her own. But it was hard to know what exactly was her own anymore, other than her body, her half-exposed, marked-up self, its bondings and reactions.

Then she remembered the fort. There was a child's fort upstream set into the embankment. Crooner had found it under some brush and snow, the bones of a small animal inside that she hadn't been able to make heads or tails of, so to speak. Something the size of a raccoon or opossum had died or been eaten there. The bones would still be inside, of course. Denise would have her run there, now, run and hide, but Ali couldn't imagine herself running through the woods, not really, and in so failing to imagine, revealed her position. Denise was credulous. Ali was not.

She walked to the house and this time left her boots on and tracked the mud inside. She packed her computer and stuffed what clothes she could into her bag without folding them and threw in her running shoes. She tucked the bag of Alph under the clothes. In the back bedroom she drew open the plastic sheeting and stared at the stacks of cardboard boxes. She recognized Denise's writing on them. *Fabrics—Israel. Soaps. Old Books*, numbered one through seven. *Winter Clothes*. Leaning against a wall behind the boxes was a large rectangular package wrapped in paper and string, marked *My Paintings*. Ali carried the package by the string out into the house and placed it by the doorway with her bag and computer case.

Shoad was up at the truck smoking a cigarette, looking to the west as if to see the water he'd promised her cresting the far hills. He'd struck an odd posture, resting his jaw in the inward-turned palm of his hand, as if he were going to shot-put his head. She pictured him turning and seeing her in the doorway, throwing his cigarette into the gravel and starting toward her. She saw it clearly, as though it were already happening. The feeling had a disturbing pitch to it, and then, as if she had to burn them off, a series of still images came to her. Her car abandoned in trees, Crooner's dog tags hanging from the mirror in a truck cab, a badly done oil painting of a blonde woman, Irina, standing next to the truck with the rust-red hood. Her brain would not be offering fantasies now if it knew she was in real danger. It would be trying to save her. But it might be doing it indirectly, through suggestion rather than direct analysis. It might, in fact, be trying to relax her analytical regions to enable itself to perform the revelatory leap required for difficult problem-solving. He'd opened the stream to make more time. Time was slowing, as she needed it to slow. Her brain, recognizing duress, was processing at higher than normal speed.

Maybe the scenarios she imagined were being produced by the drug, a manifestation of the Daffy effect so loathed in the lab. She pictured herself running, hiding, then what? Shoad would return so she couldn't go back to the house. She saw herself walking toward the bend in the river he'd spoken of, taking too long to reach it. If it wasn't there, then she'd know she was right not to go with him. If it was, she'd be in a different kind of trouble. And either way the water here would still be rising. She felt what she would feel, wet, cold, trapped in lowlands. Then she imagined she heard the water coming and the spell broke.

She would have to be careful of these visions. Alph was drawing them from commercial movies and TV, the junk novels of her teen summers. She'd lost her taste for popular horror long ago as she saw more real horrors, met more people who'd endured them. Yes, that was it, she realized. She didn't believe Denise's story because its details, the body twisting out of the fireplace and inside the forge, the serpent in the field, the vision of a chase in the ravine, these were too familiar, too easy to picture on-screen. Real terror was surely much stranger, perfectly strange, not familiar at all.

Under some compulsion she drew the knife and cut open the string and tore the paper off the paintings. There were four canvases framed in unfinished, unpainted wood. The first was of a dark, swirling chaos with red and orange toward the center. Two others seemed variations on the first, but with half-obscured tendrils of blue and yellow inside—were these pictures of the power line sparking in the field? In the last painting the darkness was crowded to the edges, outside a rectangle that made for a second frame, as if a window onto a scene. Inside were lines like the tendrils, but dozens, maybe hundreds of them, small, curving, crowded together, failing to contain a disorder of mind. Ali sensed Denise's need to turn away from the madness of the lines, the spectacle of them, yet her inability to face the endless darkness outside the frame. Written in small red letters at the bottom of the canvas, the word "south," and below, on the black outside, "north." Ali understood that she herself was there on the border between the two words but she didn't know why she thought this or what it meant.

She looked up. The rain had started again. Shoad turned and saw her. He threw his cigarette into the gravel and started down toward her.

5

ONE MORNING ON A SMALL HARBOR FERRY HEADING TO Granville Island she'd watched the boat taking its level with False Creek and felt a kind of weightlessness that seemed telling. Anja had asked if they could meet now, today, and as she'd taken the call Ali felt a flutter in her own voice. It would not be good news from the trial, of course, but that wasn't what the voice and the weightlessness meant. They meant somehow that she was getting less sure of herself and generally less certain, not just to herself but to others, as if she'd become doubted by higher powers, harder to believe in. Her decision not to seek a pregnancy returned now and then in this way, eroding her supposed selfhood, something she thought of anyway only as a cluster of changing biological conditions. But even self-betrayal is betrayal, an ancient constant that never loses its effect.

They walked along the seawall. Anja's news was that, switched to the placebo, through growing despair, Subject 11 had written less and less. The slowing made sense but she couldn't tell him that his crisis of faith was chemical. Then last week, eighteen days before the trial was to end, he dropped out and disappeared. Anja needed to know that he hadn't had a seizure, lost his memory or his mind, but he returned no calls or emails. When she went to the apartment he'd listed, she was told by a young landlady that he'd moved out, no forwarding address.

That morning at the clinic she'd received a small package in the mail, addressed to "Maker," care of her. It was a box the size of a large basket of strawberries. They took a bench seat.

"What if he's cut off his hand or something," Anja said.

"He couldn't have wrapped it so well with the other one. Maybe it's fresh strawberries. It's for me, I'll open it."

The box had weight but wasn't metal-heavy, more fruit than cannonball. The hand-printed letters in the address looked sane, unhurried.

She opened it to find a glass ball the size of a grapefruit, inside of which was one of the plastic identity bracelets issued to test subjects, with bar-coded personal and vital information. He'd twisted the bracelet once and reattached it into a loop, then suspended the resulting möbius strip inside the clear ball.

It came with a typewritten note.

Maker.
Are you there?
You've left me unfinished.
So I've left you and your pharma con.
I wanted, then needed what you were making of me.
But you weren't up to the making.
This ball is all you get.
Take it and fuck off.
No other ending.
Eleven.

"That's literally twisted," said Anja. Her voice, though not yet her face, expressed relief. "But I practically expected a bomb."

Ali held the object up against the inlet, the sky, the new ugly condos across the water. It maintained a sure beauty. Subject 11 had lost his faith, lost his sense of irony about their relative positions, lost his belief in her.

"He used to be charming," said Anja. "You okay?"

That night Anja called her at home to say that when she'd quoted the note to her unemployed classicist husband, he'd found another twist.

"He says 'pharma con' is a pun on a Greek word." Somewhere in Plato was a story about an Egyptian god who offers a king a remedy for forgetting, the *pharmakon* of writing, writing as a memory aid. The king turns down the offer, knowing it will have the opposite effect and cause forgetfulness. The king uses the same word, *pharmakon*, to mean poison. Remedy and poison. "One and both, so either, depending."

The ball sat now on a small china plate on Ali's dining table. Maybe mornings before work it would catch a little gray window-light that might, in time, disarm it.

"So it isn't just he thinks I conned him. He thinks I poisoned him."

"I don't know, Ali. I don't see how."

"Poisoned by loss. Withdrawn revelation. Before the trial he was happy knowing what he knew, seeing what he saw. Then he took the pills and saw more. Now he knows he's blind to the real size and intricacy of things. He's been poisoned with a knowledge of his blindness."

"That sounds pretty grand, actually. You haven't read the pages he sent me. He's not some great visionary. He's just a guy telling a story, and then we switched him to the placebo and he couldn't finish it."

When she asked Anja to describe the story, she said she'd put her husband on, said his name, Roland, who was better at these things.

"There's nothing so original about it." Ali remembered him now, his voice, a kind of high-snouted tone. "The usual horror themes and tropes. Violated Nature. Science and Art, fire and flood, mad-women and monsters. It clips along for a while but he never sent the ending."

They forwarded the file that night. Ali read the first page. There was already a body, a gun going off, the usual dumb mystery, cheap violence. It settled her to know that the story was only an enter-tainment. If this was all the vision he'd had, all he'd lost, she'd done Subject 11 a favor, she thought. Four days later he was dead.

She went to Carl with the news. His house had a cedar porch that in damp weather smelled like a sauna. He invited her to sit on his fraying string chairs but she stayed on her feet. She couldn't find the words at first and they ended up looking out at the neighbors' lawns and houses in the soft focus. Even at plus two degrees the gray could get so thick you expected whales to float by. There hadn't been sun for a week.

When she told him, he tried to come close but she held both palms out and took a step back.

"We have to stop the trial."

"This has nothing to do with the trial. He wasn't even on Alph."

She knew the line was coming and had tried to prepare but she hit him anyway, slapped him hard. He actually bent over briefly and said fuck.

"Now we know who you are," she said. "You're the bad guy who plays the company angle."

She hadn't known she would slap him, and having done so felt it was dopey, not genuine, a mimicking behavior. Then she thought she should feel better but didn't, especially. Maybe he wasn't the bad guy but the guy who'd sampled the drug and was now a true believer. Either way he was dangerous. As she walked to her car he straightened but didn't follow. He held one hand to his face where she'd reddened it, as if in thought.

"You've signed docs, Ali. Remember your legal position."

Beside the steps was an unpruned rosebush. The droop-headed blooms were chilled into, what, awkwardness? shame? Were they like kids staring at their feet? No, they were just blighted flowers. As she pictured them in memory now, a shadow grew over them and a whale passed by overhead.

She got into her car and saw that her removal from the place was complete. Crooner's bed and food notwithstanding, if she never returned, she might be traced only as far as her old Protegé, if it was ever found.

The back of Shoad's head in his truck was an anvil. He started up and eased forward until the chains were taut. She put the car in neutral and felt it coaxed into motion. The anvil shape might have disturbed her or else added to the feeling he was solid, could be trusted, but she let both notions pass by. He was simply part of the system of what was happening to the day. They were moving surely now and the rain thickened on the windshield. She turned the key and switched on her wipers. He accelerated as they approached the washout and his taillights nodded hard and then her car bucked and skidded sideways but they were through it and coming to the paved road. Her wipers and the truck's up ahead moved in different phases. In brain metastability tests subjects were asked to move their fingers like windshield wipers. She turned off the wipers and the rain on the glass hid her. She looked at her hands, as if they might tell her something. Then she saw on the floor the map she'd used to find the house. It was from a local gas station. Shoad's taillights slurred on her window, soon he'd stop and come for her. She grabbed the map, looking for the road, for a bending river to the west that would confirm his story, but she couldn't make sense of it. There were more rivers in the area than she'd realized, but she couldn't find the one in question, in doubt. Some roads weren't numbered and the numbers of others couldn't be followed through their intersections. They seemed to mass like capillaries or neurons. There was a knock on the glass and she dropped the map.

She lowered the window. He stood hatless in the rain. The water on his face made it limestone.

"The road's already worse. Asphalt's split open. You won't make it through. I'll tow you all the way."

"I forgot about the gears," she said. "I need to stay with the car, it slips out of neutral."

"Not by itself."

"It's the clutch. I have to keep my hand on the stick."

He looked at her, likely trying to decide if she expected him to believe the lie or thought she was explaining something she misunderstood, trying to decide if it was worth correcting her.

"It makes no difference. Brake when I stop. Don't try to steer."

They pulled out onto the highway and climbed to speed. The road was empty and the water slanted hard across it. Above were outriders to a black sky, dark clouds flying low from the south and then the black clouds burst. Every rain is all rains past but this one stood alone. She studied the map and looked up now and then at the tailgate of the truck and the chain connecting her to it. The map would not clear for her. She searched for the one town she knew, called Werso or Worso, but it wouldn't appear. A rain is different stood in than moved through. The other names meant nothing. This was someone else's rain.

The radio. She hit the scan button. Around the dial it ran and on the third revolution caught a voice. A woman said, "We cannot advise. The connections are generally down . . . I won't talk just to keep talking. The authorities have not been in touch. I'm only the producer and we have no information as to this event. There is no 'we.' I cannot advise." The voice went silent and she turned off the radio. Ahead the truck bucked on the broken road and then a half second later she felt the jolt under her as her body shot forward and sprung back and up away from the seat. She rolled down the window for a few seconds to look in the side mirror and saw the dark storm bank marcelled as if atop the heads of classical gods. Before her the truck bounced hard again and now she tucked her chin and when the car shot up it slackened the chain and then slammed it straight and the truck skidded slightly out of true, then hit another washout in the thawed pavement and this time as both vehicles lifted she saw something appear over the lip of the tailgate. The rain obscured her view but something had clawed there, two fingers in the bed hooked the gate. This was an illusion, she knew, and so she didn't believe it though it fixed her, she couldn't look away, couldn't move, even knowing there was no logic in it, not even a horrible logic, and then the fingers were gone.

When the brake lights came up again she slowed the car. What she needed from Alph was a hard jump cut, the getting to the next thing was hell. He turned left along a road that ran into trees at the base of a hill and they stopped. Brown water pooled off the shoulders and curled around the trees at the bottom of the slope. Shoad was unhooking the car. The rain was gone. He stood and beckoned her. She got out and stood behind the open door.

"Too much mud to tow you up. Get your bag."

She got her bag and computer from the backseat and closed the doors and watched him unhook the chains. She climbed into the truck, the mismatched hood laid out hugely before her. She heard him drop the chains into the bed and then he got in. His hands on the wheel were enormous. As they started up the hill she turned and saw how perfectly her car sealed them away. No one could get past it. She should have left the keys inside but they were in her pocket. The paintings were locked in her trunk. Then she remembered the fingers and looked into the bed just as the climb steepened and a set of clawed antlers slid back against the gate.

Where the road sprung a little higher they found better purchase and enough speed to carry them through the softer stretches as the truck tore up the surface. They began to plane out near the top and she saw rising ahead not farm buildings but a huge creature. Here it came, then, a final, heaving enigma that she would not survive. As it grew before them the shape resolved into a sculpture made from antlers wired together to form, through some closed loop of conception, a giant deer buck. It was about ten feet high at the shoulder, fourteen or more at the top of its rack. It faced the entrance to the yard as if to stand off visitors. The lines and proportions were exact. The head, she now saw, was slightly tilted, the shoulder striated, as if the body had been captured midmovement. There was life in the object. Inside it the horns were a frenzy. They passed by.

The yard was more or less as she'd pictured it from Denise's story but the barn looked new. A weather vane on its roof spun crazily, she couldn't tell what it was. Over the house the wind tore smoke from a chimney. They stopped before the house and Shoad stared out for a moment.

"I'm sorry," he said.

He got out of the truck and walked into tall, matted grass at the corner of the house. On mounted pipes he'd tied a rope. He picked it up and lifted it from the grass until he'd walked it to the end and held the open collar. He untied it from the rope and brought it to her.

She held it. The collar was muddy and wet. She nodded.

"I gave him bread. Watered him." What a strange way to say it, as if Crooner were a farm animal or a houseplant. "He might come back."

He would be trying to find his way home to her, and if he did she wouldn't be there. She pictured him standing at the door, barking, lying down.

"You should have left him in the house," she said.

"He wouldn't come in. He held still for food. I tied him. Maybe the barn. We'll look in there."

Ali was still catching up. Crooner had been here but wasn't. Had Shoad made the stag and how and why was it absent from Denise's account? Where had the day landed her? Where was the forge?

Shoad was in the rearview, walking to the barn. Something shivered in the side window and there it was again, a wire of lightning in the black distance.

She had a memory of crossing the yard, trailing Shoad, but no sense she'd actually done it. She'd been sitting in the truck, looking at the collar, and the next second she was standing before the barn. It stood in a rock-salt light. A concrete floor extended past the walls. The wood looked reclaimed, old, mismatched, only partly painted, with fresh gleaming galvanized nailheads. The planed timber boards joined truly. A pile of ash and scorched wood sat beyond the far end.

The swinging door was ajar. Shoad pulled it open and hit the lights and they stepped into the space. The barn was not a barn. There were no animals—Crooner wasn't here either—or stalls, no hayloft, no sawdust and straw on the floor. They stood in a workshop that gave way to a sort of gallery. The sculptures were wood and bone, copper, clay, forged metal. There must have been thirty or forty. The figures were human or nearly so, emerging from some chaos or returning to it, in agony. Their faces contorted in sole notes of pain. Air ducts led to a far wall and a huge fan high up that turned slowly and strobed the figures in light and shadow so that they seemed in motion. They were mismatched in size and height, the larger, standing ones maybe seven feet, others only three or four. Some were on their hands and knees, some lying on their sides. In many the bones were half-exposed, partial skulls, rib cages made from wood or curving antlers.

"Who are they?"

"I don't know. I dream them."

There were men and women, two children she could see. He said they weren't separate pieces. He called the whole thing Descendant.

She said something she herself didn't hear, could not recover. Then another question.

"What's happening to them?"

"I don't know. The same thing happens to all. Has happened or will happen soon."

The words led her to one clear thought. There was something monstrous about Shoad—Denise was right—but in showing her these creations, he wanted Ali to know it. What else she needed to know, to find a way of knowing, was if the monstrous was *of* him, of his nature, or only *in* him, as it might be in anyone under the common burden of those awake to certain truths. There was some receding shadow upon the edge of the distinction. He wanted her to see that truly monstrous things are real, even when they're not.

"They began after the accident," he said. "A road in the Black Forest. I hit a deer. Then came reconstruction. My face. I learned to speak again."

He said that before the accident he was a sculptor of abstract forms, "a sculptor of ideas," but that after the weeks in the hospital, with each successive surgery, each anesthetized dropping-off, he became ever more crazed with the forms of living things. The life survived into the sculptures. She'd never seen anything like them.

"You have these lives in you," he said. "These people. You know them."

"I've never dreamt about these people."

"They're strangers you recognize."

He presumed to know her forgotten dreams or unadmitted fears. She recognized the pieces, not as sculptures but as living-dying things. Moment to moment she was getting no more used to looking at them. They seemed about to turn their eyes to her. The standing and crawling ones stirred in perpetual advance. Here was a problem to record, that if the drug expanded an imagination already apprehensive, it could, in so many words, disturb you to death. But the record didn't matter now. The record was well past mattering.

She needed out and said so. For a second it seemed he might touch her, take her by the arm, but then he presented his back and he was leading her into the yard. She saw her footprints in approach as they returned the way they had come, to the truck and past it, over new ground, onward to the house.

6

HE CAME AND WENT, MAKING TEA ON A WOODSTOVE. THEY were in a large central room with a stone fireplace full of embers. She was sunk into an armchair. The handle of the knife on her belt pressed on the ball of her hip.

He put two cups on a coffee table and sat opposite her.

All day, little rounded stories had simply come to her, alive, dragonflies lit on the hand, each with its color and engine. Now she heard Shoad's. He said he'd been living in France and Spain for a summer, looking at prehistoric cave art. There'd been the deer through the windshield in Germany, a return home, here, a place he'd moved to years ago to be alone with his work.

From the end of the couch he angled himself at her across the shared table, regarding her from just above his high knees, one of which he'd grab to pull himself forward whenever he took a sip from his cup. She found herself refining her sense of his manner of speech. The words and their sounds came slanting across the gaps of dysarthria or aphasia, the sentences neurotraumatically clipped. Their compression had force. She had never understood before the thinness of conjunctions.

The sky was beginning to clear. He studied the trapezoid of sunlight that had narrowed and hardened around them. The set of his eyes, the indentations half-rhymed, rhymed again with the slight asymmetry of features not fully repaired. His face and his interest in cave art made her think of a photo on the wall of her father's study, a shot of the earliest known artwork, a once-headless human statue carved from a mammoth tusk thirty-some thousand years ago. It was discovered at the onset of World War II in a cave in southern Germany. After the war, other pieces were found, fitted together, completing the head. It turned out to be that of a lion. The earliest artwork was a hybrid, a kind of monster. The repair lines were there in the picture, somehow both ancient and new.

"Where are you from?" he asked.

She answered the usual way, as if he'd asked a different question. She said she was a researcher at a pharmaceutical company. Her training was in genetic science, her thing now was the brain. She used the word *hiatus* with a vague but present sense of its inaccuracy. He sat there across from her, point-blank. The hiatus had brought her here. She found herself mentioning her father.

"He's coming to visit," she said. The transparency of the lie seemed of no concern to him. "He'll arrive tonight. I left him a note letting him know I might be here."

In the pause he took in her deception. It was as if he could take hold of her lies and pull her closer with them.

"You don't know the Dahls," he said. "You came after they left."

"We spoke by phone. Quite a bit, actually. How well do you know them?"

She tried not to seem to be gauging him. He no longer looked away from her. The muddled expressions of his speech and face could retract, she saw, leaving a plain, unsettling regard.

"Stefan is a friend. He came here to help. After the accident."

The wind sounded, beating the house. Beyond a skylight a fleet of dime-edged clouds shot by, and a sensation formed as if her brain were growing down her neck, through her shoulders and arms. The effect was of extending the feeling of normal thought, its housing in the skull, into new territories. Was she thinking faster, better? Shoad's few words opened in all directions.

"His wife is sick," he said. "She sees demons."

Stefan had been checking in on Shoad's house while he was in Europe. After his return he visited every second day, in duty, a good Christian neighbor. Shoad was still physically weak and Stefan helped around the yard. Stefan had bought a donkey from a rescue service and sponsored its boarding at a stables, and he suggested it might make dependable company. He knew that Shoad's prescribed therapy included writing in a journal and speaking aloud, and reasoned that it would give him a set of ears to talk to. Together they built a stall in the barn and closed it off from the workshop, repaired an old fence that marked the overgrown pasture, arranged for feed deliveries. Stefan collected Aurelius, a large-headed thing with huge black eyes in a face like a furred instrument case. Together they groomed and dewormed the animal, which took to following Shoad around the pasture and watching him from the fenceline, braying in joy or aggrievement. After sunset Shoad would eat his supper in the barn with Aurelius, telling him about his life, things no one knew, and about sculpture and the human arts. He understood that the animal was lonely, and he would either have to get another donkey or return Aurelius to the stables.

Stefan came by with materials for Shoad's work. He had begun the stag sculpture, made of antlers and false antlers he constructed from wood, clay, and epoxy. If Shoad was still at work when he arrived Stefan would visit Aurelius or occupy himself with work in the yard. He never left without speaking. Shoad came to realize that Stefan needed someone to talk to about Denise, someone he could trust. She had started into a delusional phase and seemed to be off her meds, though she wouldn't admit to not taking them. Shoad suggested he bring her to visit Aurelius. Shoad had been to their place three or four times since moving here, though not since the accident, and Denise had asked about his life, his sculptures. Though he kept to himself and didn't mind being thought of as the local outsider, the Dahls had no investment in feeling apart from him, and now it was hard to reconcile his memory of Denise with the woman Stefan was describing.

The next day they arrived. He watched them from the picture window. She wore a long denim shirt, untucked, over a billowing, rose-patterned skirt with a crooked, scissored hem. She looked around the yard and seemed to fix on the weather vane. Shoad met them at the door and stepped back for them to enter but Denise would not come forward. She said nothing at the sight of him, said nothing to Stefan when he asked her what was wrong. Shoad offered her something to drink. She went back to the car and wouldn't get out.

A few days later the stories began, relayed by Stefan, of a Russian bride named Irina.

Stefan now devoted his time to Denise, and Shoad was left with Aurelius and an isolation he was used to, had sought most of his life. As if to produce company, his dreams became peopled with figures he recognized as those who'd come to him in the drugged sleeps around his surgeries. He had half forgotten them but now they returned and asked to be given material form. He began to sketch them, even as he worked on the stag. Rather than visit, Stefan called the house. He said less and less until the only things between them became unspoken. In time the calls stopped.

Shoad had built the stag on a base that sat atop skids. He hauled it with his tractor to the front of the yard. He couldn't say why he'd made it or why he'd positioned it there but it somehow displaced the turbulence he felt at the memory of the accident and its aftermath. He and the animal had happened to each other, a chance intersection of two beings that only one had survived. Their coming together had changed him wholly, not just his ways of saying but of seeing too. His work was filling with animal forms, simple enough, and with something inside them not otherwise seen. There was no way to say this even before the accident, and the way of saying it now was through the pieces themselves. His old works had been stillborn.

"The new ones are alive. They carry death inside them."

So he said, or seemed to say. His words were too simple for their volume of meaning. He barely spoke and yet the story came to her whole. In the variable speeds of the mind, her perception outran time. Had he said all this, and so willingly, or had he sketched a story that Alph had remade in great detail? She tried to stop listening. As Shoad sat before her, speaking, memories glinted and disappeared. A neighbor's mean boxer tied to a sapling. Pigeons wheeling over rooftops of some foreign city. She could see them there against the wall. Her father, young, watching TV in a motel room chair.

Shoad took a sip and continued.

Stefan drove into the yard. He stepped from his car absent of the usual forced good cheer through which he tried to convince himself he occupied some world different from the one he stood in. Even in his posture he seemed troubled. Months ago, when he'd first visited after the accident, Stefan had neither reacted to Shoad's appearance nor pretended not to notice it. It was as if Shoad's face was of no matter to him, as if he'd seen real monstrosity and this wasn't it. Now some distance, Denise, had formed between that Stefan and this one.

They walked to the pasture and said hello to Aurelius. Stefan looked confused, as if unsure of why he'd come. His movements were muted. He declined an invitation to the house. Shoad described his renovation plans. He referenced the walls Stefan would know, walls Shoad intended to knock out. He described the ironwood posts he'd procured to buttress the beams, the position of the fireplace he'd build. Shoad led him around the property, pointing out the work he'd done. A newly mounted yard light, a new well cover. He walked him to a stand of sumac, the deadwood cleaned out and piled in the open, in need of burning. Together they heaped the wood into a pyre. They gathered hoes and blankets from the barn and gasoline from the machine shed and poured it onto the pile. Shoad lit a match and tossed it. The wood fired in a great convulsion and they stood before it and Stefan began to talk. He said fire was where it all began, the troubles Shoad had no doubt suspected. He had always known his wife was holy but she was prone to visions that were not, or so he believed. It was natural for him to reject the visions. They isolated her from him. He felt they stood against him, so his position was determined. Stefan didn't tell Denise's story so much as confess the ways in which it confounded him in a series of unconnected pronouncements about fire and visions and the pitch and length of strange Russian vowels. Shoad couldn't follow him but felt he shouldn't interrupt. It was as if Stefan were speaking neither to him nor to himself but to a third party unknown between them.

Because of her illness, Stefan said, they had backed out of a planned African mission in the winter.

"I can't reason with her about her Russian friend," said Stefan. From his pants pocket he produced a necklace with a locket. "She said her friend gave her this. I've never seen it before. Denise doesn't wear jewelry." He handed it over. "You see those words there, on the clasp?" Shoad could see there were faded characters or numbers barely impressed on the cheap metal but couldn't make them out. "I guess you don't read Russian."

"Never made a study."

"I looked at the words under a magnifying glass. They look maybe Russian." There were no words on the locket itself. It was empty. "When we bought the place there were all sorts of things that would just turn up. One time in the walls I found insulation cinched around a water pipe with an old wristwatch. Maybe this is something like that. Maybe she found it in the walls."

Though Shoad felt the heat on his face and through his clothes, Stefan put the blanket over his shoulders and cut a figure in the light, holding his hoe like a staff.

"My wife has visions, Clayton. She's unstable but she has the greater faith. I wait for revelation but it doesn't come to me, maybe because I fear it. And so I sift through fallen things looking for evidence. I try to fill my heart with goodness but I don't know how to be open to revelation. I believe in it, I think I do, but it doesn't choose me." He seemed to be working toward a question he couldn't find words for. Shoad imagined the question concerned the impossibility of absolute trust in a God never present to the senses. "How can we know if the presence we feel is of God or the Enemy?" Stefan said he felt the Lord only when in a state of prayer, but his wife had had even this beautiful gift poisoned by disease. For years they prayed aloud together every night, prayed in their shared language and in tongues. "The gift of tongues sounds different in different people," Stefan said. "I know the sound of her gift like I know the voice that comes to me in my thoughts. But one night her tongues changed, another voice came. And I knew what it was, this language. She was speaking Russian. The spirit of her friend, her dead friend, real or not, lives inside her."

With the new spirit in her came no easing of the willfulness Stefan had never been equal to. In different hours she could be one or the other, almost herself or almost another, truly foreign woman called Irina who enraged the Denise he knew for her fate and her acceptance of it. Surely Irina was just a picture on the internet, and yet Stefan too was divided against himself, wanting his proof, something that would after this dark interval finally again bring their beliefs together, even though to want evidence was to want a confirmation of a suffering outside of his wife, a suffering and murder and the revelation that Shoad was not who he seemed to be.

"I confess to wondering," said Stefan. "I come here to your place and I know the truth, but at home I see her suffering and I want another truth."

But even if he could find proof that Irina had been real, there'd be something more terrible. He would be forced to confront something else he couldn't accept, that his wife now carried the souls of two tormented women. Shoad understood that Stefan wanted to find evidence of Irina and to have come to believe in her. But to find it or not, neither result would release him.

"I can almost see her, Irina. Sometimes the way Denise looks at me, her eyes, they're shaped wrong, flatter to the brow, and she holds them on me for just a second. Then she turns away and she's gone."

After Stefan left, Shoad walked the perimeter of the fire, looking for stray embers. Now and then he found one and stabbed it out with the hoe. He tried to imagine what might be done for this man who would confide in no one else. He thought of the word *mission*. His own mission was to help Stefan and Denise, but he had no idea how to reach them.

That night when Shoad undressed he found burn marks on his legs, red lines in curls and flares, like ancient letters painted with a thick brush. The heat had burned through his canvas work pants and left the pants unmarked. Only in the cool of the bedroom did he feel the burns alive.

The last thing Stefan had said to him, "To remake the house, Clayton, build it simply. All things toward God."

"I can't tell you more," he said. She understood him to mean he wasn't up to it. He seemed depleted, his shoulders rounded in resignation.

He left the house to check the sky and the water level in the ravine. Ali sat in the cool room and the remainder of story. Her memory wasn't of hearing it, but of having been present at the events, there by the fire with Shoad and Stefan, there with Shoad that night in his room. On her shins she felt a phantom heat. She could picture the burn marks on his legs that read to her as math and science symbols. One was shaped like *psi*, phase difference. Another was *theta*, time constant. *Eta*, hysteresis. And *alpha*, the false positive rate or fine structure constant or a constellation's brightest star. Alph produced the alphabet and fitted the characters into her thoughts.

She picked up the two empty cups and took them to the kitchen, rinsed them in the sink. The stream died in her hands—she'd forgotten there was no power, no pump—and something about the water on the base of her thumb looked wrong. Or it looked as it should but felt wrong, given where the hand was wet. As if her nerves were reading sensation through a new, fast-evolving system. What would it be like to lose this, to be on the other side, after weeks of this feeling, to be blunted back into common, unremarkable days? You might choose to pitch yourself off a bridge.

She looked for Shoad through the window. The weather vane on the barn had almost stopped spinning and now she could see it was in the shape of a soldier, a man with a rifle. He wore a cap or helmet of some kind. Or maybe not soldier but hunter. Only now she noticed the top of a smokestack above the roofline.

The rest of the story, the part Shoad couldn't bring himself to tell, wasn't hard to put together. She had Denise's version and the evidence of this place, the sculptures, the new barn, the scorched wood, and Shoad himself. Denise had omitted from her telling all contradicting details. Her Shoad was not a keeper of animals, not an artist, no one with a use for a forge. She would have driven into the yard, imagined a communication from her imaginary friend, and somehow spilled fire into the barn. Aurelius had died in the fire, the barn had burned to nothing, had had to be rebuilt. Stefan, if he came at all, would have witnessed the aftermath. And whatever the time between then and now, the Dahls were not in West

Africa. Denise was likely a new patient in some long-term care facility, and Stefan would be living near her, looking daily for signs she'd return to herself.

A few hours more and the pill would wear off. Would she retain this comprehension and what was she blind to? She felt herself lagging behind some important understanding, something right in front of her that she couldn't see. A need for revelation connected her to Stefan. Like Shoad they were part of the pattern. Both needed to step away from their fears to sort the false from the real, the consoling illusions from what was unsettling or unendurable. She felt the quick in her molecular and genetic levels, the decouplings, the triggered gene expressions. Of course she couldn't really, but she did.

As in fourteen percent of the subjects, a headache announced the onset of the peak effect. Next might come more intense visual disturbances, scintillations, cuneiform patterns overlaid on points of focus.

A flashlight stood lens down on the counter. When had he collected it? He was thinking ahead, thinking better than she was. Other things were out of place. A slotted box of cutlery on a stool, a canvas ball cap propped with a plate in a dish rack. Sitting on top of a covered wicker basket with a decorative floral inlay was a yellow plastic pill dispenser.

Across the room, a door ajar. She saw a glimmer on a blue wall. She walked over and opened the door.

The room held a small table, a window onto the yard. Against the blue wall opposite the window was a stepladder and an old cardboard suitcase with a faded Fragile sticker on the side. On the wall itself were a few photographs, tacked polaroids connected by angled lines that as she came closer resolved into writing, the minuscule jitterscript she recognized from the note he'd left for her. The polaroids were placed it seemed randomly on the wall. She recognized the barn and weather vane in one shot, a view of the house from the yard entrance in another. Two photos were unreadable, extreme close-ups of surface textures, maybe wood grain, maybe fur. Above the others was a picture of a smokestack streaming grayblack. Where the photo ended, the written lines took up the path of the smoke and drifted toward the ceiling. She took in the words at eye level. They began on the margins of the house shot and extended in three parallel lines to the barn.

> The sculpture must not stop. To see past plane and volum. The time around the moment. A stranger in town with blue sleeve. She handed me Samuel three 19. "and the Lord was with him and did let none of his word fall to the ground." So who is it with me.

From the barn to the wood grain the lines angled downward again.

> In a crow we know what to look at dimension perspectiv. The tree near the window. The crow in the tree is and is not bigger than the barn. He would paint the crow if he painted who is with him. The sculpture is a prison. The life inside is long-tailed. Like zoo animal. Like wartime animals starve. The skul is a prison.

The handwriting would be part of a therapy to address his lexical agraphia. Of course he would make of it a locally open book. You could know him by his spaces, his workshop, his living room, this study, places Denise had never set foot in.

She read into the crowded margins of the photos and saw that the lines crossed into the pictures in places. In the slatted walls and tire-rutted foreground she looked for references to family, friends, a deep past, but the cobalt lines floated in a shallows of personal time. The depth was only in his need for words, the need was ancient human, there in the early brain. Language began a hundred thousand years ago, writing eight. Again she thought of the earliest art. Representational cave drawing, adornments made of bone and antler, an awareness beyond sensation, into reflexive consciousness, a kind of early selfhood.

Her father had taken her caving once.

Lined into taut, parallel strings of words, Shoad's fragments assumed a disciplined force, not the obsessive massings of hypergraphia. She'd seen such tiny writing before, in galleries, cramped into notebooks, in the reproduced pages of famous men. Dostoevsky, Van Gogh. Lewis Carroll and his ninety-eight thousand letters, a number she remembered from her own childhood obsession with Carroll and his Alice, whom she used to like to think she was named after.

Above the smokestack, the top corner of the wall was barely marked. She mounted the ladder, followed the smoke plume where it broke into skeins trailing into clear space, and read what seemed the most recent entries.

The sun hit the ice. Meltwater rush in the stream. Smell
of first things. Thawing things thawed on the

bank. Digging at the source.

The source a humanform. He found a hand, the arm, the head he backed off the shape. The smell brought him backed off again. His own sound sounded strange.

The light shot into him falling

So the day's thaw had revived him in the light of creation. He'd described it all in the third person, as if trying to get outside himself. The word "humanform" seemed to refer to his sculpture, Descendant. She noted a few more dropped letters. The more energy in the writing, the more urgent, the more mistakes he made.

The vertigo arrived with a half-formed memory that wouldn't come clear. She hung on to the ladder, then step-floated down as if onto the moon and said a simple "ouch." She had never been prone to bad headaches. It didn't help that she could picture the brewing storm in her brain, a storm aware of itself just got more agitated. She sat on the hard chair and felt Crooner's collar in her back pocket. She withdrew it and with no regard for the mess she was making rubbed the dried mud from the leather only to reveal strange dark discolorations.

When she closed her eyes she was falling so she opened them and tried to focus on what was before her, the shard of pain in her head. She was already passing through the living room before she realized she was walking, looking for medicine, and then she was back in the kitchen holding his plastic med dispenser shaped like a multistory building sheared in half. The pathways inside formed a maze. Each compartment was marked with an hour. The pills were of every description. She worked at the casing, unroofed it.

Only one compartment was empty—he'd missed at least two doses, which made sense, somehow, on this clockless day. Whites, blues, yellows. Rounds and oblongs, precisely machined edges.

She recognized the Gilshey brands and their knockoffs but saw nothing for her head. He must have been in near-constant pain. Meds for sleep, digestion aids. Meds for joint inflammation, depression, and others she didn't know what. She wondered if a small dose of Alph would be of use to him in finishing out the kinks in his speech. More likely, on a calm day, a day not like today, it would help the depression with the elating wonder of simply seeing more, creating more. Maybe all the pills could be cleared away if he took a hit of Alph with his breakfast. The hell would be the headaches and the coming off. He'd recover speech and end himself.

She had a moment of panic, then remembered that the stash of Alph was in her suitcase. The sudden adrenaline should have dulled her pain but it worsened.

She put the dispenser back on top of the basket, took it off again and set it on the counter. She tried to think precisely about what she was looking at. *Wicker, weave,* the words seemed to cluster in little near-likenesses and the word *cluster* took her back to the headache. She lifted the lid off the basket.

It was full of old pill bottles and packets. She searched through the drugs, in vials and small boxes. Over-the-counter cold reliefs, topical ointments, allergy pills. Expired, most of them, now that she checked. Lemon cough drops. Letters she couldn't read became "Lozenges" when flipped. There was nothing to touch what was happening to her head. And then there, at the bottom, a broken silver packet of capsules. She turned it over and saw the word "КОДЕИН."

She stared into the mystery of it. She ran her finger along the date crimped into the edge. Whatever they did to you, these Russian ones, they could do it yet.

She needed to move but she stood there.

And whatever the effect of the drug КОДЕИН, it was nothing compared to that of the word itself. It named one thing, enacted another. The row of strange characters gave her certainty. Certain knowledge in a half-familiar word. Then the six Cyrillic letters drove the sense into questions that wouldn't stand still.

She had suffered common ailments. Irina.

There was something growing here, growing near. She was failing to react self-defensively. She knew this and yet she just stood.

She wanted to swallow the foreign word. Or Alph wanted it. She had always believed there was a genius at work in the chemicals themselves to combine and play toward a final balance. A compound of well-being. Imagine a state in which one might know about the way of things, of cruelties and neglect, and still feel well, feel joy, even happiness. Fear could always come over the top, but there were glints of evidence in the research and in her of something like calm amazement. She had thought that the final word, the name for this shared solid state, for our dreamed-of one lasting knowledge and belief, would be *peace*. But maybe the word itself was a compound, some mix of native and foreign characters and the histories trailing them. Line up the letters in just the right way. Train the palate to say it. Repeat.

She turned from the counter and looked into the living room where they'd shared tea, an empty room, a sense of contained design, trying to locate herself. What did she know for certain? Her father lived in California. She'd come here from Vancouver, where she was born. But where had she arrived? She pictured the map of it fading even as she saw herself heading east, ducking down into the Dakotas, through Chicago, Michigan. Then, as she followed herself along, the forests and fields ran to a kind of empty, unnamed space. She was forgetting the present. As in a dream, she didn't even know what country she was in.

Days ago, crossing the continent. She could see herself from some elevation. She held both views in mind, looking out from her skull here in Shoad's house and looking down at herself as if through a transparent ceiling. A part of her was in a tree, maybe a red-tailed hawk on a limb. Then the hawk flew off and she was almost where she was.

Look how alive, these walls at the end of the world. Even at the end we imagine some other ending.

This house. She really had to get out of here.

She thought of Crooner's collar. Now she understood. The discolorations were burn marks.

A presence was moving behind her. It cast its tall shape on the wall.

She couldn't turn to face it but then did. There in the window, standing up inside itself, was a silhouette against the low sun. From behind the barn the column of smoke rose higher than she could see. He rounded the corner in stride. He was coming across the yard for her.

7

SHE'S LYING IN A ROOM AND SHE'S RUNNING. THERE'S A TV playing in the corner. She's cold and wet, her feet stabbing along the streambank. The light in the ravine, in the room, is dim. The stream is more than a stream, she's running against it. The screen, at an angle, plays old footage, some black-and-white interior. The sense of someone else in the room, watching the screen, the sense of the top of a head above a chair back.

The oncoming water bends before her. Her feet are numb, she's sliding stride to stride. The waterrush covers the sound of her breath but she feels it leaving her in explosions in the air, the need to cry out and the need not to. As she runs she remembers lying in a room, a TV, a memory so sharp it's semi-actual, lying there remembering running here in the ravine, but she can't remember what happens next.

A man on TV standing on a stage in black and white with curtains behind him and she hears now distant laughter, entertained-audience laughter. He disappears or becomes a war scene slanted away from her in green spotted color and she feels greatly fatigued. A man with a rifle crouches on-screen. The head moves in the chair.

She's having to scramble more than run. The water has claimed the flats and shelves and forced her up the bank so that she's crossing slopes of mud in a continual fall and climb, and when she's highest above the water she sees its strength, the rapids formed along the rising verges. All is pure duration. She allows no full thoughts, no language for thought. The run west has slowed to nothing. She needs to make it higher, to the narrow strip of woods, but she can't get enough purchase. How far has she really come? The bank draws her back down and she hooks her elbow around a young tree and wedges herself there, resting.

The first sharp report. A dull cracking bores through the sound of the current. Then it comes in twos and threes in tight succession, and too late she looks upstream to see the wall of water high above her, breaking off the young trees on the slopes of the ravine, snapping them with the force that meets and covers her and no wonder she can't remember.

Past the way she came, past floating wooden swing seats and mailboxes, the column of smoke shunting into view and away, passing swallowing whirlpools in themselves swallowed, the highest reaches of treetops at eye level, a skunk belly-up and half cut in half by a snare loop, past the barriers to nonsense, a rumble as in train sounds, she tumbles under the surface and up again, catching discontinued scenes that seem clipped from a reel, reeling past crows hopping in branches in stark alarm, a coyote going under, its tail blooming on the surface and the cold meltwater pinching out all feeling and order. Under and up again, stunned too cold to draw breath, and her leg catches on some submerged trunk or footbridge, garbage floating past, a wind chime of seashells draped on a dead cat, tent flap, paper yard lamp, ornamental dice. The river lifts her onward again and bends her with it, sweeps the low sun into her eyes and she thinks there must be a falls ahead. The surface is not constant, it moves at varied speeds. The cold has kept at bay a knowledge now rallying to her consciousness that she's struck or been struck by something. She's bleeding from her shoulder or neck and when briefly the water runs deeper and flattens she sees or imagines the narrow furl of blood in the mudbrown current, loses it again when the surface folds, and the blood brings the feel of the wound, and the wound some body sense, space and volume, breath, at last, and the motions she's been making all this time, buoying her past impossible matter, a power cord coiled on a limb, hollow plastic buddha bobbing upright in the roil, unbroken window or hothouse pane shimmed into a trunk like a serving tray, a slope-roofed birdhouse drifting by, a beak popping out of the hole. Her limbs move without her. She can see her hands but not feel them but the seeing is clouded now and for a time it seems she's not carried at all but watching the land move around her as if out the car windows in an old flick hurtling into plot, into story, end of a story, so that now the cold is blinding and each solarized moment is beaded in her eyes, and she closes them and sees here at the end a dead man in a glass ball turning and the skull is a prison.

The through-force had released her.

She'd washed up in the low crotch of a maple on the edge of a field. Gray muck covered her, the plugged diamond bark.

Below on the hillside the brown water eddied against the higher trees, their trunks and limbs mudslick and heavy, a tired platoon from the trenches. The light was clean, of morning, the shadows solid on the moving surface reaching tree to tree, branches in dark connection like newly dead thoughts. She saw things in their relation and in relation to what wasn't or once was or would come to be.

A door rafted by, kicked off a treetop, and spun back into the current.

A huge bird lifted above the ridgeline and turned, progressing in slow loops. As it grew closer she saw the black-and-white underside as it seemed to stop midair in the apex and became a serried portal to a world of clear, dark sense. Without the strength to form the words, she opened her mouth to call the clarity down to her but couldn't sound the appeal.

She thought again of the creatures unknown to her. Did one of them feel her existence? She listened to distinguish water from wind. Somewhere underneath them both was her breathing and thinking of it made all the sounds seem doubtful.

The mud on her clothes was stiffening now. The sun was low but warm.

She shifted her weight, touched her neck. The wound was clotted or caked. There was pain in her legs and forearms, in her hands, but they worked. She bent her knees and swiveled to face the drier ground above her, and slid and landed on all fours. She crawled higher and saw two fingers out of joint. After a time she was drying on dry ground and she sensed a breathing presence over her but couldn't even gesture at escape and didn't know if she wanted to. She curled and slept there.

She dreams she is slumped sideways in an armchair, one leg dangling to the floor. She feels heat from a woodstove. Crooner lies against her leg, his fur, his weight heavy on her naked foot. It's daytime. There's something in her lap that she wants to see but she can't make her eyes look downward. Instead she is looking across the room at an opposite wall covered in empty black picture frames, all askew. Crooner is panting in his sleep. He is running in his dreams, running or in some nightmare. Her eyes feel freer now, she looks a little lower, sees her knee, the pages in her lap, and the panting grows louder and louder and she wakes.

PART II

Decor

The first dreamer was given the vision of the palace, and he built it; the second, who did not know of the other's dream, was given the poem about the palace. If this plan does not fail, someone, on a night centuries removed from us, will dream the same dream, and not suspect that others have dreamed it, and he will give it a form of marble or of music. Perhaps this series of dreams has no end, or perhaps the last one will be the key.

JORGE LUIS BORGES, "Coleridge's Dream"

THE LAST THING MY MOTHER SENT ME WAS A PICTURE SHE'D taken of a cuneiform tablet in a small museum in Anatolia. At the top, a loinclothed king or god in profile, perspectiveless, the sun and moon above, and below, columns of tiny scratchings, letters, language leaping from stone. The image was badly lit. She must have stood to the side to move the glare from an overhead bulb to the margin of the tablet. I can picture her looking into the window of her phone, taking a side step, tapping the screen. She wrote, "The work's going well, though your father still seems to think the problems in refugee camps owe to a lack of decorum and matching eating utensils. We're sightseeing for two days. Tomorrow off to those big old slabs," meaning the stelae at Göbekli Tepe, site of the world's first religious temple, which they never did see. How bluely ironic that this last dashed-off email should have attached to it an image of a language grown from pictorial symbols carved on a hard slab of reality very like the headstones that serve now as their alter-presences. And cuneiform, so beautiful. From drawings in sand to sandstone to granite, Hittite and Sumerian to Semitic symbols to Greek, ox/house/camel/door became *aleph*, *beth*, *gimel*, *daleth* became *alpha*, *beta*, *gamma*, *delta*, the signs moving back and forth from yard to shelter, nature to artifice, country to settlement. In their origin alphabetical letters had the breadth to mark both the wild and the cultivated.

The NGO called me in Montreal, first with the news, then with the arrangements. I flew to Halifax to meet the so-called mortal remains, held steady through a small service, and saw them into the ground. When I looked up, suddenly orphaned, I decided to take to the skies.

In time I was living with a petite Londoner in a one-bedroom apartment in La Latina, a neighborhood in Madrid. We sampled the city cheaply, hitting the discount hours in museums and bars, attaching ourselves to English groups on architecture tours, attending street protests, chanting in bad Spanish. On TV, soap operas confused us and soccer billionaires scored goals and then tore off in some direction as if chased by guard dogs. She worked as a copy editor for a travel magazine. For a few weeks she indulged me in language games, with imposed restrictions. No definite articles over dinner ("Please pass a pepper grinder."), only one adjective for the weekend ("Then how would you describe me?" I asked. "You are insufficiently friended."). No one-word utterances. Responding to any question of five words with a rhyme ("Do you like this dress?" "... The hemline's low. I'd prefer less."). I reasoned that the games marked us as distinct, kept us quick. Then the challenge of them became limiting, like badly fitted clothes, binding the limbs in mismeasured forms. For a time it seemed we'd never free ourselves, that we'd go mad together. We stopped having sex. And so we called off the games. It took a while to break ourselves of the habit of listening a certain way, for lapses or possibilities. We went silent, hours at a time, and, on the other side of silence, broke up.

Or that isn't what happened. What happened was she realized she could no longer watch me sit motionless. To her I seemed to move at a great speed while reading or staring out the window at the crowds in the El Rastro flea market. She said, "You sit still the way other people run for their lives." She thought I'd turned sitting into an act of cowardice, a way of avoiding hard truths. One day the truth was that she had fallen for her Spanish teacher and was moving in with him.

Alone, I cut all expenses. I quit smoking, lived on pasta and butter, but in the end my means ran down. As I left for good with my duffel bag, my landlord, a sad-eyed Italian Spaniard, held open the door and clasped me on the deltoid. "You are real. Real poets do not pay rent." He'd seen me reading poetry and assumed I wrote the stuff. In truth I am only a failed poet. A failed many things. Bartender, textbook editor, doctoral student, orchestra publicist. I have no talents but reading.

I landed back in Montreal, living in a former professor's basement. He was the closest thing to family I had left. A memory disorder had forced him into early retirement. Now his old students took turns going with him to medical appointments and grocery stores, looking after him in exchange for a basement room. Most hours of the day he was himself, lucid, funny, the Dominic Easley we all knew. But there were slips and lapses, especially in the evening, after wine. One night as we walked through the residential streets he tried to introduce me to his neighbor, a large woman out inspecting her garden. The neighbor and I understood even before Dominic that he'd lost my name, and as I said who I was, it was he who listened with the greater interest. That night in the basement I had never felt so unknown, even to myself. The feeling wasn't loneliness but rather two emotions held together, one sadness, a simple word that simply applied, and the other something borrowed from Dominic, a distilled sense of being, of possibility, as if I had entered a state of perpetual, dreadful expectation.

Contained in that dim basement I felt something in approach. Then, out of nowhere, a stranger named August Durant sent me an e-ticket to Rome and an offer of six hundred USD a week to stay with him and conduct what he called "literary-detective work." He stressed that he wasn't hiring me as a sexual companion. I would put my one talent in service of solving "a mystery of dimensions unknown" even to him. I was without other prospects. Either I found paid work or I'd become accommodated to the sorry view of myself as destined for still more years of drift and small failures, trying to stay out in front of hard truths. But a detective. Hack gumshoe or houndstooth or hard-boiled? Would I be figuratively armed? Would there be a good story? Would its end be mine?

Words grow out of the world and then back into it, made of the very history they string together. An enduring one comes out of the Old English *morðor*, the Old Norse *morð*, and several related variants, meeting the line from the medieval Latin *murdrum* and the Anglo-French *murdre*. The word is there very near the origin of stories, right after first light, and now it's all through every story, even when it doesn't seem to belong and we imagine we don't see it.

Durant knew me as the author of an online rant I'd gone so far as to give a title: "The Poet at the End of the World." There had appeared on the internet a new poetry site called Three Sheets. The anonymous host posted only his or her own poems, most short, some untitled, and yet amid all the traffic noise, the page drew a surprising aggregate of readers, for a poetry site. At first these readers were other poets and academics, who within six weeks built two new sites devoted entirely to the verse of the mystery poet who for a time was called the New Anonymous, or Nanny, for short, and to the enigma of his or her identity. Theories sprung up around the names and cities and historical events alluded to in the poems. Something calling itself the Group Against Three Sheets (GRATS) arose to attack Nanny for "a mockery of the provocateur spirit" and to pronounce Three Sheets "insufficiently political in its conception." Another, the Group Against the Group Against Three Sheets (GRAGRATS), the name and acronym chosen, as its founding manifesto stated, precisely for their absurdity, considered the anonymity central to what came to be called the Project, and defended the poet's choice to remain unnamed, and even insisted that there be no provisional designations, and so asked that people stop using "Nanny" to mean "the anonymous one" (uncapitalized), a corrective that somehow became widely adopted. (GRAGRATS) chose the symbol @ to designate the poet. The rest of us just called him or her the Poet.

One morning in the Montreal basement I'd taken a stroll past the Sheets-inspired sites, read the latest skirmishes, which usually amused me unintentionally, and came away wanting to throw stones at both sides. In any country, debates among poets are comically vicious, the stakes being so low. Though I'd intended never to add my voice to the babble, I couldn't stop from saying what no one else would say and posting it on the Sheets Project Meta-Site of Record (SHEPMETSOR). Roughly reduced, my point was that the debates over Three Sheets were being conducted almost entirely by people with no feeling whatsoever for poetry, mostly academics and bad poets, and were these people capable of reading better, they'd see that the Poet was addressing an audience in the habit of filtering out bleatings such as theirs, and that, in fact, the most coherent theme or subtext discernible in the Poet's work suggested not a communal, consensual, or debatable set of ideas, but rather a soul's draw toward a single, fixed mystery.

"The mystery itself is unnamed. Is it a lost loved one? a lost god? All we find is an absence. Absence is the most present thing in the poems." I'd fallen into a conviction and was more or less stabbing the keys. "Most of you are failing the Poet and the poems. As readers, you are thin where you should be thick, and otherwise thick through and through."

That last line now embarrasses me. I don't sound like myself, even myself in prose. Dominic chose not to call me on the brattiness of the tone, or the generalization I'd made about academics, though he was a better and more soulful reader than I. He read Durant's letter of invitation, looked in on Three Sheets, and pointed out that I was entertaining a solicitation from someone unstable or at least very likely in one of the categories of thin readers that I'd attacked.

"If you need the money, though, you can always tell yourself that this Durant must concur with your reading of the Poet, and so taking his money might not be ignoble. And anyway, it's not just money, it's Rome!"

It was more than Rome, in the end, but in Rome it began.

The next week I handed over my room and caretaking duties to a former classmate and flew off, anticipating disaster. Dominic had gifted me a few nights in a budget *residenza* in Trastevere. I had been to Rome once before, with no money, and seen the sights, sipped the coffee at Tazza d'Oro, felt the black cobblestones in the soles of my feet, in my throat, under my eyelids when the last stranger home turned out the light in the room for males in a hostel near Termini Station. I'd been alone then, in my early twenties, and now eight years later was alone again. Being always in silence had left me without a means for any human gesture toward comprehension, and the traffic and murmuring tourists only sharpened for me the silence of the buildings and stones, and cast me, in some faux-Romantic sense, with the dead.

In my small room I consulted my laptop to see what was happening at Three Sheets. There had been no new posts in a week, an unusual but not unprecedented quiet. When the site went still for a time I imagined the Poet entirely unplugged, reading old books, then wandering on a farm or in village streets somewhere temperate. He/she lived in a moderate climate, I deduced, but came from an extreme one, which was why the "runt days" with their "uncentered bubble of light"—winter days, surely—seemed to her/him "a native, wet element." Only a nonnative would feel a damp cold as "native." Of course the Poet might have been imagining the damp, or remembering a place where she (let's say) no longer lived, but the description had appeared in February, with a topical reference to fires then ravaging Australia ("an outback town in cinders").

Durant's email notes had been short, not unfriendly but neither giving anything away. Before accepting his offer I'd found him on a faculty page at a private school in California I'd never heard of, Larunda College. The page had no photo and only a brief professional biography. August Durant had studied genetics at Berkeley and the Max Planck Institute in Leipzig, and had taught at the University of Michigan for twelve years before moving to Larunda, where, it seemed, he taught very little. He was affiliated with universities in France, Holland, and England. The linked CV gave me a sense of his age—judging from when he finished his graduate work, he'd now be in his early sixties—and listed dozens of publications, the titles of which meant nothing to me except one on the American poets Wallace Stevens and John Ashbery. It was odd that he'd written an academic paper on poetry, and odder still that he'd listed it among all the articles on evolutionary biology and DNA transference on his CV, where it would mean nothing to his professional standing. He must have been proud.

The CV hadn't been updated in three years. What had he been doing recently? I used Dominic's access to online academic searches to learn that Durant had coauthored a successful and sizeable research grant on something called "molluscan phylogeny" (I couldn't remember what *phylogeny* meant and could have sworn there was a *k* at the end of *mollusc*). He'd published a single paper, back in the first months of the grant, but nothing since. A distracted program assistant at the biosciences department told me that Durant was on leave. I said I was considering an application to Larunda, and she offered that Durant's leave was "indefinite." He was not available to supervise research. "Is he retired?" I asked. "You can think of him that way," she said.

Apart from his professional life, there was scant evidence to read of him. Surely he knew even less about me, yet he seemed to have great confidence that I was his man, whether or not I knew it. "You can ask me whatever you like," he wrote. "The plane ticket would have proven to most that I'm serious. All it really proves is that I have enough money to play my hunch, and anyway, even once you realize I'm serious, you still have to decide if I'm someone you can work for." He was right, but now that I'd used the ticket, my concern wasn't that he'd deceived me but that he'd learn I was a less talented reader-detective than he'd imagined. There's a degree of

cowardice or fraudulence in every reader who feels the need, upon
closing a book, to open his mouth.

I cleared my throat and dialed his number. The voice that
answered, in English, was certainly his—I could tell somehow by
the vigorous, uninterrogative "hello." As we spoke I could picture
him, strong, sharp-eyed, square. He sounded like John Huston in
Chinatown. The call was brief. We arranged to meet the next afternoon on a patio bar on Piazza Campo de' Fiori. The presumption
that had led him to send me the ticket was there now too, even in
his attempt to reassure me.

"Anyone my age and with my way of seeing the world is bound
to be a little complicated. You'll need confidence for this work,
James. I like boldness. So tomorrow check out of your hotel and
bring your bags with you. You'll know right away you can trust me,
and you'll like me, if that matters to you, which it does. Then we'll
begin our work."

After the call I allowed myself to admit further doubts. Not just
that my talents were less than he imagined but that the enterprise
was absurd. I looked up *absurd* on my phone. It's from the Latin
absurdus, meaning "dissonant" or "out of tune." Couldn't Durant
hear the notes? Because he presumed to know me well from a letter
I'd posted online, I decided that his judgment was suspect. He was
a truster of appearances. No one is transparent, though they may
evidently be mostly joyful or not, mostly good or not, and so on.
There's always more to the story. To allow myself one generalization, people who express presumed certainties to strangers are
often, at some level, fools.

My doubts made me miss the Londoner, so full of purpose, clear
of mind. She'd studied mathematics and told wild tales about string
theory to rewrap with fine gold any loose thought I'd strung with

poetical catgut. Upon learning from her that forty is the only semi-perfect number in English whose letters fall alphabetically, I thought I might say it to myself in times of confusion as a sort of mantric assertion of linear clarity. But then I started seeing it everywhere—it leapt from screen texts and formed in the fragments of sound broken off from the noise of the day—so that "forty" represented for me everything from the number of horses in the last five Grand National races to the percentage of my country's commissioned soldiers listed as casualties in the First World War to the number of light-years from Earth to the planet 55 Cancri e to the number of days and nights of rain it takes to float an ark. I retain facts pointlessly—the Londoner thought I was "on the spectrum," I told her the internet was to blame—but now and then, as if of their own accord, the facts try to arrange themselves into meaning. These little flights of free association, these high-lateral cha-chas, as I thought of them, came unbidden like a kind of seizure, and I had no choice but to wait them out. The more duress I felt, the longer they lasted. Maybe they cleansed the carbon buildup in the brain's exhaust system, but they contained unlikely, surprising linkings, and in their wake I experienced a sudden clarity that could last for several minutes. The clarity didn't always feel good.

Except for a few flower stalls, the market at Campo de' Fiori had closed for the day by the time I arrived. The rich light on the buildings was as I remembered it. Durant had told me to look for the most crowded patio at the northwest corner of the piazza, the one the tour books listed. He'd be sitting in the otherwise identical neighboring patio, likely the sole occupant, and that was, in fact, how I found him. He spotted me first or at least was looking right at me as I approached and picked him out, a man even larger than I'd imagined, standing to greet me, with full, light brown, combed hair—I wondered if he was one of those late-middle-aged men who are proud of their hair—wearing black plastic old-style glasses over blue-gray eyes. Striking eyes, wolfen. He would know their effect. His clothes were casual, coarse cotton. He was smiling.

"You knew me by the duffel bag," I said, shaking his considerable hand. We sat.

"And you don't look Italian, or walk Italian. There's also a picture of you on the internet. You must know the one." It was a group photo. The Londoner and I met the other six when we were detained together by Parisian police as part of a mass roundup of climate change protesters at a meeting of big oil executives. We decided to gather again in Amsterdam a month later to join an alternative energy march. That's where the picture had been taken, before we really got to know each other, which is to say, before the Londoner and I split from the others and moved to Madrid. I never thought anymore of those temporary friends, except the Londoner. I'd chatted with her briefly one Paris afternoon and in all of ten minutes she made a marching activist of me.

Through our first shared drink the conversation with Durant had no shape. I learned in passing that the room I'd have in his nearby apartment had a great street view, that he'd been in Rome for nine weeks and planned to stay several more, that his feet were suffering from a new pair of shoes, that he hoped, when his time in the city was over, never to hear another underpowered motorcycle. I nursed a beer, he a glass of Madeira. There was something more to these preliminary exchanges than simply to put each other at ease. It was understood that we were each gauging the other, each allowing time to find what would serve as an acceptable, reproducible version of ourselves that we could then play at length.

I was fully aware that, against my will, I was constructing a persona—one that would not disappoint Durant, that seemed up to the job he'd offered me, but that too seemed authentic for being slightly peculiarized, as in my unwillingness to fill all silences with speech or ask the obvious questions—and that he must have been doing the same, though I couldn't detect anything in him but a genuine interest in me, in my carry bag, which I'd picked up in Madrid from a Moroccan, and in the city around us. That I couldn't detect a forced interest meant that he was older and more practiced at the art of false presentation, or that he was less self-aware than I hoped, and didn't know that we are only being true to human nature to fashion outward selves far removed from whoever we are when alone in the dark.

All this traveling I'd done—Paris, Amsterdam, Madrid—what had I learned about myself, he asked. I said I was neither searching for nor escaping anything. I just wanted to know what places were like, at least while I was standing in them. I didn't say, as I might have, that I'd been unlocated since my parents died in a car accident.

"Your posting argues that the poems at Three Sheets are all directed toward a single, fixed mystery. It suggests you see beauty in the idea of a search. You're looking for a direction. I have one for you."

What had I written about a search? My little online piece had tumbled off the top of my head. I'd tangled myself up in Dante, the canto about Ulysses's last voyage from *The Inferno*. The old sailor gathers his men and sets off for "the world beyond the sun," meaning the west, where the sun sets, the unknowable distant point where things end, the day, the light, life itself. Was this the direction Durant had planned for me?

"Why bring me here? Why couldn't I work for you from Canada?"

"Because the best discoveries are sometimes made when we're not working, when we're relaxing, talking about life and love, and I'm paying you for those conversations, too."

We looked out at the passersby, the rooftop gardens on the buildings across the piazza. Several young Romans sat on the base of the statue of Giordano Bruno. Harmless teenagers, smoking, playing cool, feigning boredom. The light was clean. Durant waited me out. I finally asked him how he became interested in Three Sheets and the Poet.

"I discovered the site in a sidebar. I forget what I was reading online, likely something about Wallace Stevens or Elizabeth Bishop, and a fragment of poetry popped up and caught my eye. And so I looked at the site and the more I read, the more the work got hold of me."

"The site's gotten hold of a whole lot of people. Does it bother you that you might be part of a virtual cult?" My ground had been marked out by the online post, but now I stood on it, chin raised. I already knew that Durant liked this image of me.

"Let's face it, the Poet's work is at best uneven and pretty elusive. Half of it doesn't even make sense. My relation to him—he's a man, let's agree—is more personal." He measured my expression, which I tried to keep neutral. "I know how that sounds."

He said that I could lay claim to "the sharpest post" on SHEPMETSOR. And I had no institutional affiliations that might skew my readings, no publishers to protect, no tenure to win. As far as he could tell from his internet searches, I was a perfect co-reader, and he needed a reader. He said not his life but "the makings" of his life were, as it were, "at stake." I wondered if he'd introduced "the sharpest post" and "stake" intentionally.

"The Poet's work has started to feel directed at me. Either I'm lost to delusion, and you might be able to help free me of it, or there really is a connection, and you can confirm that what I'm seeing in the poems is valid." He took me in unblinking as he spoke, never once looked away. "Of course, you wonder what I'm seeing. And of course I can't tell you or I'll have planted the reading in your mind. I can only ask you to tell me what you see, though even this is an interference."

If he wanted me as a measuring instrument, then already the needle was in the red. Superstitious readers project more meanings onto pages than they find in them. It is possible to see anything in language if you look with a particular slant and intensity like the one he was now leveling at me. Whole interpretive fiefdoms are built upon professors seeing gods in their porridge.

He looked off to the square. A young, hairy-legged couple in shorts had bolted from the neighboring patio and run out to flag down a dark-skinned man in a blue summer suit. There was surprise and delight all around.

Durant's hand fell off his glass, as if to make a gesture, but he changed his mind and simply took hold of it again.

"You must have some questions for me," I said.

"No. But I do ask something of you. If you're still considering this job." Before I realized the question had been sprung, I answered, "I am." Why I said this I still don't know. If anything, I was inclined at that point not to become involved in the man's suspect enthusiasms. Maybe I was just intrigued. Or maybe I didn't want to walk away from the money.

He said that he'd pay my first installment regardless but wouldn't hire me until he'd seen me read. He meant this literally. He needed to physically see me read a poem and then listen to my response, without aid of commentaries or search engines, and without the time to revise.

"You mean right now?"

"Yes."

In Dominic's Contemporary World Poetry graduate course, he'd made the class perform spot readings and then graded our discussions. Among students and his colleagues he was quietly denounced for the practice, but it was in those sessions that I learned to focus, to find meaning and test it, to find a way of seeing and a language for saying what I saw. But sometimes I saw badly, or not at all.

Durant produced a paper from his pants pocket and unfolded it, passed it to me. I recognized the poem, "The Art of Memory." It had appeared in the late winter on Three Sheets. It hadn't made much sense to me at the time, and it wasn't my kind of poem, but I performed the trick I'd learned of faking to myself a silent enthusiasm, which sometimes triggered an actual one, which made me read better. What did I see? A simple rhyme scheme. The speaker addressing an absent lover, a woman who maybe knows something of the sciences ("The world, its laws slipped / into you like light through a lens to a point / of resolve"). He remembers them standing with a guidebook in the shadow of a bronze statue, and she says, "The sun winks and we play blind." The ending:

> Who wrongs
> us when the body, its own authority, is undone?
>
> Who made the laws of art that the bronze
> of the burned man should be shaped by fire?

We spent our day here burning down, drawn
to drink as if to douse the very pyre
here remembered, then to lose our calendared days,
our lined and numbered cosmos, the entire

thing. You were leaving, and left. I remain.

I read it again, then began. I said I could see why the Poet didn't
often write in fixed forms. Even this loose terza rima wasn't han-
dled very well. He'd chosen it presumably because the poem was
partly about forms (the statue, the body, the poem), and forms
breaking down, someone burned at the stake, commemorated in
bronze, and the lovers' bodies no longer answering the laws they
once did. The iambic pentameter of the first tercet falters in the
second. I talked of the kink in the rhyme scheme.

Durant barely nodded. He was waiting to see if I could reach
beyond the undergraduate-level answer I'd offered him. I
continued.

"The lover being addressed seems to love science. The speaker has
a weaker eye for science, and questions art. There are a few tired
conceits at work. Fire as a principle of both destruction and creation,
of lovers' passion, etcetera. There's an ambiguity in the 'pyre / here
remembered'—is 'here' the statue, commemorating a death by fire, or
is 'here' in fact the poem itself, commemorating their lost passion?
The meanings coexist. And we get the full sense of that by noting the
title. 'The Art of Memory' alludes to the art advanced by the man
represented in a bronze statue in the very place he was burned at the
stake. Giordano Bruno. The poem is set here, in Campo de' Fiori."

When I'd first read the lines, months ago, I wondered whose
death? whose statue? But reading them now, the answers were

clear, though about Bruno I knew only that he had devised elabo-
rate memory systems, and that because of his heretical theories of
astronomy he was publicly executed by the church.

Durant raised his glass to me but the test wasn't yet completed.

"The lover says, 'The sun winks and we play blind.' It's the line
that first caught my attention in that sidebar on my screen. Have
you heard the expression before?" he asked.

"No. In context—I'm guessing a bit here, the poem is obscure in
places—but it might mean that truth reveals itself but we sometimes ignore it. The idea is that the lovers have had a truth revealed
to them that they've been ignoring but that one of them is no
longer going to ignore. Presumably, given the tired figures, the fire
and so on, it's that their love has lost its passion. It's dying."

Even when I hadn't fully grasped the poem I felt the loss in it.
After loved ones die, every last antacid ad is heartbreaking. In the
first weeks after I was orphaned I couldn't read poetry or prose.
The Londoner brought me back by leading me to Three Sheets,
and because so many of the poems either made no sense or were
less than excellent, I deputed them to express my emotions for me
in little combustions I could smother with cold, analytical words if
they grew too hot. One day in that Montreal basement the fire
nearly caught me (the stale fire metaphor clearly has) and it took
my online rant to extinguish it.

"The poem's autobiographical, don't you think?" he asked.

"We can't possibly know."

"He's writing about his experience. Lost passion, lost love. He
was here."

"We don't know that. To avoid fallacies, we shouldn't assume he's
writing about his life. Or at least not literally. It's the safer
assumption."

"So your training tells you. Mine tells me different."

Some echo in the comment landed me back with the Londoner in Madrid. We ate dinner at a small wooden table, our money and time running out. I'd wanted to tell her that she was the only woman who'd ever inspired me to poetry or song, inspired me to risk failing. I wanted her in words but couldn't have her there. It was a way of saying I loved her, though of course I would never admit to speech such a worn term as *love*, and so I felt both love and my inability to say it either straight or slant. She put her knife down and sipped her wine, close-set eyes, soft breath of a face. Before she took up her knife again I reached across the table and grasped her hand up high, near the wrist, and squeezed it. I meant to communicate my love and protection—her life had left her in need of protection from recurrent bad luck—and she looked at my hand on hers, then up at me. She wanted me to say what it meant, this touch. But I couldn't say a thing, and let go.

Now I sat looking at Durant's hands. He held one in the other, pressed a thumb nervously into his palm. The certainty struck me that Durant himself was the Poet. Who else would have taken such an interest in my posted rant? If I had to guess—so easily I stepped into the same trap of biographical conjecture—I'd have said the Poet was male, yes, and at least in his fifties, given the recurrent theme of aging as a kind of decline. And a man alone, often addressing an absent "you" who seemed not at all metaphysical. And Durant himself was a genetic biologist, and so might have known a woman with a scientific eye like the lost lover in the poem. And even an anonymous poet must want to meet one live reader.

He sat up slightly higher.

"There's a poem by Czesław Miłosz, the Pole," he said. "He imagines this square here, and then takes us to where he's writing the poem, Warsaw in 1943, during the first uprising. The ghetto is on fire. Outside the ghetto, couples ride in a carousel and the ashes from the fires drift to them in what he calls 'dark kites' and they catch them like 'petals in midair.' Miłosz has the authority of the survivor, of witness. The poem, as poem, stands or falls on those petals. But because he sees them with his own eyes, the charred petals are floating before us too, in the very words on the page." I didn't know what to say. I had no compulsion to say anything. "Whether a poem is about love or historical atrocity, and whether or not the poet was really there, it has to come from somewhere real. Warsaw, this piazza, or a coil in the heart. I know you understand this."

I understood less as the day went on. We left the café and through the Renaissance streets I followed him, or trailed him, more precisely, his person and his meaning. He allowed anything to come to his attention, voiced every thought and half thought. He must have been very lonely for someone to talk to as he met the city, a feeling I knew from my first visit there. But always I was on guard. The café meeting had been measured and planned, performed. Was he setting me up for more lessons as he stopped and bought us gelato or as we paused before the facade of a church? "Santa Maria dell'Orazione e Morte." He pointed with his cone to the terrifying winged skulls on the doorway. "The place is dedicated to the burial of the dead. It inspires mortals to pay their tithes and eat their greens." An underlying seriousness always there in his voice or expression enabled him to joke without disarming awe, even while ice cream melted onto his hand.

"In case you're wondering," he said, "and you are, I'm not the Poet. And the job is still yours if you want it." He was striding again, looking into the ancient stones passing beneath him. "Don't decide until I show you the apartment."

Those first days in Rome now in memory seem painted, the perspectives mastered to a mathematical exactness of light and
shadow, the Della Francesca'd faces and fabrics somehow coloring even the sounds, the streets, voices speaking a language I
didn't know. A kind of dark comedy crept into the hours. Words
became prime elements, reduced not to sense but the urge to
sense, the need to say, the need to share in the act of saying. Or
maybe it wasn't quite like that. Sense came in fragments that
combined or didn't, somewhere between Piero and Mondrian. I
felt outside of my own experience, not unpleasantly, even as I was
included in company. Durant had been absent for most of my first
two days in the apartment, but on the second evening he invited
me to dinner. We were seven on the rooftop of the apartment
building, I, Durant, and five of his acquaintances from the building. Yves was a Paris-based travel writer on sabbatical with his
wife, who was Greek and who was never properly introduced but
seemed to have once worked as a photographer. Their friends
Patrice and Anton, a gay couple, both pilots for Air France,
agreed about not much except the strength of their pilots union.
The only Italian, Carlo, who owned the building, was about
Durant's age. He resembled, it must be said, Mussolini, with
even something of Il Duce's ridiculous bearing, at least when he
thrust forward his chin to offer up the final word on Arab uprisings, the compromised Italian press, or the quality of the Super
Tuscan blend. He hosted these rooftop dinners for his tenants
every second Wednesday night.

Though I'd just started work—my only instructions were to
read Three Sheets "for patterns" and to "profile" the Poet, as if we
were out to catch a serial killer—Durant had insisted on paying
me in advance for my first two weeks. I'd been poor for months,

so sitting there with four hundred euros in my pocket I felt good, trusted, valued, but also misjudged, soon to disappoint. Wanting to impress Durant, wanting to misrepresent myself impressively, made me feel younger than I was, needy and lacking in seriousness.

The talk moved between languages—Italian, English, French—until someone remembered me, who spoke no Italian and spoke French like a camp counselor played guitar, and shifted them all back to English.

"Explain your joke," said Anton. He was narrow-featured and tended to burst staccato into conversation and then pay no attention to whoever took up his point.

"I don't think I can," I said. "It wasn't very witty. Do you have summer camps in France?"

"We have camps, yes. I thought you said 'campos.' A field. I thought you were insulting the farmers' way of speaking. Or perhaps just the French. When I visit Italy I often hear these insults."

"I'm sorry."

"Then you did intend to insult?"

It would be more accurate to say his features were pinched.

"I'm sorry others insult you," I said.

"You shouldn't apologize for others. It leads to confusion and disastrous political ennui."

Yves was asking Carlo about property for sale in Turkey. Carlo's son would spend his summer away from university studies renovating a building in some gentrifying neighborhood on the European side of Istanbul.

"The seller was a nervous man who inherited the address from his mother. He saw risk everywhere," said Carlo. "The risk of Islamicists, reformists, a police state, a racist-nationalist government. Of the surrounding economies, of earthquakes. Stupidly, he told me of his fears. The price for the building was attractive."

The word that came to mind was *retrench*. I wanted to go to bed but I saw Durant glancing at me, gauging. He wanted to see what he'd paid for. And now, Yves's wife was asking me for my feelings about Canada.

I said I had complicated feelings about it. I found it a highly agreeable country, comparatively strong by most meaningful indices, education, health care, crime and penal stats, collective rights protections, and so on, though it had never resolved or acknowledged its abhorrent treatment, ongoing, of native peoples, despite which, given the general failure of nations in their treatment of native peoples, it was the very global example of multicultural success that other countries, especially the US, claimed to be the exceptional, exclusive, or pinnacle—pick your figure of speech—examples of. For a few moments as I spoke the others listened but then drifted into other conversations. Even the Greek woman, with the countenance of a listener, seemed somehow to be listening to her left and right. Though he wasn't looking at me now, I sensed that only Durant was paying attention. And yet, I said, not really aware that I had these precise opinions, compared to most countries with strong educational systems and a history of at least some leisure class, Canada persisted in a cultural adolescence, with a huge, silent gulf between its artists, few as they were, and their audience, brought on primarily by a vapid cultural commentary. All of this complicated by new technologies and a fracturing of the impulse toward serious attention.

"So your experience escaped shallowness."

I had no idea what she was talking about. It turned out she was under the impression I'd recently visited Canada.

"I'm Canadian, not American."

"My mistake," she said. Then she asked if I'd ever visited the United States and what were my feelings. Then she interrupted my nonanswer and asked again about Canada, its vast regions and overwhelming vistas. I brought it all around—a trick I had learned on other trips outside North America—to a few stories about encounters with bears. Suddenly the whole table listened in. The stories weren't mine, though I put myself in them. The mother black bear following me (my former friend Derek) up a tree in which, I (he) saw too late, her cubs were lounging. The grizzly I (a guy in one of my literature classes whose name escaped me) met on a mountain path, where I (he) froze, unable to back away, until the grizzly turned around and left the way it had come, as if it had forgotten its car keys. The polar bear who walked into the bar up in Churchill, Manitoba, where I (the CBC camera crew) was thawing (their equipment) out. The stories were all implausible and true. I survived in each one. By the time I'd finished them I felt surrounded by a borrowed northern gravity.

Carlo's son, Davide, arrived, introduced himself to all, and sat across from me. He looked like a buzz-cut soccer star, straight off a poster for the Azzurri. As if we'd been speaking for hours he told me he found Rome tame and dull. He was leaving for Istanbul the next day. He asked if I played music.

When conversing with nonnative English speakers I often have this sense of having missed a transition, and of unexpected echoes. It changes my own way of speaking. I didn't really know how I'd occasioned the bear stories, for instance, and now I expected bears to return as a topic in some unlikely way, just as guitar playing was about to.

"I play guitar badly, like a camp counselor."

"In Istanbul," Davide continued, "I busk on the great street Istiklal with my friends. We play gypsy style. We're very good. Even the gypsies admire us. I'll send you a link."

In this way my email address was brought forth. On the back of his business card, I printed it like a seven-year-old practicing his letters, and handed him his own card. On the front side was a badly drawn figure of a very long-clawed hammer or a very thick-stringed instrument.

I asked Davide what he was studying. He said it didn't matter. He was going to drop out of school.

"Though I haven't told my father."

He said this in full voice, with his father ten feet away, talking to Durant, paying his son no attention. I wondered if Davide hoped his father would overhear him or register unconsciously what he was saying, but then it seemed he simply knew exactly how much volume he could safely get away with, in the way local taxi drivers measured small spaces at high speeds.

All at once the voices fell silent and Durant looked at me.

"James," he asserted in a voice that made me want to deny that I was James or had ever met him, "your bear stories are amusing but they don't really display your greater talents." He said that they'd recently had in their number a Canadian who claimed to be a clairvoyant. She'd announced that they all had known one another in a previous life. "She called herself a seer. And here you are, another Canadian, a seer of subtexts, a maker of connections. I wonder what you're thinking about all of us."

Durant valued the idea that he'd been right about me.

"I'm thinking I'd like to be invited back next week and should dodge the question."

"I wanted to ask her how a clairvoyant knows about past lives," Patrice said. "Maybe our beloved dead have these Wednesday dinners together, too."

"We know something about one another"—Durant was still addressing me—"but we'd like to know more about you. Tell us about your origins, your family."

"I don't talk about my family." The words were immediate, sure, and yet they surprised me.

"How intriguing," said Anton flatly. "One of you must be a monster. Was it Daddy?"

"Then what else is in your heart?" asked Durant. "By 'heart' I mean 'memory,' of course. Which poems have taken up there? Recite one."

As I pictured myself pulling the folded euros from my pocket, rolling them tightly, stuffing them down his throat, I tried to fend off the request by reminding him I wasn't a poet, that my connection to poetry was now professional and so to call it up socially would be to mix business and pleasure.

"I'm sure Patrice has landed many planes in heavy weather but let's not have him land one here tonight," I said.

It turned out that everyone at the table had in their hearts and on their tongues a little poetry, or in Davide's case, banal song lyrics. The poems tended to be very old, things learned in school, I was told, and as they were approximately translated seemed to be full of stale, romantic imagery or clunky metaphors about the stages of life or the horrors of war. When someone forgot a word or line, the others imagined possibilities, sometimes from what were apparently well-known advertising slogans or catch lines from popular television shows. There was much laughter.

Davide sang his lines in a surprisingly good voice, uninflected with earnestness.

Then it was my turn. I had very little to offer. A few years back I had tried to memorize not whole poems but stanzas that I liked. Did I still know them?

I offered a few lines from the American poet W. S. Merwin, from a poem called "The Dreamers."

> a man who can't read turned pages
> until he came to one with his own story
> it was air
> and in the morning he began learning letters
> starting with A is for apple
> which seems wrong
> he says the first letter seems wrong

They waited me out for a few seconds, expecting more. Yves declared the stanza a "paradox" but didn't explain what he meant. Durant asked why I found it significant.

"I don't find it significant so much as . . ." I almost said "beautiful and true." "Language belongs to a lapsed world. It can't quite reach what it grasps for."

"And yet," said Durant.

"And yet in this stanza language describes what it says can't be described."

"To what end?" Carlo asked. "Language is a problem. We all know this. Poems should be about the heart or the world, not the words in between them."

"That is a stupid thing to say," Davide maintained in a calm voice, without looking at his father. He glanced at me apologetically.

"Promise me, son, that you will write a song about the word *pollice* the next time you hit one with a hammer."

He said this as I've written it, in English except for the Italian word *pollice*, which I assumed didn't mean *police*, though that was the image I pictured, Davide hitting a policeman with a hammer, then singing about the words involved rather than the act.

For a moment father and son looked silently at each other and then Italian broke loose. They spoke rapidly, passionately, almost murderously, until Davide got to his feet and left without saying good night.

Carlo poured Durant and himself more wine.

"I'm sorry for my son. His boyhood will not end."

The rest of us cast around for suitable comment, found none. Showing great valor, I thought, I stepped into the conversational breach.

"Merwin was unlikely to offend. Or so I thought."

"*Or so*. No more bear stories, please," said Anton.

He tended to address his drink when he said these things.

"What have you pretended to misunderstand now, Anton?" I asked. The others, even Patrice, I noted, seemed delighted.

"I'm not the pretentious one."

Patrice explained that Anton thought I'd used the Italian word for bear, *orso*. He apologized for his copilot. I wondered how it was sitting with Anton, this third instance of someone apologizing for another person. Patrice explained that Anton was bitter that Air France had without warning informed their pilots that all communications to towers globally were to be in English.

"His ear for English isn't precise. He's worried there will be incidents."

I pictured Anton, upon the wrong angle of incidence and some misidentified English word, flying a plane into a woods full of *orsos*. I was exhausted. For three days I'd been reading poems, looking for patterns, hearing echoes. The work survived into my off-hours.

What I needed, in fact, was to hear banal song lyrics in a good voice without earnestness, maybe on a beach somewhere with the waves being waves.

I stood, waved, gave a little bow. I apologized to Anton for whatever misunderstanding was about to ensue, thanked everyone for their company and mindfulness of my unilingualism, and walked off, crawled through the dormer, our entry/exit point, which led into Yves and his wife's rented apartment, which led to the hallway and stairwell and Durant's apartment, and my hard bed, where shortly I curled up in a dark full of floating foreign syllables.

On my third day in the apartment a woman appeared. As was his habit Durant had gone out for the afternoon and I was at work in the little station he'd prepared for me, a desk with a printer in the corner of my bedroom, with a window to my left looking out at the opposing windows and flaking stucco of the rust-yellow apartment across the narrow street. For only a few minutes in the early afternoons the sun would drift between the buildings and fire them to a light I'd seen before and marveled at, but never contemplated. In sunlight the walls became the very planes upon which, to their makers, God's energies met those of common, untabernacled man. I had already come to love that window and the street's thin slot of sky, and I was sitting with a stack of poems from Three Sheets, waiting for the full sun, when I heard the front door being unlocked and opened. I bent back to the lines at hand, a short poem called "July" that seemed to be telling me something I couldn't quite hear, when a voice spoke from my bedroom doorway.

"So you're the new me."

I turned to find a tall young woman, maybe a little older than I. Her face was slightly tapered, fine-featured. Sunglasses propped on her head pulled her brown-blonde hair back to reveal a widow's peak that returned the eye, pleasingly, to her face.

"I'm Amanda. He didn't tell you about me."

"James."

"Any breakthroughs, James?"

I was trailing the moment, aware of looking, and of her awareness of being looked at.

"A lot of leads," I said. "I didn't know anyone else had had the job."

"Then you weren't meant to know. He won't be happy that we've met. I won't tell him if you don't."

In their set position the edges of her mouth curled slightly upward so that her expression ran against her tone. They present all at once, the proportions of beauty, but it's the incongruences that mark them out and steal into us. That's not at all why Yeats was so attached to the idea that "there is no excellent beauty without strangeness," but it's what came to mind.

She delivered unprompted the account of how she had come into Durant's employ. Seven months ago, just after she'd graduated with a master's degree in something called Truth and Justice Studies, Durant emailed her with the same job offer made to me. They'd exchanged comments posted at SHEPMETSOR and he said he liked her description of the poems as "mysterious little buildings with their doors ajar." Durant flew her to France, where he was working, and they both transferred to Rome, just before she quit the job. "We were becoming too attached." That she said all this so freely, so fully, and so soon upon meeting, should have left me wary of her, but she seemed without guile.

She excused herself and went about watering plants while I sat staring at the doorway where she'd appeared, failing through vertigo to connect my recent life in a Montreal basement to the one I was now living, though in both all I seemed to do was read. My first impression of her hurt slightly, in that I was sure Durant must have realized upon meeting me how far short I fell of Amanda's easy confidence, and very likely of her abilities. I am twice as present on the page as in person. If the same was true of her, then compared with mine her interpretive skills must have been of a different order of sophistication. Besides which, she had studied Truth and Justice, two nouns in that category of words I'm ashamed to utter for my lack of service to them as principles. Only the shame counted in my favor.

In a minute Amanda came in and watered some fern-looking thing beside the dresser.

"August doesn't notice plants. If I don't do this, they'll die. It's why I still have a key, our last arrangement, though I think he's forgotten it. I doubt he knows when I've been by."

"You only come by when he's out?"

She finished watering and stood there, just beyond arm's reach. I had not been this close to a woman paying attention to me since I was last in Europe.

"It's easier. He's out every afternoon. I see him sometimes for dinner. He likes to know that he hasn't stranded me here." She now worked in a bar that catered to Americans. In time she intended to head north to The Hague, where she had some connections, to see if she couldn't scratch up some social justice internship for one of the tribunals. She made it sound like migrant labor. She held a dented tin watering can. "What are you working on? Can I ask?"

I told myself it would contaminate the experiment to reveal my thoughts—for this reason Durant left me alone by day—though in truth I was afraid she'd be unimpressed. I was considering the possibility that the poems were posted in an order designed from the outset rather than randomly, which would mean that, because certain details seemed to allude to current world events, elsewhere in each poem would be lines that had been preselected. Upon this idea, I was extracting the most telling words in a few poems I'd marked by the date of their first appearance on the Three Sheets site. And I'd come to one that held me in its little mystery, door ajar.

"Do you remember 'July'?"

"Let me think. A swimming pool. And a bird. What else?"

Rather than hand it to her I pulled the poem out and slid it to the edge of the desk. She put down the can and moved one step closer. I read along with her, my eyes on the poem, my focus caught in lonely adolescence.

> That summer the heat wouldn't quit
> and the water in the 1963 blue
> concrete pool climbed
> to 89 degrees a robin
> appeared on a branch in the stairs
> landing window with so many
> twigs in his beak so symmetrically
> held that he presented long
> whiskers and a helmet of horns,
> looked, in fact, like a Kurosawa
> character. I am telling you
> they were exactly measured
> and held just so by a force
> whose agency is at work again
> now in this question you ask of me,
> its dimensions concealed from you.

Ridiculous, really, the
accidents of likeness,
that you should want to know
the magicked secret of it all.

"Right," she said, "'the magicked secret.'"

"It's beckoning us to solve a mystery. The poem's showing us
the concealed dimensions but we aren't seeing them. Or at least
I'm not."

She was still focused on the page, but she blinked,
deliberately.

"The poem is complete," she said.

"What do you mean?"

Now she looked out the window. The rooftop shadows claiming
the walls meant I'd missed the minute of perfect light. She took
hold of the pot with the ferny thing and held it up in front of her.

"Let's not name this plant." (I couldn't have.) "Let's look at it.
We can touch it, put it in different lights, care for it. But we don't
ask what it means."

I was looking at her, not the plant, but she kept holding it, so I
looked. It was, all in all, a plant.

"Yes," I said. "Well, I don't think the Poet is at quite the same
level of creative power."

She set down the pot.

"The speaker in the poem is writing about the mystery of likeness. In any given case, is the likeness of one thing to another an
accident or not? He's been asked a question he doesn't want to
answer, which means there is an answer, and yet there's the mystery of the memory it brings on, the bird unknowingly having
made a new face for itself. That's all, it's complete."

"You think I should just let the poem be."

She picked up the page and was handing it to me when the light through it revealed the notes I'd made on the back of the sheet. She turned it over and I watched her read. *Date of the pool, hot summer, house with a landing, thermometer reading in Fahrenheit. So a US American house. Two-story. I picture it mid-twentieth century. Not suburban, maybe somewhere in the West. Can't say why I think this.*

"I should be going. Will you look after the plants now?"

"I'll forget them, too. I know that much about myself. Why did you quit the job?"

Her expression shifted minutely—toward doubt?—and she looked down to the page in her hand, as if surprised to find it there, and handed it back to me.

"These poems," she said. "The moment you touch one, turn it over, it gets ahold of you. Whether he admits it or not, that hold is why August gets up in the morning. It's what he doesn't know that matters to him, not the answers to puzzles. He thinks he wants to find the Poet, who he's convinced lives in Rome—it's why he's out every afternoon, playing hunches, sitting in cafés, staring at the people gathering at statues—I bet he pulled that trick on you, too, didn't he? 'The Art of Memory' in Campo de' Fiori?"

"Yes."

It was all much bigger than poetry, she said. Durant was convinced that the Poet possessed something of his, a great, specific loss.

"What are you talking about? What has he lost?"

She took the can and walked back to the living room. Watching her walk away only intensified my wish to follow her meaning. She stopped and turned and seemed to be having an argument with herself. The winning self nodded and spoke.

"'The sun winks and we play blind.'"

"Is the poem quoting someone? Who said it?"

"He did."

"Who did?"

"August. To his daughter. In their last conversation before she went missing. Three years ago." She winced slightly to hear herself. She had come to the apartment to say exactly as much as she'd said, but she was betraying Durant. "Don't tell him we've met. Or you can say we've met but that we both insisted there be no talk about the poems."

A missing daughter. Durant had impressed upon me the seriousness of the work, but I hadn't quite believed it connected to anything real. I stood and started toward her. She drifted away slowly so that my path pushed hers to the doorway.

"Missing how? Did she run away?"

"He gives few details and there's nothing online. She was in her thirties. She seems to have walked out of her life and never reappeared. Private detectives found no trace. Then there's me, and now you."

"How did you learn all this? Is it in the poems?"

"He told me in one short, drunken conversation. I found nothing of her in the poems."

"What about the sun winking?"

"I don't know. Maybe a coincidence. Or maybe he thinks he coined an expression that in fact he overheard. Maybe it's out there, circulating like an old penny."

The words in her answer impressed themselves visually. I pictured the *coin* in *coincidence* and then saw the *penny* and it dropped.

"You're not telling me everything. I need the whole story."

Whether the whole story was Durant's or hers, she seemed to be calculating the cost of telling it, reading numbers on some invisible meter. She offered to meet me the next afternoon in the park of the Villa Borghese. She pulled the sunglasses down over her eyes, a way of announcing her exit, or of preventing me from reading something in her face.

My life falls to its rhythms, some common to many, some mine alone. Breaking the rhythms, taking my eggs poached for once, changing the route to a job, choosing to stop loving or stop failing a loved one, I inscribe a new line in my brain. It's the patterns that I can't get outside, whether I recognize them or not, that define me. To see my specific self—sorrows and fears and pathologies— reflected in external reality effects a recognition. Some such moments calm me. Others do me in.

My father was a military man. He and my mother had taken early retirement in a town near the base in Nova Scotia where he'd last served. I grew up many places, but this last town had become familiar and I knew it wouldn't be lost to me as the others had, even if, and sooner than I imagined, it would come to contain the greatest loss.

One week each summer and Christmas, Montreal to Nova Scotia, back.

In every sense he was a hard man to know.

My parents were United Church Protestants. When they both turned sixty-two they moved to Turkey for a year to work for an NGO in a refugee camp near the Syrian border. The circumstances of their deaths were ambiguous. They were found sitting inside their car on a dirt road, a few kilometers past the last cotton field, where the stony desert took up, dead of blunt force trauma. I had the accident report sent to me and translated. In separate sections, it described the conditions of the vehicle and of its occupants. I read about the car but only glanced at the second section, not allowing myself to read left to right, up to down. Instead I cast my eyes over the words, registering random phrases. The white Kia outwardly showed no evidence of having hit anything. Inside, matters were different. My parents seemed to have met a very sudden stop. They were dashed on the dash, steered into the steering wheel. Neither had been wearing a seat belt, a detail underlined by hand in the original document, as if to explain their fate or to blame them for it, yet they always wore seat belts and the car's annoying reminder bell was in working order, a signal detail, though what it signaled I didn't know.

Normally, they were buckle-up folks, my parents. Resourceful, tough, good in crises. They strapped themselves in, lashed themselves to masts in storms. In their third week at the camp one of their colleagues was killed when his car, leading a van of police officers to a food-collection point, tripped a thousand-pound bomb placed under the road by the PKK, Kurdish separatists "agitating" for a homeland. Before the day was through they'd contacted the man's wife, a woman in Pennsylvania they'd never met, and arranged immediate support for her, somehow collecting names and numbers of the couple's family and friends. After which my father set out himself, on the same road, overland at the bomb crater, to organize and secure the food transport.

There were dangers everywhere. A Turkish nationalist group in the area had been implicated in the murders of Christians, some of them foreigners, and Al-Qaeda and ISIS had begun setting up thereabouts to promote their specific lunacies across the border, inside the civil war in Syria. I asked them to return to Canada but my mother said, as if she had no say in it, "Your father wants to see this through." For him, the world was complicated but life was not.

Life was an enactment of duty to principles. He regarded my central passion—literature—as an indulgence, unforgivably inward. The inwardness was a kind of selfishness, even a cowardice. When I started graduate school he was warily proud, and my quitting it confirmed his assumptions. He believed I would never have a steady job, let alone a career, and whether or not I married, would never surrender my self-indulgence to the building of a family of my own. In so many words, he said all of this, said it once, on what would become our last Christmas Eve together. With some embarrassment, some pride, I'd produced at the table a little magazine in which I'd had three poems published, a magazine of the kind read only by the other contributors, though my parents wouldn't know that. My idea was to suggest I was making some headway in the writing world. My mother hugged me. I can still feel her bracelet pressing into my back. He looked at the poems, not seeming to actually read them, said I was just "playing a game," and announced he had to say his piece.

I was hurt but not angry. I still don't know if he was right. I've written just one poem since. That night I tried to tell him in words other than these that I agreed, that to write poetry is like playing a game, a board game, but it's play in service of the real, a game in which the win is the defeat of the game itself. In the last move the gaming piece (imagine a stone) leaps from the board into the world, the real, the physical, a red quickness, the actual, and the game becomes a kind of miracle, rules broken and laws suspended. It's a lesser miracle, but one connected to the greatest of them, the creation of life itself, in which inanimate material, a stone (imagine a gaming piece), is struck into consciousness and set down in the home space, the world.

"Words," he said.

The final word was his. Though he'd worked his whole life, and
lived modestly, my parents' worth when they died was under six
thousand dollars, not enough to cover their funeral and the estate
lawyer. It was months before the NGO, on an audit, discovered the
missing funds. Near the time of their deaths my father stole from
the organization almost forty thousand lire. His defenders argued
he must have been paying protection for the organization, though
no one could say to whom. Other details emerged. Expensive new
windows and a stack of rugs and blankets in their apartment in
Gaziantep. A tight schedule of doctors' appointments for my
mother. Everything seemed telling at one moment, meaningless
another. To repay the missing funds, the organization sold their
car, still in good working order.

Fourteen billion years ago the universe began with form but no
predictability. In time, patterns formed. Complex systems. Life.
And inside it all—I hear it—howling chaos.

Durant called my cell later that afternoon to ask that I meet him
for dinner in Monti, near the Santa Maria Maggiore. It was only
while I was in the taxi, as the driver called out to friends along the
street, as if Rome were a village, that I had enough distance from
Amanda's visit to think clearly about what I'd learned. If Durant
saw allusions to his daughter in the poems, he would want to test
his readings—he was a man of science, after all—but there existed
no empirical measures of meaning in language or art. Had he
brought in Amanda, and now me, to confirm that the poems had
something to do with his daughter or to rescue him from going
over a final edge?

I've been calling her "Durant's daughter" but before I left for
dinner I played detective and tried to hunt up her name. There

was nothing online so I called Larunda and spoke to what sounded like the same program assistant I'd spoken to days earlier. I said I was from the Petros One Group, a(n invented) private insurance company, and that I had to file something on behalf of August Durant but was unable to reach him. Again I met with resistance. "I just need to finish a form," I said. "A certain interval has passed and I need his daughter's first name. It's illegible on the document I have." She said, "No chance."

He was waiting for me at a window table, more than halfway into a bottle of red wine. The moment I sat down I sensed someone had preceded me. He received me with his usual warmth but did I detect a slight strain in his smile? Or was it that I saw him differently now? His voice was already full, but crisp—there was no suggestion that the wine had brought it forward—so maybe someone had been sharing the bottle with him. And then, yes, I noticed the stain of a red drop on the tablecloth, under the edge of my plate.

"I hope you haven't been waiting long."

"Not long. Have you had a good day, James?"

"I can't say. There's no way of taking my bearings."

"Well, let's stop working, then. Have a drink and let the mind unclench."

Durant's side of the conversation was wonderfully far-ranging. Tracing how exactly a comment about the wine had taken us to serial-killing lions, I found that his connections moved associatively, playfully, like my cha-chas, rather than logically. The route went more or less from the 2008 Le Cupole Rosso Toscana to its label's color of red like those in the frescoes in the Palazzo Massimo alle Terme to cave paintings to the life of cave dwellers to the fear of cave bears to predator habits to anomalies within predator populations to serial-killing lions. By the time he took a pause we were onto a second bottle, our plates were lined with small rabbit bones, and it was time for dessert. What struck me then was the size of the man's passions. He took a huge interest in the world but his enthusiasm was disciplined. His nature wasn't acquisitive so much as embracing. When he held up his glass he seemed to read the properties not just of the wine's color, but of the light that revealed it. He wanted to know life in all its registers. How else could someone who had suffered such a loss let himself be opened by poetry?

"When did you first learn of Three Sheets?" he asked.

So we hadn't stopped working after all.

"A girl I was living with told me about it."

"How did she come across it? Could you ask her?"

"We're not in touch. Likely someone sent her the link."

He nodded.

"They say it's organic, the way information travels on the internet. But it's not. It lacks the full range of human emotion and intent, the nuance of the conversational gambit, or the necessity to share that binds a speaker and listener. I must sound like your grandfather."

"Studies show a decline in oral skills among young people in recent decades. And so-called social skills. Sort of what you'd expect."

"But you have the skills, James. Where did you learn them?"

"I don't know. I was very shy growing up. I learned to listen. Then in school I learned to converse, debate. I had a few professors who expected words on demand."

"And so you have political skills, wouldn't you say?"

"I've never thought of them as political. I try not to play angles on people."

"And yet when you sat down here, you asked if I'd been waiting long. It wasn't simply a polite inquiry, was it?"

It was what my mother used to call a "God-in-the-garden"
moment, my thoughts rendered naked and ashamed.

"I sensed I was entering upon someone's exit."

"There's your sharp intuition at work. You sensed an absence,
someone missing."

"I suppose. But it's no concern of mine."

"And so why ask the question? It must be that you wondered if I
was meeting someone specific, someone you know. Am I right?"

"If you weren't right then I'd think you were paranoid."

"You've met those in the building. But who else do you know in
Rome except me?"

"I'm not sure how well I know you. Maybe I know no one."

"There, you see? A politician's answer."

He took an interest in the dessert menu and recommended the
amaretto semifreddo with chocolate sauce.

"She likes you," he said. I took a sip of water to stall the moment,
as if the gesture might help me decide what to think, but the
motion of my hand up and down seemed only to give away what I
felt. Confusion, a tinge of guilt, anger. "She thinks you're better
suited for the job than she was."

"There are no innocent conversations, are there? Drinks on the
piazza, dinner on a rooftop, and here now, it's one constant performance review."

"She's not an investment analyst. But I've been right to put
money on you."

"A spy, then."

"Not a spy either. This afternoon I remembered about her watering the plants. I invited her here and sure enough she'd just met
you. She says you looked at one poem together but she wouldn't
give you a reading."

"Did she tell you which poem?"

"You doubt what I'm saying, but she wasn't spying. We have to trust each other, James. I'm relying on complete honesty from you."

"But you won't tell me what I'm looking for."

I wondered if it was hard for him not to tell me about his daughter or if the undisclosed story sheltered him, the unsayable private in the place of telling all. I was the one being duplicitous. There was nothing good about the feeling, except a kind of self-punishing guilt I didn't understand but was used to.

"I don't tell you out of respect for scientific method," he said.

"A politician's answer."

He smiled.

"Write something up by the end of the week, just a report on what you're seeing, even if it's not much."

"I have to say, August, I'm beginning to think this isn't even about the poems." So I was being dishonest, trying to open an angle. "It's like I've been selected for training toward a job I can't know."

"Maybe I'm a guide of some sort."

"Or a spymaster."

"Spies again. I hope your other hunches won't come from the movies. Your objective, ours, is to solve the mystery of the poems."

He topped up my wine. I was learning his conversational habits, the way he'd counter anything that might seem a criticism of me with a kindness. But the kindness itself was often complicated, reminding me who was paying the bills, so he wanted the criticisms to stand. It was hard around Durant not to see myself as I imagined he saw me, a young man with ideas and plenty of feelings but few convictions. And not so young as to excuse the fact that I engaged with the world more fully through the mediating plane of language than I did directly, standing in the rain in an ancient city, as he'd found me the previous night when I'd gone out for a walk and gotten turned around in the streets near his apartment, and ran into him by accident (or so he said) as he was out to buy coffee. He led me back under his umbrella, talking about the patterns of Roman rain. He must have seen that even my willingness to challenge him was only a way of pretending to gravitas. We were both aware that at any moment I might be lifted by a breeze and carried away.

The next morning I began to write a profile of the Poet. In the forty-three poems so far posted at Three Sheets, he presented two personae. One of these, evident in just four poems, could not be biographically approximated. The voice was genderless, its concerns not at all personal, and in fact seemed intent on superseding the personal to play a kind of avant-garde jazz, drawing its notes mainly from pop culture, history, the languages of one arcane knowledge or another, and the sounds of pure nonsense.

The dominant voice in the other poems, I still thought, was of a likely white, likely North American male, in his late fifties or older. These poems tended to be in free verse, lyric, prose-dominated, with similar line lengths, the occasional suspended syntax, small tensions formed at line breaks, variously parsed, annotated, or end-stopped. Often the reader was wrong-footed, then rebalanced. Because of their little mysteries the poems managed to be slightly larger than they seemed, but much depended on whether or not the mysteries were earned.

On questions of poetic principles, the two voices could not easily be reconciled. The suppositions underlying them, about language, convention, the very nature of meaning, these were opposed to one another. And yet I felt sure that the poems were the work of the same (very likely) man. What they shared was the woman

described, addressed, or remembered, a woman I now couldn't help
but think of as Durant's daughter. It was possible to construct a
montage of stills about her, a few dramatic scenes. Sometimes she
was even quoted, as in "The Art of Memory" and in what I thought
of as its sister poem, "In Cities."

> Seven cities in three years with this same
> street holding light at the penned
> unseen dog's angle of howl. Turning left
> out the door, then west at the fourth
> corner will run you past the same
> bar with the tree overhanging
> the parking lot and the women's darts league
> playing for keeps on Tuesday nights.
> Much of this, imagined and half-forgotten,
> imagined and said and they're serious, the darts.
> They're in the air here tonight,
> where the barkeep serves the house wine in
> flasks, and the parking lot is an
> alley lined with mopeds,
> the tree a tree, and the howl is in the
> pitch of the roofs opposite just now
> catching what you once asked while
> looking off at them. "How many lives
> can I walk away from?" Meaning
> not yours, as I thought, but others',
> mine. And I had no answer for
> you or the penumbral rim of lighter
> red around the drop you'd spilled
> on the white cloth.

I got up from my desk. I'd read the poem maybe two weeks earlier, but somehow the last lines hadn't come to mind the previous night when I'd seen the wine stain, like a drop of blood on the restaurant linen. Because the slightly uncanny coincidence had to be meaningless, I attributed it to that suggestible mindstate we find ourselves in when traveling or reading, in which days fold on themselves upon synchronicities. Many people know the feeling, one that in the past I had tried to disarm with research. But the explanations for coincidence—probability analysts talk about anomalous statistical clusters, mathematicians predict the logical frequency for seeming miracles, psychologists speak of cognitive bias—are all inadequate. Such moments are among those we file away as interesting and inexplicable, and best not made too much of in conversation if we don't wish to be teased by others who pretend not to know what we're talking about. I told myself I should expect such echoes, given that I was both away from home and reading intensively, which is to say, there was a lot of the world streaming through me.

Part of that world was Amanda. I'd failed all morning not to be distracted by our planned meeting. What revelations might she have for me today? She had knowledge I wanted and a confession to offer, should she decide to tell me about her meeting with Durant. For the first time in months I looked closely at my face in the mirror, a good way of quieting my imagination and resetting expectations. I'd always hoped I'd be more attractive as I aged—my best features are character ones, the squared-off eye-nose combo, the mouth a notch too wide and disrupting the line between chin and barely pronounced cheekbones—but still in its youth the face was unremarkable and, I thought, a bad champion of my capacities.

On my way out of the building I ran into Carlo. The top buttons of his safari shirt were undone to display a jointed necklace made of some nacreous stone polished to the same reflectiveness as his bald head. He asked where I was going and offered a lift. His car was parked in a gated courtyard on the next block. The moment I saw the '65 Aston Martin I knew it would be our topic of conversation. He asked if I recognized it. I said James Bond, and so on. We discussed Ian Fleming, his favorite author.

"People think he was just a writer," he said. "But first he was a war hero, a man of action."

I said that, in fact, Fleming was the hidden commander behind the Dieppe Raid that killed nine hundred Canadians in 1942. The raid was a disaster, poorly planned and supported, and the losses were viewed by some as a cover for an attempt to steal one of the German four-rotor Enigma machines used by Axis powers for passing coded messages. It turned out Carlo knew about Enigma machines, too, about the Italians' failure to update their naval versions before World War II, and the British intelligence successes in cracking the code. He had no time for fascists, he made a point of saying. One day, he said, he'd show me a painting of Bletchley Park that hung on his office wall.

"Are you meeting someone in the park?" he asked.

If I said no he might invite himself along, but my meeting with Amanda was no business of his. I said I just wanted to take a walk to help sort my thoughts.

"Grass and trees," he said. "Bletchley was all grass and trees. Very good for hard thinking."

When I closed the door I thought he'd speed off like an asshole but the bright silver car just pulled away and slotted into the traffic like a cog in a rotor assembly.

The park was full of young families strolling, couples and tourists on rented bikes, older tourists on small motored trains, and possessed the distinctive Italian features of unkempt grass and foliage. What is it about city parks that their every color and point of light return us to our moods? And yet the feeling was so familiar to me, from so many parks in so many cities, that it made me only more aware of myself and my history of moody park days, and removed me from the natural beauty itself. It said something about me that I still recalled from years earlier my visit to the Villa Borghese, and especially the Bernini sculptures, as a distinct experience that really did seem to bring me closer to the Maker, not Bernini but Whoever was at work in him, Someone Who'd mastered Nature, and now had, through intermediaries, taken on Art. Not that I would ever share such a thought, so easy to dismiss as empty or pretentious, or to ridicule in any number of ways.

I stood before the statue of Byron, our meeting spot, and looked back through the shaded path. There she was in the distance. Somehow in our short time in the apartment I'd registered her walk (I must have seen all of three full strides), and now it was her movement that marked her out among the others, straight-backed, with a sure but light unhurried step, her feet seeming to come off the ground even as they fell to it under a print skirt with blue tiger stripes. Her head was up, eyes no doubt forward, taking me in, as characteristic in my attitude, looking out in bafflement from a stillness, as she was in hers. I tried to look away but failed. As her face came clear by degrees I saw she was smiling at me, though there was something else there, some unsettling counter note, and I was further surprised that she didn't slow but came straight to me, put a hand on my shoulder, and kissed me on the cheek.

"We've been found out," she said. She spoke in the manner she strode, directly and with purpose.

"I know. He told me."

We began walking. Her friends would expect her in thirty minutes outside the zoo. She talked more about Durant, a more precise timeline of her history with him, his way of accepting unfavorable readings—

"Where did you go to grad school?" I asked.

"Small place in Oregon."

"Are you from Oregon?"

"Michigan."

"How did you end up in Oregon?"

"I don't want a speed date, James. I need to explain something to you."

"Why don't you email about it? We can use this time to enjoy the park together."

"So you'd rather be told something important by email than face to face?"

That I was silent at the question only supported the possibility that I was not a serious enough man to be in her company, but she seemed to soften then and began the explanation of how she ended up in Oregon. It would be another few minutes and we'd be sitting on a bench outside the zoo entrance, watching a large, apparently ownerless shepherd-collie chasing birds, until I realized that the story was leading to the thing she had to tell me.

"I went west to go to school at Rhyce College. My undergrad degree was in political science so it took some persuading to get them to consider me for a lit degree, but I told them I wanted to write about the decline of the political novel in American litera- ture. I made my argument to a man named Carlson Werling, in the English department, and said I wanted to study with him. The political novel was Werling's specialty. I appealed to his interest, to his vanity, really, and he pressured to have me admitted. What he didn't know until a few weeks after I got there was that I wasn't interested in studying the political novel, but in studying him. Like a lot of faculty and administration at Rhyce, Werling had done work for the CIA. Before teaching he'd been in Central America at the same time my brother was. I thought it was very likely that he knew my brother, or knew of him, and he might know who murdered him."

The shepherd-collie stopped in its tracks, as if it had been listening, and stood in profile twenty feet before us, staring into space until it forgot why, then put its nose down and trotted off. I seemed to be looking at Amanda's knees where they appeared beneath her skirt, knowing this focus could be misinterpreted, that it was certainly no place to be looking in such a moment, and yet feeling trapped in a kind of precarious apprehension, unable to look back into the park. And now she was looking at me, I sensed, looking at her knees like a horny schoolboy. Through some intervention of grace, my face turned up to see hers, and it forgave me, without expecting of me anything like a verbal response.

"Marcus and I had different fathers, different last names. When I got close enough to Werling, and had had enough afternoons in the faculty lounge with him to ask about his time in Guatemala, he began to tell stories. At first he fell into a kind of pathetic attempt at intriguing evasion, as if he really knew too much to say anything, but when I pretended to let it drop he acquiesced to tell me he'd been contracted to 'liaise' between governments after the US paid to set up surveillance systems abroad following 9/11. They wanted foreign governments to spy on their citizens for themselves and the US, exactly the story Marcus was working on. I spent the next few days making calls, connecting dots. At some point Werling must have gotten a phone call. He was in trouble. And he dropped me instantly, or rather, he had the department secretary drop him as my advisor. Another professor in the department guided me to Truth and Justice Studies and arranged for a prof over there to mentor me through a thesis. I transferred, different department, different building, and never saw Werling again. He took a leave in midterm and didn't return until I'd graduated. I wasn't going to get more from him, but I knew I'd looked in the right place."

She took out a pack of cigarettes and offered me one. I declined.

"My Italian girlfriends have me smoking," she said. "Here they come."

The women smiled broadly. Their clothes—one wore linen pants, the other a skirt—weren't especially stylish but looked better just for being Roman, on Romans. We stood and Amanda introduced them as Detta, who took off her sunglasses and smiled at me, and Cinzia, who left hers on and nodded. Detta said something in Italian and laughed.

"She wants to know if you speak Italian," said Amanda.

"I learn more by pretending not to." This was understood to be a sporting lie, and they laughed again, and Cinzia said something and now all three laughed. I should have been enjoying the moment but was still thinking of the revelation about Amanda and her brother.

"We only tease you," said Detta. "Not polite. We didn't know Amanda has a boyfriend."

"Does she?" I turned to Amanda. "I'm disappointed. Will you tell me about him?"

Now I was in confederacy with the Italians.

"Will you come with us?" asked Cinzia. The temples of her shades disappeared perfectly into the blonde streaks in her dark hair. I felt overmatched even by the tortoiseshell plastic.

"He has work to do," said Amanda. She took from her woven bag an envelope. She said Durant had given it to her shortly after they came to Rome and she told him she was leaving the job. It was his thesis on Three Sheets and the Poet. "You should read it now. Let's meet tomorrow night, after eight."

"Why can't I go to the zoo? Let me go to the zoo."

"Don't tell August I've given you this." She placed the envelope into my hand.

"I won't. And listen." I leaned in and whispered to her while raising my eyebrows to the other women, asking them to forgive me, and I could see that they did. "This isn't the place to say it but I'm very sorry about your brother."

She administered another kiss, and for a very full measure of dappled time, I watched her and her friends walk away.

Maybe for the first time in my life I sat on grass beneath a tree. What I'd just learned about Amanda was strange, having met her friends in that moment was strange, the city, the park, the place I was, strange. What wasn't strange was the shameful ranking of my concerns. I told myself I was just understandably lonely, and so my thoughts were fixed on my chances with Amanda when they should have been aligned with her feelings, her grief and anger at her brother's death. But because in recent months my rankings were often a mess, I found something reassuringly familiar in my hateful self. Knowing you're superficial doesn't make you any deeper. Were my base motives—and they were base—simply money and desire? Or was my real motive hidden beneath poverty and loneliness? Whatever was going on, I had a very serious problem with the surround. As if to demonstrate, I took out my phone and checked my email. The only message was

from a "D. Scirea." "I just found your card. I was going to send
music, yes? My father is an asshole. Yours, Davide." I opened the
link and a few seconds later was staring into my little phone
screen at buskers on a daytime street somewhere, presumably
Istanbul. Three musicians, two guitarists and a drummer with a
single drum, all wearing porkpie hats. The one who looked something like Davide as I remembered him played guitar. The
phonesound was small but I could make out the gypsy jazz, as
he'd called it, the instruments in tight formation. People stood
around them in a half circle. At one point the camera, or phone,
more likely, wandered over the heads of the crowd and turned a
full three-sixty, taking in a pedestrian street locked with hundreds or thousands of people, as if it were a stadium exit after a
game, though the traffic was in all directions. Just before the
camera came back around to the band, I saw a phalanx of men in
white helmets, holding shields, standing by. Why were there riot
police in the middle of all this? What was about to happen? The
clip ended before the performance had. Another meaningless
fragment of random capture, broken off and drifting.

With the tiny music still in my head, I took up Durant's letter.

Amanda,

Across the street below my window an artist has put out a
tray of flattened paint tubes, a jar of turpentine, and a small
painting of a woman. I walked by them earlier—the fresh
smears of color on everything, the painting, the tray, the
tubes themselves. Now a dog has stopped at them, sniffing
at colors he doesn't see, and yet knowing in his way things I
cannot. What's the difference in smell between two shades

of blue? And here I am, no different, nose in art, thinking I
see things as they are but intuiting other wonders all around,
unavailable to my senses.

Even if it weren't anyway so stale an expression, to say that
the Poet's work "speaks to me" is inadequate. It can't describe
those first moments in which I felt the poems knew me not
anonymously but personally. The first line I came across led me
to "The Art of Memory," where I heard myself quoted, through
my daughter. *The sun blinks and we play blind.* I was elated, I
laughed, I recall talking out loud to myself, even a kind of singing. This went on through the evening and night until morning,
by which time I'd read all the poems at Three Sheets, and as
much as I could of the commentary at SHEPMETSOR and the
other sites. I made pages of notes by hand. They were mostly
questions. Who did she leave in the bar in Campo de' Fiori and
why? Who was the Poet? and so on. I started seeing connections
in other poems, references to places she'd been in the past few
years, even the general times she'd been there, and to other
words and private jokes shared between us.

In "Relief" the Poet writes of a man meeting a woman, a
stranger, in a café, and the disquiet he feels, the ghost of
familial love there inside the romantic attraction. He's sure
they must be related and wonders who might be their
common ancestor: "What coalescent event binds us?" Surely
only a geneticist would have this way ("coalescent event"?)
of expressing the idea. I've felt this precise strangeness
myself. And I once explained to my daughter that the current we feel whenever we fall into attraction with someone
is in fact genetic conditioning, the species trying to shuffle
genes yet another way to find ever more advantageous

mutations. The idea is so antiromantic that she ridiculed me about it in a running joke. I remember she remarked on the word "coalescent," meaning "bringing together," and she objected to the fact that things proceed in variations on an original copy. In a sense she objected to nature.

Models of understanding are ways of seeing a thing, not the thing itself, and so in some instances can be applied, with modification, to new questions. The models that suggested themselves were those I know best: those describing patterns of codes and transferences.

Over many days I began to hunt for these codes. Imagining ciphers is the stuff of madness and popular novels. But if we geneticists hadn't gone looking for codes we wouldn't have discovered the underlying mysteries of life, which surely bring us as close to the Great Explanation as anything these past many decades within advancing human knowledge. Some geneticists are hubristic enough to imagine that they have stolen fire from the gods. The truth is we don't even know how to conceive of gods, let alone their places and secrets. We're some more clever than others, but we're all dogs of a sort, sniffing at colors we can't see. And yet among our senses, a few have been granted by nature, others won by our pursuit of them.

I chose the two poems called "**Decor**" for special attention. They stand out for their titles, of course, the repetition a kind of underscoring, a way of the Poet's insisting upon a significance. In ways I hadn't seen yet, I thought, they must be something of a like pair. It occurred to me to focus on the title itself. Without much effort I derived from "Decor" the anagram **Coder** and this seemed a confirmation that at least

I might be on the right path (or maybe I'd been on the verge of seeing the word "code" all along, which is why I played my hunch). But **who is the Coder?** (Now there's a question for the ages!) That was simply another way of putting the question I already had in hand. Then, an adjustment. What if the anagram was in fact not Coder but **R Code?** This made immediate sense. Given the hours of her girlhood I spent teaching my daughter about genetics, to us the term R Code means **recombinant code.**

I tested various models: gene conversion, transpositional recombination, and (this seemed promising, given that I was finding all these wonders at an internet site) site-specific recombination. But the model that fit best with my premise was the simple **DNA crossover** in homologous recombination. Have you ever studied meiosis, Amanda? In sister pairs of chromatids aligned side by side, at a point called the **chiasma,** the pairs become connected and exchange a segment of DNA. Just picture two trains, one bolded, side by side in a switching yard. Each train has ten cars. The bolded cars are numbered one through ten, the others, A through J.

1 2 3 4 5 6 7 8 9 10

A B C D E F G H I J

Suppose that the back halves are exchanged. We end up with these trains (DNA segments):

1 2 3 4 5 F G H I J

A B C D E **6 7 8 9 10**

This is (very roughly) the process of DNA crossover at the chiasma.

You might know that in poetry the term "chiasmus" refers to a **reflecting rhetorical device**, as if a mirror has been set down in the middle of a line or stanza. The primary early source is Scripture:

A   B   B   A

the first shall be last and the last shall be first

The ABBA structure can be made more complex, as in ABCDDCBA, or disguised through separation, so that each letter is on a different line or so the ABCD is in one line, and DCBA in another. If the poems contain any such principle, we must then look for **chiasmic phrases**—sequences of **words, sounds, or meanings presented in one order, then its reverse.** In recombination, the code would be the same at the chiasma, but it made sense to take guidance from the poetic sense of the word. Should I find matching word sequences, I'd then transpose the line endings following each to make new lines, with new meanings. Through this method, based on **a natural phenomenon within creation itself,** I might find the hidden code.

All that prevented me from glazing over—scientific or technical language tends to leather my brain—were the irritatingly bolded words, the text version of Durant's full-voiced pronouncements, and the building evidence that he'd made himself open to a kind of lunacy that brought false traces of his daughter. His need to argue for the traces was desperate and sad, and I wondered if his social manner, warm but challenging, was more than just a way to keep his workers on task. In testing me, he kept us both distracted from the possibility that he was irreparably heartbroken.

Upon a stray thought I wondered if Amanda sensed as I did that we might make a beautiful advantageous mutation together.

A breeze reached me but failed to stir the pages in my hand.

Both "Decor"s are nine stanzas of nine lines (they're terrible, pointless poems, I think you'll agree), which makes the fifth line of the fifth stanza the middle line of the poem. And in the middle of this line, in each poem, we find the key.

After weeks in open country I hit town with its yowling
    corners and hotel room phone looking as do
the plastic key fob and newspaper at the door like a movie
    prop. I'm one city nearer you but a call is unlikely to
save me, father of nothing now, no one I haven't already here lost
    within sight of home. Lost too amid too many markers.
Everything moves toward one of two conditions. The name
    said or not. There's forgetting, yes, but there is no
place without thought of itself in a wind. One of two conditions.

And, from the second "Decor":

How to say I met a casting director without getting your
    hopes up.
The traffic here is a kind of weather. How to say, Mother, he
    took an interest.
The part of the footman's mute girl in prison. With no text
    per se my

audition was stunning and two weeks ago, okay, but still
    they are unlikely to
forget me, Father. Already I've known the one absence I'm
    imprisoned
within is how he put it. To have trouble finding the words
    makes sense
for a casting director and so we are alike, he and the mute.
    There are no
true clichés in this business, he said rotely. Other parts often
    come open.
Auditions are best done on-site. The weather here gets tied
    up in arteries.

Each middle line is long, eighteen syllables. Extracting the
middle word sequences we arrive at

    A   B   C   D
[of nothing/now, no one/I haven't/already]

and

    D   C   B   A
[Already/I've/known the one/absence]

Now we do the train move, switching the cars at the point of
chiasma and sectioning out the mirroring material to construct the new lines. After extraction and transposition they
read:

save me, father. I'm imprisoned

and

forget me, Father. here lost

Was I to enter a whole new order of despair? Or were these accidents of language, products of over-reading? Because I couldn't
bear the one possibility—that my daughter was "imprisoned" or
"lost"—I chose for weeks to think that I'd imposed the patterns
and connections. I know that fragments of language travel on
invisible vectors and reproduce as if through binary fission at
incalculable rates. There are rational explanations for what
would otherwise seem inexplicable coincidences of this sort
within language and outside it. In fact I was researching them
on the day that "August" appeared on Three Sheets and cast me
into the dark certainty I've lived in since. Somehow, though
there'd been a "June" and "July," I hadn't anticipated a poem
whose title was my own name. I quote here only the first stanza.

You let his name slip. I made you describe
him. You said a bend in a road, a single
blue tie, walls covered with images of gas
clouds spooling two hundred light-years
high tacked up by this man who long ago
walked out of the straw upon his schooling.

Coincidence does not extend this far, Amanda. Her favorite
view was at the bend in the road at the crest of a hill that looked
over our acreage to the sea. The blue tie was the only one I

owned as she was growing up, and she laughed at me whenever I wore it. Deep space photos that I'd tacked up covered the walls of her bedroom. And it's true, a scholarship allowed me to leave the small Nebraska farming town where I grew up.

Imagine my horror at seeing myself. But you can imagine, can't you? I sense the poems reach you, too. I think that you feel something of my loss for seeing what I see. Your distress—it's obvious to me—is a bitter comfort to me, I confess. If a mystery grows large enough, if there comes a point after which there's no hope of explanation, then our troubles are vaulted to the realm of . . . not the metaphysical, a dated category I have never accepted . . . but the omniphysical, what the anthropologist Lévi-Strauss called "the one lasting presence" that might be there at the end of all inquiry, a presence not that surpasseth understanding but that surpasses current understanding and, I admit, even given the exponentially increased pace of intellectual gain, likely always will.

The disappearance of my daughter as a causal event could be brought to hand with enough evidence, but the everlasting condition of her absence will never make sense, not to me. And so, on the good days, the poems at Three Sheets can seem to understand me. Even as they wound, they can seem to be my friend.

Can you sce thcm that way? I ask that you don't let go, don't abandon them out of fear for me. We can encourage each other. We have been made to matter to one another in ways no one else could comprehend.

I'm sorry that the poems have caused you the pain of empathy, but I must tell you that I've come to treasure our like-mindedness. There is no name for this state as it has evolved in me in recent weeks. To me, the closest name is "Amanda."

And so the letter ended where it began, upon Amanda. Durant was like someone out of Nabokov, afflicted with a referential mania. He'd offered a plea for mercy in the guise of a pattern analysis, with circumstantial evidence, weak and incoherent. Was his daughter a character in the poems, the "you" being addressed, or was she in fact the voice of them, telling him in code that she was "imprisoned" or "lost" (and which was it?)? Maybe the details in "August" could be fitted to his past, but blue ties and deep space posters aren't uncommon, and the other poems, objectively read, supported none of his imaginings. He had read cleverly and wrongly. It seemed obvious now that he'd wanted Amanda and me in Rome not just the better to guide our work but out of sheer lonely despair.

I tucked the letter into my pocket and sat there, the park and the city resuming around me. Above the trees the very sky seemed material. What I thought was this: my parents are dead, the Londoner is lost to me, Dominic is fading and will soon forget us both. The two people I felt closest to in that moment were Durant and Amanda, and sitting in the olive light of a stone city, I knew them hardly at all.

The rest of the afternoon was free. I wasn't prepared to return to the apartment and risk letting Durant engage me in talk. He read me much better than he read the poems. I walked south toward Piazza di Spagna. The traffic and jostle of Roman streets require of pedestrians an alertness that should have simplified my thoughts—I'd learned too much, too suddenly—but in fact the walking opened an

emotion I'd not wanted to confront. I was angry at Durant. It was
small of me, I conceded, to be angry at a man carrying a great loss,
but by involving Amanda and me in his troubles he had found a way
to prolong his pain and make it more acute, luring us with money into
what I could now think of only as a kind of sickness. But guilty anger
is not a clarifying feeling. I suppose because I have a northern soul my
idea of clarity opens in my mind vast landscapes, reaching to horizons
and the most distant geological times, places almost untouched by
human event. The true north. And so Rome, historied, cultured and
culture-defining, was not likely to afford me the kind of space I
needed to see these questions clearly.

Or that's exactly wrong. The clarity of empty vastness was only
an idea that didn't hold up to scrutiny. I thought best amid clamor,
especially virtual clamor.

Using a street map called up on my phone, I headed south
toward the Spanish Steps, looking furtively into the faces of those
I passed. How many of these people were like Durant, recon-
structing their losses in the shades and surfaces of their days?
How many saw in the available light ghosts they knew by name?
In a big enough city, a pedestrian city, I sometimes imagine I see
the same face over and again, but always a stranger's face, though
less a stranger on every encounter. A face strange yet familiar, as
if from my other life in a parallel universe. The recurring face in
Rome was of a dark-haired, slender man just slightly older than
I, maybe in his midthirties. There he was coming down a side
street or looking out from a doorway. At a table across the bar,
crouched by the tire of a car near Durant's apartment, in a gallery
queue. He was usually well dressed, sometimes casually so. On
every instance of seeing him I was aware of my *failure* to see, of
having grouped a series of first glances into a type based on a

general similarity and so overlooking each distinct feature. It was what everyone did, this lazy way of seeing. It was what poetry should have saved me from.

And yet there he was again entering the Japanese paper shop where I stopped to buy a small notebook and pen. He was half turned away from me, examining a display of ornate leather blotters and fountain pens. (How could there still be a market in beautiful writing objects?) This time I really looked. Who was he? Or rather, who was this version of him? I held to my guess of his age. He couldn't have been forty but neither did his face hold youth. He wore a long-sleeved cotton shirt with a mandarin collar (also called a Mao, a Nehru, or a Japanese ((was this coincidence?))). A thick watch with a metal band. No wedding ring. His shoes looked handmade, of the kind that could be cheap in a poor country but very expensive in a place like Italy. The oddest thing about him was his movement, or lack of it. He was still, even facially, as if not only assessing the pens but also intently listening to them. Whatever they communicated, he turned and left the store without even glancing farther inside.

I walked to a small church and sat for a few minutes on the steps in the shade. A young mother with two little boys walked by, laughing at something. They were good little boys, I could see, and there was a sureness in their goodness that I envied.

At random I took streets without consulting the map, and walked myself lost. Durant's letter, the pained, skewed vision of it, was all around me now in the city itself, both an element in which I was suspended, and an endlessly complicated, unfolding event. For the first time I sensed what it must be like for Durant to believe he'd found a voice directed at him personally, a kind of singing inspired by the particular spirit of his lonely nights. Meanings, such as they were, came on delay, and so I was eight or nine strides past the entrance to a watchmaker's shop before the recognition hit me. As I'd passed I registered a set of steps curving up into the dark and a glass case recessed into the space with watches and escapements mounted against a bright red cloth. All of this perceived in an instant, the same instant in which I saw, reflected in the glass, the familiar face. He would have to have been inside the open entrance with his back pressed to the wall. I stopped walking.

Moments later I was in the watch shop, one small room, empty but for me and a large, wattled man behind a desk with a single lens strapped onto his eye, bent over his work like Polyphemus counting sheep. He said nothing, didn't look up. I returned to the street and looked for the man with the mandarin collar but he wasn't to be seen. I walked back the way I'd come for two blocks, turned down a new street, narrow, in shadow. Whether I was trying to find or to lose him I couldn't say. I was following a following, led by a fascination even as I fled it. As my eyes adjusted to the shade, I spotted him up ahead, across the street, his shirt almost the color of the water-stained wall he walked beside. There was no one else around. I could run and catch him (it seemed he was now trying to escape), but did I really want to confront him? Just then he turned and stole a quick look over his shoulder, directly at me. I realized that the other times I'd seen the face were in fact as I'd first imagined. It was the same face, exactly, and in his eyes the stranger carried his recognition, or more than that, his *knowledge* of me. As he moved away again he came to a bright cross street and rounded the corner. I ran to catch up and as I took the corner he started down the Spanish Steps.

They were crowded but I saw that by keeping to the nearest side I could make ground on him. He moved along a railing, about a third of the way down, and descended past a garden, then took the main steps at an angle. As he turned sideways to squeeze past an elderly couple, he looked back and saw me, I think, and must have seen that I had a clear path to intercept him, though at no point did his pace quicken. He altered his course laterally, keeping level, and made his way just in time to allow a wedding party ascending the steps to come between us. Amid the celebrants and photographers I lost sight of him and made the error of moving into the stream rather than continuing down the side. When a way finally cleared he was gone. I descended to the street. He should have been visible in one direction or another, but he'd vanished. I returned to the steps and sat.

Surrounded by feet and languages I closed my eyes and tried to think of a northern landscape. Miles of perfect focus in a cold, dry air. On the distant horizon something took shape, like letters of an unknown alphabet, growing, nodding in rhythm. The first humans to the New World brought dogs with them across the land link. When I'd asked about his work one evening Durant showed me pictures from his California lab, including one of a skeleton of a prehistoric dog with grooves in its shoulders where it had been strapped to its work. Besides the heavy load, the dog carried tuberculosis. It was possible, Durant explained, knowing the genome for the dog from its bones, to know its snout shape and hair color. It could be simulated exactly with the right programs, or could be cloned and so repeated on earth seventeen thousand years after it died. This strong, coughing dog. "These are the facts," he'd said. "We can literally make the past get to its feet and look us in the eye. Or some of it."

I called Amanda, got her voicemail, but on hearing her voice found myself unable to say anything. Whatever I was involved in, it wasn't about the open exchange of information. I needed time to think but time in itself wouldn't be enough. That must have been why I'd followed the stranger.

It was late afternoon, late morning in Montreal.

Upon answering, Dominic sounded weak, I thought, or uncertain. I told him it was me, but he said nothing in response, so I kept talking to give him time to come around. I reminded him that I was in Rome. Dominic loved great cities and the idea of them. Many of his stories began like old romantic novels. "Once in Jakarta . . ." "Once in Cairo . . ." The stories were never about literature but instead some intriguing person he knew there, dinner at a consulate, drinks with a despot's most dangerous enemy. The accidental impression was that he'd lived a large, unlikely life that he could not, in fact, tell you about fully, out of duty to some unnamed political principle or silent calling. As his memory declined, the stories began to lose the outlines of sure character. They developed hesitations, small corrections, then larger ones. Some were obvious conflations he wasn't aware of. Over time the unreliable stories came to damage the old, stable ones I'd always assumed were true. I wanted to save them for him, the real ones, and usually tried to steer him away from new tellings. But to what end? Robbed of the pleasure of telling, in time all he'd have left were verse recitations learned in childhood.

"I'm supposed to be spending my days in a room solving the mysteries of poetry. But it's not working out that way. Things have gotten complicated." I hoped the sound of my voice would help him locate himself but given what I was saying, I might only have been further confusing him. "How are you, Dominic?"

"I seem to be the same, but more so. What's happening to you?"

"I'm not sure I can explain it." I said that the Three Sheets site had induced in Durant a feeling of secret communications directed at him personally. And given the volume of commentary around Three Sheets, I wondered if the same thing wasn't happening to other readers, who instead of admitting these feelings in public forums obsessed about the Poet. The whole thing suggested a shared madness.

Until I said it, I hadn't known that's what I thought.

"Then you've discovered something, haven't you, James? Even if your terms are imprecise. Where are you?"

"In Rome." Already he'd forgotten.

"Rome. Do you know the Italian writer Chiaromonte? I met him there once. He claimed that Shakespeare understood madness, but in the centuries since, we've eliminated it from our understanding. This hum of rationalism we're stuck with—it forces madness to out in irrational rebellions and destruction."

"Things were pretty destructive for the Elizabethans, too. And we hospitalize and treat the mentally ill instead of killing them. And even if I believed in such a thing as irrational understanding, I'd still have no idea how to explain this particular weird phenomenon."

"I accept that." He paused. Now he was all too self-aware. "Do you know your Roman pagans, James?"

"I haven't met as many locals as I'd hoped."

"Symmachus wrote that 'It is not by one way alone that we can arrive at so sublime a mystery.' He's arguing for the proliferation of gods in Roman religion, against the gains of Christianity. It's centuries old, this call to open up other ways of knowing."

"I'd be happy to arrive at a mystery, as long as it took me in. But I haven't arrived anywhere yet."

"Be patient. We have to prepare ourselves to receive great understanding."

"Dominic, I'm being followed."

"What's that?"

"Someone's following me. I think. A man. A stranger has been following me almost since I got here."

"Oh. Well then, you really must get to the bottom of that."

The moment we signed off I began missing him. I pictured him staring at his wall calendar, failing to make sense of it. Even within an ordered system, things get complicated very fast. There are more possible moves in a game of chess than there are atoms in the solar system. And that's within the squared square of a chessboard. Imagine the square of a boxing ring, the number of possible movements of feet and hands available even to just one fighter, Muhammad Ali exploring the possibilities for deforming the face of his opponent. In the so-called game of the century Bobby Fischer made a move no chess grandmaster would expect, sacrificing his queen for a long-term material advantage. The Londoner had a red T-shirt with a picture of the queen's face deformed as if with blobs of clay. When he was twenty-two Ali changed his name from Clay. At the time he won the game of the century, Fischer was just thirteen. His twenty-six-year-old opponent, Donald Byrne, taught English at Penn State. His specialty was Keats.

I felt someone looking at me.

The street was an ever-changing sameness. No one paid me any attention. For the few seconds of bounding thought I hadn't been paying attention to myself and a part of me was still floating. It must have been from my imaginary, elevated position that I glimpsed the watcher. I was thinking of the chessboard squares and the rectangles on Dominic's Gardens of Quebec wall calendar, and suddenly my focus was on the ordered lines and rows of windows in the corner building at the foot of the steps. There, in a

second-floor window, a movement. A man turning away, disappearing. I hadn't seen him fully but he'd been watching me. It was
the stranger with the mandarin collar, the Follower—who else
could it have been?—waiting me out. There and not. And from my
first visit to Rome I knew it was not just any room. The building
was the Keats-Shelley House. The presence had been looking at
me from the room where Keats died. Of tuberculosis.

I ran into the building and up the stairs and stood in the foyer to
the small museum, the only way in or out. A young woman waited
at the admissions table, not knowing what to make of me as I stood
puffing, out of breath.

"No rush," she said. "We don't close until six." Her accent was
British. Given where we were she assumed I spoke English. I paid
the fee and went inside. In the first room were three middle-aged
couples and a sleeping white dog. The apartment ran to smaller
rooms, left and right. I went right, through a small library, to Keats's
little room, with the floral reliefs on the ceiling that were his last
vision. It was empty. I stepped to the window, leaned over, and
looked. Yes, the spot where I'd been sitting was visible. I waited for
a chill to come over me, the certainty that the figure in the window
had been the ghost of Keats himself. But the place was only as it
seemed. There is nothing as truly dead as a museum. I looked in the
other rooms but of course the Follower was gone. I walked out, past
the manuscripts in the poet's handwriting, past the glass case mor-
bidly displaying a lock of his fine hair. What could Durant do with
the DNA? Might he be able to bring two tubercular creatures back
to life? And what would the young Romantic poet, only twenty-five
when he died, make of such a wonder?

I told the woman at the entrance that I'd been hoping to catch up
to a friend and described the man with the collar. Had she seen

him? She had not, but then she'd been away from her desk for the few minutes just before I arrived. She invited me to check the guest register, in case he'd signed it upon leaving. There were about a dozen names for the day. Some had written comments, in German, Italian, most in English. Some had left email addresses to be informed of coming events. The most recent had signed his name pretty much incomprehensibly, something like "Elias Hepner Voth." The "From" space Voth had left blank. In the "Comments" he'd written, semi-legibly, the words running together, what might have read, "In our Pantheon. Silence." followed by an email address: "Rememberthepoet@ostia." At a glance there was nothing strange about the entry. Keats was certainly in the pantheon of poets, and he'd praised silence for its eternity, most famously in "Ode on a Grecian Urn." But the cursive was uncertain. The opening *I* was in an archaic hand, weighed down by the bulb of the loop. The *I* might, in fact, have been an *O*, and the long trailing skirt on the *n* might have contained another letter. The longer I looked, the more I thought the line read, "One hour. Pantheon. Silence. Remember the poet@ostia." The fact that the words seemed as if they'd been written in haste only intensified my sense that they weren't about Keats at all, but addressed to me. Once I'd accepted the second reading it came to me—I admit I felt a bit sick at the realization. Ostia was the Roman suburb where Pasolini, poet and filmmaker, was murdered in 1975, or at least where his body was found on the beach. A teen hustler was convicted but, if I remembered correctly—I wasn't about to consult my phone to find out—the killers might have been anticommunists, or extortionists who'd stolen some rolls of his last film, the one with all the sadism.

If I was right, I'd been warned to keep quiet, pricked with a pointed allusion. "Rememberthepoet@ostia" was a death threat.

But who would deliver a warning this way? I assumed the threat was empty but couldn't hazard Amanda or Durant, or myself. Back on the street, I didn't take my phone from my pocket in case someone was watching me as I stood there, looking the length of the Via Condotti. The city suddenly seemed as it was, not a place of tourist sites but of sight itself, millions of pairs of eyes, all with their points of view, different light shows playing in each skull. It was hard to imagine that amid all the beauty and history and grappa I could be worthy of anyone's attention. Maybe I'd been mistaken for someone else. Maybe just as Voth's face had at first looked to me like so many others', my own had triggered a false recognition in him. But then why deliver the threat by conjuring a poet's murder? Had he wanted to be spotted and hoped I'd follow or chase him? Had he staged the whole thing? If so I had played along perfectly, even positioning myself below the window in the Keats House. But why not just confront me? No, he wasn't expecting me to come after him, but once into it had improvised beautifully. He must have needed the hour to prepare for the meeting. His game was up, after all, or at least headed that way, and by stalling he maintained an essential advantage. He knew who I was and likely where I lived, and I knew only his face.

Pasolini. Dominic had once told me to read "The Religion of My Time" but I saw nothing much in it, at least in translation. I'd seen a few of his films and forgotten them. It was the facts of his life that I remembered. Before the future antifascist was born, his father had captured the fifteen-year-old who'd attempted to assassinate Mussolini, and the kid was lynched on the spot. As a soldier in the Second World War, Pasolini was taken prisoner by the Germans but escaped disguised as a peasant. Later he lost a teaching job and his place in a regional Communist party to charges of public indecency and corrupting youth, a charge (maybe warranted) against poets from Socrates onward, and he moved with his mother to Rome. In time he became Pasolini, neorealist; proponent of "contamination," the conjoining of the sacred and profane; atheist lover of Christ the revolutionary; defender of the proletariat, though his films spoke only to the educated elite. He kept getting hauled off to court, a true *provocateur.* (Like Socrates. And—why did I know this stuff?—even more like Apollinaire, another poet, novelist, dramatist, intellectual of a sort, who was born in Rome, moved to France, caused trouble, and was once accused by police of stealing the *Mona Lisa* ((begun in Italy, finished in France)). As Pasolini had been a soldier in the Second World War, Apollinaire was a combatant in the first. A year before Mussolini received almost exactly the same wound, an exploding shell drove shrapnel into Apollinaire's forehead, though he survived. In that same year, 1916, he published *Le Poète assassiné. The Poet Assassinated.*)

These goddamn cha-chas. My father thought my memory was a curse.

The Pantheon wasn't far. There was time to walk there. I set out, in hopes that I'd misread the entry, and decided I could live a satisfactory life never knowing whom I had chased that afternoon, as long as it was a long life. I pictured this life as a clean line extending before me the length of the street and to the horizon, which I couldn't, in fact, see, falling into the earth's curve along a bending plane true to some mathematically sound aspect of space and gravity. It was drawing me, the clarity of this line, drawing me along the streets, down Marzio to the Obelisk of Montecitorio, with its bronze ball and spike, a sundial, which I must have seen on my first visit, though I recalled it not at all, and along to Via dei Pastini, where I took a hard right and had to imagine the line doing so as well, to the Piazza della Rotonda and the thing itself, the Pantheon. The great assertion of balance, of classical proportions, of the very shape my mind would normally assume after one of its spells. The line ran straight through the high doors.

I crossed the crowded piazza and passed through the grand portico, into the murmuring geometries of the ancient space. Of course it was full of tourists wearing knapsacks, taking pictures with cellphones, as it had been when I'd first visited, and I longed now as I had then to experience the place in silence. All was echo. The babble sharpened my unease that I was about to meet Voth, or maybe that, amid all of these people, I might miss him and have to face the threatened consequences. I looked for the shirt, the collar, the general impression his face had made. I reasoned that, to be seen, he would stand in the least crowded area of the floor. The humanity was thickest around Raphael's tomb. I looked elsewhere, kept my eyes on those not in groups and not staring up fixed by the two panels of the dome illuminated by what seemed especially intense sunlight coming through the oculus, and for a moment I myself was unable to look away from the brilliant plate of light. From nowhere came to mind lines from the cryptic anti-Semite Ezra Pound: "But that the child / walk in peace in her basilica, / The light there almost solid." The child was the daughter he had fathered with his lover and more or less abandoned to poverty. Pound had ended up like Bobby Fischer, raving against Jews and his president. But I could feel that the light surpassed the hate and madness, surpassed all poison. The light was sound.

Who here, if anyone, was alone and looking nowhere, or searching the crowd as I was? There were two or three dozen seated on the long wooden pews, their backs to me. At first I missed him. Then, scanning again, I realized he must be the man with his arms outstretched along the back of a bench. His shoulders pushed his shirt up into folds that obscured the collar, but this was him, surely. In one hand he held a paper or pamphlet.

Before I could approach he was standing and in motion, his back still to me as he stepped into the throng. I kept my eyes on him and began forward. He had channeled into a slow counter-clockwise flow. I reckoned I could intercept him and started away upon the angle. Though still at a distance, he was almost in profile when I plowed over the little boy. I felt him against my hip and then looked down just as he bounced to the floor on his bottom. He wore short pants, brown, and an odd cloth cap that made him seem older than the five- or six-year-old he was. We were looking at each other with equal surprise when his face began to crumple into what obviously would become in moments a wail. And yet when I squatted down to him and said I was sorry, the sound of my voice seemed to stop him. Maybe he didn't speak English and found the experience of being addressed nonsensically too interesting to eclipse. In any case, when I smiled, he assented to do so, too. It wasn't clear to whom he belonged. I helped him to his feet and now he was looking over my shoulder. I turned and saw that he was staring up at the circle of light on the dome. "Beautiful," I said. And he said, in some Germanic tongue, what sounded like "Gott in heaven." Then, with no note of hurt or embarrassment, he toddled off toward Raphael and stood at the legs of a young couple who must have assumed he'd been by their side the whole time. The woman dropped her hand and felt for his head and hat absently, her eyes steady on a gesturing tour guide.

The episode had taken less than a minute but when I turned to look for Voth he had disappeared. I paused on each face but he was nowhere. I let the crowd move around me in its circles and eddies and was suddenly overcome with inspiration or light-headedness. In the second-row pew I found the paper he'd been holding. It was the information flyer from the Keats House, with the young poet's likeness badly hand-drawn on the cover. Inside was printed Keats's last letter, written as he was dying to his friend Charles Brown. "I have an habitual feeling of my real life having passed, and that I am leading a posthumous existence." He writes of finding it emotionally difficult to read or write. "Yet I ride the little horse,— and, at my worst, even in Quarantine, summoned up more puns, in a sort of desperation, in one week than in any year of my life." I pictured him in his bed, writing, dying, punning for his life.

My hip retained the sense memory where it had knocked up against the little boy.

I could handle a few blind-side collisions, I reasoned. In this one I'd lost track of Voth, or whoever he was, but it was the little boy, now gone, whose absence I felt. It hit me, under that beautiful light, with something like shock.

Now and then we find ourselves in story. Events, some of them causally connected, begin to seem inevitable. Their presentation becomes distinct. Maybe a theme emerges. But because life is not literature, we drop out of the story before it ends.

The next morning I sat in my patio chair, sipping coffee, scanning the intersection of small streets for Voth. It seemed obvious from the perspective of a new day that the man hadn't actually been following me. Suppose he was alarmed when he saw me following him and so evaded me on the Spanish Steps. Suppose it was a coincidence, hardly inexplicable, that I'd seen him in two tourist destinations on the same afternoon. The idea of his having been a significant stranger struck me now as ridiculous. Would

the face keep repeating if I was looking for it? In memory, the
passing faces, like the patios, all looked much the same.

My phone buzzed on the iron table. Amanda's text: "hope you've
read the letter. now see Streams, posted last night @ 3 Shts. Drnt
just called to say the dream in the poem is his daughter's." Half a
minute later she sent a second text: "meet me tonight at the fountain of piazza di santa maria. trastevere. 8:10."

I called up Three Sheets and read the new poem.

Streams

One afternoon, more than a year
ago now, the physical world
opened in that familiar
astonishment for what I knew
even then would be the last time.
Growing old is not a diminishment
but a closer knowledge of streams,
then the returns
of moments now undressed.

Afterward she talked of a dream
she'd had of a city Marseille
and not Marseille. A skulking dog
she followed in a port slum street.
They always know more than they're saying,
she said, meaning dogs, but only a
little more. She said for striking
you cannot beat
the eyes of a certain North African man.

I said I'd never been to Marseille
or North Africa. So many
places I would never see I
once assumed I would. What
I didn't say put a vast watershed
between us and sounded like
four feet in stride
on stone and the
panting hanging panting
moving there.

Thematically the poem was clearly in the same category—older-man-feels-loss-of-power (physical/sexual) or OMFLOPPS, as I called it—though obviously not of the quality as certain sonnets of Donne and Shakespeare and many poems through the periods, including instances well-known in Eliot and the Yeats of "Sailing to Byzantium" ("That is no country for old men" and so on, "An aged man is but a paltry thing, / A tattered coat upon a stick" and so on), but—

I was becoming the dullest of creatures.

Durant thought the dream of the dog was his daughter's. He'd hired me for my reading, but writing up responses to the poems had induced in me the same kinds of misperceptions that afflicted him. I couldn't even read a line in a guest book now without feeling it was directed at me. My only honorable course was to finish my report, tell him that Amanda had told me about his daughter, out of concern for him, and that I rejected his thesis, tell him of Voth and the mistake I'd made to think I'd been followed, a mistake brought on by having made myself suggestible, even a tad paranoid, and then leave the job. That would mean leaving Rome, and Amanda.

I spent the afternoon working. I gave readings of certain poems, outlined recurring themes and seeming recurring characters, then pointed out exceptions, reversals of the usual use of "I" and "you." I laid out the various tested theses about topical lines, titles, influences and allusions, image patterns. A separate section formed on poems that simply defeated me, that I had no idea how to read. Among these were some of my favorites, maybe oddly, but they dopplered past my sense-making faculties. Because he'd featured in my recent hours, I quoted Keats, from another of his letters: "O for a life of Sensations rather than of Thoughts!" What I really felt, but couldn't say, was that in writing the report I was leaving the real things out, like those thin readers I'd complained about online. The truth was that every second poem at Three Sheets, even ones I thought weren't good, induced a pinch of heartsickness I didn't understand but recognized physically as the sensation of pain touching belief, the raw incomprehensions of feeling that Durant sensed I valued, and for which he valued my judgment. I ended the report by saying that I saw no hard evidence of his daughter in the poems. "You asked if I'd ever heard the expression 'The sun winks and we play blind.' You and she once shared the line. But even what we imagine to be our most private expressions are not, in fact, exclusive to us. They're out there, and if we really need to, we'll find them. What we do with the finding depends on our need to believe, to believe in a thesis, a god, a truth, a longed-for possibility. I'm sorry, August, but it's my considered opinion that the poems at Three Sheets have nothing to do with your daughter."

And so it would be finished. I'd give him the report in the morning. I'd collect my fee and arrange to ship out.

I left the apartment before Durant returned and arrived thirty-five minutes early for my date, as I humored myself to think of it.

At the edge of the piazza I sat trying to put all thoughts out of mind by contemplating the real things there before me. What mattered was matter. I watched the day's last light as it played on the stone and flesh. How had one emerged from the other? What a miracle that a human should stand up from the very mud of creation. Scientists had a term for it—*abiogenesis*—which I'd come across one day when looking up the word *hylozoism* (the idea that all matter possesses life). Maybe we're all seeking out other matter as if to find the home from which we've been made lost by creation itself, all displaced—and here's the irony built into everything—by that First Seer, Metaphor Maker, that First Poet, who said, Let there be light. And breezes, mud. And patios with white awnings, tourists with knapsacks and purses, water in half-liter carafes, the clock tower and clock reading 8:06 beneath the Madonna and Child on the campanile, grayblack cobblestones, and Amanda. Let there be Amanda. And there she was.

"I'm tired of walking," she said. "But I'm more tired of bars. Would you object to coming to my apartment?"

"As long as you have designs on me."

She smiled, tolerantly.

We headed uphill to a house across from what might have been a school (it might have been anything, like most buildings in Rome. Where were the hardware stores?). As she unself-consciously led the way in a black summer dress, she said that Carlo kept offering her apartments in one or another of his buildings, but she liked her little place, and anyway found Carlo "an old creepster." On the top floor was her single room. The walls were yellow and umber. A small upright bookshelf, full of books, marked the living area. She said she had no wine or beer, which I took as a hopeful sign that maybe she didn't often have visitors. A love seat faced the only window and that's where we sat, angled toward each other, glancing now and then at the early night sky.

I gave her back Durant's letter.

"What did you think of his R Code theory?" She started right in. I could feel, or imagined I could feel, the heat from her legs.

"I think he hopes to find his daughter. The hope has made him inventive unto a little nuts. People in distress see as they need to."

"But now the new poem. He told me he took his daughter to Marseilles when she was young and she befriended a street dog. For years the dog showed up in her dreams. Now there's the dog in Marseilles in a dream in a poem. You can see why he finds it significant."

"It's just a fragment, something familiar. I could watch the nightly news and see ten fragments of my own life if I looked for them."

"And you don't sense anything else in the poems?"

"Well, reading them in the way I've been asked to did toss me into a spiral yesterday. For a while I thought someone was following me."

An expression of specific concern came over her, as if she'd been worried I might be followed. I told her about Voth, and the warning I'd decided I imagined, the threat I'd read into a line in a guest register. She looked more anguished than surprised.

"James. You need to trust me. You have to stop reading the site. Don't visit it again. Ever." She held her hands to her face, then threw them down and said, softly, "Ouf."

"What aren't you saying?"

"You'll think I'm as inventive unto nuts as he is." Her hair, loose, no longer pulled back by sunglasses, so the widow's peak was gone, accented her face differently. It was as if I'd brushed grass from a stone and found an ancient goddess looking back at me. No, what an inane image. She seemed older, more deeply beautiful, less striking than she had earlier, less successfully serious, a little weary from need and intent. "Do you read science fiction?"

"No." I'd had some luck with speculative novels but more often whenever I'd tried to read the so-called classics of the genre, I'd been unable to draw my eyes across the page. The silly made-up names, the plastic dialogue, the alternate histories and magical technologies *that seem to describe where things are actually going!*

"Do you know Stanisław Lem? His novel *Solaris*?"

"I've seen the movie. American, not Russian."

With a look of self-amazement, she said that Three Sheets was something like the planet in *Solaris*. Anyone who tried to penetrate it began to see their own lives communicated back with terrifying veracity.

"It isn't that readers project personal meanings onto the poems," she said, "or not just that. It's that the site really does seem to know them."

I wanted to stop her from saying anything more, to protect us, but I couldn't respond.

"It will happen to you, too."

"I've been reading Three Sheets for months and haven't caught a glimpse of my life."

"Well, I've seen mine." She looked out the window at the sky getting darker. "I see Marcus."

If she pressed the point any further I would have a hard time, in trying to avoid saying she was delusional, not telling her that because of her brother's death she was simply in a state of high vulnerability, like Durant, and so prone to misperceptions. It was understandable, I'd say, though of course it wasn't, not really.

"This stranger following you, that was inevitable. Have you read the Three Sheets chat rooms lately? The talk is getting really concerning. Someone worked up a profile of the Poet, more or less like yours, that he's middle-aged male, likely white North American, maybe living in Rome, and people began hunting through the postings. Now August has been named and there's a theory that he's the Poet. Your follower is probably just the first one to track him to Rome. Before long we'll end up meeting some pretty desperate people unless we cut loose from him."

Maybe it was her way of putting things, saying "we" instead of "you," promoting a note of shared romance, that kept me from feeling her degree of concern. What if we were just a couple of suggestible dopes, Amanda and I, knocking around in a crazy world?

"So you're visiting the chat rooms," I said.

"No one comes right out and admits it, but that's why everyone needs to talk online about Three Sheets. Each of them believes in this secret communication, but they're afraid to say so. Instead they debate about the poems and build up profiles of the Poet."

It was the theory I'd presented to Dominic. She drew her feet up under her, which had the effect of tilting her slightly in my direction. Her posture was exactly that of the Londoner in our pre- and postcoital talks on the rented Spanish couch. We weren't bed loungers. We made use of our few rooms, reading at the kitchen table, having sex in the shower, watching TV shows on the couch, talking at the kitchen table, watching sex between people in a shower or in bed or on a couch on her laptop on the couch. The memory belonged to some other life.

"I can't get free," she said. "I've seen details in the poems, things about Marcus, and now I can't stop looking for more." She said he was killed in Guatemala City when a pallet of construction bricks fell on him from the roof of a restaurant where he had lunch every day. "Same patio, same chair. The official version is, a kid working construction, twenty. The pallet was on scaffolding. The kid claimed to be trying to secure the platform but it tilted and the pallet fell perfectly off the side. From just two stories up. Most of the bricks weren't even broken." Marcus had just written her that he had evidence and the names of Guatemalan government and military figures who were using the US-funded surveillance apparatus to identify and detain human rights activists, some of whom had died in custody or been found dead in the streets. "Marcus died before the list could be published. It wasn't in his effects."

Suddenly I was cold, sorrowful, still. She looked at my chest, as though it might offer what she needed, then up again. Out of nowhere, the way of things could come crashing down on us. We all knew this fact and worked hard to forget it. You could make millions from people's need to forget the way of things.

"I need to stop talking for a while," she said.

She disappeared into some isolated *penetralium* (great word, Keats, in a complaint about Coleridge) of her thoughts. There we sat, sometimes looking at each other. A minute passed. I didn't move or speak or check my phone. Then I felt it coming on, a dread truth I hadn't been willing to admit, but just in time she reached across and cupped a hand behind my neck.

The word that came to mind—nothing to be done—was *penetration*.

The first time I woke it was still dark. I knew instantly where I was and felt wonderful. When next I woke the sun lit everything and I lay in pristine confusion. I rolled over and there she was, head on pillow, looking at me. She smiled. Her face seemed a little fuller, her eyes somehow a different shape. She unfolded herself from the sheets and walked out of the room in the underwear she'd slept in. More even than the sex, which we hadn't actually had, just a kind of making out, gropings and glimpsings, what felt like teenage prewar sex, then falling asleep together half-clothed, this was so far our most intimate moment. She returned with a sheet of paper and we sat on top of the covers, shoulder to shoulder. She looked down at the page—there was a poem on it—and said that it was why she couldn't let go of Three Sheets.

The poem was "Seconding." I remembered it from the site. To read a poem is one thing; to be directed to it, another; to be directed by a new, half-nude semi-lover, a thing of a whole different order.

A former general back home in the jungle
capital from DC where specialists made
the first breaches in the wall around
his forever silent teenage daughter
inquired about transforming the vacant
third floor of the old municipal building
into a school for children in need, not
knowing that the floor processed
cocaine. The lords kidnapped
his wordless girl, left her in a stream,
though death was not by water. And now

the general is talking. In the beginning
we killed one, he says, though which
one is debated. By the third day
and thereafter we killed without
distinction. In the end we killed our natives,

Americans, Dutch, the British,
Canadians. We killed wives and daughters,
uncles and mothers. Workers, piano teachers,
men on the road.

The Turks we killed and their enemies.
The Spartans, Persians and Prussians
and Mongols. We killed ancient mud
warriors carrying spears. Their final words
covered the earth in languages. The elephants
they rode. Their caged birds.
You have to understand we killed
them all many times over, as I will now be killed.

Words recorded by a visitor
to this country of punctuated endings,
in his blue notebook stolen from the bag
at the scene not secured by police who
didn't ask questions.

"Marcus."

She nodded. I reached to touch her but she shook her head. A dull longing to put my feet on the ground, a longing made all the duller by my clichéd condition to have been born into a safe class in a safe country, a good family, born lucky. By degrees, many Westerners feel the same. We are our own country, the young, dumb-lucky educated Westerners.

"Which details?"

"The jungle capital is Guatemala City. The killers. The blue notebook, which would have contained the names."

"Not the general and his daughter?"

"He never mentioned them. But don't tell me there's still room for coincidence. I've been reading around, trying to figure it out. That's what I'm doing with my days here, searching online, emailing contacts in Holland and Central America, trying to find the identity of the general. He might know who killed Marcus, or at least maybe I can get the same story he did."

"With the same result."

"Not if I don't travel there."

"Did you ever see this notebook?"

"He always had one with him. A blue one was in a picture he sent me the week before he was killed. But it wasn't in his belongings they sent. I asked about it. The police claimed there was no notebook at the scene or in his room."

"Is this the only poem about your brother?"

"Before 'Seconding,' every now and then there was a phrase or line that seemed sort of loaded, but they showed up in the more obscure poems and I wasn't really sure what I was seeing. I was actually afraid to see more. It was like any day there'd be a poem called 'When Marcus Was Killed Under a Ton of Bricks.' And then this."

She got up and stood by the window and lit a cigarette. She said something about the sky and I tried to make a note to myself that there's this in life, too, there's murder, killing upon killing, but there's also seeing this person in this moment. If only I could see her against a window once a season, life would be easier. She stubbed out the smoke and returned to bed. Before reading the poem I'd been planning to keep some light in the hour, some hope she'd find a way for me to stay in Rome without money. Now the breathing fact of her was overwhelming. I turned and held her and when she started to cry she pushed me away and let the tears come, then go, closed on herself. At some point she raised her knees and hugged them and dropped her head to her legs in a kind of cannonball-tuck position.

I was looking at the part of her I could see, more or less at her thighs. I tried to take them in as part of my sense of her. Those thighs are Amanda. Those feet. That forearm. Amanda. So clearly all three syllables. She could never have been Mandy. Three syllables, the same vowel in each, an assonant echo inside the whole—

"Penetration," I said.

She turned her head to me, made a sort of cautioning expression.

"Penetration. It's hacker language. You didn't tell anyone about the notebook, but you must have written about it. In emails to the police, you just told me. You've been hacked."

We looked at each other, a distance of about eighteen inches.

She paused, then slowly nodded.

I had it, I had it.

"I have it."

She said nothing. I kept my eyes on her, thinking it through, as she must have been. Her round belly, its single roll of skin, heaved a little.

The theory had weight. People of political interest are flagged. Their online habits fit them into a profile. False sites are seeded, sites for, whatever, eco-activists, currency traders, poetry readers, a site exactly like Three Sheets. But why? Could people be reliably manipulated through a website? Of course they could, if it was one they visited daily and it presented with some authority or inviolable mystery.

Not quite believing myself, I laid it all out for her. Her thoughts were divided, I could tell.

"Me with my Solaris effect, you with your conspiracy theory."

"I know, I know," I said, the theory still building in me, cumu-lonimbus, airy and full of violent consequence. "But still."

She got off the bed and left the room and I realized I could never truly know what it meant to her to have solved the mechanism, if not the whole mystery itself, if that was what I'd done. The solu-tion connected to her brother's murder, to emotions I couldn't know. I tried to isolate what I did feel about the possibility my own computer had been hacked. I should have felt violated, but didn't especially. Maybe I didn't believe my theory, or did believe it in the abstract—big data trawlers could see all—but not the actual. I had no deep secrets or pictures of inflamed privates on my laptop, but the thought of some stranger looking around in my emails new and old, between me and Dominic, me and the Londoner, seemed too unreal to anger me. To make it real, when Amanda returned I imagined a third person with us, hiding somewhere in the room. Did I want to brain them with a bottle of Peroni, or ask them to leave, or just let them listen and watch? Neither. Nor. All. I couldn't decide. The real world contrives to be unbelievable.

We wouldn't tell Durant just yet. We agreed to test the theory's holding capacity, though how, we had no idea. A way forward would come to us if we stopped looking for it.

"Tell me about Michigan," I said.

The verb *surveil* is young, a 1960s back-formation of *surveillance*, itself young, nineteenth century, though from older fragments, the French *sur*, meaning "over," and *veiller*, meaning "watch," from the Latin *vigilare*, to "keep watch." As I noodled around online in Amanda's bed, learning all this, these unsuspected links between, say, *surveil/watch* and *vigil/witness*, with their half-opposing con-notations, I pictured Voth's reflection, there or not, in the window of the watch shop, and felt I was skirting the labyrinth again. One of these days my cha-chas would dance me completely out of sense. Maybe they already had.

Alpha, beta, gamma . . .

"Detta," she said. Somehow we were dressed and walking now, eating so-so pastries, watching the rhythms of the traffic shooting along beside the Tiber. "Her brother works in cybersecurity."

She began to tap Detta on her cell, paused.

"Is it safe?" Holding up the phone.

Seeing it in her hand made me think again of my mother, tapping me on her cellphone when she'd sent the picture of the cuneiform tablet. After they died I dreamed of my parents, one or both, almost every night for months, and was still dreaming of them in Rome. Dreams are ours alone. Never to be spied on, stolen, and never really to be shared, even when we try. If we're lucky something in the waking world, some artifice, roof of wet cedar shingles, sail of meringue on a passing dessert plate, poem, maybe a poem about a dream of a dog in a port slum street, will seem to have the impress of the dream, and for a short time we can set the secret inside the found shape, and imagine that we are known.

We took a trolley car north and walked to the wide mall outside the entrance to the MAXXI museum. In the courtyard was an enormous, maybe one-hundred-foot sculpture of a human skeleton on its back, all its bones present and exact except for a long, sharply pointed god's doodle of a witch's nose. We sat on a low wall in the sun and watched people walk around the skeleton, interested but not visibly moved. Were they thinking of mortality or thinking about the artist thinking about it? Some leaned in very close, inspecting the bones, the materials. I was reexperiencing the thought of my parents lying on their backs, struck and struck until struck dead, working backward to them getting out of the car, my father hit hard in the face, unconscious and no trouble, my mother next, the both of them dragged back into the car, and then I stopped thinking altogether, closed my eyes and listened to the day, to my breathing, and opened them on the curving, white museum building. I told Amanda the museum was audacious simply for being contemporary and in Rome. We discussed ancient capitals, how age and beauty are oppressive, and nostalgia to be feared as a bearer of troubles, losses, animosities, and gilded never-weres.

Or else they died in a car accident. I got some purchase on the idea and decided I could hang on for the day.

Detta's brother, Pierluigi, a suave, young hypomaniac, turned out to be a lot of work. She'd told us he had a disorder, which she had trouble translating but seemed to be a kind of compulsive talking problem, which would be worse when he spoke about the internet. As he emerged from the museum and crossed toward us he looked somehow both fashionable and genuinely (as opposed to fashionably) unkempt, like an undead model, the summer-weight gray sports jacket wrinkled and unevenly faded, tie improvisationally knotted, blond hair wilted from the over-application of some product. He said hello and explained without prompting that he worked with the museum, building the database and conducting penetration tests and vulnerability assessments. It took him some time to convey this because though his English vocabulary was good, his pronunciation was god-awful, as if he'd never heard the language. Amanda addressed him in Italian, which she spoke musically but not well, it turned out, because they settled on English.

We outlined the Three Sheets phenomenon and my theory. We asked about hacking. Suddenly he became very animated and, oddly, more fluent. His hands began moving in little circles before him, slightly out of phase with each other, as he started to talk about himself. As he spoke through his lunch hour and dinner that night at Detta's apartment (Detta helping in real time and afterward with the clarifications), and then again in an email sent in the middle of the night, when I was asleep, written in a mix of English and idiomatic Italian that I used Detta and an online site to work through, with a few interpolations of my own, I developed a composite sense of his thoughts, and a very clear one of the ways his condition presented.

"When you think of the 'hacker,'" he said or wrote, "you will imagine subcultures, crooks and perverts, the geeks in the basements. But these groups overlap like it's crazy. Political, criminal, government, black hats and the white hats, hats of other stripes and races." Sometimes his fingers held a cigarette, the smoke sailing in little loops as he performed his hand circles. "No matter how strange we are, always there's someone who feels like us. We can find these people online. My people are called Keyholers. The name comes from the spy satellites. We are nineteen, in Italian branch. We agree in words and thinking. In English they would call us 'hacktivists.' Why have I never met you, Amanda? Are you two lovers?"

She smiled and asked if we could record him on our phones. He nodded.

"Detta has mentioned you often. We were bound to meet," she said. I put my arm around her waist, a move not native to me. Pierluigi seemed to be looking at her clavicle and nodded at it, and kept nodding for maybe twenty seconds after she asked if there was any way of finding out if our computers had been hacked.

"In Keyhole language, what we do, hacker practice, is we call 'entering all.' We are the sailors. We sail on virtual wind. We are"—this took many tries to arrive at—"'lifted up into the god prospect.' Like satellite cameras we can see at same time great distances and smallest movements far below. We see search trends within masses, hear music in the tap-tap of the password," he said. He talked about his special connection to the world, the hunger that develops once you realize you can know more and more. "It's like religious, the hunger, but the faith is not being blind. It's all right there in one *grosso* evidence field."

Detta got up from the table (there were four of us, it was evening now) and began massaging his shoulders, trying to relax him, slow him down, but he stopped only to scold her jokingly, in English, for not having introduced him sooner to her North American friends. Around his sister he seemed to speak with more control but then couldn't stop himself from accelerating. I wanted to pour cold water over his head to save him from his all-seeing vision.

"Hackers know the living and dead. We're all the same, no clock time. We float with ghosts and angels and some of them turn and look in your face from the screen, and you know inside them. I am a secret inside a secret."

Whenever he started into what seemed to be an answer, he lost track of the question. He never once answered a direct question about anything. I began paying more attention to Detta and Amanda. Their silent exchanges were about managing Pierluigi, Amanda nodding interrogatively at his third empty beer glass, Detta shaking her head slightly. I was worried about him, too, but admit to hoping for some signal about me. Did Detta know Amanda and I had slept together? But then I barely knew it. It was sleep, after all.

Detta put her hand on her brother's arm and asked him again to assess our theory. Could he determine if we'd been hacked?

"Of course they are hacked. Everyone is hacked." He explained the mechanism. There were dozens of ways into our files. Even clicking on an unsubscribe button could open the gates. "You know

Troy, story of the horse. You're all hosts for remote-access trojans. Someone controls your computer camera and microphone. They've installed the keylogger and tracked every password you have."

The information seemed sound but his certainty felt unjustified and made me doubt him. I had no idea what to believe now. He began talking about hacker intuition, an ability in some hackers to predict keystrokes, words before they even formed. The Keyholers all had some version of this talent to predict.

"But then the thing. It came to us all in the same time. We all had it before anyone spoke. If you see ahead in time, even just for a tick and tock second, you also see, not so clearly, what's longer away. It's a vague shape but all of us have seen it and all of us are scared. I'm telling you. We've seen the end of time and it's much closer than you think."

Of course he was an apocalyptic. So many troubled minds washed up on the same shore at the end of the world. He explained that when the Keyholers understood they were all seeing the same thing, they agreed not to talk about it, not even with one another, and because it had a shape, they'd all draw what they saw. One day, on an agreed-upon minute, they all uploaded their drawings. They were the same shape.

Detta tore a page from a notebook and Pierluigi worked over it for two or three minutes with a sad intensity. When he finished he stood and left the table. Detta, Amanda, and I stood over the sketch.

"We all see it," Pierluigi said from across the room. "It comes to us in dreams but also when awake and offline. We wonder who else outside our group has these visions."

"But what is it?" asked Detta.

"It's obvious," he said and refused to say anything more.

I'd been hoping to return with Amanda to her flat but our night ended with her leaning into a cab and kissing me, briefly. I arrived home to find Durant making tea in the dark. He asked how things were "progressing on all fronts." It seemed a veiled question about Amanda. I said I'd had a breakthrough but couldn't tell him about it yet.

"Well, if you've enlisted her to help you, I'm all for it."

Our agreement not to talk in detail about what I was finding had started to claim more conversational territory. I was tired of the circumspection.

"For a while yesterday, I thought someone was following me." I described the episode with Voth, and confessed I was still conjuring spy scenarios. "I could have misread what was happening."

His face gave nothing away, not even concern. A cone of lamplight from the main room cast his shadow hugely on the kitchen wall.

"I'll get you a security escort for a few days. Carlo knows people who do that sort of thing."

"No thanks."

He held the ear of the teacup in one thick finger.

"It's prehistoric, an adaptation, the sense we're being followed. A part of us is still on a plain somewhere, moving through long grass, easily spooked. But sometimes . . ."

He looked like he was about to start into one of his lectures, but his expression changed. He drained his cup and set it on the counter.

"You owe me a report."

"It's written. But today I have a better theory."

I saw doubt or regret pass over his face. He said we'd find a place to meet the next afternoon, wished me good night, and disappeared into his dim room, no doubt to reread "Streams" and nurse the code hypothesis that carried all he had left of hope. How could I take it from him?

In the morning I heard him leave. From my bedroom-study I looked into the narrow, quiet street and heard his steps receding on the stones. There was no one in sight, no locals or tourists, no Voth or whoever had or hadn't been following me. Things were half-defined all around.

I opened my laptop, stared at the screensaver, the bare trunk and branches of a dead staghorn sumac tree. The Londoner had sent me the image on the day she left. She said it was the most peaceful thing she'd ever seen and she hoped I'd draw peace from it. The sumac, which I'd always found slightly disturbing, now seemed to be staring back at me one-eyed from a knot or wound below the most dramatic of its staghorns. I switched it out for one of my screensaver photos of poets' faces. When I was in a northern mood I chose a Swede or Scot or one of my countrypeople. The southern faces ran clear to Zimbabwe's Zimunya. The poets had little in common. I chose the first up alphabetically. *A* is for Ashbery. He was young, mustached. His first book of poems was *Some Trees*. His name sounded like a tree. Ashbery replaced sumac.

There were no new poems at Three Sheets. I checked SHEPMETSOR and followed links to letter exchanges. A woman in New Zealand was finding tide charts useful in understanding the poems. A prof in Calgary had put the site on a graduate syllabus. Someone in Leeds was arguing that "Nanny/@/The Poet" (which he refused to stop using) was a desperate and implausibly successful stab at "aura buzz" by a publishing house in its death throes, and predicted there'd soon be a great reveal and volumes for sale. A singer-songwriter in Dublin had set one of the poems to music. I clicked on the video link and made it about twelve earnest seconds into "Invert Program" before I couldn't take any more and stopped it in midpennywhistle.

I felt a long way from recent events, from Voth and the Keyholers. Said together they sounded like a band out of a Pynchon novel. How could they even be real? But the world was such now that characters and events once thought to be broadly ironic and clearly imaginary were part of the given. They showed up in our towns, sat at our tables. We shared a weakening sense of the discordant. You caught a frequency, something you thought of as your life, and then the interferences began.

I looked at Pierluigi's sketch. The shape was familiar but hardly unusual, rectangular, humanly designed. Within the borders, certain geometries held but things got more complex, maybe crazed. The sketch had a terrible innocence about it. Had the other Keyholers really seen this in their dreams? How could the apocalypse look so clearly machined? At the end of all things, a great bar code.

It came to me not what the drawing depicted, but what Pierluigi would think it depicted. He'd sent me and Amanda an encryption program, which I installed before writing to him. He replied immediately.

"yes! integrated circuit!"
"So how could this be a vision of the end?"
"the circuits are in everything, James. everywhere in the place and time. you have to forget your ideas of 'end.'"

He was about to start firing again and so I cut off the exchange and forwarded it to Amanda and Detta.

A minute later Pierluigi sent me a version of his diagram with English labels added. Now it looked like a satellite photo of a railway switching yard or palace compound or suspected missile site. The parallel lines were apparently diodes. The things they connected, capacitors and resistors. The larger structures or open spaces were marked variously as silicon ingots and composite crystal assemblies. I returned to the unlabeled diagram and sat with it. The shape and pattern were everywhere, not just in circuit boards but in marked-up calendars, stuffed bookshelves, lines of prose or justified verse, and yet the drawing seemed particular, of something very close by.

It sat horizontal. I held it at arm's length, raised my arms slightly. There, on Durant's wall. It had been over my head the whole time. Since moving in I'd looked once or twice at the framed drawing or diagram or maybe print of a painting and assumed it was abstract art, slightly too busy and geometrical for my tastes. The design echoed Pierluigi's drawing: tight, parallel, segmented lines connected by thinner crossing lines, some of them forming a well or knot (or composite crystal assembly). The dimensions were proportionally about the same. Each image had sets of horizontal rows. The wall-art version was colored, with precise resolution, so that what looked like shading in Pierluigi's rectangle were, in the picture, arrays of the finest lines, like hairs strung between the rows or maybe rhizomatic growths in a sub-strata not representable in 2-D.

With my phone I took a picture of Durant's artwork and sent it to him with the text "Research question: What is this? Thx, J."

Beyond being a misfit, Pierluigi was also very likely a clinical paranoid, but his vision made me test my own beliefs. I didn't believe in reliable foreknowledge of the end of the world, beyond what any sensible person already possessed, the knowledge that it would someday end, badly. I did believe in a widespread and justi-fied renewal of common paranoia brought on by the obvious, sorry truths, collapsing polar shelves, persistent evil, the fact that most lives were now being tracked and subject to algorithms that could predict their behavior with a high degree of accuracy.

On this last point I believed, maybe hoped, that many people would unplug, refuse to be configured as market data, that there would be an ever-growing back-to-the-earth movement, but (not my hope now) given the scarcity of available earth to get back to, competitions would form, market logic would take hold, legal language would shift, and even some of the enlightened and peace-loving back-to-earthers would become militant in defense of their needs and unalienable rights as they viewed them. I believed in a coming chaos that could be forestalled only by even worse possibilities, nuclear or biological apocalypse, mass raining death or global natural disaster brought on by, say, a meteor of the magnitude of those that had already caused extinctions and in fact, with a glancing blow, had brought about the moon and oceans and nudged the planet off its axis, forming seasons and, in a sense, earthly time.

But did I *really* believe in the likelihood of these doomsday scenarios?

In a great vastness the size of my body I was alone with the question of what I believed, and so checked my email. Durant had responded.

"That thing on the wall over your desk came with the apartment but it looks very much like a synteny graph I once worked up to represent the history of the black death genome as it morphed over time into other plagues. The enterobacterium is beautiful. So is the graph. The contagions are not, of course, and they just keep coming. We're due for a big one soon. You still want to meet? Bring Amanda if she's free. Let's say three in the Protestant Cemetery."

Amanda found me at the gate on Caio Cestio. She took my hand and looked at me earnestly but didn't kiss me or say what the look meant. Then she let go of my hand. I sensed she regretted our night together and wanted to signal as much before saying so. In emotional self-defense I tried to focus my attention away from her. We stood near three *carabinieri* with their peaked hats and white straps running diagonally across their chests. I couldn't imagine why military police were guarding the entrance to a cemetery. My Rome guidebook had mentioned that, more so than the *polizia*, the *carabinieri* are the subject of popular jokes, a tradition deriving from northern snobbishness at the many southern rural men who join the force to escape poverty. I was working through some connection between the *carabinieri* and Pasolini when Amanda brought me back.

"I never wanted this to happen." I thought she meant us, but she was speaking of Durant. "Our theory will crush him."

"I think he's pretty resilient."

"He's built everything on one hope. I can't even be around him without feeling like a stand-in."

He didn't so much come into view as make an entrance, an effect I would have thought impossible to produce while coming down a long city street. He walked fast, as people never do around cemeteries, and sort of swept us into the grounds. We were three abreast, Durant in the middle, but I felt the way he inclined toward Amanda. I'd never seen them together. The connection was clear, a father-daughterly affection that ran both ways. He said he liked to come here because the quiet helped him think.

"I've just spent a few hours with colleagues at EMBL, the European Molecular Biology Laboratory in Monterotondo. They're doing amazing things in marine metagenomics." He said he hoped with his mollusc work to secure an affiliation with EMBL that would allow him to stay in Rome another year. His description of the laboratory, his friends there, the work they were doing, microbiological genetics, continued unbroken for several minutes. "I need to land a new fellowship to pay back my research team the funds from the last mollusc grant. That's how I've paid you both, by the way. My life lately is one big shell game. But the world is not, is it, James?"

The question almost literally tripped me, caused a hesitation in my stride before I recovered. I didn't understand it or why it was addressed to me, but already he'd moved on. He was talking now about yet a different set of colleagues, these ones at another Roman university, Sapienza. We'd made it deep into the cemetery along one of the paths. Durant paused for about twenty seconds and even the quiet felt commemorative, the cypress trees shouldered together like the graves in the crowded precincts of death.

What a terrible idea to meet here. We should never have agreed to it.

Now he was talking about the cemetery itself, its famous dead, its poets, including Keats and Shelley. I recounted popular versions of Shelley's death by drowning, and the one about how, during the cremation, a friend snatched the poet's heart from the fire and later gave it to Shelley's wife, Mary, who kept it for thirty years in a copy of the poem "Adonais" and only later had it encased in silver.

"There are those who still believe that snatched-heart story," said Durant. "There's no underestimating people's gullibility. Mary must have been in on the mythmaking. She'd have done better to focus on her novels. What a mess she made after *Frankenstein*." Now he turned to me. "So what do you have to tell me?"

Seconds passed and I found I couldn't speak. Amanda rescued me. She told him that she understood what it felt like to see a lost loved one in the poems and told him of her brother and said she'd begun to see Marcus and his death at Three Sheets. She explained how her own theory of the Solaris effect had been displaced by a new one that I'd struck upon. Durant stopped us and took her hands in his.

"I'm sorry. So sorry. I misread your distress. I should have seen that it wasn't about me."

She absolved him with a soft smile and I thought he was going to hug her but he just lowered his eyes. He began walking slowly now, and led us to a bench on which sat two fat pigeons that vacated it only when we stood over them. We sat, me between them.

"Your theory, James."

As I spoke he looked at me squarely, not even glancing at Amanda. I said the theory's improbability was part of its power. Without describing Pierluigi's suspect authority or apocalyptic take on things, I evoked his expertise and his support for the idea that private details from Durant's and Amanda's lives had been extracted and used against them.

"That's it?" He smiled slightly, as if relieved. "The government's in our underwear drawers?"

"Maybe more than one government or corporation if your underwear's deemed threatening. Imagine the Poet, or someone he hires, or some program, tracks discussions, flags certain people. Biographical details are gathered from the virtual debris field. New poems are written from these biographical fragments, ever more private details of these selected readers' lives. And why? To infiltrate the minds of people posing threats. To lead the eye, misdirect their dangerous attention."

Neither of us had moved, but he seemed closer to me now, his regard farther away.

"So you think Amanda and I were prompted into each other's lives, the easier to control? You're right, it's a little far-fetched." He turned to her. "Given what you've just said about your brother and your own investigations, I understand how you could be seen as a threat. But how am I?"

"I don't know," she said. "Maybe it depends on why your daughter disappeared." His involuntary response, to lift his head just slightly while blinking and keeping his eyes shut for a moment longer than normal, somehow suggested that he was confirming something to himself. "Was she a threat to anyone? Will you tell us about her?"

As a way of gathering himself, he clasped his hands behind his head and straightened his spine, brought his elbows together and looked from one to the other. Then he crossed his arms and stared straight ahead. He told us of a young family, an early death, a move to California, single parenthood.

"What do you think happened to your daughter?" Amanda asked.

"The truth is she disappeared on her own but then stayed that way. From the outside it looked like her choice, so I've been unable to get police involved, just private investigators who find nothing."

"Did she work with secrets professionally?" I asked.

"She worked in the drug racket. So, yes. I like to think that if there were whistles to blow, she'd blow them."

I asked if he or his daughter had ever written in emails or posted online the details he'd found in the poems—the blinking sun, the blue tie and spooling galaxies, the dream of the dog in Marseilles— but he didn't answer. We waited for a group of teenagers to walk by, smoking, loudly talking and laughing. One of them, a skinny young guy wearing what looked like tie-dyed medical scrubs, smiled at us. A friend handed him something and the kid skipped over and asked in English if any of us had a smoke. Durant looked at the ground, as if alone, and I saw in his face the answer to my question—yes, the details had been or could well have been communicated online—as Amanda got a cigarette and lighter from her bag and gave them to the kid. He lit up and offered her a few coins he'd been holding but she smiled and shook her head, and he glanced at Durant, realizing then that he'd blundered into something, and handed back the lighter and made a little involuntary gesture, his hand with the smoke cocking slightly and his eyes flitting away. He nodded and was gone.

"Let's walk," she said.

Durant stood and looked back in the direction we'd come from.

"There's a theory that Shelley was killed by government agents," he said. "The idea is they rammed his boat and he drowned before he could publish 'A Philosophical View of Reform,' with its arguments for women's rights and the formation of trade unions. It's where he wrote that poets and philosophers are the unacknowledged legislators of mankind. And in fact, after he died, the thing wasn't published for another hundred years." He actually raised his finger to stress the point. "But he wasn't murdered. He'd just had his schooner refitted and it was a bad job and the thing was made unseaworthy. A storm blew up. He drowned. No plot. No conspiracy of interests." Whatever the truth was behind Three Sheets, he said, he didn't believe that any "Shadowy Apparatus" could be so nuanced in its manipulations. "These people you describe know money and tradecraft, but they think hearts and minds are things to be won. It's laughable, the idea that they're practicing mind control when they can't control crowds in public squares. They don't do subtle nudgings, James."

Maybe Shelley wasn't murdered, I thought, but over the centuries writers and poets were murdered by governments all the time. If not Shelley, then Lorca, then Mandelstam, then Neruda, Saro-Wiwa—

"I know plausibility isn't what it used to be," he said. "But the problem with your theory is the poetry. Slogans control people, not poems."

And yet we were all in Rome because he'd read "The Art of Memory." And Amanda's search for evidence of her brother's murder had been directed by a poem mentioning a Guatemalan general who possibly didn't exist. What if these two, my American friends, had been led to look in the wrong places? I held to my theory but left him unchallenged. He was moving now, inviting us to walk, struggling, I thought, to find the energy he'd had when our meeting began. Whether he knew it or not, his physical self suggested we were closer to the truth, which meant his daughter wasn't speaking to him in poems, which made it harder to believe she was alive.

We returned to the gate on Caio Cestio. Amanda gave us both a hug and left for work. We watched her leave, trotting across the avenue and walking, turning a corner, and I heard Durant take a little inhalation. I pretended not to have heard and gave him a moment by walking up to the *carabinieri*, three of them talking at once, and asking if they could tell me the name of the street we were on. One of them did so and then their conversation resumed and I returned to Durant.

"You have a lot in your head, James. You read well, think well. But that's not what we're here for, is it?" Again I'd missed something. I thought reading and thinking well were exactly what I was there for, why he'd hired me. "I'll see you tonight at the apartment." We came and went in each other's days too frequently to bother with greeting or parting gestures, but now he gave my arm a brief squeeze. He walked back into the cemetery.

I stood for a while, without destination. In time I went through the gates and looked for him. I needed to ask what he'd meant in telling me the world is not a shell game, and in hinting I didn't know why we were there. I expected to find him lost in thought, staring at a grave marker or a tree trunk, more alone than he'd been in years. But though I walked the circuit of paths, I couldn't find him.

An hour later I was back at my desk, sitting in general uncertainty. The meeting had revealed gaps in my understanding, in my knowledge. I went online and tried to learn about what Durant had called the "mess" Mary Shelley had made after *Frankenstein*. He must have been referring to her later novel, *The Last Man*, apparently a futuristic, philosophical, gothic thing about the end of the world brought on by plagues in the twenty-first century. Critics agreed that she didn't really have control of her material. Looking up at the framed art, the one Durant had likened to a graph of plagues, I thought of nature and art sprawling beyond their understood forms. How could we grasp radically new creations from inside our moment in time? We didn't know our world any better than did Shelley's twenty-first-century characters, flailing around in a sprawling plague novel.

I'd been absently scratching my shins. I rolled my pant cuffs and examined the little marks I'd raised up. A few of them had a pleasing Greek alphabetic character, lazy *zeta*s and *pi*s, or so I imagined. I thought the trouble was less likely bubonic than allergic, the issue of Italian fabric softener. I showered and found a pair of unlaundered jeans. The brand name was Viral.

It used to be we saw beasts in the shadows, gods in the clouds. Now we'd shaped the common mind to accommodate new visions carried, according to Pierluigi, on microchips, bringing us news of the end. But was the end there in the information carried on the card or in the chip itself? Plague or integrated circuit? Of course the end of the world could spring as easily from the natural world as from the artificial. From the ox or the house, the camel or the door, *aleph* or *beth*, *gimel* or *daleth*, the letters in some tongue to come would bear the last word on us all.

In one of his dinner-hour holdings forth, Durant had told me of a magical microchip designed by the military of a country he couldn't legally name. The chip could identify any virus introduced into its circuitry through a liquid solution. "Think about resistance. These soldier-scientists can use the microchip to design vaccines or treatments to ward off biological weapons and outbreaks. One kind of resistance put in service of another. How hard it is, James, to bring together usefully the biological and the mechanized. Usually they collide like a car into a tree, but this little technology might save us from a great plague."

The comment had stayed with me but only now did it set off a cha-cha. I thought of Camus, hero of the intellectual Resistance during the war, and author of *The Plague* (a novel inspired partly by his struggle against tuberculosis), who was killed when his editor drove him into a tree. Some things I made studies of, and some just stayed with me in sharp detail for reasons that weren't always clear. The car crash produced memorable ironies and coincidences. Two women passengers in the backseat were unharmed but a dog traveling with them, name of Floc, which can be translated as something like "splat," was never seen again. Camus had a fear of cars but died in a 1956 Facel Vega, the fastest four-seater in the world (how shameful that the names of the car and the dog were in the record I read but not those of the women). Though it took two hours to extract his body from the wreckage, in Camus's pocket was a pristine, unused train ticket to Paris, the car's destination. Nearby, in the mud, was found the unfinished manuscript of the novel he was working on, *Le premier homme*, raised from the earth as its creator was returned to it, by the doctor who attended the scene, also named Camus.

Camus is sumac spelled backward.

The car crash has variously been attributed to a blown tire, faulty bearings, and—where had I read this? likely somewhere online— the KGB. I recalled that Camus had published a newspaper article criticizing the Soviet foreign minister, who didn't much like artists and had chaired a congress that denounced Shostakovich, and warned against the dangers of jazz and rock music and the cave-man orgies they incited. Camus accused the minister of ordering killings during the Hungarian uprising. The theory is that the minister, unhappy with his critic, ordered spies to doctor the tires of the Facel Vega.

Like my parents, Camus was a victim of either murder or a car accident.

I found myself searching through my files on Three Sheets, choosing the one tagged "Political" in my pointless sorting system, trying to find the poem that was floating in mind now, half-remembered. I'd read it once and never again, maybe, subconsciously, on purpose. When I found it I sat back in my chair and looked for a few seconds at the view out the window of a burnt umber wall.

Reunion

My family was randomly generated
My generation is overfamiliar with the image world

Leading members of my family imagine a world beyond the
    sky where we go after

Dinner went well I thought, despite a bad start
That comment about the royal accident, the tunnel and the
    tree
Was a sumac forking against the night sky as the courses
    came and

When was the last time this mode of thinking worked
In light of the image world. I know my lifelong presences
Better now as cyberfolk, wish they'd known their dead this
    way

The table was long and complicated, extended across zones
And tongues quoting lines from the Bible, the Koran, the
    minutes
Of the accident in the park. A distant cousin fell to sneez-
    ing, an Algerian

Reaction to the tree, dramatically rising up and leaving the
    table
As we rushed around carrying whatever was fragile came
    down
In sheets and inside now chills, trigger-eyed blessings fired
    off all

Around with real violence until you
Can't think in here. I'm looking for my cyblings.
I mean you know what I mean.

And there it ended, like an imprint of my confusion, or a spirit waving at me from the edge of a dream. If I stared long enough at the spirit—I cannot explain this—it had my father's face.

Though "Reunion" had been posted recently, after I moved back to Montreal, I hadn't remembered it well. It was the kind of poem that didn't linger past the experience of reading it. Yet now I felt called back to it, so the lines must have made a claim on me without my conscious knowledge. The scene presented a dinner party at a family reunion. The speaker thinks of absent family, some dead, some he knows distantly, and siblings he feels connected to mostly through the internet. The reunion includes Christians and Muslims and the conversation gets heated just as a storm kicks up and people rush around saving things from the table. Or something. If I believed my theory, there were details from my life here, but also a new false detail that could direct me away from an important truth. I read and reread it. A heat formed around "the minutes / Of the accident."

On my laptop I had screenshots of the accident report in Turkish and a text of the translation. The document was titled "Kaza Tespit Tutanağı," which translated as "Minutes of the Accident Report." Was this a chance echo? On my first and only reading, I'd allowed myself to wonder why my parents hadn't been wearing seat belts. Now I gave the record the full attention I hadn't the heart for when it was sent to me. The telling line was stark in light of the poem: "Araba park halinde, motoru çalışır vaziyette bulundu." "The car was found parked with the engine running." If they'd died in a crash, why was the car in park?

Apocalypse. From *apokalyptein* (Greek), meaning *apo*—"from" + *kalyptein* "to cover, conceal." The world had ended for me almost two years ago when I got the call from my parents' colleague in Turkey. With the Londoner it was brought back to life. Now in

Rome in my little room I felt death-haunted and electric. Things had about them a nimbus of fatal promise, possibility. I wanted to sleep with Amanda again, more than sleep. I called her and she reminded me she was at work. I told her to phone me after her shift. Almost in the same motion I tapped end call and pressed redial.

"Can't talk I said." There was music in the background.

"I'm taking the night off. Where should I go?"

"Your voice sounds strange," she said.

"How did you first hear of Three Sheets?"

"Same as August. In a pop-up on my computer."

The Londoner had shown it to me, sent it to me, kept drawing my attention to it.

"I want to be alone with you." I needed to stop thinking. "What's the Palatine?"

"It's a hill with a lot of old rocks that used to be buildings."

"What should I do?"

"Detta and Cinzia will have fun plans. I'll have them call you."

"Something's got me thinking apocalyptically. I need something present, and real, and not too beautiful."

"If you want real ugly you could always go out to Ostia and watch men in Speedos play volleyball."

"Ostia is where Pasolini was murdered."

"They play on little fake beaches beside the real one."

"He was a neorealist. He conjoined the sacred and the profane."

"You'll get me fired here."

"He was a champion of the common people but they weren't his audience."

"Your tone sounds sort of flat. What's wrong?"

"Something is about to happen. Something really big."

"What are you saying?"

"My parents were murdered. I've never told anyone. I've never told myself."

She said nothing for several seconds. I heard her tell me to stay on the phone. I heard her talking to others, her manager, I guess. She asked me where I was and told me to stay there. I tried to say I was sorry, that I hadn't known I was going to say that about my parents, but she directed me to other topics.

"Tell me more about Fellini."

"Pasolini. He always connects in my mind with Apollinaire, another dead poet nobody reads. Do you know him?"

"No. Tell me."

So I did.

Against instructions I left the apartment and walked up the stairs to the top floor. Yves's wife was coming out of their place.

"James."

"Hello. I'm sorry, I don't think I ever learned your name."

"Anthoula."

"Anthoula, hi. I was hoping to find a way up to the roof that doesn't involve going through your apartment." I saw her look at me more closely now, my clothing, maybe for signs I was drunk or in some kind of emotional trouble. "My girlfriend's coming to visit and I was hoping to take her up there."

"Oh. Well, there's no other way up."

I asked after Yves. I was polite. I tried to concentrate on how she looked. Was it Greek? If I didn't know her or her name, would I see her and think Greek? Mediterranean? Her face was dark and slightly masculine, handsome. She looked very specifically like herself.

"No one's permanent here," she said. "We all just rent from Carlo. I find him charming and brutish. What about you?"

"Carlo reminds me of some of my father's friends. They were all military guys."

"Brutish Canadians. I can't imagine." We smiled. "I'm going out but I can give you the key. Just drop it in our mailbox and I'll pick it up when I come back."

As if to refuse I shook my head but at the same time thanked her. I feared she wanted to talk more. I was not present to myself or to her. I was floating somewhere over a rocky plain. Feeling transparent, I patted my pocket and withdrew the cellphone, pantomimed answering it, said, "Hello, hi!" Anthoula pressed the key into my hand. There was everything despicable about my behavior. She whispered she'd be back around eight, holding up eight fingers. I offered a foreshortened bow to thank her again, asked my nonexistent caller to wait, and kept thanking her until she waved me away. When she was in the stairwell I put the phone in my pocket and said in full voice, "That's right. Just keep following— Yes, just follow— I don't— There's— Yes . . . No . . . Yes . . ." until I was sure she was gone.

I hadn't really looked at the apartment as I passed through it on the night of the dinner. The main room was orderly, dull, a faint smell of coffee. Late light streamed in through high porthole windows of colored glass, casting blue swirls on the walls. To be alone in a strange room felt nearly right. The only book to be seen sat on the little dining table. It was in French, a catalog of photos from a gallery show of Anthoula's work. The pictures were of electrical fields or firing neurons laid over barely visible human faces or portraits, heads and shoulders. In the figures obscured by the webbed lines the eye kept capturing faces and losing them again, like flashing memories of someone half-forgotten. The faces felt dangerous. I closed the book, opened the dormer window, stepped out. The table and chairs were in place, their legs loosely tied together with nylon rope, the whole assembly attached to a satellite dish, as if they were being held hostage. I took a chair and looked out at the city from three stories up. Higher roofs all around, green shuttered windows, cream brick walls. Yellows and umbers were everywhere but did I detect my love for them fading? I'd needed to be alone but out of Durant's place, outside but not in the street.

Amanda's brother and my parents had died in accidents that weren't accidents. But imagining the accidental as a principle removed from intention overlooks the role of design inside chance. The degree of accident isn't the same in every crash or chance occurrence. Whatever killed my parents, their last weeks and days were shaped by thousands of intentions, their own, their agency's, those of refugees, agitators, soldiers, rogue leaders, and all the rest. My parents had only wanted to establish a small spot of order amid chaos. I knew a version of the feeling.

My detective work, conducted to solve an unknown crime, if there'd been a crime, had pointed me toward atrocities, in Guatemala and Turkey, so distant from each other that the discovery of a link between them, if that's what it was, promised a dark sudden knowledge. Since learning of the disappearance of Durant's daughter I feared I'd find in the poems evidence of a murder. Now I was facing murder itself. The social constant of it, the standing condition. Murder in history, murder in nature, not in art. Never until now had I admitted that murder, the real thing, might know me personally. It had known my parents even before they died. They struggled for others against murder and neglect, starvation, hopelessness. There was murder inside their convictions, murder in their eyes and hearts. Murder is with all who, by circumstance or choice, have their feet in the real world. My parents died for the hearts of, and maybe at the hands of, desperate souls.

Pigeons wheeled through the sky. The world, ongoing, verified nothing. It wasn't even something to look at. I felt a small breeze, felt a shiver on my thigh, and the breeze died and the shiver returned and I realized it was my phone. Amanda had said she'd call me again as soon as she arranged to have someone take her shift, but I didn't want to talk to her or anyone now. I didn't want to hear my own voice. Wrapped up in words, I had failed the people I most loved.

I felt at the beginning of a long period of self-recrimination and raging decline, when I might become a danger to myself. Somehow knowing what was to come, placing myself on my personal time-line, allowed me to feel need. Though I still didn't want to hear my voice, I now needed quiet connection. I checked the phone for a message, found none, checked my email, which suddenly made me feel not at all alone, given that someone else might be reading it, too, if not now, then in the future.

The only message was from Dominic.

"I don't know where you are—are you here in Montreal?—but you should know I have to sell the house. I need daily care, and you and the others need to live your lives. Think about books/furniture you might want."

One by one, or two at a time, people leave. I put the phone away and stood with my hands in my pockets, looking off at the colors and planes, not seeing a thing, and this interior blankness was clarity. The paradox, that clarity can strike us into confusion at the yawning gulf between what we thought and what we've learned, between seeming and being, the long then and now. The powerful asymmetry of *as* and *was*, *was* and *is*. Then the pigeons shot overhead and turned, seemed to stall for a moment, and came rushing back toward me.

I WOKE TO A VOICE, SINGING. THE CALL TO PRAYER THROUGH the open window, desert air at dawn. Şanliurfa, southern Turkey. Day one.

I'd landed at night, found a bus. Unlit, isolate buildings rose up out of the desert. Four boys on bicycles, riding no hands, flew down a steep on-ramp to the highway. The end of the line was a turnout near a shut-down gas station, still on the outskirts of town. I got off in the dark with an old couple. A car was waiting for them but they saw I was stranded and talked to their driver, their son, I think, and he took me with them farther into the city. No one spoke English. When I said "Canada" they each said it in turn. They dropped me at another gas station and the son walked me to an intersection and began chopping the air with his hand, and said the name of my hotel, and I walked a long time, my bag slung over my shoulder, staying on the only lighted street even as it turned until finally other lit streets ran across it or joined it or led off and away. Then I was walking past people in doorways and dim recesses, walked with others walking. Now and then a man would come alongside for a few steps, always with the same words, "Hello what is your name?" in a hurried, movie English, and I gave it and he smiled and said goodbye, expending the last foreign word, falling back, falling in with others. One of these, a boy who said my name over and over but wouldn't say his own, led me to the hotel.

The night clerk was still on the desk in the morning, the same polite, unsmiling man who'd photocopied my passport and pushed it back to me with a coupon for free tea in the courtyard. His face shone and I wondered if he'd shaved in the night. He asked if my "people" had arranged a "fixer" and I said I'd arranged my own. The assumption I let stand was that I was another journalist covering the refugee crisis, the Syrian war, or the infiltrations into the local population of jihadists, or the Turkish gangsters I'd just read about looking for Westerners to kidnap and sell to internet executioners at the border. On a map of the city I had the clerk circle the police headquarters. Unprompted, he also circled the market, the castle, the sacred sites. He said it was best to eat at the hotel. I thanked him, started away, and then stepped back and showed him a picture of my parents on my cellphone. I said they'd once stayed there and did he recognize them. The impression, I think, was that this question was unrelated to whatever I was in town for. He hesitated over the possibility, seemed to want to help, but shook his head.

I took breakfast in the courtyard, with the free tea and wealthy Turks. I was the lone white Westerner. Before I left Rome a police official in Urfa named Erkin had assured me over the phone that I'd hear from the investigator in charge of my parents' case. Someone called twice from an unknown number and hung up at the sound of my voice. Only when I was on the flight did Erkin leave the message that the file was closed. "It was accident. No more investigation." I called him now, but someone else answered, a man with no English, and this time I was the one hanging up. Before my bread and tea were finished I emailed Erkin, asking if he himself was the officer in charge. I didn't say that I was in his town. I hoped to gather a few facts locally, before anyone knew I was there, and present them to him in person.

After I told Durant that I had to "leave his employ" to learn about my parents' deaths, that though I had little hope of finding anything I needed to be on the ground in the place where they died, he said such a trip would be "pointless and perilous." When I wouldn't be dissuaded, he offered to accompany me. "I won't have it," I told him, forcing a smile. "Much too dangerous. And I've already arranged for help in Urfa." To justify paying for the flight, Durant would declare it part of the Three Sheets investigation. He and Amanda saw me off at the airport, and I tried to voice my affection but could say nothing, couldn't touch them—I wasn't equal to the moment—and just nodded and walked off to the security gate.

I was making up my leverages on the fly. I knew next to nothing about this part of the world in the here and now. The analyses in the press were contradictory and alarming and changed daily. The Canadian government warned off all travel to the region. I fell back on my more comfortably confused sense of the deep past of the over-recorded Tigris-Euphrates basin. The earliest stories extend an Old Testament time that corresponds not at all with the historical record. I'd left my laptop with Pierluigi to scrub clean so back in my room I studied sources on my phone. I learned that the whole fiction of the city's most famous local son, the prophet

Abraham, born in a cave only steps from my hotel, was invented to provide grounds for land claims. And even the fiction itself, half-familiar, failed to interest me, though I tried to brush up on my patriarchs and kings. Here was Nimrod ordering the construction of the Tower of Babel, destruction and languages scattered, etcetera. Here was Abraham on the point of sacrificing Isaac and so on. There was Nimrod sacrificing Abraham in a burning pyre and God interceding, turning the fire to water and the embers to fish and there it was outside my room window, Abraham's Pool, with its pilgrims feeding the sacred carp.

Amanda and Durant wanted twice-daily updates. I wrote that I was meeting with a former colleague of my parents' who'd offered to guide me around for a day. Gail van Wyk was the South African who first told me about the accident and arranged for the paperwork and body transport. When I called her from Rome she said she remembered me, of course, and thought of me and my parents often. I asked for help. She would drive in from Gaziantep, arriving at noon, and stay in a house near the museum where my mother had written her last note to me. We'd arranged to meet at the cuneiform tablet.

From a cab I watched the city pass in scenes of small gatherings. Spice vendors with carts, stacks of aluminum pots, a chicken-wire pen full of pigeons overseen by a boy hammering a copper dish. Old men on low folding prop stools, absently rubbing prayer beads. It was this motion, the beads shaken and rubbed in the hand of a mustached, middle-aged man on the sidewalk beside me as the cab waited for the traffic to clear, that announced an impenetrability. As the street curved up a slight elevation the city of half a million looked more like a town, its sure limits on all sides ending abruptly at empty desert plain. The world out there offered no recognitions, only the sense that I was unequal to it. My father would be surprised that I'd come. He'd expect me to fail. To fail and then write full-heartedly and to no effect about the failure.

The museum's ticket taker doubled as a guard. I showed him the picture of my parents—it was a shot my mother had asked someone to snap of them, standing outside the gate at the camp, and one of the rare recent photos of them together—but he didn't speak English and we were unable to get past his idea that I was asking if these people were in the museum now. He gestured with an open hand and shook his head. What was I expecting him to tell me? The museum was a part of their last hours. Maybe I wanted to know if their picture set off a memory or reaction.

It turned out I was the only visitor. I couldn't muster an interest in the statues of wild boars, early Bronze figurines, Iron Age adornments, human remains in cramped exposed graves, six-thousand-year-old pottery, obsidian tools and seals, all of it found locally. These pieces struck me not as artifacts but as facts, hard, stark pieces broken off from a dead reality. Some of the explanatory texts included English, some didn't. My father would have read one or two, discovered his boredom, and given up. Likely he'd have taken a seat on the concrete bench, stared at the late Hittite relief in 2-D of an archer, God of Nature, standing beside or on the back of a stag, and waited for my mother to finish. It was strange to picture them here but for some reason wasn't hard to feel their presence, and because of it, the only item I really took in was the cuneiform tablet. It was larger than I'd imagined, the size of a sidewalk restaurant placard advertising lunch specials, which for all I knew it could have been, and the letters in their neat rows were alien beautiful, notched into their tight rectangular fields. My mother had found it beautiful, too. The moment I realized I couldn't stand the beauty, Gail van Wyk walked into the room and said my name.

"We came here when the refugee camps started. The usual agencies were on the ground early but the Turks wanted to run everything, pay for most of it, and they did a good job at first. Our role was limited. Your father's strengths were organizational, with him in command. That wasn't an option here, and maybe he overstepped."

She was driving me to Çodhir, the camp where my parents had helped with the delivery and distribution of food and school supplies. The camp administrator had agreed to meet us. Gail was in her fifties, I guessed, with black hair, a sun-damaged complexion, a habit of lifting her chin slightly as she spoke, as if steadying herself. She lived alone in Gaziantep and would soon fly back to South Africa.

From her bag she produced a computer hard drive and handed it to me.

"What you asked for. I couldn't get into your father's email account. There's a password. I don't know why the police never asked for this."

"Maybe they already know the real story. Or maybe they don't want to."

"Or maybe they don't care. The Turks can afford to choose their friends, and a Christian aid group, they think they don't really need us. This country is hard to understand. People in the know can't believe what's happening in Turkey these days. But not even Turks in the know can believe what's happening in Iraq and Syria. And here, Urfa and the southern towns, now they're crawling with ISIS. The Westerners are getting out."

Almost an hour out of the city she asked if I wanted to see the accident scene.

"Is the road somewhere near?"

"We're on it." The spot was unmarked, of course, and unmarkable. There'd been no other cars for miles. Stony desert, a sky white with dust. "Somewhere on this stretch."

I asked her to pull over. I got out and she waited for me. In the car I'd begun to sweat but the heat and wind dried me, it seemed, instantly. I walked into a field of burnt grass and stone that ran in every direction to the horizon. It was no place for an ambush. They must have been followed by car, forced to stop, or maybe someone pretended to have broken down and they stopped to help. I took a short panoramic film with my phone, put it away, stood still awhile, trying to feel what it meant to be here, where they ended, but the feeling wouldn't come and I didn't know how to look for it.

Of the camp, nothing can be written. Nothing so sure as a city struck onto a desert, behind armored trucks and razor wire. Nothing as straight as long rows of eleven-by-thirteen tents with blankets strung between them for shade. Nothing as present as a woman with wide-set eyes and blunt fingernails across the table in the operations trailer, asking me to call her Didem. No textures so grainless as the voiced summaries of paperwork detailing delivery schedules and costs, originals and duplicates, signed by my father. No place to linger, though that is all that happens there. The camp defeats description as it defeats everything, no other side to the stopgap. The camp is there full stop.

"Meaning what?" Amanda asked.

"Meaning we found nothing. I met no one who knew them and as far as Gail could tell, the paperwork contained no clues. I've got nothing to present to the police but lines from their own accident report."

The word was *prolepsis*, a prefiguring of a future knowledge that arrives suddenly, without conscious reflection. The idea was that Three Sheets knew us and we were on the verge of understanding how. But the idea was false.

"Maybe ideas aren't real," I said. "And what we mean by reality isn't an idea at all. Not an idea, not a hunch. Reality just shows up all at once." She indulged me by saying nothing in response. "What about you, anything to report there?"

She told me that Durant couldn't let go of his search. He'd hired Pierluigi to hack Three Sheets. I tried to tell her that here, in southern Turkey, the thought of these internet mysteries, emptily timeless and placeless, seemed to belong to so small a sense of the human that, if they would only become material for a second or two—a gnat weaving the air—I would extinguish them, smudge them out in my palm, restore nature to reality, and release us all back into the wild.

"I say, respect the gnat. Gnats are people, too."

"I didn't mean to disrespect them," I said.

"And thank god for molluscs while we're at it. They're funding the good fight."

"In this corner, the vast and shadowy complex. In the other corner, clams."

"I hope you're being careful."

"I hope so, too. And I send you a semi-chaste hug, Amanda. But I really don't wish you were here."

In the courtyard I had just started into my lamb dish and was taking some comfort in the thought that I was not of little consequence in the world, but of zero consequence, when two policemen walked in and spotted me. One was in uniform, one in jeans and a bulletproof vest. The other diners, couples at three tables, stopped talking and watched. There was a long moment before the men crossed and stood at my table and the uniformed one said my name. I nodded. He was tall. His face was narrow and pockmarked, so that he seemed to be assessing me from over a rough terrain. He handed me a blank envelope and they left. Inside was a typed note signed by Erkin.

> You gave no indication of a visit to Urfa. Since the death of your parents the only new informations are missing funds from their Christian organization. There are presently no reasons to open the case. You serve your mother and father by not pursuing questions.

> You will understand I am too busy to see you. You will understand that you are not safe here. This letter is my courtesy.

I put the letter back in the envelope. The diners resumed their evenings.

That someone had marked my arrival, my name, and Erkin had taken the time to compose the warning, suggested that a next event awaited. In literature, letters are so often plot devices. I sat there thinking of letters in plots, the letters in *Othello*, love letters in Tolstoy, a stolen letter in Edgar Allan Poe. Somewhere Poe writes that perfect plots are unattainable "because Man is the constructor. The plots of God are perfect. The Universe is a Plot of God." What would Poe have said of the Universe in his last hours, dying in the streets of Baltimore, cause unknown, and for reasons unknown, wearing another man's clothes?

As if to court the next thing, I went walking in the near-empty streets around the hotel. A young man with a vendor's cart tried to interest me in a scarf. He spoke enough English to ask where I was from and wanted to know if my country was filling with Syrians. Already he'd wrapped a scarf around my neck and head in two swift motions. He asked if Canadians thought all Muslims were terrorists—his understanding came from American TV shows—and I assured him most Canadians were better informed than to think that. He held up a mirror and there I was in a blue keffiyeh, looking ridiculous. He said, "But you are not believers." I gave him about five dollars in lire. I said we didn't have to share religious beliefs or even hold such beliefs in order to respect those who did hold them. It occurred to me we couldn't extend things much further, not into either of our orthodoxies, not into the place of women, for instance, without ruining the fellow feeling, and so that feeling was ruined anyway, but I smiled and said it had been nice talking with him and moved on.

I unraveled the scarf and draped it around my neck. In defiance of good sense, I turned down a stone alley and came out on a quiet street that afforded a view of the hill and fortress that marked the south edge of town. I walked in what I guessed was the general direction of the hotel and thought about human event grown so complex that no human and likely no god could comprehend it and then I stopped walking for a moment and heard steps behind me and then they stopped, too. I turned to see a man about my age standing and looking at me at a distance of six small parked cars. There was no one else in sight.

"My friend," he said. "I am talk to you."

His beard wasn't full. I tried to find significance in this detail. I checked for human shapes in the parked cars. The ones nearest were empty, those farther down the street, obscured.

"You are James." He held his hands open before him in a gesture of weak surrender. "I am for you."

"How do you know my name?"

"I come from camp. I know your father."

He came closer and stopped just past arm's reach.

"I not tell you my name. I am help."

He said that he and a friend had met my father three times, helping him unload supplies. My father asked them if any of the trucks were arriving with less than full loads and they described such trucks. Then he asked them about their families and lives.

"What happened to my parents?"

"I am safe." He withdrew something from his back pocket. "Please."

He pressed it into my hand, a crudely rolled, bent-up cigarette.

"Is to read," he said. He looked briefly down into his palms and mimed reading a book. He turned and walked back up the street.

"Wait. Stop," I said, but he didn't stop, made no gesture toward me, didn't change his pace at all. He disappeared down a side street and was gone.

In my room I unrolled the thing, tapped out the dry, odorless tobacco, and saw hand-printed there in tiny, elegant, almost illegible English letters an email address, a name, "Burhan Rihawi," and "Istanbul." In ten minutes I'd composed on my phone a simple email in English, explaining who I was and asking to meet. I sent the note off into gray, unimaginable space.

In Istanbul I walked for hours. Things happened more than once, each moment contacting all others, happened then happened again when I reviewed my phone shots and footage. Crossing the Galata Bridge with its hundreds of fishermen lining both sides. Standing before mosques watching tourists and the devout take off their shoes. Blue Mosque, New Mosque, Süleymaniye. In the spice market, politely declining. Taking a ferry to the Asian side. Across a city four times the size of Rome the carpet salesmen kept pace with invitations and questions and all claimed to have brothers in Toronto or Vancouver. The street dogs were always in pairs. In the Hagia Sophia I dutifully lost my sense of perspective. Most beautiful, along one side where workers were sprucing up the hand-painted tiles and frescoes, a black scaffolding towered, one architecture imagining the other, or as if in a sultan's dream of New York. I wrote the line in an email to Dominic and he replied, "That should be 'emperor's dream.' The place was built during the Byzantine, not the caliphate."

The fourth day I spent in Davide's small apartment, still waiting for a reply from Burhan Rihawi. I hadn't slept well or enough. Davide was out late, away early. The couch was too short. At dawn the amplified call to prayer seemed emitted from the kitchen. Obvious thoughts beset me about the relation between deprivations, mind control, faith. Each morning in the laneway below, a man towing a fruit cart called out. Later came another man with a cart of junk for sale. I peered down from my little balcony and in the shape of the cart, the laid-out positions of copper wire strands, a green toy handgun, a piece of what looked like an old radio, I saw again a version of the image that haunted Pierluigi and the Keyholers. An old woman in a headscarf appeared in the window across the laneway from me and lowered a small wicker basket four floors. The junkman took the alms and moved on.

An email arrived from Gail. She'd found copies of the information forms that my father had designed for the volunteers from among the refugees who were helping with the food deliveries.

One had been filled out by a Burhan Rihawi. From the form and internet searches of place names I put together a profile. He was from the city of Al-Hasakah, where anti-Assad infighting had broken out along religious and ethnic lines. Sunnis, Kurds, jihadists, Assyrian Christians. In a nearby town eleven nuns had been kidnapped and disappeared, and although all sides protested, the nuns never turned up. Rihawi was Sunni and spoke Arabic, Turkish, and English. Given his date of entry to the camp, he was likely among a group who fled the city when the Kurdish military took over their neighborhood. The story was of shelling and killing, no electricity, trouble finding food, and the men volunteering or getting forced into militias.

As I related the details to Durant he interrupted me.

"And you think it's safe to meet this man based on an exchange with a stranger who wouldn't tell you his name."

"I don't always trust my instincts, August, but I hear them out. They seem to know more than I do."

"Well, instincts or intuitions must have a drive for self-preservation."

What I didn't tell him was that the instincts that had led me to fall in love with the Londoner were now telling me she was not who she'd seemed. Hours earlier, playing a grim hunch, I'd sent her a short, newsy email and received a message that the account had been deactivated. I searched around online and found just one mention of her, on an eco-activist site listing the names of "possible infiltrators" into activist-protest groups. I examined timelines. We'd met after I asked the Turkish police to send me the accident report for translation. It had seemed a chance meeting. Her leading me to Three Sheets was an expression of understanding, I had thought, as was our lovemaking and movie watching.

Believing against myself, I spent the afternoon fixed in small devastations. From the Latin *dēvastātus*, meaning "laid waste." *Vastus* meaning "empty."

At dark I was half-drunk in a sixth-story bar with Davide and five of his friends. An open-air view to the south. Out on the Bosphorus a cruise ship completely out of scale with the city was attempting a three-point turn. I'd eaten too little. Three bottles of Efes returned my thoughts through warped glass. The slight rocking underfoot might have been an earthquake or the music from the club below us, or it might have been me as I thought of the passengers on the ship deck looking at the vast, breathing city, wondering if they'd missed anything in their three hours ashore.

I'd lost most of their names, Davide's friends, but somehow I knew they were two Turks, an Italian, a Swede, and a Czech, the last three being women, the Swede being Davide's girlfriend, the Turks being in Davide's jazz band, me simply, barely, being. The Czech woman, Adéla, asked me what Canada was "like," thereby opening that familiar twenty seconds during which foreigners are willing to contemplate my country. I said, "Canada's a place where if you come home and find a bear in your living room, you're not *entirely* surprised." They turned out to be less interested in bears than bear spray and a minute later they were telling tear gas stories. Months ago they'd all been gassed together in Taksim Square and Gezi Park, and now there'd been more clashes, more water cannons. But the stories were about ghost gassings, the ones that caught you unaware, the sudden, faint irritation of the eyes and throat when you turned a corner or stepped out of a store.

"You think you're imagining," said the Swede. She was big-eyed, dark-haired. She looked Turkish, in fact. I might have had the nationalities wrong.

"Someone coughs, maybe you. Then others start coughing," the drummer.

"There's always someone who panics a little and runs away," said Davide.

"Then the coughing gets worse. But meanwhile others aren't coughing at all. They're just buying things or having conversations, maybe looking at you funny," said Adéla, who was looking at me funny, I thought.

They started to list places where they'd had this experience. Gas real or imagined outside the Pera Palace Hotel, up north outside Kanyon Mall, at the funicular station at the base of Tünel.

"Maybe the little burning in your throat is just a rumor," said the second guitarist. He had rings on the fingers and thumb of his right hand. They were all nursing their drinks. They weren't drinkers or couldn't afford to be. "But the rumors are usually true. Like the rumors the police are out of control in some other street. They're in squads, they're gouging out eyes. Which is true. It happened."

"Beating people to death or near death," the Italian, which was true.

"Leaving them for dead on burning trash heaps," the Swede, truly.

"They're all the same," said Davide, meaning the police.

"Well, no," I said. It was an outrageous statement, this no, and demands were made that I explain myself. I said that we all knew of police corruption and brutality. Some or all of us had witnessed or experienced this violence. But there were also stories of justice-seeking police, heroism, protection of the innocent, and self-sacrifice. To say of any outwardly similar group of humans that they were all the same was to ignore nuance, shade, a more precise kind of perception. It was bluntspeak.

"But bluntspeak, as you call it, has force," said the second guitarist. "The world will end in bluntspeak."

"Yes. And because of it," I said.

"There are bad cops and a few good cops, you're saying," said the Swede.

"Yes, but also the bad and the good are sometimes within the same cop, though maybe not in any kind of balance. It's hard not to think of them all as one thing when they wear uniforms and erect barriers and act as one. Maybe I'm just remembering a poem by the Italian filmmaker Pasolini after riots in the late sixties in Rome when students fought the police. He sided with the students' cause, but with the policemen in the fight. He saw the police as disadvantaged, uneducated farm boys, the true proletariat, fighting the children of the privileged."

"Simplistic and condescending," said Adéla, though she was smiling at me.

"Yes," I said. "And no." I don't know why Pasolini kept coming back to mind. I didn't like his poetry or his movies. I think I admired his conviction. Even his hair had conviction.

I asked them to forgive me. I said I'd come to Turkey in hopes of settling a personal concern, and my hopes seemed to be riding on the possibility that police in the south would prove honorable. To my disbelief, Davide then told everyone the story of my parents' murder. It turned out he'd heard it from Durant, who'd asked Carlo if he could ask Davide to look out for me. I'd never heard the story, of course, in the sense of having it told to me rather than by me or in my head in fragments. It was hard to listen to. I didn't correct the errors in his version. The other five muttered in sympathy. Adéla leaned over and gave me a hug. I felt a sudden love for them and felt at the same time how shallow it was, or maybe not shallow but tenuous. We were attached by chance, on one small node of connection. They reminded me of the crowd I'd known briefly with the Londoner. We were all roughly the same age, and though from different countries, all poor and hopeful, meeting as partial representations of ourselves, combining and recombining, looking for meaningful arrangements. The word I'd learned from Durant was *coalescent*.

It was the drummer, thin-faced, wearing the same dark porkpie hat I'd seen in the street video Davide had sent me, who produced the pill and laid it on the table.

"Welcome to One Two," he said.

I regarded the thing, rectangular, beveled, yellow, looked up at them all. They were looking at the pill, smiling. Davide explained it was a new street drug, origins unknown. It had appeared first in Amsterdam or Berlin and made its way south as far as Cairo. Now it sat between us, troubling no one, it seemed, this thing in plain sight.

"You're in a dark time in your life," said the drummer. "The pill will help you through."

I didn't know what it was or what it did or, really, who had given it to me. I picked it up and held it before my eyes, as if inspecting a strange insect, put it in my mouth, swallowed it. The others raised their bottles and glasses to me, and I to them.

My dreams that night almost killed me. When I woke they had balled into a headache so intense I couldn't move. In the dream that stayed with me I was walking in a landscape dark with

floating petals of black ash. I stepped a few feet in one direction,
then changed course and set off in another, then another, unable to
find open air or the promise of light. At some point a shape
appeared and began to grow before me, a human shape, coming
closer, a woman with a skin of dry mud. She took my hand and led
me into a cave, along a firelit rock face. We came to drawings of
horned animals I couldn't name, and she held her palm before me,
showed me the cake of ash in it, and then spit into her palm and
began to rub out the drawings. I understood that one by one she
was extinguishing not just the drawings but the animals themselves, not just the animals but the species. I squeezed her wrist but
she was too strong, her hand could not be stopped, and as she
moved along the wall the animals grew more and more familiar,
they stood, their heads turned, they looked out at us with familiar
eyes, our eyes, blinking. We ourselves were there on the wall, she
and I, watching us disappear ourselves at the end of the world.

The headache had receded by the time I woke again. It was late
morning, I knew, maybe noon. Somehow I'd slept through two
calls to prayer.

The experience of lost time is a dissociative amnesia of the kind
reported by alcoholics and alien abductees. I had no memory of
having left the bar or walking to Davide's place, no idea if I'd done
so with him or alone. Had I seemed drunk to others? Balanced of
mind and body? I might have done anything and not known it. Was
some Istanbul cop right now stringing together security footage of
me scaling a wall or smash-and-grabbing window sweets from a
baklava shop?

Davide was out, presumably renovating his father's building. He'd
left a note apologizing for leaving just a single egg for breakfast. I was

looking at the French coffee press or whatever it was called and then I was sitting in the sun at the little table on the balcony without any memory of having made the coffee. I looked at the floor, which I must have just crossed, but didn't even have a sense memory of my bare feet on the wood. I grew very still, told myself not to move. Somehow I'd wandered into a Godard movie. The term *jump cut* seemed especially unpleasant there on the third-floor balcony. Through a narrow gap between buildings I looked off at the Golden Horn, minarets in the haze. I closed my eyes.

When I opened them Davide's girlfriend was standing at the balcony door, smiling at me. She wore a red T-shirt and white pajama bottoms. Terrifying. Was she real? Her smile fell and she said, "You look confused."

"That pill I had last night."

"Oh, the One Two hangover." She came and sat at the table opposite me. Her hair was all over the place. "The first time it happened to me I thought I'd been trapped in a French New Wave film. I thought this must be how Jean Seberg felt in *Breathless.*"

"I just had the same thought. Godard."

"She was killed, Jean Seberg. Did you know?"

"No. When does it go away, this feeling?"

"Half a day, a full one. Some say the pill works for days. Stories differ."

"Did I leave with you and Davide last night?"

"You left alone. You were asleep on the couch when we came in. Should I make us some breakfast?"

"There's only one egg. He left a note for you. What happened to Jean Seberg?"

"The FBI tapped her phones, followed her constantly. Then they planted a story in the press that her unborn child wasn't fathered by her husband. She went into labor early and the child died. That was the beginning of the end of her. For years she was suicidal on the anniversary of the child's death until finally, on one of those anniversaries, she overdosed herself to death." Strange phrasing, I noted, then remembered she was Swedish. "All this because she supported the rights of natives and blacks."

"Surveilled to death. Are you an actress?" She laughed but didn't answer. "In my condition, is it safe to be moving around?"

"It's safe, yes. You know what you're doing as you do it, even if you don't remember. Davide loves One Two. He's involved, buyer and seller. He wants to be a player. Davide the drug lord. It's stupid. It's not him."

"Maybe he wants to piss off his father. He seems to hate Carlo."

"He doesn't hate his father. He hates himself for loving him. It makes him bitter."

Now that I looked at us, we were both fully dressed. Apparently I'd elided two conversations.

"I think I'll go out for a while," I said. "I'm sorry I don't remember your name. Unless it's Anna."

"Yes! That's the One Two. It makes you know more than you know."

One Two had me in trouble. As soon as I left the apartment it seemed I was sitting on sloping grass in Gezi Park, looking out at Taksim. There was a rally of some sort, a lot of men, all men, carrying red flags with yellow sickles that looked very like the national flag, though with some slight differences I couldn't locate. There were more than a hundred of these men, maybe more than two hundred, and they seemed angry. Many held up large poster images of someone I assumed was a political candidate or dead victim. Beyond them were riot police, and around the rally and the police walked passersby not paying them much attention.

I tried to hold a sense of continuous memory. An old man crossed the square, a face with the half-cloaked world in it. On his head he was balancing a tall stack of pretzels, *simits*, they're called, and he walked past me up the slope and began trying to sell them to people seated at the patio tables outside a tea kiosk. A young waiter appeared and I expected him to shoo the guy away, but instead he beckoned him and bought one of the *simits*. Then he went into the kiosk and came out and handed him a cup of tea and a cigarette and the two of them stood there looking out at the park and the square, talking, and when the tea was gone the old man went on his way, paying nothing. Simple transaction, made in kindness and respect. I'd never seen anything more dignified.

A strong urge overcame me to record the scene in writing—when had I last had this urge, not to interpret but describe? It had been a few years, my early twenties, back when I thought I might someday be a poet—but I had nothing to write with. I climbed up the slope, took one of the patio seats, ordered tea, got a pen from the same young waiter whom I was about to sketch in words. From my back pocket I pulled out the folded boarding pass from my flight of four days ago and stared at the blank side.

After fifteen minutes I'd written one line. "The sun is warm." I couldn't get past it. I tried again, stayed longer, until clouds moved in and the line was no longer true. I was not a poet. I'd already reconciled myself to the fact, but not to those parts of myself, griefs and dreams, I seemed to need fixed extra-cranially, in something beyond myself. The poem I'd wanted to write was about more than the waiter and the old man, even as it would be, like all poems, at

the same time, about nothing. It was about those two things. I
needed very badly to write about everything and nothing.

As the waiter cleared away the teacup and left the check, I was
breaking down, becoming a mess. In time I was aware of a hand
on my shoulder. The waiter was trying to comfort me. He spoke
English but I'd seen him with the old man, I knew him, and I
knew he wouldn't ask what was wrong. I was sure he understood
that once you try to answer, once you truly commit to such a question, you'll never reach the end of what needs saying.

A muddle of streets ran downhill off the square. With no memory
of leaving the park, I'd gotten lost. I needed to hear Dominic's
voice but, overburdened, couldn't risk feeling his decline more
acutely. I pictured myself down at the water, signing up for ship
duty, entering a seagoing adventure, as likely a prospect as any. The
next minutes, the next years, were blank, as if I were already dead.
I needed to feel more settled before calling Amanda. I'd got myself
turned around, passing the same antique shops twice. I chose an
uphill path. By the time it plateaued at an intersection of fruit
stores and cafés, I was out of breath and feeling better. I sat in the
doorway of a closed dress shop and called Rome.

"Okay, where are you?" she asked.

"I don't know. Maybe the fringes of a neighborhood called
Cihangir. I ingested something strange last night."

She led me through my explanation, that I'd taken a drug and
woke to find the moments in my day randomized and not quite
making sense.

"You were making sense last night. Have you checked out the
address?"

"What are you talking about?"

It took a minute for each of us to understand what the other was saying, longer than that to believe it. The previous night she'd called my cell and we had a version of the conversation we were now having again. Things had come about. They were hurtling toward a conclusion, and I would be standing there for it. She backed up in her story but spoke very quickly. She said that Pierluigi had enlisted all branches of the Keyholers in a hunt for the Poet. Someone in the Berlin branch discovered a likely internet protocol address and a corresponding actual one in Paris. Two members of the French branch staked out an apartment in the Eleventh Arrondissement with a lone occupant, a tall man, who they believed might be the Poet—

"Hold on. How did they find him?"

"I don't know. Software and intuition. The Germans set up a dummy metasite and mined it and followed the hits. The Italians planted stories and worked out timelines. The French circumvented a googlewhack. They all followed the money. What does it mean? I'm not into geek procedurals."

"The Poet is a tall man in Paris."

"Not anymore. They followed him and took a picture. Yesterday he went to Charles de Gaulle and boarded a plane."

"A plane."

"Maybe this is all a goose chase but if the Keyholers are right, you could be in danger. Pierluigi got one of the Istanbul hackers' sisters to meet the plane and follow the Poet into the city, which she somehow successfully did. Or at least the guy she followed looked like the guy in the picture."

"Here."

"The tall man is in Istanbul. Since yesterday evening. See your emails. I already told you to come back to Rome. You asked me to send you his picture and address. You said you think you've flushed him into the open, that his appearance connects to your parents. You're already determined to confront him. You already think this is your one shot."

Inside the lost time I'd had a phone call, I'd sounded lucid, a thought I had to process along with the news about the Poet. That he should be in Istanbul wasn't a coincidence. My emails were encrypted but I'd had dozens of conversations, in person, by phone, about my hacker theory, the Keyholers, my trip to Turkey. And of course I left a data trail everywhere. It was easy to assume he knew it all, knew where I was staying, what I looked like. It was natural to think that he was here for me. I'd followed my father, who might have been murdered, and murdered for a reason, and so I'd made myself a threat like he did by coming to Turkey and asking questions. I'd hatched a notion. And I was the solitary, with no protectors, no family or real lover or close friends except a man across the ocean losing his memory. Did he think I could be bought off or threatened? Made to drop my investigations? What leverage did he have? Was he violent?

Ludicrous. Root meaning in "sportive, jesting," from the Latin *ludicrus*, from *ludicrum*, meaning "stage play."

The picture had arrived in my inbox just before midnight. The graphics told me I'd already opened it. I called it up again and there in my little phone window was a tall man apparently in midlife, midstride, approaching the camera. His head and hands were large. A high forehead, pronounced brow, notched at the eyes. Short hair, maybe light brown. His nose was slightly out of true. He was dressed in brown pants and a faded red canvas jacket.

The man—or was it the photo?—looked vaguely familiar. According to my search history I'd already called up the phone map for the address. It was in the Beyoğlu neighborhood, not far from Davide's place. I told myself, unbelievably, that I had to get the drop on him. This was the extent of my plan. I worked my way across the high streaming traffic of Tarlabaşi and looked back to see if I could remember crossing the wide avenue. I had it for a second and then it was gone. As I headed north into the little streets I felt in need of a revelation, a useful cha-cha, but cha-chas could not be induced. My thoughts were now desperately linear, blind baby vipers at speed. I was prose-headed, story-bound, seeking logical connection as I navigated by phone through the neighborhood's mix of old, condemned-looking buildings and renovated ones with fresh plaster faces covering the cracks that seemed to run vertically on every structure. I came to the street but wasn't sure the phone had it right. It was unmarked, dead-end, two blocks long.

I approached the building. There was no number but Pierluigi's friend's sister had said to look for a "flock of birds" above the doorway. I stared up at a horizontal line of three blue-and-yellow ceramic tiles with dozens of black chevrons or birds in flight painted on them. I realized I'd seen the motif before, above the entranceway to Durant's apartment building. Back in Rome the black marks on the blue and yellow had reminded me of the birds in Van Gogh's *Wheatfield with Crows*, likely his last painting. Van Gogh, who wrote that he wanted to be "a poet" of landscapes, died two days after receiving a gunshot wound he said was self-inflicted. Through his agony he told his hosts not to blame anyone, which led to speculation that he'd been shot, maybe by accident, maybe not, maybe by a local farm boy. In the 1950s someone even confessed to the shooting. As I looked up and thought of his last crows, they seemed obviously in their flocking beauty an ascension in the heart, and I was sure his death wasn't suicide, which left accident or murder, the question I couldn't get free of, and so landed me back in my shoes.

From the windows of the upper floors plastic sheeting billowed and snapped in a light wind. All but one of the ground-floor windows were tacked over with plywood. The one next to the front door was wide open, likely why the door was closed but unlocked. I stepped into the dark foyer, where dim light revealed openings on either side of a staircase. The whole building felt empty and I began to suspect that Pierluigi's friend's sister had steered me wrong. Without bothering to be quiet I walked into what used to be an apartment. The floors were scarred and dirty, the kitchen appliances pulled out from the wall. There was no furniture. In one of the corners were graffiti drawings and writing in a penciled script but there was no sign of recent habitation. Apartment to apartment, the story was much the same, down to the graffiti.

The discovery was on the fourth floor. I entered an apartment identical to the others, but in the living area, near the window, were a green sleeping bag, a small flashlight, a half-eaten loaf of bread. I registered all this in an instant and then I was on my knees, searching the sleeping bag, and there I found a notebook. Glued onto the hard cover was a postcard reproduction I recognized as Velázquez's painting *Head of a Stag*, which the Londoner and I had seen in the Prado museum. The composition, even the texture, the colors, retained the breathing life of the original, the moisture in the fine chin whiskers. It was as if I'd come across the animal in a woods or the museum.

The stag's head marked a spot. It made the notebook seem the center of something, the home space in the game. The beauty of the little reproduction held me. The word was *execute*. Representational artists *create* an original, which is in fact a copy of the world, and sometimes *execute* a copy, after the original. But the idea of execution doubled when I recalled why the Londoner disliked the painting. Velázquez had rendered the stag at the request of his patron, Philip IV, who sometimes wanted portraits of animals he'd killed. "So of course the stag is regal," she said, already walking away, into the next gallery. "The forehead furrowed like royal satin, the horns a crown. The powerful kill the innocent and force artists to play along." She was prone to these broad declarations, assigning values always through this way of understanding. By turns her views were enlightening, self-evident, lacking in nuance, but her conviction was soulful. Too bad for me if I loved two souls at odds, hers and that of an artwork she didn't like. Power presumes to bend art and nature.

But nature, and sometimes art, can resist. If she was an infiltrator then her disgust in the Prado was an act. But it was genuine, I was quite sure. She hadn't betrayed me, after all, I decided, or at least only in the conventional, sexual sense. My nature now had me flipping through the pages in the notebook. Most were empty but near the back was a page of handwriting, letters in minuscule script. I tilted the book to catch the obscured windowlight. The words were English. The first line:

The sun is warm.

Had I already been here? Had I come last night, read these first four words and unconsciously recalled them an hour ago in bright Gezi Park? Or had the Poet sat here in the plastic-filtered light, just as I had sat in bright Gezi Park, both of us inspired to the same assertion, then both falling to our native confusions? The other words were set down in fragments, little bursts of meaning and half meaning that didn't come together.

The border mass pension. You missed your foreigners.
Potatoes that fortified your military. Graves are turned up.
Like the garden. As you called the thin winter. You thought
  of them.
Dashed the thought against hutments. And fences.

Deer of your retirement. Today you won't be forgiven. Your
sanctioned en masse. Bring yourself close but the sun warms
mercies. Across your memories of the open wild.

There's no place for them now. You feed them all on the backs
of your hands. What this is today the trucks. And it's a good
day. Inspired habit of saying all others.

All the lost in all times have known.
Knowing are coming this is today.

The words, like the day, had fallen out of sense. The day, like time,
like the city, was prone to radical emancipatory outbursts. The lines
looked randomly generated, as if by an algorithm, but there was
something here too private, too intimate, and I felt it drawing me
downward. These weren't recorded thoughts but the rudiments of
thought itself, an innermost sound. I couldn't read and I couldn't not.

I reread the page several times. There was an order to things but I
couldn't know it. Reality was unsecure. It could shift in any direction.
It simply *was*, not *was as if.* The idea of *as* always stands in the way of
the real.

And so it was not *as if,* but that he really *was* already coming up the
stairs before I heard him. My instinct was to hide and wait for a
chance to make the stairwell but hadn't I come to confront him? If

he'd been following me, he would know I was here. It seemed obvious now that he'd chosen this time and place to meet me. But why this building? Because it was abandoned. Because someone could die here and remain undiscovered for days or weeks, if the wind was right.

The steps were in steady rhythm, passing the third floor. Timing my footfalls with his, I left his apartment and crossed into the one opposite. The room was veiled in plastic sheeting. I turned my shoulders, stepped through. Everywhere were power tools.

He made the top of the stairs and I took a tool in hand, its name lost to me, and he heard me and approached. His form was vague behind the sheets. Then he stepped through and I knew him.

We went down to the street and sat in the open sun.

I explained all I could.

"All these buildings, we get squatters," said Davide. "I get to know them, let them stay as long as no one steals the tools. Some come for the protests. When I'm done my work, my father sends his crew in and they chase out the squatters."

"Have you seen the one here now?"

"It's been empty. He must have come last night. Like you said."

"How many buildings around here are being renovated?"

"Many. Thirty. Fifty. The world is buying the city."

"This can't be a coincidence. He chose the one you're working on."

"It's strange if he had money to fly here and take a taxi from the airport."

"What do you mean 'crew.' Who are your dad's crew?"

"I just clean the places and do general repairs. Then he sends in the guys for the wiring and pipes and plastering and painting. They make the big money."

"Where does he find them?"

"Same guys always. They're American. He flies them all around. He doesn't care about local workers. Sometimes he pays off the unions."

It's only when you leave the sun and stone that it becomes hard to know what's real. The doubt is ancient and ongoing, from Plato's cave shadows to current anxieties over the smooth fictions of government, media, even fiction itself, the suspect common surround.

That afternoon I moved into the derelict building. From the junkman with the cart, who was younger up close than I'd realized and who tried to interest me, sans English, in what seemed to be the hose of a hookah pipe, I bought a plastic pen with an elongated picture of Atatürk on the side and copied out the words from the notebook page. I bought fruit and bread in the neighborhood and at evening walked with Davide fifteen minutes to his apartment for ablutions and a change of clothes.

I stayed awake most of the night, under a blanket of Davide's. Next to me were my cellphone and, I confess, a long screwdriver, weapons-grade. I had no choice but to embrace the lonely absurdity of my position. My parents' decades had been as chaotic as mine, but the tone they managed was sure, constant, polite, not especially funny, never absurd. Their need for meaningful work had taken them to the most fraught border in the world. My need for meaning had landed me in the dark with simple tools. The Poet failed to appear.

The next day Davide and I worked our way down to the first floor, pulling out wires, sweeping up glass and plaster, repairing nothing. He spoke of playing music, of working for his father, who paid him well for unskilled work but didn't respect him or his friends. In the afternoon two of them dropped by, the drummer in the porkpie hat and the second guitarist with the rings. They hugged me in greeting and Davide invited me to take a break with them, but I stayed and worked on the poem I'd found, if that's what it was, trying to make it make sense.

When he returned Davide questioned my move into the cold, plumbingless building.

"If the squatter is a poet, maybe he came to find me," he said. "Maybe he wants the One Two. It's good for the imagination."

"That wasn't really my experience of it."

He said there were three illegal labs in Europe. They shared information and agreed to keep the sale price as low as possible. Whoever was behind the drug viewed it as enlightening, community-building.

"One Two is the future. Our future. The young."

I tried to imagine a future in which the recent past had been lost to collective gaps in memory. Who wouldn't want to forget periods of trauma or embarrassing fashion? But we remember with more than our brains, I told him. And anyway, we are both our actions and our memories of them. It was hard enough to hold an identity together in the new century without voluntarily fracturing the self.

"Maybe we won't know who we are," he said. "But we'll know who we are not. My father and his friends are very sure of who they are. They could use some doubt. All they have is greed and fear. This is my last job for him. Then I disappear."

At dark I was alone again, waiting for the Poet's return, reading the words from his notebook over and over by flashlight. I began to form a sense of the man in the photo. I wanted to believe he understood me, that he wrote the poems under some injunction or debt, half against his will, more or less as I read them, though he was or once wanted to be a real poet, and even he didn't know the full dimensions of the machinery of deceit he'd been made a part of. Maybe out of necessity, I convinced myself he hadn't come to Istanbul to harm me. He wanted me to know I was known.

With my Atatürk pen and a small notebook of my own I worked on the scrambled words, trying to make them come clear. The phrases and lines seemed shuffled out of an original order. The idea bore some relation to anastrophe and hyperbaton, figures of speech in which words in a sentence or line appear out of their usual sequence. The intended effect was to produce altersenses, competing levels of meaning. I tried arranging the words into short lines. I could fashion no obvious rhyme scheme, find no pattern in the sounds, but the echoes of meaning were localized, so I attached one fragment of sense to another that seemed promising. My notebook pages were soon a mess of circles, numbers, lines, and arrows. Every time I thought I was making headway, the sense would break down, but with every attempt one certainty grew clearer: the poem, if I could only rescue it from chaos, was about my father.

After five hours I had fourteen versions of the poem. In the sixth hour, past midnight, I finally cracked it. I called it "Çodhir."

> The sun is warm. Across the border mass
> graves are turned up like the garden
> potatoes that fortified your military
> pension. You missed your foreigners,
>
> as you called the thin winter
> deer of your retirement. Today

you thought of them, dashed the thought
against hutments and fences.

You won't be forgiven your sanctioned
mercies, your memories of the open wild.
There's no place for them now. You feed them
en masse. Bring yourself close. But the sun warms

all and it's a good day, inspired habit of saying,
knowing on the backs of your hands what
all others, all the lost in all times have known.
This is today. The trucks are coming. This is today.

It wasn't much of a poem, and I couldn't say who'd authored it, but in the sense that I'd discovered it, or the makings of it, it was mine. I would likely never show it to anyone. I looked at the words on the page, the letters in the words. I tore out the page and in the light of my cellphone app held it up flat, near my eyes, and looked at the impressions of the ink in the fibers, little sculpted shivers of the human need to say. The letters, not the poem, seemed evidence of One Great Meaning. Call it God or Poet, Designer or Intender, many believed it was a fiction from the outset. Others believed that, even if long ago a sure, final meaning had departed the world, the world still vibrated from the departure. Did I believe this or just need to believe it? There, in that night, I believed it.

I stayed three nights in the squat. The Poet did not return.

I had to tell Amanda that I'd failed. Because of "Çodhir," the failure was enormous and I felt it personally now. He must have found the poem's details in my correspondences—though I couldn't recall ever having written to anyone about the potatoes my father grew or the deer he liked to call his "foreigners" that he fed in his backyard in Nova Scotia—and in leaving the lines for me, he'd let me know there was a poem to be imagined and answers to be found. In his signs and wonders and failure to appear he should have seemed an absconded god, but instead I thought of him as someone like me, flawed, by turns inspired and confused, needing to make contact. Or he might not have been the Poet at all.

"If he'd gone there to find you, he would have by now." I pictured her standing at her bedroom window, listened for the sound of her drawing on a cigarette, her way of being alone in the intimate presence of another. Then I heard others laughing. She was at work. "We should have told the Paris hacktivists to grab him. Now even Three Sheets has gone dark."

"He must know that Pierluigi's guys tracked him."

"I think it's over, James. I think he's gone for good."

Durant called with the same conclusion. In the late afternoon, from the rooftop bar of the Goethe-Institut, I looked out at the amazing city, as if to find perspective.

"We'll never know what we nearly discovered. Amanda says you found a poem about your parents."

"More like the makings of a poem. I think he left it for me."

"Did it feel like a kindness or a cruelty?"

"Both."

"Yes," he said, then "Yes" again. "It's time for you to leave. I'll send the ticket. Amanda tells me you've been into some strange drug. Make sure you don't try to cross borders with it."

He asked me to read him the poem. In my own voice it struck me differently and I formed an intuition and had to stop midway and tell him I'd get back to him. At Davide's place, on his laptop,

I plugged in the hard drive Gail had given me, from the office computer of Believer Missions (Global). At the password prompt I typed "thesuniswarm" and there it was, my mother and father's shared email account, open before me. I'd been given the password so indirectly that I had to assume someone was in danger, me or whoever had left the notebook.

Mixed in with NGO correspondence were personal messages, some to me, from me, that I barely remembered and hadn't been able to reread since the deaths. All outgoing messages featured the Believer Missions (Global) electronic letterhead. Only in the last email my father sent did I find anything unusual. The message had no saluta-tion. Unlike his other messages, signed with his name and military rank, this one was unsigned. It read: "Discovered. Who can I trust?"

Attached were four photos. Open wooden crates containing artillery shells and, given the wiring, what seemed to be suicide vests. The writing on the shells was in Cyrillic.

I crossed Tarlabaşi and entered a large hotel, the Marmara Pera, and took a room. In the lobby I found a telephone for guests. I called Gail in Gaziantep and asked her to phone the number from a public landline. The call came through in forty-five minutes. She recognized the email address where my father had sent the pictures as that of Oliver Mantz, an elderly man in Leeds who'd lived for years in Turkey and helped NGOs and Western companies with "back-channel communications."

"Oliver knew who could be trusted with information and who couldn't."

"He sounds like a spy."

"I don't think he was but he knew them all. He retired back to England after we all arrived. He may never have read the message. What did it say?"

"It's better if you don't know. I'm sorry I involved you in any of this."

In the hotel's "Connection Room," near the steady industry at the front desk, next to a broken coke machine, I sat at the common terminal and did internet searches with promising word combinations made of "artillery shells" "Cyrillic" "suicide vests" "southern Turkey." I surmised that the arms were Russian-made or Ukrainian. I learned that everyone imaginable was running weapons through Şanliurfa Province. Arms dealers, local officials, Turkish gangsters, Russians to Assad, Americans to the Kurds, Turks to the rebels. Profiteers shipping to the Islamic State. Those quoted invoked God's name. And I learned that two months after my parents died, police discovered an apartment in Gaziantep being used by ISIS, packed with suicide vests and weapons artillery with Cyrillic lettering. These details sat at the bottom of a story only one day old about a suicide bombing in the Şanliurfa town of Suruç. It had killed thirty-two students who were about to cross the border to help rebuild the Syrian town of Kobanî. The police were already claiming that the attacker was a Turkish member of ISIS. The government had blocked social media sites containing photos from the scene. Already happening in different parts of the country and all over Istanbul were antigovernment protests against, variously, control of the internet and the flow of information, and a perceived alliance between the Turkish government and ISIS formed to weaken Kurdish forces. A side note to the coverage was that in retaliation for the bombing two policemen suspected of helping ISIS had been killed by Kurdish gunmen outside the camp of Çodhir.

The hard drive itself felt like a bomb. I could tell no one about the arms photos without risk of endangering them.

I found Davide at the building, finishing up. I thanked him for letting me stay with him and for his good company. We talked about our futures, which seemed featureless.

"You should be careful about selling One Two. You don't seem the criminal type."

"Neither does my father." He was polishing the banister with a blue-and-white rag that looked much like the bandana he wore to keep his hair from his eyes. "If I get in trouble he'll pull his dirty strings. Every country, he buys off men in suits and uniforms."

"Then you're not really free of him."

"I'm not so young, maybe. I know it's not so easy to be free."

I climbed to the top floor, gathered up the Poet's notebook and sleeping bag, and carried them down to the foyer. Davide asked if he could have the sleeping bag. We stepped outside. In the full light I checked for new voice messages, there were none. Then I erased the saved messages, including one from Amanda, and the address book and photos and clips, including the film taken on the road where my parents died. I called the cell provider and canceled my service and asked Davide to give the phone to the junkman. I kept the notebook for myself.

"Have you solved your mystery?" he asked. He looked painterly in his bandana. Out of nowhere I felt an affection for my generation. A gravity could form around the right Davides in many countries, in the spirit of wanting to piss off fathers. He was a flag.

"I don't even know if there's one mystery or more. I don't think they'll ever be solved. And I'd like to think nothing at all for a while."

He said his group would be playing on Istiklal that night if I wanted to come by.

"I'd like that. But in case I can't, I'll say goodbye now."

"Come find us. We're going to a protest when we're done playing."

We shook hands and I wished him well.

I lasted less than an hour free and unplugged. At the hotel computer terminal I discovered three emails. Durant had sent my ticket and I had it printed off. Amanda wrote that she'd pick me up at the airport in Rome. She said Durant had become a little distant, detached. "Something's going on in him and I bet even he couldn't tell us what." She said she'd be leaving Rome in a few weeks. A friend had offered her a place in Amsterdam. "And after that," she wrote, "I don't know any little bit of the future."

The third message was from Burhan Rihawi: "Meet past Akşam tenty minute tonight tea in Passage Hazzopulo?" In a few clicks I learned that Akşam is the evening call to prayer. I replied that I understood and looked forward to meeting him. I said I would wear a blue scarf. Never had I felt less prepared for anything. I'd even lost my blue Urfa scarf.

Half an hour later at the common terminal I sat trying to grasp the numbers. Number of millions displaced. Number of dead. Number of tens of thousands of photos of tortured corpses from the prisons. The numbers were obscene. How many raped, suspected number unreported. Number dead by sarin gas. Trying to memorize the numbers was obscene. Trying to imagine any of it was an absolutely necessary impossible presumption, a morally responsible prayer for and reprehensible insult to the dead. To be defeated by the numbers was pathetic. Failing to be defeated was unconscionable. The number of Syrians arrived in Istanbul since the conflict began was estimated at two hundred thousand. Many were housed in communal apartments and *cemevi*, gathering houses, and some lived under cardboard in the public parks. Most didn't speak Turkish. Maybe half had come across mountain passes and were not counted in the numbers. The sum of their prospects was zero.

The world and its collapsed distances held comic farce one minute, suffering the next, the new tonal discord of living. Inconsonant ironies, asymmetries, mass crushing need.

I considered bringing a gift but I'd never before been faced with meeting so unknown a stranger. As gifts I liked to give books, but I didn't know if he read, or what, or in which of his three languages, though I presumed Arabic, or if he read outside his religion, Christians or Alawites or authors of no faith at all. And what were his politics?

To stop my thoughts I left the hotel and walked down to Galata Tower and sat in the square taking in the people taking in one another. Human wiring isn't built for these disjunctures, meeting or even just seeing so many people in so many places in so short a time. The countless foreign territories, lost clans, glancing moments at different latitudes make the idea of home provisional or reduce it to a jagged atavism. I walked to the base of the bridge and caught a tram across to the old city. Near the Grand Bazaar on a small market street I bought scarves for Dominic, Amanda, and Durant, a blue one for myself. For a full minute I stood before an intricate carpet hung outside a shop. The owner appeared, a short man of about forty, wearing an inexpensive sports jacket over a striped sweater, a choice that seemed neither fashionable nor practical. In English, he asked me inside but I told him I had no money and couldn't buy anything more, holding up the scarves. He shrugged, went back into the shop, and came out with two cups of tea. We stood sipping and he told me about the carpet. It was from Kurdish Iran, made in 1944. It cost nine thousand two hundred American dollars. If I examined the patterns, he said, I would find them symmetrical in shape but not color. He pointed out a motif along one of the inner borders, taken up with variation on the side opposite. He said he lived half the year in Paris, and was in fact Turkish French. Making a frame with his hands he identified an area of the carpet containing the maximum number of subsymmetries. He remarked on the unknown maker's use of scale and interposed spaces. He spoke four languages, English his least favorite. Of greatest effect, he thought, was the random ordering of colors and design elements in the outer border to slightly disrupt the visual field and create accidental echoes and hierarchies. He said, "The carpet brings God into the room."

The word was *decor*. While still understanding nothing, all at once I understood everything. The poems, the cities, the painted tiles. The murder upon murder upon murder.

It all came on the sound of his voice, almost imploring me to see, and the balanced complexity of the carpet as he portioned it out for my understanding. Feeling on the verge of levitation, I handed him my cup and thanked him. I said he'd been a great help to me in ways I couldn't explain and he laughed and even the laughter felt corrective and clarifying.

In forty minutes I was at Davide's apartment. Anna answered the door. She was holding a bottle of lemon water and she wore a red sweater with a lemon motif. Amid the echoing lemons I realized I knew almost nothing about her. She invited me to the balcony but I stopped and stood in the living room.

"I've just come for a minute. At sundown I'm meeting someone in Passage Hazzopulo. Do you know where it is?"

"It's across the boulevard."

"And it empties onto Istiklal, where Davide's group is playing tonight."

"You have mastered the facts, James. I'll go watch them for a while. They're good but they're as good as they're going to get."

"I'm leaving tomorrow morning. Tonight I'm staying at the Marmara Hotel."

"Why are you telling me this? Is something wrong? Have you taken a One Two?"

"No, I'm fine. I gave away my phone but I have email access at the hotel. And a phone in my room."

"Is Davide looking for you?"

"I just saw him earlier. We've said our goodbyes. And now I'll say goodbye to you, Anna. Be happy and remember yourself."

She and her lemons laughed.

"Is that a Canadian saying?" She kissed me on each cheek. "You're strange. I didn't notice it before. But strange in a nice way."

I hesitated, leaned in, whispered.

"Remember what you said about that actress, Jean Seberg. It's still happening. There's someone with us, someone we can't see. Someone's listening to us right now. Maybe watching. In these buildings. Carlo's buildings."

I stepped back. Her look was of shock. She was processing, a little lost, her mouth slightly open. If she thought I was paranoid, it didn't show. She nodded and gave my forearm a squeeze.

Wearing the blue scarf I entered the Passage Hazzopulo twenty minutes after the evening call to prayer. A young wrangler ushered me to a wicker stool at one of the many low tables and I sat there under a spindling tree, trying to look Canadian. I saw no other white Westerners, no obvious tourists. Most were young, under thirty. The overhead lights had come on and lifted high colors from the blue bowls and green cups people drank from. I

felt a quickening. I was thinking both forward, in anticipation of
meeting Burhan Rihawi, and backward, about the carpet sales-
man, regrettably nameless to me, wondering what neighborhood
he lived in, if he had a family. Did he walk home alone after closing the shop? Did he like to stop somewhere? Did he look around
in a place like this and see design and intricacy even in the ran-
domness of so many small shops crammed together in the senseless desperation of small commerce? Did he see more shape in
things simply for knowing more about carpets? It had value
beyond itself, the deep knowledge of a made thing.

I thought about surveillance. The tapped internet, smart-
bugged buildings. Even there in the open air I felt anonymous
one moment, watched the next. And I was being watched. I'd
been looking back the way I'd come when I turned to find a fat
black dog standing at my table, as if to take my order. It looked
me in the eye without real interest and limped away down the
passage just as the waiter approached.

"She says hello," he said. He was slight, another young man, with
a black stubble beard. "She eats too much. Soon she can't walk."

"Does she belong to anyone?"

"We all give food and water. She's the passage dog. The police
shoot her in the spring but a doctor fixes her for free." He extended
his hand. "I'm Burhan."

"Oh." I stood and shook his hand. He had soft, generous eyes.
My father had known this face, looked into it in the days before he
was killed. "I'm sorry, I'm James, I thought you were the waiter."

"I am. Would you like coffee, maybe tea?"

Our conversation progressed in one-minute spurts as he took
and delivered orders at a dozen or more tables. That he'd arranged
to meet me here suggested some slyness or uneasiness. He didn't

know what I wanted. I'd said only who I was, my father's son, and that I'd like to meet him. If he knew anything about my parents' deaths, he would have been keeping it to himself all this time. And in any case it made sense for Syrians to be wary, even in Turkey.

"I'm sorry we meet here. I use my friend's computer. I read your email yesterday."

"This is fine, Burhan."

"I work very late."

He and the other waiters fetched the tea from a little shop down the passage, where it narrowed and there was barely enough room for the two-way pedestrian traffic as people stopped to look at jewelry, clothes, ceramics. It developed that he'd been working these tables since he and his family arrived from the camp. In Al-Hasakah he'd worked in a hotel and learned enough English and Turkish to get this job. Now he worked twelve hours a day, six days a week. He never elaborated on his answers unless I kept asking questions, but he answered every one of them. He said he knew that leaving Syria wasn't temporary, though that was what other refugees told themselves. A number I remembered, nine million displaced.

"Before the fighting we live with our neighbors no problem."

"How did you meet my father?"

"I help at the camp."

He went off to clear a table. His movements were efficient and precise, he'd done them many times. He returned and stood holding a tray of empty cups. He told me he'd never met my mother, that she worked outside the camp.

"You are a son," he said.

"Yes. I am." He seemed to be trying to see my father in me. I had the sense it wasn't obvious. "Why did this man in Urfa give me your name and email address?"

"I have friends there. We all feel the same."

"What do you feel?"

"Your father help me. I help you."

"How did he help you?" He looked at me directly, gauging something. "I'm sorry to ask, Burhan, but did you know they died?"

He set the tray down.

"Yes." He sat across from me. "Yes. He told me to send him my place number, where we live here, and he would send back."

With his hand he made a motion of writing in air.

"You mean a letter."

"Yes. I write him letter but no letter come back. My friend wrote they died."

I outlined the circumstances of the deaths and said they seemed not quite to make sense.

"I'm worried they were killed by someone. Murdered." His expression was already sorrowful and the word had no outward effect on him. He knew it from the inside and heard it every day. "Can you guess why they would have been killed?"

He lowered his head, alone with something that I felt should belong only to me, though his feeling of loss would attach to other sufferings much greater than my own. Resignation to fate, the bow of its spine. He took out a cellphone, tapped it a few times, and handed it to me. On-screen was a photo of shells with Cyrillic writing, one of the very photos attached to my father's email. He tapped to another picture. Suicide vests.

"I help at inspection station, outside camp." He said the food trucks arrived at the inspection station full but left half-empty. He took pictures of what was off-loaded and, at the camp, showed the photos to my father.

"He want to know if I was secret, did anyone saw me. Yes, they saw me. I show the pictures to many. He said send to him the photos and take my family on the bus to Gaziantep, next day." My father staked them to a new life. He gave them money, a lot of it, to continue their journey and find an apartment and work in Istanbul. "I never see him again." His face was muted now, as if obscured by a haze of pipe smoke or as if I were remembering it years into the future. "I'm sorry to you, James. Your father save my family."

He knew to leave me alone. He took the tray and left and I watched him catch up to his work. Now and then he glanced at me from one table or another. He was an innocent. His innocence had orphaned me.

Someone had been bought off by jihadists, maybe the same someone who'd murdered my parents, someone who needed the truth to stay hidden. Then what? Had the someone himself been killed? Whom had he betrayed?

Though I hadn't ordered one, Burhan brought me a *pide*, a flatbread with cheese and some kind of ground meat inside. I looked at it. Who deserved such an offering? I resumed watching him work. To settle myself I tried calculating his wages. He must have made nearly nothing on tips from students nursing tea. He worked seventy-two hours a week. He would barely see his family. This place was his life.

He sat with me again. Were his eyes really generous or did I need them to be? Other than a hardworking victim of history, who was he? I wanted no unearned sentiment, no easy affection. Even more than I wanted to know him well, a man like any full of contradictions, I wanted to know he was, like us all, guilty.

"I think of seeing your father," he said. "I think of my children and they should meet him. Now is not possible. But I will tell them someday."

He showed me another picture on his phone. His wife, Maira, wore a sweater and simple cotton pants, no headscarf. She looked twice Burhan's age, though more likely she was our age or younger. She stood with either hand on her two children, a boy and a girl, maybe five and six years old. He said their names were Amal and Samir. It seemed impossible that I could be connected to this family in any way that mattered, but in fact I was connected only in ways that mattered.

He asked for my mailing address. That I didn't have one was an irony I chose not to voice. I wrote out Dominic's address in Montreal, though he was selling the house, and he wrote out his and we made a show of folding the papers and putting them safely away. I promised myself to do as my parents would wish and send them all gifts when I got back to Canada. We'd begin a simple letter exchange, Burhan and I, and we wouldn't let it falter, just a note twice a year, and when the children were teenagers maybe I'd return and meet them. I'd be in another life and maybe they would not be, and maybe that was as they'd want it. Or maybe I'd leave in a minute and never have contact again.

We said our goodbyes and I started away toward the narrow end of the passage. There, watching me, the only other white Westerner in sight, was the Poet.

I followed him out onto Istiklal, into the stream, the thronging tens of thousands. He was half a block distant, a head above most of the rest. He glanced left and right, the face at angles, expressionless. The forehead was not so large as it had seemed in the photo and I couldn't make out the notches at his eyes, but it had to be him. I'd flushed him into the open by moving out of the squat and giving away my cellphone, moves that forced him to watch and track me in person.

At Davide's apartment I'd laid out my evening not for Anna but for him. I was sure that he or someone in contact with him would be listening, surveilling from hidden devices, from the appliances and lighting fixtures, the art on the walls, or by whatever means the dated, clumsy, Cold War comical spying tropes had been accelerated into the new reality.

We were headed toward Taksim. The moving crowd had weight and through-force. On the street's south side the flow moved east, north side west, though in any location were crosscurrents and tributaries coming from side streets, or wider openings where people massed and eddied. A multitude, face to face both highly particular and undifferentiated. A man with a monkey on his shoulder stepped from the doorway of a tobacco shop and disappeared. Women in jeans or chadors or floral cottons, yoga pants, Saudis in black abayas. Eating baklava, hoisting kids, drinking from plastic cups, carrying shopping bags. Through the din came the bell of the funicular. The tram moved by on the rails midstreet, kids hanging off the back. I passed smiling young men in groups of three and five, a tourist couple struggling for direction with their laminated map. Buskers at intervals, playing jazz or Turkish songs, two African men on instruments I couldn't name, a family of peasant musicians with a small boy bongo prodigy. The flow diverted around a thick ring of onlookers surrounding a large group of chanting protesters. The chant was loud, stadium ready, and at one point a cheer burst forth and the watchers raised cellphones and cameras like chalices and the hundred or more of them joined the chant as others in doorways filmed it all, and filmed the police filming them. From a large white truck, a water cannon sat at the ready, trained on the protesters. The riot squad stood only feet away and extended in rows along the next full block, down the ranked side streets into staging areas, their shields before them, the white helmets with blue stenciled numbers all lined at nearly the same level. I looked into their dangerously bored faces. They looked back and saw nothing. They were young like me and Amanda, like the Londoner, like Davide and his friends, like Burhan and Maira.

Was I chasing, following, being led? I tried to make up ground, skipping into each brief clearing, but the crowd was thicker now and I had to keep my focus level on him. Other Westerners and tall men appeared up ahead and marking him became harder. I focused on his brown hair, cropped and unshaped, as if he'd shorn it himself, his skull—yes, I saw it now—slightly offset at the brow. When I glimpsed him whole I saw he wore brown pants and a rust-colored shirt that was stained or textured or frayed through in places. But the hair and the colors of the clothes repeated with slight variations in the crowd. With Taksim in view the tall man who seemed most likely to be mine drifted left and entered a one-story building, stone, vaguely, dumbly Spanish colonial to my unschooled eye. A tasteful plaque at the door designated it as the French Consulate. I stepped into the small entrance. He'd passed through the security station and was walking out into an enclosed courtyard. I nodded at a security guard and moved through a metal detector. In the courtyard people sat at candlelit tables. Whoever they were—consulate staff? diners?—none looked my way. The Poet was nowhere but I saw a door closing in another wing of the building. I trotted to catch up and stepped through the doorway to find a small gallery. A placard fronting the exhibit announced a forty-year retrospective of some photojournalist agency. He wasn't in the first room—no one was— but other rooms extended off this one. I walked into the space, surrounded by images, shots from El Salvador, the West Bank, the Philippines, New York, Cairo, wondering at my trust.

Suppositions present themselves to be tested. Suppose there exists a mind. Suppose it can know your heart, your great loves and losses. Suppose that it watches and listens, not just watching but leading the eye, seeing the eye being led. Suppose it flags people of interest and has the means to prompt these people into each other's lives, to control them through their secrets and unexpendable pains.

Suppose you'd never claimed your grief.

I crossed the first room, entered a second. There was no one. An opening to a third gallery was across from me, and two openings opposite each other at the far end of the room. If he wanted to and was quiet, he could stay out of sight. I moved quickly into the last room, saw no one, came back into the second space and walked its length. At the far end I saw a possibility. A hallway ran off the last room. I came across and turned the corner to find a short dead end. He stood with his back to me. He faced a narrow wall with a picture collage mounted next to a window that looked out at the crowds moving by on Istiklal only meters away. I stepped forward and came up beside him. The images were anonymous cellphone shots from the Istanbul riots. Water cannons firing, clouds of gas, improvised masks, fists, bleeding, phones upon phones.

The faint scent of wet soil, a barnyard note.

"So many cameras," he said. The voice was deep, the speech not native English, I guessed, though I couldn't quite place it. I had a sense I shouldn't look at him or press him so I bent closer to the collage. Some shots were stills from security cameras. I pictured walls of screens, silhouetted heads in dim rooms. So many cameras, so many cities, I thought. The streets thrashing like they're trying to wake from a dream. The world as one big sleep lab.

Against my will, the words "big sleep" opened a cha-cha. I thought of Raymond Chandler and his best-known detective novel. I remembered that Chandler began as a poet but discovered he lacked talent. He enlisted in the First World War with the Canadian Expeditionary Force, at the onset of the Depression lost his job as a California oil executive because of drinking and womanizing, and published his first novel, *The Big Sleep*, when he was fifty. His detective, Philip Marlowe, is thought to be named after Marlowe House, which Chandler belonged to while in school in England, and which itself is named after Christopher Marlowe, murdered Elizabethan dramatist and, allegedly, spy for or victim of a shadowy government agency. Chandler advanced the detective novel for being less interested in plots and resolutions than in everything else. I couldn't recall a single snappy line from his fiction, only that he once wrote that the ideal mystery was one you would read even if the end was missing.

I waited for the Poet to say something, maybe about Durant's daughter, Amanda's brother, my parents, whistleblowers all, it seemed, the real missing and the real dead in their real big sleeps. I waited for him to tell me that history now stole from the cheapest commercial fantasies. They kept each other running, events and their mockeries. Fantasies kill.

From the street came a dull roar, what might have been a low cheer a few blocks away. A shuddering energy moved through the windowpane. Outside, the crowds moved as before.

"What's happening?" I asked. "I mean, exactly what?"

Now he looked at me as if he'd just realized I was standing there. His eyes were dark mouths.

He said, "This is the new weather." I thought again of human systems grown so large no one can know their nature. He bent

forward and examined one of the pictures. A protester with a bandana over his face sat against a concrete wall. There were burn
marks or bloodstains on his arms. "I know this one," he said. Did
he mean the picture or the protester in the picture? "Two days after
this was taken . . . This boy's dead."

Of course he was. All was murder without end. For some reason
I thought of the two versions of "Çodhir," the one in the Poet's
hand and the one I'd made from his words. And now I preferred
his. What did I mean? I meant that knowing there was an order to
put the lines into, I wanted the disorder after all. Not chaos, but
order-into-chaos. I wanted to bust up the decor. If you trust the
decor you're a fool.

I turned to him but he stayed facing the collage. I reached across
and grabbed the front of his shirt—when I touched him I felt a
kind of spark in my skull—and pivoted him toward me. He had
weight, substance. He was bigger, stronger, but he allowed this. I
felt that if I pushed him through the window, he'd allow that too,
and the allowances were infuriating, but he took my hands, turned
them open, pushed me back one step. He pressed down on my
shoulders, as if telling me to stay put.

"Who are you?" I asked. "Are we in danger?"

Nothing in his face seemed expressly unkind, I thought, and at
that moment an explosion sounded and the window shivered in its
frame. The glass misted over and then it blew open and I was thrown
against the wall. The back of my head hit something hard. I didn't
lose consciousness but it was several seconds before I put together
what had happened. The jet of water had struck me in the chest and
was gone again within moments. As I looked around I saw the Poet
was gone too. My hands were bloody, glass in the palms. I got to my
feet and looked out just as he ran into the thick braid of turmoil

where the police and citizens fought. When he reached midstreet, as if they'd been waiting for him, the police line surged forward. There was another loud crack and more shouting, people running, falling, being run over, dragged off. A cannon stream knocked them down and then it was all short bursts, the way the cops ran, sudden percussives, the way they fired, shooting gas at angles from antlered guns. At close quarters the weapon of choice was their boots. They stomped and kicked like common thugs. Through it all a tall man fell—was it him? I thought so—and was circled and claimed by cops and I couldn't see a thing.

I ran around to the entrance and passed beside the metal detector. The guard was at the door holding back people wanting shelter inside. He looked at me gravely and held up a hand. When the cannon swept by again and cleared petitioners from the steps he unlocked the door and opened it fast and shoved me outside. My eyes and throat closed immediately. I tried to look across to where I'd seen the Poet on the ground but the space now belonged to the police, in helmets and gas masks, advancing in ragged phalanx, gathering the citizens they could, dragging them behind the line. I fell into a thin, broken file, people crouched and clutching blindly, fetal, crawling. One of them poured water into her eyes and then handed me the plastic bottle and I did the same and passed it on. All of us were coughing. Out of the gas and water the masked cops were coming at us in twos and threes like figures in a dream, selecting at random, pulling us away. One of them pointed at me and came running, another cop behind him, passing other protesters. They were after me and I turned to run too late. The lead cop had me by the hair and kicked at my knees until I fell, and the two of them grabbed my arms and started dragging me just as three men with T-shirts wrapped over their faces ran at them. Someone took up my legs. I couldn't breathe and tried to say so but nothing came out, the experience was beyond words in that moment. Then all in an instant my feet were on the ground again and the young men hurled themselves at the cops and knocked one of them down as the other retreated and signaled something to the troops behind him. I was free and the masked young men were beating the cop when the water hit us.

I shot backward along the brick street and the pain seemed both general and multiply located, both sudden and timeless, and in the tumble I was there and in the future something like the one that came to be as the water advanced upon me and spun me, wouldn't let me go, and I passed by people running, catching discontinued scenes, reeling past people carrying others by the legs and arms, people tending others down the side streets, a column of smoke shunting into view and away, past barriers, shouting, and came to a stop. I looked up at apartment windows above the chaos, people standing behind them, closed away, and the figures were shadows, the shadows various, observing the spectacle.

THE WORLD CONTINUED TO ACT UPON ME. I INFLUENCED events very little. Unlike in literature, character was not fate. Fate was unbelievably itself. Staring out from the unlikely present I found each possible future equally implausible, though one of them began to take shape along the Canada-US border where, under a concealing canopy of maples, I rented a house in a woods. I lived off a small sum Dominic advanced to me from his will. In early November came the days of first snow. The place had a busted furnace and a woodstove. I burned firewood and sawed and chopped to replenish the pile, a daily routine in my unpeopled life. In the mornings and late afternoons I handwrote stories I found hard to believe, including the one you're now reading. To protect the vulnerable, I changed details and names, including my own. Amanda is not Amanda, Durant not Durant, the poem "August" not "August," and so on. These measures are acts of delusion or faith in the idea that an audience awaits and some reader somewhere will see what's true.

Amanda and I didn't get our Italian reunion. From Istanbul I flew to Rome but never left the airport. A man with aviator glasses peeking out of his shirt pocket seemed to be following me through the Fiumicino terminal, or at least he was always behind me as I detoured, ducked into a washroom, stood a distance from the screens listing baggage carousels. I left my bag unclaimed for several minutes, waiting for him to claim his and leave, until finally we were the last two waiting, pretending the two last bags weren't ours. I claimed mine, went through security, headed straight for an Air Canada desk, and booked a flight to Montreal.

For six hours I camped out near the gate. Nothing that could be called my state could also be called stable. In a wifi lounge with free stations I wrote to Amanda and Durant, explaining nothing in detail. I wrote of a change of plans, of "forces able to inhabit our obsessions," and sounded unreliable to myself, knowing I couldn't explain the further intricacies of what I knew or how I'd come to know it. In my bag was the fugitive hard drive. "Reality and paranoia both present a seamless fabric of truth and fantasy," I wrote. "Implausibility is no longer a measure of anything. If it was the Poet whom I met in Istanbul, his presence there was like his presence in the poems. I have to believe that he communicated to me, though I can't know the full meaning of the communication." He had broken some protocol and taken a risk to make contact. He had wanted to be known, or for me to know that I was known. And he'd succeeded and paid for it. Under the cover of riot control, using police thuggery, the Shadowy Apparatus (I used the term ironically and not) had reclaimed him and had tried to claim me.

Half a day later I was back in Dominic's house, helping him organize, pack boxes, and decide what to do with the materials of his life. My last email exchanges with Amanda and Durant were written and collected on Dominic's laptop. I learned that Pierluigi and the Keyholers had gone dark, fearing reprisals. No one else took cover. Amanda was looking forward to The Hague. A friend who worked on political killings in Guatemala had promised to give her access to secret records. She still hoped to learn who'd killed her brother. I said I was getting off the grid, and wished her well, and asked her to imagine a day when we could meet again. Just picturing this day, I said, would bring it closer.

Durant decided to stay where he was for a few more weeks, dismissing my direct warning that he move out of Carlo's building and return to his life in California. "But I need a new point of focus, James. I've decided to resume my work on genetic transferences. The unknown world is endlessly interesting." Without prompting, he confided that, in his quiet times, he hoped his daughter would return to him.

I understood hope, the need to believe in whatever thin evidence of fixed meaning could connect the future with a past that seemed to go on forever.

In the woods I lived bookless, offline. With no cellphone or computer I sent my mailing address to Durant via Larunda College in an unsigned, handwritten letter, glued and taped at the seal. At random intervals I checked the mailbox I rented in the second-nearest town, where business was slow and I could see if anyone was watching, but there was no reply.

In time the work of writing prose and of pre-grieving Dominic, whom I knew I would never see or speak to again, changed my imagination. I was no longer subject to cha-chas, or at least their character matured. My lateral thoughts seemed to fire to more purpose, as if they'd finally left their youth. And living alone without human contact for days at a time, with no screens, no voices but those from a radio I seldom turned on, set my brain waves into a pleasing rhythm as they formed and rolled and broke upon the shore of my new world.

At night I walked along the edge of a ravine behind the house, then into woods and fields. The stars, if not the satellites, hung above in a trusted disregard of me and my little world. At their unimaginable distances they offer a picture of a cosmos that could never have been. Some stars are already long dead, others extinguished more recently, all have shifted, but there they all are, seeming present. Knowing of the lie inside the heavens (knowing not the specific lie but of the lie's existence) layers the simple amazement of stargazing, one of the few things we have in common with the earliest humans who, if they believed anything could be told from the stars, saw in them not the past but the future.

And yet when I got turned around in the fields one night I used the North Star to mark my direction and find my way home, an experience that reminded me of navigational poetic images and recovered something of those readings at Three Sheets—the site's very name used seagoing imagery—that had drawn me in the first place. I thought of Dante's story of Ulysses's last voyage, into the unknown world, and of canto XX of *The Inferno*, where Virgil leads the poet through a treatise on seers and diviners. For Dante a prophet was above all a great reader, someone for whom the book of the future, the *magno volume* of God's mind, lies open. All these challenges to God and His knowledge landed people in one or another circle of hell. I understood something of the dumb vanity of those who seek omnipresence and all-knowingness. Not that I believed in Dante's God, or even that of my parents, but some otherworldly dimension had been added to my pre-existing sense of wonderment. I had always found my transports in the physical and experiential world mediated through arts and technology. Now as I wrote I felt the company of distinct presences. These can't be described as angels or demons because the presences weren't divine or diabolic. They had no designs on me. The closest word might be drawn from that set of terms for *ghost*, except these beings weren't supernatural, but supramaterial. The phenomenon eludes direct description.

I came to believe in the there/not-thereness of invisible beings. They were with me all day and began to appear in the stories I wrote. I chose not to think of them any differently than I did the people who had been visible to me, and to one another, Durant and Amanda and others, or than I did my mother and father, still near me in the dark.

And in spite of myself and of Dante, for weeks while writing I began to see scenes from the future in vivid, waking dreams. In one of these I was in the parking lot of a diner somewhere in the west of this continent. With me was Amanda. It seemed we'd just met up. As we approached the entrance, the glass door opened and a woman about our age, maybe older, stepped out. She and I looked at each other and she hesitated for just a second in a moment of recognition or false recognition—we both felt it—and then passed by. I didn't turn but watched her reflection in the door as I held it open. In the parking lot the woman looked at me briefly, then got into her car. I joined Amanda inside and she gestured with her head and eyes to the end of the diner. There, in the last row of red-and-chrome booths, Durant sat not just by himself, but existentially alone, his face barely familiar for being totally open. He looked at us the way the woman had, and again a recognition sparked and died. He didn't know us, or didn't know how he knew us. Moment to moment the dream formed in front of me as I followed it in prose, but it stalled there before we approached him and, while other waking dreams have since come and gone, dreams in which I am absent except as the engine of them, and that suggest possible worlds strangely connected to one another through me, it all ended in that place, and my two American friends never appeared to me again.

PART III

The Boy in the Water

1

SINCE THE SUMMER CELIA TURNED TWELVE HER FATHER
had taken her on expeditions. He led teams of interchangeable
members, opening plague pits in London, coring ice in Siberia,
hose-blasting permafrost in the far north full of perfectly intact,
extinct creatures, while some grad student who'd pulled the duty
to look after her demonstrated the care involved in brushing and
screening soil for the tiny bones of long-gone lizards or birds.
Three Junes ago they revived the practice for the first time since
she left for university. Now he was summering in France, living
alone in the Cévennes. A team had come and gone. Once a week
he visited friends in a lab ninety minutes away in Montpellier, but
most days he spent in the mountains, on foot.

She pictured him wandering out of the mellifluous French landscape and into a cold, soundless house full of other people's furniture and dishes. He'd have dinner with a magazine splayed open
beside his plate, following the plot twists, red herrings, and cliff-
hangers in *Nature* and *Science*. The rest of his time was a mystery

to her. Before a visit she liked knowing the sum of his hours, the daily whole she was being added to. It was strange to think of a day as a sum, but there was comfort in imagining numbers unattached to time and money, luggage charges, seat designations next to sneezers, infection and mortality rates.

She'd been in transit for fifteen hours and had slept maybe two. In final approach she looked down at morning in Paris, bright city, oddly flat. The Eiffel Tower, so small in person, like a male movie star. Even the high-rises of La Défense seemed like just the beginning of a vision, a dream interrupted, sketched out and half realized at a safe distance to the west of the old realities, the beautiful districts, proportioned, ornate, storied in the richer sense.

On the ground things were loud and chaotic. That her suitcase seemed heavier on this side of the Atlantic complicated the boarding of trains. When she finally took her seat on the TGV she turned on her phone. The only new text was from Indrani, looking after Hartley for the week. "Walked him, he pooped. Now eating popcorn in front of HBO. He's coughing up kernels on my rug." She almost laughed, almost cried, good lord. She fell asleep at three hundred kilometers an hour.

At the Montpellier train station he was lit with a kind of chemiluminescence. Something just below the skin held differently. "You look good, Dad. Great pigmentation." He said he had something exciting to tell her.

They drove through a landscape of hard plains, rock outcroppings, sudden sheer faces. His hands cupped the steering wheel, left wrist curled at eleven o'clock, right at three, then to the stick shift, then back. He glanced at her repeatedly as he spoke. She watched his avid blue eyes, his long jaw working the words and lines. He said a local friend had given him a map of the unexplored cliffs and he'd been investigating as he could. The hikes were physically hard—was she in shape?—but his joints liked the climate. He could still balance on a foothold, still scramble on loose ground. After a couple of weeks the friend, a German he wanted her to meet, told him to focus on the least accessible of the promising rock faces, and several days ago for three hours he'd cut a path that emerged above a treeline. After no more than a minute along a barely navigable ledge, he came to a deep, uncrossable crevasse, and there on the other side, a cave mouth.

"There seems to be no research on this cave. I'm sure no one knows of it. And it's perfectly protected. If it opens up, if it doesn't just run to a full stop in the dark, there could be thousands of years of artifacts inside. Tens of thousands. Neanderthals and humans lived around here at the same time. I've been waiting for you. Tomorrow we'll climb with a ladder. We'll go in together."

He looked at her a long time and the car drifted to the shoulder before he corrected it.

"Okay. That's pretty exciting. Wonderful."

"Wonder's the very thing that makes us human. There are lots of theories about Neanderthal extinction but it came down to a lack of imagination."

She'd imagined her arrival, an embrace, an almost wordless greeting, and a slow gathering of the moment. Now she was here and there'd been no arrival. Their reunions often began on the topic of her sister, but Chrissy was generating little concern these days. Still he might have waited to tell her about the cave. Maybe he was afraid of recognizing her, or of failing to—she was aging, changing, about to enter important years for a childless single woman with a career—and so he'd put something between them that they'd have to pass back and forth. She'd wait a day before getting around to life updates, a new position he'd approve of at the company, a brief romance come and gone, a health scare come and gone. She supposed she wouldn't tell him about an unwanted pregnancy come and gone. Or at least a surprise pregnancy, and given the precautions a bit of a mystery one. It seemed to have come and gone on its own, as if it had nothing to do with her, or as if she had failed a test of grace, not that she believed in grace or even really understood what it pretended to be.

"They died off very suddenly, the Neanderthals. Twenty-eight thousand years ago, in Gibraltar, staring at the sea. They weren't crossers of oceans. Leaps of faith didn't occur to them. Whereas we *Homo sapiens*, well, here we are."

Here they were, driving down into a gorge of steep light. A whitewater river ran next to the road. She watched the crests and considered his hopes that the visit might be marked by a great discovery. His world had always been larger than hers. His enthusiasms had taken him to the top of the extinction field. Her mind didn't work the same way. When she was being hard on herself she would say she was, as a scientific researcher, at best only dogged.

They were barely to his house, one-story, terra-cotta floors, at the base of a mountain, and she had just showered and changed clothes when he announced they were going out to have dinner with his new German friend. He said the friend wasn't a woman, no, and that Celia would see right to the heart of him, this man, and find there "a nest of essential questions." She pictured such a nest, tangled into smooth form, saucer-shaped, grayly reflective. She'd noticed this about herself, how her mind became suggestive and picture-prone when her sleep got messed up. Her body thought it was still in Vancouver. She used to trust her body, its distant early warnings and blunt reminders, but lately it had struck its own secret agenda and lost its sense of humor. It would arrive properly rested in a day or two. Until then she'd have to float around on her own, a hovering face, talking and smiling, waiting to close its eyes.

The nearest village was stone. It must have once been merely itself but now was picturesque. Red roofs crowded together in some ancient improvisation below a huge chateau estate with its own forest. The chateau, their destination, had been divided into apartments, most of them owned by what her father described as "kick-about heirs" of the French upper middle class. Their host, Armin Koss, greeted them in the ungroomed gravel parking area and led them through enormous doors into his first-floor home. He was thin but strong-looking, about forty, his face darkly tanned. His body and hands moved with casual precision.

The apartment opened onto a stone patio at the back of the chateau. At dinner they sat overlooking a little river and a pretty falls about thirty meters upstream. They spoke of air travel, her father's summer house in Oregon, a resident species of bat, the local watershed. Twice Celia caught Koss looking at her fingers on her wineglass, once at her breasts, and momentarily losing his focus on whatever her father was talking about, sonar or rock erosion. When her father paused to eat, Koss asked Celia about her work.

"She can't tell you much," her father said, mouth half-full of trout. "Private companies. They feed on secrecy clauses and blood oaths."

She smiled. It struck her that she didn't really know where she was, the name of the town, the history of the chateau. It was unsettling, the state of not knowing. She was expected to speak.

"Whatever moves the ball down the field, as one of my team leaders says."

"I don't understand," said Koss.

"The ball is knowledge," she said.

"The ball is profit. It's not knowledge. It's not even pigskin. It's boner pills."

Only now, in the pre-twilight, did she notice that his hair had grown wispy.

"This is an old argument between us," she said. "I work as a researcher for a drug company. This is my ongoing sin. Lately I've been reading about stimulated astrocyte cells and anhedonia, the inability to take pleasure in pleasurable things. The wine's good, isn't it, Dad?"

"They're not even properly medical." His forehead was pursed in a familiar disbelief. "My dear brilliant girl here is in the so-called lifestyle drugs division. The motto is 'Longer Living, Better Life.'" She expected him to add his usual line, that her "monkeyshine operation" really "puts the sham in shamanism," but he left it out this time.

"For the record," she said, "I'm not brilliant, never was. But I began as a virologist. Dad wants me to work at a university and practice some imaginary pure science that will save us from the coming plague to end all plagues. He doesn't know that lately I'm doing that very thing for my profit-crazed company. We hope to find a wonder drug and sell people their lives back."

"You're doing viruses? Is that true? Why didn't you tell me?"

"I just got here."

He straightened in his chair and nodded, as if judiciously.

"I'm sorry. Sometimes I won't shut up. Armin, tell Celia where your money comes from."

When he drank or his blood was up her father was prone to blunt questions and commands. Koss seemed unsurprised. He said that "as a child" he'd designed an early, long-lost generation of video games. Bigger talents had surpassed him, and now he was simply at work "practicing enlightenment." The phrase sounded more North American West Coast than German, but maybe the distinctions were dated.

"Armin spends his days following his passions. Art and wine." The two had met at a nearby farmers' market. Koss said their first shared interest was a local terroir that produced the very Mas de Daumas Gassac she was drinking. Her father had never had a tolerance for spiritual types, or artists who hadn't lived in caves and been dead for seventeen thousand years. She guessed that the men had been brought together by loneliness. The rest of the chateau was dark. There had been only one car in the parking area. The other tenants were apparently elsewhere in these months.

New sounds reached them from the water. Five or six teenagers, boys and girls, were wading in the shallow river above the falls. Celia could barely see them, bodies dimly lucent and contoured under a nearly full moon. Her French was minimal and the kids were a little too far away, but the voices were full of laughter and daring.

"I don't know much about gaming," she said to Koss. "Even the old kinds. I mix up how things move, horses and bishops."

"Gaming is a beautiful distraction, nothing more. My big success was a kind of murder mystery in an old house. The player moves his character through the rooms, spots clues or false clues. He turns around suddenly to see shadows disappearing down hallways. And of course there are bodies. One at the beginning, more by the end."

Her father had entered the kind of shaped silence that often preceded a pronouncement.

"What was the best clue?" she asked.

"The clues changed play to play, but I took some pride in the distant barking dog. The player might think to ask why it was barking and why it suddenly stopped."

"I don't suppose it just dozed off," said Celia.

"The point of the game is to produce fear you don't have to be scared of. Empty fear is like humor. It makes life richer by opening the spirit."

"You won't believe it, Lia, but Armin has been teaching me about spiritual practices. It might be the wine every night but I seem to be buying in."

He was right, she didn't believe it and wouldn't indulge him.

"Aren't the most popular games pretty violent?" she asked. "Some fantasies inspire kids to join armies."

"Designers find the criticisms . . . innocent. These worlds aren't real."

"But they come from somewhere and they go somewhere. For things that aren't real they make a very large wake in reality."

The wake from his lucrative murder game was currently topping up their wineglasses.

"Maybe you're right," said Koss. "Yes, I agree. Of course."

His assent was transparently false and she saw immediately that Koss intended the transparency. And he'd calculated, correctly, that Celia would catch it and her father would not. The man was sly, she decided. Whatever he was doing in their company, he'd been doing it at half speed.

"Of scientists, I know the chemist Kekulé," said Koss. "His revelation about the structure of benzene came to him in a dream of a snake eating its tail. The symbol is called the ouroboros."

"I'm named after him, you know, Lia. After Kekulé."

"The self-consuming snake appears in many cultures." Koss was evidently a sampler of wisdoms. "In the ancient world. In the Book of the Dead. In Hindu folk myths it represents creation calling itself to life."

"Beautiful," said her father. She had never heard him utter the word, not even to describe an arrangement of nucleotides.

"And here I thought benzene was just a petrochemical carcinogen," she said.

Something in the teenagers' voices changed. They were no louder but a new random cadence had taken up. One of the boys leapt out past the falls and cannonballed into the water. The drop was five or six meters. He surfaced with a yelp and then another launched himself out and down.

"They'll break their necks," said her father.

"They're there almost every day this time of year. Now they seem to like jumping in the dark."

She knew the desire, or had once known it when she was their age. By the local standard in Vancouver she'd been wild for a couple of years after her mother died. Drinking, having sex with boys whose last names she didn't know from other parts of the city, once with an older man who'd offered her a ride in his Jaguar. He asked her not to leave footprints on the wooden dashboard. She'd almost ruined her grades, everything, her chance at life, as her father had put it. Of course, looking back, she could see she'd just been angry at Fate. Furious, actually.

"I walked down there," Koss continued. "This was in the spring. I would have thought the water was too cold for swimming. We talked for a while, me and two of the girls. They're local kids. They assumed I'd come to complain about the noise but I just wanted to invite them up to the chateau. They were interested but too shy, I think. They were sober. There's no law against diving as far as I know. I suppose their parents are just happy they're not fucking. Though of course they're doing that, too."

In her father's expression was a sudden fascination. The near-naked humans, jumping and howling, made for a primitive scene. He would be thinking about the cave he'd found, calculating whether to mention tomorrow's expedition to Koss, which she hoped he wouldn't, and how much he'd had to drink and whether he could trust his calculation. Or was he just remembering a swimming hole from his youth?

"What are you thinking about?" she asked him. He looked at her urgently, as if he didn't know where he was. It was a woman's question, she supposed, though not of the kind she would normally ask. He wouldn't have heard it for years.

"I was thinking that video games, the entertainments, they separate fear from awe. Last week Armin pointed out that the word *reverence* is from French and Latin—"

"Cognate of *reveri*," said Koss.

"Yes, reverie, which is what you caught me in, dear. To be in awe of, or in fear of. And the worship of the thing that strikes awe or fear. This can't be good for us. But then, seeing the kids out there, risking their necks and whooping and laughing, I wonder if maybe fear does belong with delight."

"I suppose we have to factor in boredom and stupidity and mating displays," she said. "These are part of the species, too."

Koss caught her eye and held it, trying to load a sexual charge into the moment. Through her blank stare she saw the charge die on his face.

By now the kids had all jumped into the pool. One of the boys climbed onto the rocks, scrambled to the top, and waded out to the lip of the falls. He was about to jump again. He paused for a moment with the rushing water folded against his calves, and stood tall and seemed to look their way, aware of his audience at the distant candlelit table. Celia counted five heads below in the water, two of them bigger, male. She realized she'd been hearing only two male voices. One of the boys must have been soft-spoken or silent. She wondered which one, and who he was inside.

And then the boy on the top was gone. She had expected a shout before he jumped but he simply stepped out, surely too close to the rock face, and fell inside the falls themselves. Or he must have. His descent wasn't visible. One of the boys in the pool below began swimming toward the falls with his head up, looking, ducking into the water and surfacing again, swinging his head this way and that with the long, wet hair whipping around, and only when he was before the crashing falls did the other head emerge, back with the others, who yelped with delight. A brilliant trick, to have fallen secretly and swum undetected below his friend. One of the girls, Celia guessed she was the jumper's girlfriend, was less delighted. She held a hand to her face and then drew it back and hit him on the shoulder. By now the friend had swum back to the group. He raised locked hands above his head and kicked up and brought them down around the jumper's neck to pull him under—this was playful, Celia thought—but the jumper ducked and pushed him away and turned to his girlfriend and embraced her.

Koss and her father had been watching all this, talking, she hadn't really listened. The jumper was the silent boy. He knew something, she was sure of it, that none of the rest of them in the water understood. It was a suffered knowledge no one would want.

The father of her lost child was the first man she'd had sex with in three years. She'd described him to Indrani as the only man in Vancouver who in his off-hours wasn't wearing shorts, fleece, or spandex. He co-owned a restaurant near the lab where Celia often had the appetizer salad by herself. One day he was characterizing the balsamic reduction as "sugared blood" and the next he was someone she'd spent a night with. There were no actual dates. The dates were retrospective, the plates he'd set before her, the weather talk, testing together the tang of fruits through the growing season. He didn't call her afterward. She returned to the restaurant once, a week later, and the waitress told her he'd gone to Paris "to study what they do with ducks or something." The way Celia told it to Indrani, absent the pregnancy, the way Indrani laughed at the beginning and end, it was a rounded story, one of slight and comic disappointment. Indrani understood this was how people came and went in a life, or at least in Celia's life. One day in the future Celia might tell a story of the same shape about Indrani, assuming she had someone to tell it to.

Koss stood to light the candles on the table—left-handed, she noticed—sat back down and looked at her, then stood again and pushed two of them slightly closer to her until he was satisfied with the effect.

Spiritual matters put aside, her father held forth on the role of ancient pathogens in the great extinctions. This led them to de-extinction and cloning, the thought of which prompted Koss to exclaim about "the possibilities."

"It's coming fast, extinct species, even humans," said her father. "We shouldn't let *that* genie out of *that* bottle. And whatever they say, profit is the evil here."

Koss checked Celia for a reaction. Apparently she looked as she felt, plucked from one world and set down a few hours later into another where she was expected to know the local customs and rules of sport.

They cleared the table together. The kitchen was huge. It must have once served the whole chateau but now sat mostly unused and unlit, full of pointless space. In the dim reaches were black cast-iron pans and table legs. The long room had the feel of a broken steam engine. She was a little drunk, a little free-associative. A dozen copper pots hung from a metal cylinder like huge saxophone keys. A wall of cookbooks, a rolling ladder to reach the top ones. Except for the island where he'd prepared the dinner, it was all clean. She wondered if someone other than Koss was tending it.

As the men prepared espressos she drifted into the living room. On one wall were light boxes of images overlaid into senselessness, and artworks of neon lines suggesting horses' necks and women's backs, and small black photo frames without photos. She looked at these in some defiant mood, so as not to look first at the center-piece. On the floor midroom was a device about three feet high, in motion, a brass frame and fulcrum with a malleiform lever, duller, mismatched, tinted red. A ring spun on an axis as the head of the lever bobbed up and down as if hammering the stone floor or drawing oil. The machine or whatever it was possessed a throw-back, deco beauty. She sensed its weight.

Koss came in behind her and loomed at her shoulder. She turned to find he was slightly too close and storming pheromones. She turned back to the penitent machine.

"Don't tell me. I'll figure it out," she said.

"I've never been able to. It doesn't even have a name as far as I know."

"You bought it?"

"I made it from my grandfather's design. He was a soldier in the second war." She resisted doing what he wanted, asking for the full story, but then asked. "As the Russians took Berlin he was shot through the cheek. The bullet broke his jaw and many teeth and disfigured him. He missed dying by only inches, but he never felt lucky or unlucky during that time, or for the rest of his life. He didn't believe in luck." She drifted to the right as if to get a different angle on the piece and Koss stepped along with her. "He was a prisoner of war during the occupation. And his wife, my grandmother, she was left to deal with the Russians on her own. He said he used to stay sane by designing these objects in his head. Then after he was a free man, he drew them but was afraid to make them in three dimensions. He told me he thought they were connected to a madness but the madness wasn't his."

The story was not burnished. He wanted the telling to sound uncomplicated and fresh, but its ease was practiced.

"It seems to run on its own," said Celia. "In perpetual motion."

"There's a trick to it," said her father, entering the room.

"Not a trick but a secret, yes. This object is my closest connection to my grandfather." Celia and her father watched the machine but Koss didn't so much as glance at it. He was looking at them. Of the machine he must have been well past looking.

"You inherited his design talent," said her father.

"Not in this case. My blood grandfather was a Russian soldier. Brutal and anonymous. I only learned this at the end of my grandfather's life. He told me himself. Even my father didn't know."

"Good god." Her father's head slotted back a few inches as if the machine had made a threatening remark.

Koss said, "It's not such an unusual story to come out of a war, of course."

In the days ahead, what would come to her most often from the chateau was the penitent machine and the moment she and her father took their coffees outside to the table with Koss still in the house.

"I'm undergoing a conversion, dear. From a man of science to a man of god. Or at least of something much larger than I've been willing to imagine."

He could say nothing of the god, except that it was ancient, and Koss had been given to glimpse it in earthly forms. Koss had urged him to make of his remaining years the practice of a devotion to seeing the world differently. He would look for god or the evidence of god. He would study the raiments, the praisings, the showings forth, not only in the great and obscure religions but also, as Koss had advised, in nature and art. He knew how to read the natural world but had never tried not to read it, had never actually seen anything he had studied for having imprisoned it all in names and taxonomies. And it was art—painting and poetry, "that bobbing thing in there"—that would help free nature back into its innate strangeness and wonder. Of course art had its own terms but he didn't know most of them so they weren't in the way. He would sample and read, and if he ended up covered in mud and dancing around a fire, then so be it. He would find the shards of the first things.

He asked her not to look so shocked. Koss joined them at the table and began speaking. She worked at not registering meaning in his voice. The kids were gone now, night had fallen, the moon rising. She watched a bat fly overhead and disappear onto a dark shutter on the upper floor of the chateau and then realized the shutter wasn't dark but matted in bats. The night was full of textured shades of misperception. At least the bats could echolocate. She was jet-lagged in a foreign country. Apparently she couldn't even guess at what counted locally as unexpected. She'd just heard what she'd heard and now they were all drinking coffee and talking about the great extinctions.

"In your lifetime, Lia, or certainly that of the next generation, at least half the species on earth will have gone extinct."

"Parents shouldn't scare their children," she said. He missed her subtext.

"I've tried to learn these extinctions," said Koss. "The last was called . . ." He'd lost the English name.

"The end-Cretaceous event," said Celia. "I wonder what ours will be called. Just 'The End,' I guess."

"It won't be called anything, not by us. Not even by our clones." The false authority of the booze had further elevated her father's voice.

"You believe our species is ending soon?" Koss asked.

"Well. The harbingers are there. Biological, climatic, historical—"

"Conversational," she added. "Men love talk of doom. Though not so much plummeting sperm counts."

"It's time for some other organism to take over the world." Her father outlined the so-called no-analog future currently rounding the corner upon carbon emissions and acidification. "Nothing like this has ever existed before. There's nothing to compare it to. We've made something new and deadly and can't stop repeating the mistake."

"What do you think, Celia?"

She thought about dyings-off. Not the deaths of lone things but of kinds. It was perplexing that only one species should know about the past. To what purpose does one animal evolve to study the great swaths of time? Was such study driven by some shared

awareness not yet identified? We can't always find words and numbers for what we know. She couldn't find words at all.

She excused herself and left the table and walked across the pea
gravel to the low stone wall. Behind the chateau, ground lights had
come on to reveal a garden with ragged hedges and two rows of
plane trees that ended at a square fountain. On the four corners
stone lions stood astride tipped stone barrels. Only two of the barrels still fed the small, dirty pool. A stunted column of water stood
in the center. Then another rose up inside it, reaching higher, falling on itself. After a few seconds the columns disappeared.
Presumably they kept the bugs down.

She turned and watched the river. Her day had been sustained
past its breaking point. The men talked, their voices drew down
the sky. She was not safe.

After the pregnancy she had slipped into a kind of beyond, a
place she once couldn't have imagined. She had no illusion that her
father could be there with her, but she had hoped to tell him about
it someday. Now he had taken some turn of his own. She realized
she'd recently been expecting a change in him. But why the expectation? In everyone was a reservoir of intuitive knowledge. The
mistake was to think of this reservoir as magical. Around her
eighth week she began listening for intuition, which she pictured
dripping from the top of her skull, pooling in the cranial dish of
her occipital bone, then trickling down her spine to her sacrum.
She had simply found herself believing that the falling drops connected her to her deepest processes, to the possibilities in her
future, even more truly to her father. She'd made herself vulnerable
to lazy, superstitious thinking, and had failed to pay attention to
what was real, a fetus, and made some error, distracted by dream.
Though she listened, she heard nothing, won nothing, and after

she lost the baby she stopped believing in things unseen. Science, madness, religion. They all had their sorting systems, all depended on belief in things unseen, but they weren't equivalent. Who wouldn't want to believe in the soul? Who had the sense and mettle not to?

A tail of light in the river. Something caught the moon. She couldn't tell if it was on the surface or just below, or see at all what it was. It moved by in the dark. Maybe she was seeing the edge of a piece of wood washed off an upriver bank. It rolled, flashed, and disappeared downstream.

As she returned to the table a scented wind presented itself. Storms here would appear unannounced from over the mountains. They'd show up and rain floods, ruining the roads and breaking off conversations, interrupting the passage of thought.

Her father admitted he was trying to say a thing without saying it.

"You mean something like *mystical consciousness*," said Koss.

"What were you describing the other night? The Hindu word?"

"The state of absolute *samadhi*."

"I think that came up in yoga class," she said. "The words were even worse than the pan flute. I had to quit. I mean, who fails a yoga class?"

"Well, I'd never heard of it. We seem to need new things, strange words now and then. They're part of the mystery we're made of."

"We're made of gene codes and brain architectures," she said. "Including our religious impulses. You've always known this, Dad. Maybe it gets harder to know after a while."

For a moment there he was, the fixing look he used long ago when she was a misbehaving child. But the look gave way. She couldn't read what took its place. "Whoever we are," he said, "there's a core person in there, and that person is connected to elemental and timeless forces."

"How can there be a core person if they can be changed completely by a trauma or a little plaque in the brain?"

"But change is our condition," said Koss. "The only god is the one who's ever becoming. Ever becoming inside of us."

"The only thing becoming inside us is death," she said. The men were silent. They looked in her direction without meeting her eye. "I'm not saying this especially troubles me."

"We've rejected so much as a species, dear. It's vanity to dismiss the wisdoms of earlier men and women. The primitive mind knew a thing or two that seem lost on us."

So this was how it would manifest. He would speak more often of the mind, less of the bones. She had loved the bones. Through the years he'd made gifts of them, sometimes wrapped in newspaper pages local to wherever he'd made his field trip. He dedicated the bigger ones to her with a black marker: "(To Celia. Tail Fragment, Megatherium. Argentina. 310,000 years)." The last one—her final year of high school—had been a partial third metacarpal of *Equus occidentalis*, a proto-horse of the Americas, 120,000 years old, wrapped in pages of the *Klondike Sun*. She cherished the bones of extinct species for the thought of her they represented. That year she'd saved her money to sponsor a rescue horse, so he'd given her the *Equus* and not the femur from the American camel, for instance. The year before, after she came through a dental surgery she had dreaded, he chose not the rib fragment of the mammoth but its huge molar, heavy as a cantaloupe, amazing and ridiculous. The ancient, partial bones had the character of his fatherly sentiment, measured exactly in the amount she was able to accept. She kept them wrapped in burlap in a chest at the foot of her bed.

"Maybe we're not so far from watching shadows on the cave walls," said Koss. "Celia, I want to show you something." In his hand—where had it come from?—a small device. He turned in his chair and pointed it into the dark and there on a rectangle of dull plaster on the back of the building appeared projected light, a scene. As the animation began, an ache took up in her legs and back.

On the chateau wall was the chateau, the very side of it they faced. The image was silent even as they appeared, first Koss and her father, walking out to the table, and then, trailing behind, Celia herself. The scene was lit at not yet dusk. The three of them were approximately rendered. The animated Celia turned to look at the chateau, taking it all in, looking back now at the estate, the river, into the viewing perspective of the camera or whatever you'd call it. There was something slightly wrong with her. Her hair shorter, she was too tall. Their faces were about half-right. Her legs were too thin, and in fact not plausibly human, just sort of tubular placeholders for legs. This was the intended aesthetic, lazily gesturing at the real. She wore brown pants and a black tunic thing, not really her look. She sat down at the table she was sitting at, same chair. They were talking now, her father and Koss, and Koss was turning to her for a reaction, just as he'd done earlier, and was doing now, in fact, and on the wall they raised their glasses and toasted something or other. Their programmer. Their success at seeming to be. Their motions were stiff with digital algorithms. For a half minute or so they ate who knows what, a lull in the playing-out trick. Then they all stood. The virtual camera dollied in behind them as they walked toward the low stone wall and looked out at the river and the falls. The miracle of it appeared only then, for there were the teenagers, swimming in the pool. Celia

looked for the silent boy, wondered if he'd been rendered, but of
course she'd never really seen the kids clearly. He could have been
any of them, even one of the girls, given that in the water they were
indistinguishable. There was a dog on the bank, white with black
spots, running to and fro, barking, soundless. Celia was sure
there'd been no dog earlier but the dog must accompany the teens
more often than it didn't, and Koss had guessed it would be part of
their evening as, in a sense, it was.

The movie on the wall, too, was spotted now as moths pressed
into the illumination and she felt a chill of revulsion. The shadows fell left-right on the animated rock face. A figure climbed
onto the bank. It was the boy, her quiet boy, she decided, and the
dog jumped up at him freed from the earth for just a second and
he stepped back and let the dog fall clean and foursquare and
then the two of them climbed up the rocks. At one point the dog
slipped a little and the boy steadied it and gave it a boost in the
hindquarters and then they were above the falls. He picked up
the dog and held it squirming in his arms and walked out into the
river and she saw now that the river ran straight, it ran very
straight here, and there at the bottom of the frame the animated
Celia turned her head to look at Koss with a wide alarm and he
only half turned his face, not even that, only just barely acknowl-
edging her, and then lifted his chin at the scene, making her look,
so that just as she was about to turn to him now he had already
shown her his response, and she kept watching the silent boy in
the movie. It was the boy's world cast there on the wall, his silent
world was all. The kids in the pool waved their arms as if trying
to catch some kind of sense, and the dog was squirming scared,
but his tail wagged and he wanted this, wanted to be part of their
playing. She tried to picture how it would happen, the boy's

posture or whatever, what was the gamble in it, but he just took three running steps and launched off from one leg and he threw the dog forward so the two of them fell separate but level. They hit the water at the same time.

The scene was fully textured now. It played on the backs of insects, and there he was, the boy came up. The dog at first did not and then the wake just before it breached and swam downstream, then looped back and joined them, swimming right through the too-perfect circle they formed, and continued to the bank and climbed out. And then of course it shook itself and the water from its coat flew everywhere and the kids were cheering, sort of bobbing up and down and throwing their hands in the air like it was all a rave, and only then did she realize it was the first time for the dog, they'd not done this before, and things might have turned out some other way in the video. Except of course they were wrong, the happy ending was assured from the outset, and as if it wasn't false enough, the three of them at their table at the bottom of the frame also raised their hands and waved them in celebration as the kids all ducked under the surface and swam to the shore and climbed out. They turned and waved back at their audience, and for just an instant she saw it—what had happened—and the wall went dark.

"A wonderful show," said her father. Koss didn't register the comment. He was looking at Celia and she was looking at him.

"You did that on purpose, then," she said.

"Did it capture you?"

"It was very impressive, Armin," said her father.

"You've tried to hide it," she said. "The real story."

"What is the real story?"

"What are you talking about, dear?"

"The story is that we're distracted by false joy, the dog and the cheering, and we miss the truth. The truth is there were six kids in the water at the start, but only five got out at the end."

Koss turned his head slightly, as if to listen better.

"I wasn't counting," said her father.

"One of them never surfaced."

"Could this be a mistake?" asked Koss. The question had been prepared.

"Is it true?" Her father was trailing, disappointed in himself. "I missed it."

Her eyes had not fully readjusted. His face looked skyped.

"I would have us think of it as a mistake, but maybe Celia has seen the truth. Maybe even without knowing, I do this. In my little worlds people go missing."

Koss walked them to the car. He shook her father's hand and then opened his arms to her interrogatively, leaned in, held her shoulders in his hands, and kissed her on both cheeks. She stood very still.

The road was empty and dark, the headlights dim. The illuminated rock faces led them onward. He tested the high beams. They seemed to make no difference.

He said, "It had its effect, his movie. Different on you than on me."

He stared ahead, failing to work through some thought about people and their behaviors. He wouldn't know whose version of the video to accept. Koss had given ground too readily, as if to allow Celia a way out of an embarrassment. Again he had known that she and her father would read him differently.

Even in the car she felt the night chill. She watched the passing rock faces and dozed. She dreamed of floating spores, a dozen or so people standing in a field. We breathe in spores of light that tax us, thin our thoughts. Then the spores were high above and they were airplanes and the whole world was a city in wartime. She saw what would happen, her father's remaining days.

She woke to the road, the cliff wall gone.

The bobbing brass machine. Koss had said a secret, not a trick. Her body would catch up to her in a day or so. She'd have her senses about her, alarmed at the course of her thoughts just now and relieved that she hadn't gone back into the chateau and taken hold of the machine, as if to break or understand it.

When they arrived at the house she was just for a moment a young girl, coming home with her father from a sad, antiseptic hospital room. The house stood there with its darkness locked up and peering out at them. She knew what it felt like to the touch, the home darkness, and then he walked ahead and the lights came on in their wide and ancient pretending.

2

THERE'D BEEN DAYS LIKE THIS IN GRAD SCHOOL, UP BEFORE
dawn getting ready for an outing. Back then they'd all loaded into
a minivan too small for them and their four tents and propane grill
and hiking boots and at least two secreted thesis chapters to be
edited by moonlight and lantern, headed north for eleven hours,
and there they gathered, around a fire, seven students and their
mentor, Erik Bouma. The yearly weekend in bear country was
unstated mandatory. Research money was siphoned off to fund it.
Erik joked in all seriousness that it was "teamship-building," getting the word wrong, but on the third trip Celia wanted the days
for silence, or at least talklessness. For dream. Erik liked to induce
in them a shared dream, to insist they were all at the center of what
was coming, that there would be applications for their knowledge
no one could yet imagine, and then he tried to steer the dream and
imagine for them. He told stories of disease therapies and reversals,
of antiaging, memory enhancement. In their off time, he said, they
could sell their genetic science expertise in every direction. Already

he'd been offered huge sums to speak to Mounties and G-men, play the expert at drug piracy trials, authenticate unsigned de Koonings. Not all of these jobs he'd said yes to. He'd had set before him by a captain of Japanese industry a briefcase full of money to entice him to clone the long-extinct, thirty-five-hundred-pound South American short-faced bear. The briefcase, the short-faced bear, half of the dreams and their contents were stolen from movies, though they were also real, or possible.

In the pause after he said, "The future is in front of us," she almost said, "No shit," but then he added, "and so is the past." He could take some ribbing, could Erik, but he wouldn't stop with the pithy sayings. "We serve the living, the dead, and the unborn." The unborn came up a lot. Celia found she couldn't picture them except as newborns or futuristic adults of very pale skin wearing spaceship uniforms with stirruped pant legs. The real unborn, as they could be conceived of now, in their current state, were more like shapeless energies inside the living. If she followed the thought long enough they became, basically, the sexual impulse. Complicated, to be struggled with or surrendered to. Even when joyful, unstable.

Or so she had thought then. Now, in bed in a guest room in rural France, the unborn was someone specific. His name was James. He would be seven months old.

She'd left them at the campfire and gone to pee and then walked farther into the woods until the voices were gone. She hadn't brought a flashlight but the moon was bright. She sat on a fallen tree, felt the bark and guessed cedar, and closed her eyes and listened into the silence. In nature she'd learned to picture an ever-deeper auditory penetration of the darkness. Smaller sounds would take form. Others would trail the end of a breeze. At first you had to let the sound be sound, and not try to assign it to

animals, birds, jet planes, water. She found a state of nonthought
and the silence took its place. It seemed she was there a long time
and nothing emerged but a small wind, its empty wake. With
nothing to hold on to she slid into memory echoes from the day,
mostly voices, Erik's Swiss-German English, making great
claims. At one of the highway stops he had looked over at her,
standing slightly apart, and she saw a sympathy, or at least a sad
acknowledgment of her. She was not the most talented or ambitious of his students, not the easiest to direct. She expanded discussions into strange territories, beset by a kind of speculative
ethics. Not just, what are the dangers in bringing extinct viruses
back to life? but what does it *mean* to play god or, as she'd always
thought of god, nature? He probably expected her to become a
teacher at a minor university or a science journalist, maybe even
an enemy of the cause. She was learning about herself through his
view of her, as she imagined it.

She tried again to quiet the thoughts. The silence was a presence
in itself. When the wind came up she heard something inside it,
and let it be, just listening, and then she understood it was one tree
rubbing against another in the distance. It hadn't been there before.
The wind had changed. Now it was gone but something else was
there, then wasn't, then there it was again. On the edge of her
perception, miles away, a wolf was howling. She tucked inside the
furrowed note and it ran with her and died. Then the same note
grew forth again and, in a higher register, a second howl joined the
first. Soon there were many overlapping voices, calling and answering, it seemed. Asserting the only shared truth. Blood bone I am.

She stayed with the wolves for some duration, until, at last, she
could no longer hear them. Then came the greater absence, and
then even the absence attenuated to nothing. How lucky not to

have been with the group. They'd have talked of wolf studies, certainly, the meaning of howls, of pitches and amplitudes, the human measures of animal territories. Maybe someone would have brought up Prokofiev or Red Riding Hood, or Lon Chaney versus every wolfman since. Whatever the subject, they would certainly have talked. Briefly she succeeded in banishing the thought of them and now, in the aftermath, came something low, in approach. The underbrush took animal weight. She tried to measure distance with sound. She listened for a kind of breath, the huff of a black bear or grizzly, but the thing in approach was gone and then no it was behind her and she turned and saw the flashlight beam. For a moment her voice wouldn't come, and then she said, "I'm here."

"Oh thank god." It was Chandra. "Erik and Jeremy are out here somewhere looking for you, too."

Chandra was the only other woman in the group, the new student, a hard wisdom just starting to take up in her dark baby face. She was smart and ambitious. Presumably she understood what it meant that the future and the past were before her. She knew she was in a world of boys and their toys, and she had shared a joke or two with Celia. In the end, though, Celia knew, if it came to it, Chandra would always side with the boys.

"No bears. Just the wolves."

Chandra hadn't heard the wolves. When they returned to the fire, the group, Celia learned that no one had heard them. Erik asked her how far, what direction, how many distinct howls. He didn't ask her to describe the feeling of hearing them, a question she wanted but wouldn't have been able to answer. It intrigued the hapless Jeremy to suggest that she was probably just trying to scare them. He wanted to sleep with her but hadn't puzzled out a method.

Erik was sitting across the fire from her. He turned his head this way and that to address the group, his sternocleidomastoids popping grotesquely in his neck.

"Celia's not the type to cry wolf, Jeremy. It's no game to her. She believes the wolves are out there. Even if they aren't." He looked into her face. The rest of them kept their eyes forward, into the fire. "We need a few Celias in any population. They imagine just enough to keep us honest."

Her story had no defenders but she didn't care what was said about her—she'd graduate in months and Erik had already written her strong enough letters of support—and yet the pronouncement seemed to render the wolves imaginary, even for her. She found she couldn't call them back to mind, and didn't until the end of the weekend. In the years since, she had never doubted them. The wolves became more certain with time. She didn't think of them as past or as hers alone. Their offspring were still out there somewhere, nothing other than what they were. She tried not to assign meaning to them, not to read portents or to assume they'd been sounding a warning. They were wolves, not harbingers. The harbingers were elsewhere, in numbers and graphs, infection and transmission rates. They had a different pull and cast, and they grew ever closer. Soon everyone would know them. A great wing would appear in the sky and the talking would stop all at once.

After breakfast they tied an aluminum ladder to the roof of her father's Suzuki Swift and set off into the mountains to explore the possible Neanderthal cave.

She followed their route on a map covered with his printed additions and notes. They drove on the edge of La Vallée du Terrieu. He'd marked the names of each peak—Montagne d'Hortus, Pic

Saint-Loup—each perched chateau, but as they climbed on ever narrower roads the names fell off until finally the doubtful path disappeared from the map and became only a track through a field that ended in trees. Above them the forest climbed steeply to the base of an immense, white, vertical rock face. He studied the approach routes. From the trunk he took their supplies, shrugged into a small backpack. He gave her a coil of rope. He untied the ladder, put it over his shoulder, and led the way into the trees. There was little underbrush but the climb was steep, improvised, awkward with the ladder, and soon they were too spent to speak, though they had said very little that morning anyway, and before long Celia was sweating in her unbreathing layers. Four times at intervals of thirty or forty minutes they stopped to rest. "I wasn't sure we'd make it," he said. "I kept you out too late." He wouldn't normally express such a concern. He needed a simple summation with which to cap the events of the previous night, as if they could be put away. She said nothing, he let it go. Maybe he understood that she had taken herself out of play in response to last night's man-of-god nonsense. Two peregrine falcons floated on thermals at the top of the mountain.

In time they broke above the treeline, then rested once more and ate their packed lunches while looking out at the valley and the distant Mediterranean, a seam on the horizon. The set of his face was as she'd seen it at the chateau, when she'd caught him in his reverie. She let it run and in time he said he was trying to imagine the view of fifty thousand years ago. A colder climate. The trees would not be oak, as now, but pine and beech, species adapted to the cold. In the valley, deer and sanglier, and European megafauna, mammoths and giant elk. And humans and protohumans. Glaciers had pushed Neanderthals this far south, and *Homo sapiens* had migrated here from Africa. They overlapped for maybe twenty thousand years.

"They must have recognized their difference from one another." His voice was sure. He had caught his breath faster than she had. "The genetic record says they interbred. We still have Neanderthal in us. The fossil record gives no evidence of war, though it does of murder. Bones showing evidence of tool-scarring, as if they'd been de-fleshed."

"News of the day."

"We still behave this way, yes. But they were much closer to the originating moment. If we wanted to, with the genomes, cloning, we could recover ourselves—I mean ancient man—but we'll never recover our minds or beliefs. We don't even know ourselves now, most of us."

The ledge ran above a sharp drop. Navigating it required him to balance the ladder on a forearm held away from the rock face, so that from her position behind him the ladder seemed a floating incongruity, a surrealist object juxtaposed against the stone sublime. The face curved away from them for a time and then the ledge widened to a large table of rock. There was the cave mouth, across a wide cut. They walked to the edge. Her father extended the ladder and timbered it across the gap, then squatted to rest, letting his arms hang limp. The crevasse meant business. There was no telling its depth but the noon light disappeared at about thirty feet. It was maybe fifteen feet across, too far for anyone to jump, with too short a run up and no safe place to land. Maybe the cave really was unexplored.

The exertion had slightly elated her, and now in the pause before they continued she detected a hopefulness in the air that must have been coming from him. For years they'd shared a weight never discussed, not father to daughter, or adult to adult. The grief, coming so early in both of their lives, had inside it a degree of fear. But they hadn't named it, hadn't known there was anything to figure out, Celia realized, and now they understood but had no way of crossing back over the silence.

She held the ladder firm on one side as he walked across it rung to rung. Seeing him take the deliberate steps brought on her first shiver of apprehension. If one of them fell, even if they survived the fall, there'd be no way out. What exactly would the other do?

"We're being careless," she said after he'd crossed. "This is pretty stupid."

"Don't cross if you're not committed. I'll go and report back."

She threw the rope coil to him and told him to hold the ladder and crossed over on her hands and knees, looking forward. He pulled the ladder clear and laid it by the side of the cave mouth. From his backpack he produced two flashlights and a truffle pick for digging out artifacts. There was no threat in the sky, unless it was behind the mountain. No one knew they were up here.

They approached the entrance, ducked under a pediment ledge, and stood in quiet light. Only a short distance ahead the rock ceiling above them curved down to form a back wall. The space was certain and empty. It led nowhere. He said nothing, kept still. She walked in, letting him have his moment of disappointment. Near the back wall she crouched lower, turned and sat on the cave floor and looked out at him silhouetted there against the blue sky.

"It could still be your cave. Grotte du Dad."

"I feel something. Do you feel it back there?"

In fact she did feel it, a draft. She shined her light into the corners and saw that the floor opened about twenty feet to her left. She

scuttled over on her ass. The walls of the hole formed the first revolution of a kind of curved well that seemed to open into a space
beneath them.

She had no time to speak before he was with her, shining his
light into the hole.

"Holy christ," he said.

"Okay."

They were silent. She wanted to stop him from thinking but it
was too late.

"I wonder if they named it, the first humans," he said.

"Maybe they called it 'the hole in the floor.'"

"It's got a real *come hither* to it. I'm going down."

"That's too stupid even for you. It might just drop you half a mile
inside the mountain."

"That's why we have the rope."

"Oh, come on. A cave. We thought we'd walk in, we'd walk out.
Nobody said holes."

"We're prepared."

"We are definitely not prepared. We should have a team. With
radio communication, helmets, gloves, water, first aid, harnesses,
those mountain-climbing spiky things, and at least one person who
knows what they're doing."

"Humans explore. We wonder what's beyond."

She saw how it set up in his mind. He tied the rope to a stone
anchor, a kind of newel post at the top of the opening. The rope
was just something he'd found along with the ladder in the storage
room under the rented house. It was thick, but old and dry, and
would fray easily. He tied the other end in a loop under his arms
and braced his hands against the smooth wall of the hole mouth.

"Jesus, Dad. If I got hysterical would you stay?"

"You're not the kind. Now, if I get in far enough you won't be able to hear me through the rock. Give me thirty minutes. If I'm not back, then don't—do not—come after me. There's no cell reception so you'll need to go down to the car and drive it to town." He leaned to one side, extracted the car keys from his pocket, and tossed them to her. "Go to Armin and he'll call the police. Take the map so he can tell them how to get here. I'll be fine, likely just stuck with my head in a prehistoric honey jar. I'll have a sleep while you lead them up."

"Let me go instead. I'm lighter and thinner and my joints work better."

"Nonsense. I won't allow it. Much too dangerous." He suppressed a smile, clamped the flashlight in his mouth, and started down.

She'd been waiting twelve minutes. He'd been in voice contact for about eight. He'd barely disappeared when she heard his first exclamation. Right below her the ground leveled out and opened into a chamber. "I can stand up," he said. After a few seconds he said, "No artifacts or remains but . . . hold on." She stared into the hole. "There's a ledge, sort of recessed in the stone, and it's full of seashells. I need to know who put these here." She saw flashes of light come out of the hole and remembered he had a camera in his vest. He said there was a narrow passage ahead. His voice was fainter now. "I'll investigate." She asked him to describe the space and he said, "It's pretty small." "How small?" There was no answer. Four minutes later the rope went slack.

She was inside the very quality of strangeness she'd felt the night before at the chateau, with its shards catching the light. She'd seen them passing in the river, rising in the fountain. They ran along the levers of the penitent machine and curved around the bowed head of a boy. Things full of meaning but resistant to words. The presentiments had been pushed forth by a lack of sleep and the pressure of things unsaid. And again now, the unsaid or unheard. A simple human commerce stopped. What else had he said about the cave on the way up? Nothing useful now. He said certain caves were places of deep solitude, that it wasn't just fear or necessity that would make people gather out of the killing elements, but something inward that needed to be acknowledged to others around a fire. "These were the first stirrings of religion, the deepest parts of ourselves brought into the social. A collective of souls, staving off fear, hunger, loneliness, if not doubt."

She reasoned that he'd come to the end of his rope but not the end of his time. He'd untied himself and kept exploring. Near the thirty-minute mark she'd feel the tension back on the line. She'd hear him, he'd emerge. She tried to have faith in this idea and the faith or tending there opened a space inside her where the dim figure she made out was herself.

The rim of the hole was the only smooth surface, worn by thousands of years of hands and bodies. On the pocked wall above it she tried to detect the smallest movement of the stippled shadows. In its simplest form time was light, nothing more. Our sense of it changed from being with others. Others marked it, were marked by it, set it at variable speeds in the social flux. But isolated, removed from other presences, time was light and nonlight in perpetual bend and stretch.

She would deny rogue freedom to the one she most loved out of her own childish need. She sampled the idea that he was after balanced understanding, not revelation, that a word like *god* didn't need to injure her. Maybe he'd just grown tired of the terms and metaphors of science, the terms they'd always shared. A balanced understanding would close distances but in the hours since she'd arrived, distances had formed.

The shadows had notched along without detectable movement. The sun leaned on the mountain faces opposite, the distant fields and vineyards far below. From where she sat the superstitious mind would see the god in all things moving each day left to right, up to down, changing its slant with the seasons. The first divine readings would come from such a prospect. At an earned altitude, in your very body you felt great meanings were arrayed before you, you could look and know yourself. The trouble was in trying to say them, the things you came to know. She would say them only this way. Left to right and up to down.

It had been forty-two minutes. No sound for thirty-four. Something was wrong but she hadn't yet moved, weighted in place against the whirl of her thoughts. If she left the cave he'd be alone up here inside the mountain for five or six hours, too long if he was injured or in danger. The rope lay slack against the wall. The first chamber was safe, the one he'd called from, with the shells. It would make sense to lower herself into it and call to him through the next opening. If she couldn't hear him she'd have to keep calm and crawl out and timber the ladder, and cross it without anyone to hold it steady, and start down the mountain. She had to bring help before dark or she wouldn't know how to find her way back up. Assuming she could do so by day. She hadn't paid attention on the climb, only following his lead in slight variation, as she'd done much of her life.

She imagined sitting with him on a patio somewhere, beginning the story of what they'd done wrong today. It had been a mistake not to tell anyone. Was it from vanity or cool, delicious hope that he wanted this for the two of them alone? Another error, not to have planned for emergency. The previous night they should have given directions to creepy Koss, explaining that if they hadn't called him by such and such an hour he was to do so and so. Were there earlier mistakes? He should have told her of the cave before she left Canada. She would have researched what to bring, planned for contingencies. How far back could they go? What were their mistakes, through the years, and how had they contributed to this colossal miscalculation?

It wasn't yet panic she felt, as if panic were a stable marker. She wasn't hysterical. Her heartbeat was getting up there but she'd experienced nothing to cause real fear, only a duration of silence. She told herself that her father was simply late. He was often late, he lost track of the hour, though admittedly given the directions she expected him to know it had been forty-four minutes, fourteen overdue, or six if he was counting from the last voice contact. On the imagined patio she told him her calculations. A small delight held on his face. It would all have worked out, of course, so he was enjoying the story. She looked for the slightest sign that the enjoyment went only so far, but unless you knew him, by his face you'd think nothing much had ever happened to him. You'd guess he'd lived a safe and lucky life, that he felt fear only as mock fear, fright, a tingling on the skin, a shiver along the neck. Never as drops of blackness spreading in the blood, thickening the tongue, numbing the light. But he understood as she did that the world divided between those who knew and those who didn't.

She would need both her hands, so how to carry the flashlight? If she put it in her mouth like on TV she'd gag. It was too thick to fit into a belt loop but she had a belt, pretty much decorative, so she took it off and cinched it around the base and then tied a knot and looped the flashlight around her neck so that it nodded and swayed, catching random shapes in the illuminations as she took the rope in hand and felt along the smooth rock wall and lowered herself into the hole. She found level ground almost immediately and stepped forward before taking hold of the light and looking around. She'd stopped herself all of six inches before a spur in the rock that would have brained her. Another mistake, a lucky break. She ducked and moved forward and stood again. The light now caught all of the small chamber. The ledge with the shells, about a dozen, was at eye level. At its highest point the ceiling was maybe eight feet. The rope ran straight across the floor and into a low, small opening in the opposite wall, five or six strides ahead. She could not see how anyone could fit through it.

She kneeled at the opening and listened, nothing. Even the light draft she'd felt above was absent. She shined the beam into the passage and up came a wall forty or more feet ahead, but she couldn't tell the dimensions of the space. The rock was smooth, water-worn. She called, "Dad. Can you hear me?" and her voice seemed to wreck in the passageway. The rope—how long was it?— ran true along the shadowed ground. Maybe he'd seen a safe way forward beyond the end of his tether. Even if there was no chamber, even if what she was seeing was forty feet of tunnel, there must be a curve or drop or else she'd be able to see him. All she saw now was a frayed rope lying along a rock shaft.

She checked the time. Forty-six minutes, no contact. He was just ahead somewhere. If he was hurt, in trouble, time was short. She did not want to enter the tunnel. She could not go down the mountain, go to town and get help, come up again in the dark. Already she was sixteen minutes behind in whatever action she would take.

She said fuck it and sat and started in, feet first. She rested the flashlight on her chest and pulled herself along with her hands. The top side of the passage was inches from her face and she felt her short breaths burst back upon her. Her knees could barely bend but little by little she went forward, telling herself that her father had made it through so there had to be room for her. After several seconds she opened her feet and looked down along the beam. A penumbra had formed around the light on the wall ahead and so she knew that the shaft widened, though by how much she couldn't tell. She seemed to be moving on a slight downward grade. The thought to be suppressed was that she might not be able to reverse her direction. It made no difference to close her eyes so she closed them and kept moving and only when the air and the sound of her motion changed did she open them to see that she'd come out into a large chamber. She sat up, shined the beam around. The rope ran to its end midfloor. She checked her watch. Inching through the shaft had taken less than two minutes.

The chamber looked fifteen or twenty feet high. She stood, breathed. There was something very different about the space, the way it held her imagining. Against this deeper silence even her breath sounded different, muted. If she were here alone she'd panic but knowing her father was ahead somewhere allowed her to keep it together. She crossed the chamber and saw the passageway to her left. Up ahead, through another narrow space, she saw the moving beam.

As he must have seen hers. She could have wept with relief but instead felt a wave of unsteadiness, an inability to speak. She came forward. The opening to the next chamber was narrow but vertical. She crouched and stepped through.

But he hadn't seen her light. Only now did he notice the concentration spot next to his own on the omphalos of rock that hung from the ceiling, huge, rose-colored. The rock was conical, rounded at the bottom, as if shaped by intention, and she saw, felt, immediately why he hadn't been able to leave it. At some point—time was hard to reckon now—he registered the second beam and turned quickly and they trained their lights on each other. His face looked strange, as if she'd woken him from a sleepwalk.

"You didn't come back," she said. She dropped her light to his chest. He did the same. He said nothing. "Are you all right?"

He turned his light back on the hanging rock. It was smooth, vegetable, sparkling. She came forward and stood with him. He walked her around the perimeter. The rock seemed suspended, floating three or four feet from the floor. She felt something larger than fear, though it had the same intensity. It was awe, strickenness, a shiver of beholding, as on first seeing a vast canyon, maybe, or walking into a great cathedral. But here the measurelessness was directly before them, with dimensions perceived all at once. The rock's hovering shape and coloring were hard to account for, but more so its proportions in relation to the rest of the chamber. It hung exactly midspace and though its curving surface was uneven, from anywhere on the cave floor, itself irregular, the rock seemed to face her.

She stopped walking. He continued. She tilted her light up to the dome, then down, and clipped her eyes to him as he was about to round out of sight.

"Stop."

"Quiet, dear."

She came to him, held him at the elbow, trained the light on the back of his head. His hair was matted in blood that had run behind his left ear and down his neck, under his shirt collar.

"What happened?"

"I don't know. I got dizzy. I bumped my head when I fell. It's all part of it."

"Part of what? You fell? Are you disoriented?"

A short laugh escaped him. He held his hand up to ask her patience as he reached into his pocket and produced a pack of matches. He struck one. It flared and went out immediately. He did it again and again it was there and gone.

"There's not enough oxygen," he said. "This is how they died."

He turned the light into the recesses. He led her forward. At their feet she saw where he'd chipped away at the sediment. There were bones in the floor. Femur staves. Calcified splinters and broken osseous plates. Beyond, ribs breached the surface.

"Human," he said. "Or protohuma—" He didn't quite finish the word or she didn't hear him.

She took him by the arm and drew him away and as they passed by the hanging rock he turned and directed his light at it and looked a last time. She watched him, gauged his movements, as they stooped into the next chamber and crossed it. He was lurching, unsteady. Should she go first or second? She couldn't reason it through. She was breathing fast. If he went first and passed out she'd be unable to move him. She had him sit near the narrow opening. She looped the rope around his chest, under his arms, and he followed her hands vaguely with his eyes, as if drunk.

"You come in right after me," she said. "Keep your head close to my feet."

She rounded her shoulders and started in on her back, headfirst, with the rope running along her right side so she could tug it as a signal, if nothing else. As she'd feared, the slightly inclined grade was harder to move along in the confined space. She used the heels of her hands and feet to get what traction she could. When her palm touched a smoothness she thought of water, rushing water, filling the passage. He followed well enough but midway he stopped and she said, "Keep coming," and her voice died inches from her face. She tugged the rope and he started again. It seemed to be taking longer than it should have, and then was certainly taking too long, and the despair was in realizing that somehow she'd taken them into the wrong opening, but no, the rope had run to this one, so on she went, her hands bleeding now, her knees banged up, and then the blackness stood higher and she knew they'd made it.

At the mouth of the first entrance they stood in pain, crouched over, breathing hard, and now she was weeping for the air, at the daylight visible above. He went first, climbing and pulling on the rope as she boosted him. Then he reached down and helped her up. They walked out of the cave and stood looking at La Vallée du Terrieu, miles of green and sunlight.

She examined his scalp, the short, deep gash, still bleeding. With a paring knife they'd used at lunch she cut away the sleeve of his shirt and wrapped it tightly around his head, under his jaw.

"Can't open my mouth," he tried to say.

"Perfect, then. Let's go."

They crossed the crevasse and left the ladder and walked down, saying nothing.

The part she would never tell anyone, not even herself, she decided, was that the place they'd been didn't exist, not in the way the rest of the world did. Or it existed in space but not time. You could see time from the entrance but the place inside the mountain was outside of time, as if it had absorbed tens of thousands of years of human wonderment and held it, imprisoned it, and to enter the chamber was to enter the imaginings of the dead. It was a trap they'd escaped that others had not, lured by promise, filled with disorienting visions, then weakening, suffocating. The self-deceiving mind could so easily imagine a design there to hold them. You couldn't see the rock's symmetry and color and not imagine it as the shaping of an engineer, a force, a god with aspirants among humans. Some inherited groove in the brain caused people to believe that all order is intended, that balanced wholes can't form by chance and natural circumstance. They couldn't see that none of the received names, the names cursed or called out in worship, could really attach to an ordering force. Over time, she would likely come to think of the cave visit as a misadventure, a lucky escape that had sparked thoughts of a Maker, thoughts she was already putting in their place. Yet on some future nights—how did she already know this?—the sparks would come back to her.

And then, a last idea, one she couldn't suppress. It was that she was still inside the cave. She had fallen out of time, even as she descended through the woods as present in the world as she always had been. In thought, memory, body, she was nearly exactly herself. The feeling began to fade, to seem fanciful, at lower altitude, as her blood became better oxygenated, but she understood that it would never entirely leave her. It was somehow familiar, the idea that she was two places at once, or one place in two overlapping times. She must have read it in a junk novel, seen it in movies, things that everyone consumed without really remembering and that she found it harder and harder even to pretend to believe.

She'd been trotting and was too far ahead now. She stopped and looked back, waiting for him to appear through the trees.

3

HE CAME HOME FROM THE HOSPITAL AND MADE A LONG
phone call to Armin Koss and a shorter one to California in which
he arranged to take a permanent leave from the university. He sat
speaking on the phone at the outdoor dining table. From where she
stood looking at him through the open patio doors at sunset he
seemed to be addressing a mountain. Echoing the language he now
embraced, he told some administrator that the institution would
have to "convert" him. In stages the department and benefits
offices could attribute his absence to whatever they wanted, sick
leave, research leave, but after twelve months he wanted "the
honorable discharge of early retirement." He'd finish out his pro-
jects and go.

The sky darkened and held for three days. He hardly slept. Even
when the rain woke her one morning near four she went out along
the stone floor to the sitting room and there he was. The urge to
speak left them, even through the drink hours. He would start
talking about something he'd read or hoped to study but then trail

off after a minute. Every subject seemed to connect in him to
something unsayable. She could only be embarrassed for him.
Never before had he been unequal to his thoughts. In the car,
coming back from a day trip to Uzès, locally famous cathedral
tower and bright woven cotton, she asked him why so quiet.

"I'm trying to respect what's happened to us."

"You mean surviving a stupid mistake through dumb luck."

"Human nature once tried to accommodate profound experiences. Now some of us try to joke them away. Or drape them in
rational language."

He seized on the idea of this rational drapery. It was everywhere,
he said, a full decor of false surfaces, a fabric of numbers and symbols cast over creation. The man was a complete stranger to her.

They flew back to North America, same coast, different countries,
and he walked out of his life. Over the ensuing weeks he began
attending poetry lectures and readings, drawing live nudes. Twice he
gave over his home to self-described musicians he'd met at a festival
and flew to Peru to get high in ayahuasca ceremonies. He was talking
now, but differently, more present in conversation. He admitted he
was no natural artist, and his intuition felt at times imprisoned by his
learning, but he really did seem changed. For all his self-exploration
he was now attentive to her when she spoke, guessing at her unstated
concerns, an empathetic listener. There he was on her screen saying
in one breath that genetic technology would unlock the secrets of all
pathogens, and in the next that the cave must have opened something
in her, too, whether or not she wanted to talk about it, and this opening could lead to inspiration. Had she acknowledged something in
herself? he wanted to know. He blamed himself that she'd grown up
in denial of what he called her "otherworldly side." She found herself
longing for their old, loaded silences. He'd always been a gundog on

point, but he'd never before been pointing at her. The analogy extended in her thoughts to find Koss at the trigger. Koss was there always, at the beginning and now haunting her father's descriptions, something Armin had suggested, had told him on the phone or by email, someone Armin knew in Lima or LA.

Armin Käding Koss, minor internet figure. He existed almost exclusively in German. His website was under reconstruction. In the virtual strata Celia found a few small profiles in gaming and art magazines, interviews at three gallery sites, promoting shows, two of which had been reviewed. She ran the pieces through a translation program with the usual mixed, often ludicrous results. "'I like to make Sundays for free,' says Koss his owner. And he also says his client because he knows nothing." Against the random incorrectness, the accidental nonsense, she surmised and filtered her way through everything she could find. When the sites seemed to have given way to other Armins and Kosses she turned a few more pages and saw nothing and was about to leave the search when he appeared again on page eleven on an antianarchist site that listed the names of members and sympathizers belonging to a group it deemed to be, in the translation, "violent or postured of threat." The group called themselves Löschen. Koss's name appeared midpage. A new search took her to what looked to be a pamphlet or booklet self-published by the group four years ago. The booklet was online, pick your language. She clicked on the Union Jack and up came the manifesto. On the cover she recognized Koss's gestural figures, his semi-nonhumans. These ones, a man and woman, stood with their hands crossed on their chests, slightly bowing forward.

The text began on the next page.

We all must work immediately by whatever means available
to achieve Total Planet. The term Total Planet refers to the
environment and to the whole condition of post civilization,
post control complex to be brought about by a Sudden Event.
To achieve Total Planet, threats must be recognized and dis-
armed or eliminated. The greatest threats are 1) human
technology and its ruthless insistence on conformity and 2)
those sciences working against the natural world and its organic,
evolutionary means for eradicating threats.

Point two was pointed, more or less, at her and her father and their
colleagues in the plague wars. She clicked ahead and read lines and
paragraphs at random.

Voluntary sterilization will lead to humans only being born
to unenlightened parents. For this reason, enlightenment
must be brought about through force.

Total Planet can be anticipated as either enlightened survivor-
primitivism or extinction.

The enemy from within includes those employing the rheto-
ric of long reform. The only acceptable reform is in prepara-
tion of mind, body, and soul for the Sudden Event.

Eleven signatories, none of them Koss. She looked again at the
cover. The figures were from his hand, or computer, whatever, she
was sure of it. She should have been alarmed, she *was* alarmed, but
she felt too the pleasure of pieces fitting together, of suspicions confirmed. That he was or had been a fellow traveler of these particular

believers made sense. The senseless cause made sense. Even the
strange translation "postured of threat" made sense. And so, of
course, did his interest in an extinction scientist and his pharma-
virologist daughter.

What were they bowing to, his creations? The hand positions
made them look like the risen dead or extras from a sci-fi movie,
aliens greeting their master. They were bowing to the coming end,
of course. Envisioned and aided, enacted. Imagined and welcomed.

She pasted both links into an email to her father. She tried not
to cheapen with cliché her characterization of the group with
which Koss was associated. After typing the words *doomsday cult*
she deleted them. Then she wrote them again but put them in
quotation marks. She said she was surprised to find this site while
looking for examples of Koss's artwork. She understood that he
must know of Koss's anarchism, given all the time they'd spent
together, all the long conversations, but did he know it was basically an "activist doomsday cult"? How did Koss describe it?

The draft sat on her screen. She returned to the antianarchist
site and ran the names of the Löschen signatories through a search
engine. Nothing came up clear and certain. The hits were few and
there was no way of knowing if she had the group members or their
namesakes. In an email to a W. Shult at the contact link she apologized for writing in English. She identified herself as a concerned
Canadian. Could he tell her more about Löschen? Did he have any
more information on Armin Käding Koss? She pressed send and
received an auto-reply in five languages: "Your message has not
been read. There is no Shult. The group Löschen does not exist but
groups like it do. The members and manifestos are fiction. You
have encountered art. A. Koss"

She urged him to visit old friends, anthropologists and biotechnicians, men and women taking physical delight in the phenomenal world, and to see a psychiatrist.

"Shrinks have nothing on shamans. I have my guide."

"Suddenly you trust shamans. Armin Koss is no guide."

"We test each other's ways of seeing. Apparently I'm an easy read. For the first time in my life I'm close to believing in a metaphysical force."

What he needed wasn't metaphysical. As far as Celia knew it had been a few years since he last had a womanfriend.

"You should get out more."

"I'm floating in far-outness, as they sort of used to say."

"At least you're not solemn."

"You haven't heard me yet on the souls of the dead."

"Then I won't ask about the afterlife."

"When I get there we'll discuss it."

The travel was its own problem, no longer underwritten by new research funds. He had only the money he had, and he was burning through it. It shot out behind him in contrails stretching to Bali, Machu Picchu, Hatshepsut, Borobudur. He sent her photos of temples and reliefs no different from those she saw on the internet as she followed him from her desk in Vancouver. He sometimes traveled alone, sometimes with Koss. She couldn't decide which troubled her more.

"What exists right in front of us should make us believers, Lia. The endless varieties of wonder, the symmetries and echoes and patterns and modifications. Before the sheer complexity of nature, we should be stunned, fetal."

"So you see the stone gods and the altars and all of it as . . . what?"

"We mimic creations. We make because we're made. And we can deepen ourselves by encountering those things made in response to *reality at base*. It's art touching reality I'm after, religious art or otherwise. I'm not so interested in pop songs made of pop songs."

"I like *pop songs*, as you call them. And some people see gods there, too."

A scoffing laugh.

"There's a big difference between true things and their mockeries. The mockeries will do us in."

She stared at true things every day in the lab. Contagions and immune susceptibilities, genetic mutations, epidemics and reemergences, bacterial pathogens, adaptations, manners of transmission, the vulnerabilities of hosts. In some remote village a genius is born. It leaps out of its home, across species, leaps into the world. Against it stand she and her kind and they have to move fast. They have only the gathered data to draw on, a spotty battle history, clouds of fast-figuring computers.

Some distant village in Africa or Asia. What did it matter? There was no safe distance. Would she ever lose the feeling that something unimaginable was incubating darkly? This was *reality at base*.

Her father declared his last project to be finding a variant genome of the Justinian plague, sixth century, thirty to fifty million dead. New contagions were more accurately targeted if they were known descendants of old ones. In a move of stark nepotism his team offered Celia a grant to join them on a dig in Turkey, ancient Troy, working with other groups uncovering a mass grave. She declined but the award notice had been sent to her superiors in the company's anticontagion arm. Her team leader, a polite, hairless man named Didier, called her into his office and asked her to picture the towering plume of a feather the grant would add to their funding cap. They'd be gaining access to a genome that could position them ahead of market competitors. She knew there was no use getting angry with her father for not clearing the idea with her first. He would think of it as a surprise, a gift, and anyway she wanted to see the old him, at work testing hypotheses against evidence. It would be their last research adventure together.

The work would take ten days. Her father sent the ticket. She flew Vancouver-Toronto-Frankfurt-Istanbul-Çanakkale on the understanding he would be there on the ground when she arrived, though he wasn't. Two hours after she checked into the hotel the phone woke her. She picked it up, half-asleep, but there was no one at the other end. A few minutes later she discovered by email that he'd tried to phone but couldn't get through. He was sorry, he'd be late, maybe two days. He and Koss were stranded in Cozumel, where bad weather had grounded the flights. He'd attached the names of contact people on the other teams, his friends Jenny and Dresen, they'd help her. Until he arrived she'd have to be his designate.

The other teams, from Amsterdam and Indiana, got her situated on-site. Jenny and Dresen were always together, an older woman, younger man wearing identical wide-brimmed sun hats. They were hunting for ancient tuberculosis and staph infections. They set her up at the edge of the boneyard. A grid was laid over the site based on images from full-spectrum cameras. The dig proceeded steadily. She wrote to her father every few hours with updates, questions, asides about methodology and record keeping. That he didn't respond made no sense. She checked the weather in Cozumel, blue sky and light breezes. Since France he sometimes went silent, a practice Koss had effected, but he wouldn't have abandoned her, so she pictured him unplugged, in transit, heading her way.

On day three at a depth of seven feet she came to her skeletons. They were lying face to face, and as she brushed away the dirt, uncovering them over many hours from the skull down, she discovered they were buried holding hands. She saw the hands, stopped, got out of the hole, looked back down. It might have seemed like an ancient joke or sentimental ploy but in fact it moved her in a way she could not account for. There was no one near her. The light was clean. She tried to smell the sea but the wind was from the east. Then she looked back into the grave and decided she was done for the day.

She spent the night in her small room, with the sounds of singing muezzins and an English translation of *The Iliad* that some previous guest had left in the broken safe. In Homer the origin of disease was hot-tempered Apollo, "who in anger at the king drove the foul pestilence along the host, and the people perished." There was no appeasing Apollo, not then, not now. He had turned our weapons against us, taking us out. Against Apollo, the plague warriors had targeted enrichment and next-generation sequencing (TENGS). They had comparative genomics to track changes that could account for the sudden virulence of a transient pathogen. They had reverse-engineering technology, in-vitro and murine models, and Indrani's message on her cellphone saying, "Hartley just stole my lamb burger" and Didier asking, "How are TENGS today?"

By the time she arrived at the site the next morning her skeletons had been fully revealed. People gathered, took pictures, went back to work. She took a picture herself and got a young guy at the imaging station to enhance it. To distinguish one set of bones from the other he colored them in the image. Only then, looking at the bones on-screen, did she see a third set, that of a child, between the adults. The grave held a family. She pressed a hand into her hip, a gesture entirely new to her.

When she'd looked down at the couple, looked through her camera's viewfinder, how had she missed the smaller skeleton? The profound failure to see forced her to admit this had been happening recently. Since France there'd been gaps in attention. Her father's outward drift had suspended her in a state of perpetual distraction. In dreams he was nearby but not visible. She called for him but he wouldn't appear. Even when she was awake he seemed both close and absent.

She tried to locate herself in the work of securing a twenty-five-hundred-year-old killer. Upon sugarless diets, even before mint-flavored pastes and fluoride, human teeth endured. The bacterium sat in the pulp, protected over centuries by enamel. The idea was simply to pull the tooth from the skull. In a clean room in her father's lab in California, someone would drill from the root end and pull the bacterium from the pulp. Part of the pulp would be sent to Celia's lab in Vancouver. If it was well enough intact, its genetic code could be sequenced and compared to known plagues. Before her father's group published their results, Celia's company would have a few months' head start on beating the odds to design a new generation of antibacterials for one or all of the pneumonic, bubonic, and septicemic plagues.

Dresen offered to help with the extraction. He kneeled beside her in the pit and put his hands on the skull of the adult female. He'd been working hard and smelled of sweat. With slow delicacy he turned the face toward them and removed the skull from the body.

Celia got out of the hole and helped him up. He carried the skull before him, hands top and bottom, to the work tent. One of the Dutch grad students directed him to place it in front of a tripod-mounted camera. The student photographed it and cataloged the photo, and then Dresen opened the jaw. With his index finger he pointed to what seemed a good molar. Celia confirmed his choice. He produced a pair of small pliers and plucked it out expertly. Celia put the molar in a gamma-sterilized Falcon tube and marked it and against her resistance Dresen took her phone camera and tapped off a picture of her with the dead woman's skull.

"So whose tooth do you have? What will you call her?" asked Dresen. He said researchers always named their skeletons and cadavers. "It humanizes them."

"The researchers, you mean. I'm not naming her."

But she did name the skeleton, privately, against her will. The name should have been Turkish or Roman, she supposed, but what came to her a minute later when she was briefly alone with the skull, came fully and unbidden. The head, the skull, was Alice. If there could be a Helen of Troy, surely there could be an Alice.

For the next two days she helped others with their work. At night the dinner talk turned to the end of the world. Deforestation, changing fruit bat habitats, bushmeat markets, Ebola, bored undergrads or terrorists creating smallpox from the genome on the internet, the next great airborne flu. One night a journalist joined the group, Lacey Ann Kronin of the *Washington Post*, and the talk narrowed and became more responsible. Lacey Ann was writing a profile of Jenny and Dresen but asked Celia questions about her work and her father. For some reason Celia felt protective, evasive, and that night she did research. She'd written on TB, Lacey Ann, on medical marijuana, West Nile, sex workers, pertussis, arterial stents. Before becoming a science and med journalist, she was a foreign correspondent in Egypt and Turkey. Her older stories were on uprisings and protests and—here was the link—the spike in deaths from treatable wounds and diseases in Syria during the war. Attached to the story were photos of dying children, the crowded hallways of hospital wards without electricity, a doctor in a surgical gown lying dead in a street, executed for reasons unknown. After a minute Celia found she'd been staring at the straight edge of her screen. How neatly it penned up the chaos out there. The stories were smart and true-feeling. The only things not true were the endings. The reported events had no endings, obviously. Cause to effect they went on forever. She clicked back to one of the photos and found a young girl staring into the camera from beneath a wall clock missing half its face on a half-missing wall, and now Celia realized she'd seen the picture before somewhere, on some other cruise through the headlines months ago. This was the news, a succession of scenes soon forgotten. Did anything mediated actually stay in memory? In the hell wards of the mind the clocks had all stopped some time ago.

On the sixth day, as she showered, she thought she heard the room phone and ran out dripping on the tile floor but the room was silent and she doubted her senses. Upon her unanswered emails she'd passed from disappointment through anger to concern. Now in her inbox was an automatic notice informing her that the last seventeen messages to her father had bounced back. His remote server was full. This had happened before and infuriated her. Wherever he was he hadn't received her emails since she'd arrived. Yet he must have sent her messages, and they should have been getting through.

Koss would know where he was—they were likely still traveling together—but how to reach Koss? She tried his website. It was no longer under reconstruction. What she found on the home page was a large image of herself. Or rather Koss's version of her as projected on the wall of the chateau. It presented as a portrait. She was seated, framed from the waist up. She wore the same clothes she'd been given in the animation but the background was uncertain, as if she were in a room with a dark wall far behind her and windowlight crossing her figure. The chair was slightly at an angle so that her head was turned to the viewer but her face lacked distinguishing features. Maybe it wasn't her after all, she thought, maybe it was just the way Koss designed all his women, but then she saw the attention he'd given her hands, folded in her lap. They were rendered much more realistically than the rest of her, and she remembered catching him staring at them at dinner. On the little finger of the right hand was the same ring with a delicate, rectangular face that she had worn that night and wore now. She'd bought it from a crafts vendor at the Granville Market, a microchip daubed in amber.

The page had no text. She was forced to click on herself, a hollowing little tap of surrender. She learned that the image was from an art show opening in Berlin: *Apokalypse: neue Kunstwerk von Armin Käding Koss*. There she was again, Celia, or the animated version of her, this a daytime image. The view behind her was recognizably that of a cityscape, her city, Vancouver. The mountains, the squat, accordioned downtown high-rises. The image was after one of her own snapshots. She'd taken it with her phone camera and posted it in one of the online albums she sometimes put together for her family and friends. Her father must have sent Koss the password to the site. Had he forgotten or misread her response to the chateau

film? Koss's live attentions were creepy enough. Now he'd made a
project of her. Her site had five albums, over a hundred pictures. For
forty-eight of these Koss had constructed what the text described as
"memory theaters," twenty-by-twelve-inch windowed boxes, in each
of which played a short, silent, animated film. The shortest film was
four seconds, the longest thirty-two. Celia on a ferryboat, Celia
holding a bottle of champagne on the day they'd made a breakthrough at the lab, driving a car into Seattle, unsteadily on skis on
Whistler Mountain. Some were entirely fictional, Celia playing
with Hartley or swimming in a lake, and seemed intended to advance
a narrative, strike a theme, or finish a chord.

The on-screen pointer became a hand over the live link. As if
complicit in her own theft, this sure, remote violation, she had to
click on herself twice more to find a fuller text, each German para-
graph repeated in French and English. The English looked shorter
than the German. He'd written that the memory theaters were
inspired by moments in the life of a friend he left unnamed. He
didn't presume to understand how the moments came together,
what they amounted to, but he sensed in them a thing larger than
themselves. He would not call this thing meaning or story, though
it seemed to involve both. "It is a mystery, forever-yielding," said
the text. "To be revealed at the end of the future, all at once."

She chose another sample box on the site, number seven: Celia in
an orange life vest standing with strangers on a boat near Tofino, a
whale just off the stern. Indrani had taken the photo. She clicked the
play button. The camera angle looked right, as she remembered the
picture, but in the box the whale was too close to the boat, maybe
fifteen feet away. The photo had made it seem farther than it was in
truth but the film brought it too close. The figures beside her looked
unspecific, some genderless, the backs and tops of heads. They were

on the water for about an hour, she remembered. Nervous conversation, stories of past such trips. There was a couple from Chicago, a woman from Saskatoon, an elderly man from Manchester or somewhere in the north of England, but none of them was there now and the dorsal was too large. The back breached and she waited for the sound of human awe but there was silence, and then the geyser from the blowhole, a sound she remembered as if it were happening now but absent here, the spray almost not visible, not showy, and then as it crested and dropped under she saw that Koss had changed the whale. That day the whales were all humpbacks and grays but he'd made this one an orca, killer whale, apex predator, the black-white seam disappearing under the surface. The wave hit them and the camera bounced and steadied just as the whale breached again, closer now, almost right under the boat. The white patch above the eye, the eye itself a whorl, and animated-Celia turned to the camera and the video stopped. She tried to read the look on her face and decided it came off as dreadful.

Something had changed in the boat. She rolled back into the video and counted seven strangers, then clicked back to the beginning. Eight. Watching again, not distracted by herself or the whale, she saw what looked like a family of three on the edge of the shot, then the camera's dip and shift and they were out of frame until it found its position again. The tallest one, the father, she supposed, was gone. There was no reaction from wife or child, as if he'd never been there.

After some interval she got off the bed, walked across the hotel room, and sat on the tile floor with her back to the wall. She drew her knees up and hugged them and missed her dog. Whenever she got onto the floor and hugged Hartley he moved to an open space and left her feeling pathetic. She told herself never to watch another of Koss's films. By the next morning she'd watched them all.

4

Her little sister lived in Brooklyn or Williamsburg, or Bushwick, the name kept changing when Chrissy said it over the years but the apartment address was the same, a warehouse on Bogart Street. Chrissy had known no one in all the United States when she moved to New York. She'd gone simply because that was where people like her went, they moved to New York and allowed themselves to be swallowed like all those over time who had left the Mother Country for the Great Maw. Now she was living with a guitarist from Arkansas named Clete, though Clete literally wasn't in the picture anymore whenever Celia skyped them. He was always at a gig, was the story, or preparing for one or on the road. Chrissy waited tables and sold to local shops the jewelry she made from found materials. The items were simple and beautiful. She'd once sent Celia a necklace with an acorn folded into the curved metal tongues of so many broken Jew's harps.

In any season, when Celia talked with her sister, saw her face lit up by the row of small windows that ran high along the length of the apartment, she pictured the same sky over Brooklyn that she'd seen the one time she'd visited, a cold blue April sky, unevenly portioned by high-rises. On the warehouse rooftop they had drunk wine and talked about safe things, Chrissy's life and work, and New York, Manhattan in the distance at an unfamiliar angle. Until the bottle was half-gone they did not talk about what truly separated them, money, love, life trajectories, the way their father thought differently of Celia than of Chrissy, the way he'd trapped them in different misconceptions. That evening had ended with Chrissy angry and in tears, then embarrassed when she had to run down to answer her door and talk to her landlord, a Hasid named Hammuel, in Celia's memory now only red curls, white socks, and black shoes, to whom Chrissy claimed to feel very close. She'd shut the door and explained that Hammuel had always been good to her. "Some people are naturally good," she said, as if this would be news to Celia, as if she had no intuitions about people and had always to wait for hard evidence of goodness or treachery. "Others just lack decent human beingery."

When she returned from the dig, Celia stretched out on the bed and dialed and Chrissy's face surfaced on the screen. The call had not been arranged. There were never any pleasantries between them, Chrissy just started in. Now she was saying she'd given up waitressing, that she'd met a woman who wanted her to work with a "not-for-profit book-repurposing thing" called MEND, which she seemed unable to be specific about. Celia reduced her on-screen and did a quick search, trying to press the keys rather than tap them, hoping she couldn't be heard. "It's not like there's nothing meaningful in service jobs. But maybe it's time for a change." Celia pulled the screen, the camera, closer. She tried not to look down at the letters. "I mean, maybe someone else can recite the specials— What? You getting a little work done while we talk? Writing something up on your poor lab rats? You called me, remember."

"Sorry." She pushed the screen back and put her hands up in a gesture of surrender. "I should know better. Multitasking makes us forty percent slower at each task on average."

"The species can't afford to get any dumber. Though I'm all for slow if it's deep and rhythmic."

Chrissy had begun making lewd asides only recently. Celia had never heard them addressed to anyone but her.

"I'm wondering if you've heard from Dad recently."

"You're always wondering that. I should keep a chart."

In spurts of three or four words Celia read the MEND site but mostly just peeked at the pictures. The impression formed that discarded books were being put through "green-driven machinery" that pulped and compressed them, maybe into boards and walls that were shipped off, maybe to help house the global homeless. It was hard to imagine Chrissy in any of the pictures.

"Has he mentioned Armin Koss lately? The German guy?"

"Dad's German should be ten years younger. Clete and me are split for the duration. I hereby announce."

"I'm sorry, Chrissy."

"You already half knew."

"Surmised, I guess."

"I should fly off and meet this Armin. Maybe the age difference doesn't mean anything, at least not for six or eight years."

"He's not what he seems, or at least not what he seems to Dad."

"You met him for, what, two hours? Has he been sending you dirty emails? He has my coordinates but so far it's all been strictly flirtless on his part."

"You've been emailing with him?"

Chrissy said Koss wanted her version of certain stories their father had told him.

"They're about us mostly, maybe mostly you."

The imperative was to describe Koss to her sister but the terms were not coming up. Celia's thoughts coursed into new terrains that didn't seem her own. She wanted to say there was something about Koss that made you doubt basic suppositions and understandings. So knowledge advanced constantly, so what? He made you believe against yourself.

"He's no one to get close to. He's furtive, manipulative."

"Mysterious, forward-thinking."

"He's got Dad adrift from himself."

"And that's a *bad* thing?"

"Yes. It's a bad thing. It's like he's been completely rewired."

She instantly knew her mistake.

"Oh, it's his *hardware* you're worried about. You think people don't gain enlightenment, they just have a short in their circuits. Has it ever occurred to you that maybe the soulful brain is the only one that's working to full capacity?"

There would be no getting her on-side, no getting her back, now. If Celia said one more word, Chrissy would go off for ten minutes. I miss telephones, she imagined saying. I used to wash dishes in the middle of our calls. Saying, there's something about Armin Koss that there's practically no way of saying. He's stealing us, one by one.

One wrong word and she'd blow.

"Hartley says hello."

All dogs, even their names, melted Chrissy, left her at a loss for words. Celia was six thousand miles from her dog but Chrissy didn't know it.

"Unfair."

"Hartley."

"Let's see him."

"It's a standing hello. He's in Vancouver, I'm in Turkey. For work, sort of last-minute."

She found herself not mentioning how she'd come to be there. It was an oversight not to have told her before leaving. Now telling her would seem an afterthought. If you added up the oversights and afterthoughts, you arrived at Chrissy's feeling that she was the less favored daughter. Not less loved, but less thought of.

There was some lag now, some echo, between the image and the sound.

"So you haven't heard from Dad," said Celia.

"Sure I did. He's off to Berlin."

The voice came somehow without Chrissy's mouth actually moving. Celia waited for it to move but it didn't. The background color had shifted. Something had changed in the white balance.

"We've got a delay. Can you hear me?"

There was no response. Chrissy's face was tilted down, her eyes unregarding of the camera. She was inwardly drawn, seeming not so much retracted as alone. Celia made gestures now to signal the failing signal, hands over her ears and mouth alternately, but Chrissy wasn't looking. She presented the crown of her head and a slight movement registered in her arms. Now it was Chrissy who was typing. Was she emailing her? Did she think the call had been lost, that the camera was off? Chrissy whispered the words, as she always did when she wrote. Celia tried to make them out and though she could not, some sense of them seemed to hold on Chrissy's lips. Celia felt herself attended to, not as someone addressed, but as a subject, written not *to* but *about*. She felt herself there in her sister's prose. How could such an impression have formed?

"Can you hear me, Chrissy? Can you see me?"

And then her sister went still. It seemed the image had frozen, with Chrissy staring at her screen, her eyes caught in some mid-sentence, but then she blinked and her brow began to knit and the screen went dead.

She changed her ticket and rerouted the return through Berlin with a two-day layover through the date of Koss's opening. Her father would be there or not. He was lost to her or not. On the flight, with an ancient plague in her carry-on safely stowed beneath the seat in front of her, she thought of the young woman who'd heard wolves. The one who asked questions. Her intuitions had once been socially, politically conscious. Now they seemed self-enclosed. The pregnancy had turned her inward and its loss had fucked her up. Her attention since then was slightly off-true. In ways small and large people lost themselves all the time. The important thing was to recover the lost one before you changed too much and became forever a stranger to yourself.

She checked into a small hotel off Kurfürstendamm. Her room overlooked a narrow pedestrian avenue. Opposite her was a long seven-story glass building that seemed sheared in half, so exposed were the people in their offices and rooms. They moved about their day on display.

She had no thought-out plan. It was best that they all meet together, in the unfamiliar space of a gallery, where things look different by design. She pictured herself physically separating her father from Koss, taking him by the elbow. The confrontation would last only seconds, she didn't know the exact words. If she could remain calm, she might explain to Koss that her father was prone to strong bondings. She would say that strong human bondings require responsibility. Koss's interest in the two of them, her and her father, could only be called proprietary. She would insist that he release them. She herself did not wish to be the object of his fascination, trapped in a cell in his honeycombed mind.

Online the Berlin show was getting advance attention. There was the half sense, at least, of an impending breakthrough. The *Lernstoff* was agreed to be *faszinierend*. Much was being made of the elusive narrative, the *Geheimnis* of the *Geschichte*, meaningful patterns, and of the mystery of the subject, the woman, the unnamed friend, who might not in fact even exist, Koss wouldn't say authoritatively.

She looked at the building across from her with its exposed offices and thought of a lab technician moving a pipette over a field of the same repeated shape. She imagined partial exchanges with her father and Chrissy made up of past conversations and the one she wanted to have now. They're in his dining room in California. They speak of novel weather patterns, petroleum derivatives, including a drop in science funding from the oil-slick Canadian feds. Chrissy has a new boyfriend she sketches fast because he's sketchy. The daughters begin clearing the dinner table and their father notices after a minute and hops up from his chair and takes over from them. Does anyone want music? Chrissy solicits their opinions on dog breeds and the new hybrid cars. And what about her, is Celia seeing anyone? She tells them, apropos of nothing or everything, that she's what's called a private person.

Thursday arrived, still no word. She read a Berlin guide, marked it up, then skipped the points of interest in her wandering. The city came to her in sliding intensities. Roma musicians on subway cars, the traffic of prams in Prenzlauer Berg. A Russian-run market, the blunt, clay faces. She couldn't get the hang of the cyclists, she was always stepping back just as they shot across her bow. Berlin seemed too white, the way most Western cities do when you come from urban Canada. The buildings collected into an elusive character, sharing something she couldn't identify. They were unalike to the same degree. She had lunch on a bar patio. The waiter was cool and attentive.

In midafternoon she was sitting on her bed, watching the glass building. She settled her attention on two small rooms, each with one man and two women. The men stood, now and then pointing to something on their respective walls. The women sat at tables, taking notes. One of the rooms emptied out. The man in the other looked in his thirties, white skin, black hair. He seemed to speak with great deliberateness. He used his hands and chin to punctuate. The women said almost nothing, a word here and there. One woman wore a hijab. The man more often addressed the other woman, a blonde. He seemed to say a word and they looked at him, uncomprehending. He said it again. Then he stepped up to the woman in the hijab and held the back of his hand in front of her face. She hesitated a moment, then sniffed it, and they settled on a meaning.

Over dinner at the hotel she told herself to stay composed. Her presence at the gallery would be enough. She'd be recognized, standing there refusing to look into the boxes. The real thing would trump all. Or maybe she wouldn't be recognized or allowed to stand there, or even to enter the gallery. It occurred to her she had no invitation, she'd just assumed the opening was public. Did Galerie Grau on Lindenstraße have a visible door or did you have to know to press on a certain brick so a whole wall slid away? Was there a password? She pictured the black-haired Berlitz man guarding the entrance, presenting the back of his hand.

She turned on her cell and switched on the data roaming. No messages. She called up the gallery address on a city map.

There in the mirror in her neat, cramped room, she wore an auburn sweater over a cream blouse, a pair of black pants, conservative fit. She wanted to look apart from whatever were the looks in Berlin galleries. It was North American professional, her look. Serious, contained, half turned away from style. It was an outfit she wore to meet the higher-ups at the company, the level of authority above the teams and team leaders. She had always been good at reporting, the team spokesmember. She put local test results and stats in national and global contexts. She explained findings, found language for numbers. The last time she wore these pants she'd nailed it, everyone agreed. Even with no strong results she'd justified their course, the idea they could engineer a generation of prophylactics, antiretrovirals, maybe even targeted antibacterials, if only they kept funding research into ancient DNA. What she hadn't reported was the hope she always felt when talking the real language of research. Hope in the comparative analysis of gene sequencings drawn from past pandemics, hope in the measures of mass death, whispered in a nonsyntactic, post-human language. "The YopJ T3SS effector of *Yersinia* acetylates Ser and Thr residues critical for the activation of the MAP kinase kinases and the inhibitor of kappa B kinase beta and alpha." She'd presented only so much, said nothing inadmissible. "YopJ-mediated inhibition of the NF-κB pathway allows *Yersinia* to suppress expression of TNFα from infected macrophages and to induce apoptosis in naive macrophages." What could be driving this hyper-precise seeming nonsense but hope? It held in her chest, below shoulder level, a little heliated balloon of promise. Something to remember when things, as now, weren't otherwise promising. The promise of

mass salvation. Mass healing. Mass life. When she had her father
back, she would tell him about the little balloon.

She gave the taxi driver an address and as they drove she looked
down at her hands resting on her purse. Every two seconds the
passing streetlights made two of her fingers look broken sideways.
After a while the driver talked about the traffic, the weather. He
assumed she was American, asked if she knew Los Angeles, which
he'd always wanted to visit. He said they were entering Kreuzberg.
He let her off on a narrow commercial street with bright windows.
Small galleries lined the avenue. Grau was already full. People
bunched in the window, pale and narrow, and the lines they made,
their clothes, accentuated their length. She studied them as if
looking at a diorama, as if she had been transported back a thousand years from the future to observe earlier humans while standing on their cobblestones. She couldn't see Koss or her father but
sensed they were impending, that they hadn't arrived yet, and upon
this understanding, based on nothing she could detect, she was
struck with self-consciousness. She moved on, as if she had some
other destination.

The gallery next door was closed. One a little farther along was
open and apparently empty. She went inside and wondered what
she thought she was doing. She was on a rescue mission, was what,
but unprepared, at any number of disadvantages to be confronting
Koss so fully on his turf, in his city, his milieu, without his language. She was afraid that she'd fail to see what needed to be done,
or see it and fail to act, not say what needed saying. Afraid she'd
allow herself to be turned, swayed by some graciousness, fitted
with a look of true concern, fooled by a perfect, false compassion.

Already she was failing, standing in the wrong art gallery. In
midroom was a long glass case displaying open notebooks filled

with the smallest handwriting she'd ever seen jammed onto each
page. The writing was in English. She walked to one end of the
case. The work was titled *The Copyist*. The explanatory text fixed
to the glass was in German, the only English words in quotation
marks, "found art" and "unknown outsider." The artist was
nameless, maybe not an artist at all, she couldn't tell. She bent
close to the cramped script and picked up one of the magnifying
glasses resting on the case, chained at intervals. The opened
pages in the first book described Saint Jerome translating the
Vulgata from Hebrew and Greek into Latin. For centuries the
translation was copied by hand, sometimes in monasteries.

> As mendicant orders emerged, small, light, pocket Bibles
> were required for traveling. The copied text was compressed
> and the pages became animal, made from the thin, strong,
> luminous skin of unborn calves. The illuminated human fig-
> ures drawn in the margins were given rouged cheeks to sug-
> gest health amid the plagues of the times. The best copyists
> were illiterate, unable to anticipate letters or phrases or to
> think they'd found errors to be corrected. I myself am illiter-
> ate, copying what I see to the letter.

She walked past ten or twelve notebooks to the last one, at the
end of the case, and through the magnifying glass read the open
page.

> Episode One of the murder show ends with the woman just
> short of dead. In Episode Two a woman is missing, the worst
> of fates presumed. Episode Three is happening now. The
> woman is in the next room or next building, or, yes, two

doors down. The frame only appears when I turn off the screen but that hardly ever happens. The episode now unfolding affords me no escape. I press my Guide for Episode Four but it hasn't happened yet. The woman has just lost a job that she loves, the workplace she worked in is distant. She sits in a room and reads and reads and of course she is just asking for it. We have a connection, the women and I. Without me they don't exist. A movement at the window, is that you? The screen only appears when I kill it.

She stood back from the case. Now she wanted to know what she was looking at. Where and when had the notebooks been found? Was someone making money off a record of mental illness? Or was the copyist an invention, like Koss's anarchists and antianarchist? Of course he was. "I myself am illiterate." She wanted to put her fist through the case.

The moment she stepped out of the gallery a car turned the corner in front of her, emitting a high squealing, several squealings overlaid, and moved away down the street. The sound returned Celia to herself and she remembered her purpose. A young man wearing a cheap faux-satin jacket passed by, headed toward Grau. She stepped in a few paces behind him and the windowlights reflecting in the folds of his back moved and died in the rhythm of his steps. He stopped suddenly and saw, just before she did, a wasted man sitting in the doorway to the gallery she'd earlier found closed. His head was shaved. He said something in German and the man in front of her responded briefly and walked on. Celia expected to be addressed but the seated man called after the other, something like "Sie brauchen one two." She kept her eyes forward and continued. The walking man, who seemed a kind of protection now, passed by Grau and kept going. The man in the doorway hadn't noticed her. He watched the jacketed man and then suddenly he saw her and his face became a cartoon astonishment. He didn't quite meet her eye, but focused on something just in front of her, though there was nothing in front of her. Then he looked down quickly to the palmscape of his hand and whatever he saw there caused him to look back at her and stand and hurry away down the street.

She entered Grau. Viewed from inside, the crowd now had dimension. Its shape suggested a character. Part of the character was the noise it made, the high chatter babble of such spaces anywhere. Most of the patrons held glasses of wine or beer. They tended to look past one another, even while conversing. No one recognized her, apparently. She was repeatedly assessed and dismissed. Koss's name beckoned, floating in elongated script on the archway to another room. She walked under the archway.

The second room was enormous. She couldn't imagine how it fit into the gallery she'd seen from the street. She scanned the space for her father but he wasn't there. The script on the wall read *Apokalypse.* Lining the room were boxes, maybe four feet apart, more than the forty-eight memory theaters she'd seen online at Koss's site, maybe twice that many. People stood in ones and twos before them. Their gaze had a certain character of self-loss. They seemed to break from one box and step to the next without removing themselves from the viewing. Only at the first few boxes did people speak now and then. By the fifth or sixth they were into the story, putting things together.

She kept her distance from the walls, stepped into the room's open middle area. She saw at the far end a roped-off space with a stage, a small riser and three empty chairs, a podium and microphone. Soft laughter rose up from nowhere and died. Voices moved in the range of quiet to conversational. The words she could make out were foreign. She stood and took it in, the German murmur. After a time, words came clear. A young couple had taken to meeting each new box by trying to guess what would happen next before peering in. The guesses were in English—"The cave collapses," "The dog drowns," "A message from the sponsor"—and brought on little pulses of dread. They smiled and put their faces to the box and watched together. Each time, before they moved on, the man touched the woman, on the shoulder, the hip.

Now and then people crossed the floor and skipped forward or back, not noticing Celia, but most progressed box to box around the room. Still another room led off this one, she now saw. She stepped into it, a longer, narrow rectangle. Her father and Koss weren't here either. This space was more crowded than the first, there were bottlenecks forming at some of the boxes. The people moved differently, with an urgency. Some laughed nervously at what they'd seen. One woman, older, in severe glasses, held her chest in a gasp or mock gasp. There was something a little raw in the voices. The viewers were slightly losing their cool.

When the first box came open Celia let herself be drawn to it. Through the glass she saw herself standing at a window. She wore pajama bottoms, a red T-shirt. Then the scene changed and she was at a door, letting a dog out into a bright winter day, a woods in the near distance. End of box. She waited a few seconds and it played again. She tried to study it, to understand why it felt famil- iar. She didn't recognize the house. The dog looked slightly less like Hartley than she looked like herself.

The second box gave no clues, yet the feeling of familiarity per- sisted, became almost acute in its refusal to hold still. It produced

a kind of déjà vu that she understood would be particular to her
only, so strange were the conditions. Lia, Koss-Lia, was sitting at
a computer, extracting something from a plastic bag. She plugged
the thing into a port. On her screen up came a scene and the camera
zoomed in until the new image filled the light box. A woman not
Koss-Lia was leaving the same house, in summer, to meet someone
arriving in a brown-and-orange pickup. The truck stopped and a
dyed-blonde young woman emerged. End of box.

A space had opened near the entryway and now she saw on the
wall the title for this part of the show. *After James.* The words
dropped inside her for a few moments before going off. She'd told
no one the name of her lost child. She said something aloud. The
room seemed to move at great speed.

A new sound came from the adjoining gallery. The lights were
dimmed in all the rooms and people turned to face the little stage
and podium. It was rare anymore, she thought, this feeling of
everyone looking at the same thing in real time. The narrow room
began to empty into the larger one and she stepped into the human
stream and looked back. A few viewers were staying to the end of
the story.

And so she was at the back of the crowd when it began, barely
able to see the speaker. She looked for her father and Koss but it
was hopeless. A young black woman in a light blue headscarf introduced a man whom Celia took to be the curator of the show. He
wore a charcoal, collared shirt. His hair was close-cropped. From
where she was standing he could have been thirty or sixty. He
stepped to the microphone without smile or greeting. She couldn't
follow his remarks but now and then an English word or name or
quotation came clear. She heard "John Dewey" and "William
James Lecturer." She heard, in clean English, "the movie, jazzed

music, the comic strip." The crowd waited, bored and patient, for him to finish and introduce Koss, wherever he was, somewhere on the floor, presumably. All at once she felt someone looking at her. She turned, saw no one, and remembered she'd had these little moments now and then in the past few weeks. They came to her, saying, I've found you, and then they disappeared and she forgot them, the specific character of them, until the next one spoke.

Finally, without the slightest finishing gesture that Celia could detect, the curator moved away and sat on a chair beside the headscarf woman. The lights brightened for a moment and then the room went almost dark and there at the microphone, like an apparition, was Koss himself.

It wasn't clear where he had come from, a magician's trick entrance. He was standing with his arms at his sides, looking downward, as if at papers on the podium, though not quite. He looked as he'd looked at the chateau, same hair, though now dressed casually in an orange T-shirt printed with some design she couldn't make out. He rocked slightly forward and back once. When his voice came she felt the first pinch, a slight shudder. The voice sounded wrong, was mic'd differently than the others had been, and now something was stirring in the crowd. There were whispers and shushes. A woman standing about fifteen feet in front of Celia turned around open-mouthed and made a shocked expression at someone, her boyfriend, and Koss rocked back and forth. It was the same movement exactly and Celia realized only then that he was on a loop. His voice was flat and declarative, recorded, in keeping with Koss-not-Koss, false-Koss, the artist there and not, present not-present, holographic-Koss. She detected no tone of apology. Some people were pushing forward to the image, others drifting back or turning and leaving. A few looked pleased, some confused, others were nodding, apparently certain that they knew what point was being made. Celia wanted to stop them, ask them what it was they thought they were seeing.

When she reached the foot of the riser he rocked once again. She examined the others close by. It was obvious now that her father wasn't here. No one noticed her, she was among several who'd come closer to look, and just as Koss said what sounded like the title of the show, she stepped onto the riser. Holding steady through the surge in her blood to be so close to him, his presence and specific, immaculate absence, in a gesture she thought of as a refusal of her consent, she passed her hand into him at chest level and let the colors spill onto her arm and the hologram and voice continued on their loops. She withdrew her hand and looked out at the crowd. Those near the stage stared dumbly, delightedly, and seemed to think she was part of the event, as of course she must be, breaking the illusion, the continuity, in a show called *Apokalypse*. Then she saw a lone figure at the back of the room. He wore jeans and a black hooded jacket, the hood was deep, it obscured his face. Only when he lifted his hand did she see the object, and at that moment she was taken by her elbow. With the nervous look of someone appeasing a madwoman, the curator gestured for her to return to the floor.

Just as Koss's voice cut out and his image died there came the first explosion from the back of the room. The hooded man raised the hatchet again and smashed a second box, which fell to the floor, and he struck it again and stepped to a third and smashed it and now he was on the run as men from the audience rushed him and he made the door and the crowd opened like a hand.

The gallery emptied onto the street. The curator and the headscarf woman who'd introduced him were standing over the destroyed boxes. Celia stepped off the riser and passed through the room and out onto Lindenstraße. People stood along the sidewalk, on the street, looking this way and that, some still holding their wineglasses. Presumably others were off in pursuit. A young man with something tattooed on the side of his neck, parentheses, approached and said something in German, then asked in English, "Are you the woman in the boxes?" Celia looked back into the gallery through the window. The curator was on his cellphone, talking, a brief smile. The headscarf woman was using her phone to take pictures of the wreckage. She shot and tapped, shot and showed the curator, who nodded and tapped.

The parentheses man who'd approached her gave up, drifted into the crowd. When the curator walked into the main gallery, Celia went back inside. She passed through quietly and unobserved. The curator and the headscarf woman were huddled with their phones. Celia returned to the narrow room, *After James*, now empty, and looked into the last box.

In it was a flood. The water carried Koss-Lia past floating wooden swing seats and mailboxes, a column of smoke shunting into view and away. She tumbled under the surface and up again, reeling past crows hopping in branches in stark alarm. The surface was not constant, it moved at varied speeds. Blood furled in the current and the animation sped up, shapes streaked into colors, night changed to morning in all of three seconds. She'd washed up in the crotch of a tree. Shadows swept across her and slowed into real time. She dropped from the tree and crawled, mudslick, the last human. But no, another shadow covered her now, a looming human shape. She lifted her head, the video shifted to Koss-Lia's perspective, but she saw no one. She looked down at the shadow, fully there, and again looked up and now there was a small boy, looking at her. End of box.

She felt nothing or at least not whatever she assumed viewers were supposed to feel, a hopeful ending. Somewhere in the fuller story, box to box, someone would have gone missing. Who was it and had anyone noticed?

Except for possibly being cheap and sentimental, the ending didn't disturb her, not like the earlier boxes had, the ones with scenes from her real life. What disturbed her came later, the next day on the transatlantic flight. All around were screens playing the same or nearly the same movies and TV shows, staggered at different intervals, and she would not admit that her father had disappeared, would not acknowledge the dread she felt, and she looked out the window at the bright table of water, thinking, how many times in one year will I cross this ocean? The screen map was in Spanish. Océano Atlántico. When she sounded it out to herself, for a moment, she felt suddenly alone, with no one around, no passengers, no plane even, just a lofted mind, and then just as surely it all resumed around her and she remembered two moments from the previous night.

She pictured the curator on his cellphone as she'd seen him through the gallery window. His brief smile, there and gone, had escaped him, she realized. He'd corrected himself but she'd seen the smile, and now she wondered if the whole gallery had been the stage. Maybe the hologram had been a misdirection, and she'd really sold it. Had Koss vandalized his own show? If so, he must have seen her, recognized her, but instead of doing anything real like coming forward and addressing the crowd, introducing her, or at least speaking to her, he'd played his found advantage to the end.

She'd left the gallery feeling hollow. The crowd had mostly dispersed. She formed a vague intention of heading for a cross street to catch a cab. Walking behind her, close enough for her to hear, was the English-speaking couple who'd tried to guess what would happen next at each box. She recognized their voices and was happy to hear them again. The overheard conversation, little bursts of shared meaning, kept her feet on the ground.

"Where did you go?" The woman sounded American.

"I was looking for that guy who was here when I came in." The voice was maybe Nordic but his English was near perfect. "The Turkish guy selling drugs to the art lovers."

"I keep getting propositioned by Turks and Spaniards and Greeks. The continent's collapsing into Germany."

"He said he had something that makes you see ghosts."

A cab approached from the other direction and Celia flagged it. It U-turned and came to the curb and the couple ran past her, the woman nearly brushing her shoulder, and got in. As the man closed the door she stepped to the window and bent down, peering through the glass at them, but they didn't see her and were laughing with the driver, who checked his side mirror and pulled away.

Now in the plane, looking at the water, trying not to look at the screens, she was struck by the obvious truth that she was a ghost, a ghost who made her way in the world, unaware that she was a ghost. That was why the drug dealer had been alarmed to see her. He had the drug in him and knew her for what she was and it sent him down the street.

How long had she been in this state? Since the cave day. She'd first had the intuition as they descended the mountain. She was dead, not just dead inside, but dead inside the mountain. Her father was there, too, with her in the chamber. He was missing from this world, the outer one, so of course she couldn't find him. But how had she managed to book plane tickets and hotel rooms? How had she done the work at the dig and secured an ancient tooth to carry around in a bag? Now that she thought of it she couldn't remember details about the actual transactions at counters and reception desks, but then that was sometimes the experience of traveling. It suspended you in a state of nonthought, nonperception. She recalled being in the presence of others, the people at the dig and in the gallery, but all actual conversations could have been old ones that echoed in the present, remote exchanges with her father and sister. Maybe all that she thought of as recent had happened long ago. The present was populated entirely with returns from the past.

And yet here she was in the plane, in her own seat. She turned and looked at the young man beside her. He wore headphones and stared grimly ahead at his movie and seemed not to notice her at all.

"Is it good?"

He didn't hear her. She reached over and tapped his screen with her finger—had she ever done anything so intrusive?—and asked the question again.

His mouth opened slightly. He was looking at her finger, or where her finger had touched his screen, and then he touched the screen himself and put the movie on pause. He took his headphones off and looked at them as if he'd never seen them before, then looked at Celia.

"It's all right," he said. She told herself to remember this, being addressed. The young man said the movie was about an Iraqi man in Texas who returns from prison to his new hometown, where everyone else is white or Mexican. "He did time for arson but they all think he's guilty of murder but they never found a body so we don't know for sure."

Celia nodded. It all made beautiful sense to her.

She said, "It's very hard to hang on to, a whole life."

"I guess. Did you want out?"

"No thanks."

She turned, comfortably seated and alive, and looked at the sky. She touched her finger to the bottom lip of the plastic window molding. Below, the shadow of the plane moved along a bank of white clouds and she felt someone, maybe herself, looking down at her in the real plane from a distant place and time.

5

IT WAS A SMALL PLACE VERGING A SMALL TOWN. HE
entered the diner wearing a green canvas vest, cargo pants, walking
shoes, intent expression, sun hat in hand. She slid out of the booth
and hugged him, no longer than usual, and she remembered he
always felt smaller and lighter than she expected, and they took
their positions with a view of the highway and distant mountains.

The waitress was in her forties, bob cut, name-tagged Deena.
She took their orders by memory, said them back wrongly, and
took them again and was gone.

On the table the tube with the ancient tooth inside it. He held it
up to the window and looked at it briefly, nodded, dropped it into
his shirt pocket. From another pocket he produced a small spotted
doll of wire and leather and set it before her, a gift.

"A Hopi boy was selling them. They're not sacred in themselves, as I understand it, not like the larger ones. This is Little
Fire God."

She left the little god on the formica surface to act as it would.
Witness, arbiter, junk. The place was half-full, a few diners at the

counter. The neighboring booths were empty. He reached across and took her coffee and sipped it. His hand tilted slightly at the wrist, as if the cup were heavy. His movements were muted. He seemed underslept or enduring an excess of gravity.

"China," she said.

"I didn't specifically say."

"You said somewhere vast and foreign."

"With a distant early warning system for outbreaks in the remote villages and a history of controlling the news."

"China."

She'd picked up his message between flights, in Toronto. His voice had sounded doubled, as if on relay. He said if she was willing to change her route home he could meet her the next day in New Mexico. A ticket was waiting for her at the American Airlines desk. More details to follow. Here they came.

He said he'd been "spirited away." In low tones of divulgence he said that a few years ago he'd been invited to give a talk on extinctions and ancient disease at a national laboratory. He became a kind of consultant, "or really just a name on a list," in exchange for access to the world's best genetic-sequencing technology. Nothing had ever been asked of him, but last week he'd been waiting for a plane out of Cozumel and the first one to land after the storm had come for him, a small jet carrying two strangers, a government medical officer and a woman in uniform. The man and woman seemed the more plausible for being easy to picture, Celia thought, picturing them two-dimensionally. They'd called him into the field, briefed him on the plane.

Days of half-formed thoughts presented themselves to her all at once to be dismissed—the thought that he was sick or drowned or lying in thick greenery somewhere, victimized, that Koss had given him a psychoactive drug, that he'd been detained at some airport, unable to call—and yet her concern hung on, as did her childish hurt.

He said he was part of a small team of men and women with deep, specific knowledge, all of them stunned out of their lives. He'd slept twenty hours in five days. In prop planes and vans they traveled to the village and saw the results of the outbreak, mortal trouble in the many hundreds, and then to a large city in the large unnamed country, working with local virologists. The outbreak was yet unreported. The government seemed to think that containing the news meant containing the virus. He hadn't known his messages weren't getting through to her. They'd been blocked by state authorities.

"You've been in China. For the US government."

"We're cooperating."

"You mean China and the CDC?"

"No."

That's why they were in New Mexico, she realized. There was a military national lab ninety miles from the diner. It also explained why he'd known which airports she'd be flying through. She'd been tracked.

Nothing he'd said was so hard to believe, not when you were in the business and knew what she knew, true stories that other people would think were from movies or disaster-preparedness scenarios. And China was the least surprise of all. The place incubated annual flus, SARS, MERS, enterovirus 71. What was hard to believe was how he'd come to be there.

"You have government friends in bioweaponry."

"Biodefense. It seems impossible, I know. But you better be happy they're on the job."

He'd been brought to a Chinese government research center. Now he spoke of illegal foreign weapons stockpiles.

"Any country, the secret labs are all huge. Here they drive cars from building to building. There, I was left alone for a minute in a basement fridge, three acres big."

He said he wasn't sure why he was allowed to see what he'd seen except that his minder was also his translator and wasn't very good at either job. Or maybe he knew exactly what he was doing. Maybe he wanted others to know.

"To know what?"

"That a certain former superpower has acres of aerosolized plague."

The world refused to stop going on around them. The lunch counter was fuller now. Celia wondered, as she did sometimes in this country, how many in the place were carrying guns or had them in their cars. There were ten times more guns down here than there were Canadians in Canada. Knowing what a person came to know, it was work, every day, to take a generous view of the species.

"And you told your military friends here."

"They suspected but had no proof. They wanted to know if it was secure. But empires break apart. Nothing's secure. It only takes one drunken idiot. And we all have stockpiles of those."

Deena brought their food. Out the window was a narrow band of notched, vertebrate clouds. Her anxiety from the past few days was now redirecting or changing to something else, the usual abstract horror with too many points of focus.

He said the outbreak was of some new virus, a variation on something itself still not clearly identified. It killed its host slowly, the better for wide transmission. Of bigger concern, it seemed airborne. He'd been to a makeshift ward holding thirty or forty patients, more streaming in each hour. He tried to say he wasn't a medical doctor, but his handlers dressed him in a biohazard suit and marched him out with these people in their tortured postures. All ages, weak and dying. Reverse-pressure air ducts led to a far wall and a huge fan high up turned slowly and strobed the figures in light and shadow so that they seemed in motion. Their faces contorted in sole notes of pain. He was having trouble telling her the specifics. He said he wouldn't speak of them again.

He asked if she'd seen the strange sunset last night. In fact she had. It had stood ominously, high paneled darks in red, behind the scene she watched from a Santa Fe motel balcony. Pickups and family vans pulled in and out of a parking lot between a True Value and a Liquor Barn. She was jet-lagged and grimy—she had rerouted, her bag had not—and didn't need a sleep aid, but out she went, across the lot. She returned with a screw-top bottle of California merlot and sat on her little balcony, and the sun was still hanging on, and the voices seemed to come from the electric lights, and for a few seconds she couldn't have said where she was or the day or month.

When the air chilled she moved to the bed with the bottle half-empty. The TV's aspect was set wrong, everything flattened, the alarmed weatherwoman's map of North America looked stepped on, while on other channels wars raged, refugees gathered, men cracked jokes, polar bears almost drowned. She was lost in the channels when her phone buzzed.

"It's Hartley," said Indrani. "He's gone." She went over the events repeatedly until Celia had to tell her to stop. She'd taken him up to North Vancouver, to Lynn Canyon Park and their usual spot, creekside. Indrani sat on a large round rock and checked the cell reception to make her weekly call to her brother. Celia knew the rock and could see her vividly, right down to the incipient varicose vein that ran over her shin where it emerged from her skirt. Hartley stood staring into the white water for fish to bark at, ignoring a small group of young people, university student types, who were cooing at him to visit. Only when they broke out sandwiches did he consent to be friendly, walking over, wagging vaguely. A few minutes later when she clicked off the phone she noticed the kids were gone and so was Hartley. She called but he didn't appear. She assumed he'd followed them out. The light was dying and the park would close in minutes. By the time she got to the parking area, her little blue Yaris was the only car. She stayed by it until a bald man in a uniform came to tell her to leave. She explained about Hartley. He closed the park gate and let her backtrack to the creek in the half dark. Of course Hartley was nowhere. "The guy said it was the kids, you can't trust the kids around here. He said there'd been no sign of cougar." Indrani was speaking too fast, in the voice of a woman who'd just lost her only real friend's dog. Together they formed a plan. Indrani would return to the park the next morning and hand out pictures of Hartley with both of their phone numbers. For a few minutes they couldn't stop repeating assertions about the complexity of large parks and the stupidity of certain dogs, and then Celia needed to get off the call. She showered and slept and her dreams wrung her out.

Her bag arrived at the motel room door just before checkout. She changed clothes and set off for the town whose coordinates he'd texted to her. A cheap paper map led her to open desert road, where fragments of the previous night's dreams returned. She'd been on a rocky plain somewhere with smoke in the distance. There were

women in black chadors walking ahead of her and she was a trotting, panting animal, behind them. The women slowed and
looked off along the length of their shadows in the lowering sun
and the horizon turned silver and when Celia looked back to the
sun the women were gone and she felt herself pulled along by a
torrent and she was Hartley, running west. The thing that was her
and her dog passed into the city, their city, creek to river, river to
harbor, out past Burrard Inlet into English Bay, the Georgia Strait,
south past the Gulf Islands, across the border into the Juan de
Fuca, and out with the tide to the Pacific. She floated without
effort, unafraid, and the tide shifted and she washed up on a wide
empty beach, scenting something wonderful on the air. She woke
up crying but still dreaming and in her dream she walked out into
the night along neighborhood streets of sleeping arts-and-crafts
houses and then she was on Jericho Beach sitting on one of the long
timber logs laid out parallel to the waterline and looking at the
freighters dimly lit against West Vancouver, tucked into the pocket
of the measureless feeling she'd had looking out from the cave
mouth in France.

She checked her speed, which seemed wrong, and then remembered the numbers were in miles, not kilometers. She thought of
caves and towns, places people gathered against fear. In the West
of the new century was a state of incipience so pervasive that when,
every so often, close to home, you lost something, when it slipped
over the edge, gone for good, you felt the shame of relief finally to
have had your fear endorsed. Only then, in the diner, with the
whiff of disinfectant rising from the formica, did she remember
that in the dream she'd detected a faint note of urine, as if some
animal, four-footed or two, had marked her dreamscape as his
own. He had spread his entire genome into the imaginary earth.

We used to think our bodies and lives were ours alone. But even the stories of them were told and read differently now in the languages of science. Today a life seemed borderless or the borders had been redrawn by technologies and their mock infinitudes. Consciously or not, we kept emitting ourselves. Even our traumas, it turned out, imprinted genetically. Our sharpest memories could be pissed along, if not pissed away. And so the smell. Someone in his unique code, there and fully absent, had been with her on the beach in her dream.

He said he had pictures to show her and passed her his phone. He'd taken them thereabouts the previous day, shots of petroglyphs and presumed sacred places. She paused over a young boy riding a donkey, the only image with life in the frame.

"My picture albums online," she said. "Those were mine, for us."

She could read his every motion so that when he sat back and cocked his head to look at her the way he looked at a problem in the field, shards that didn't add up, she realized it hadn't been him. They arrived at the next thought together.

"Your sister, she doesn't always consider the consequences."

"She does, actually."

Koss had given Chrissy a way to infuriate Celia through the pretense of claiming her for art.

"I thought you'd assented. I'm surprised Armin didn't tell me he'd contacted her." His very name uncolored things. "I know you think I misread him, Lia. It's hard to accept that you might have a point. But he gave me a lot of direction."

"'Gave.' Past tense?"

"In Cozumel he told me he was disappearing, wouldn't say where to. In the art world, you disappear and people sell it. The story, the mystery, the disappearance itself. I think he might be at the chateau. Or else he's here somewhere, in America." He glanced out the window, as if Koss might walk by. "I'm told you routed home through Berlin. You saw the show?"

"I thought I might find you."

"The idea was I'd collect you in Troy and surprise you with a trip to the show. It's in London next, *Apokalypse*. The gallery wants to play up the mystery-woman angle. They want to make you the new Mona Lisa."

She was a better Picasso, all cubes and planes, having lost perspective on what used to be her life. Along the row of booths she could see the tops of a few heads above the seat backs, dipping to the forks and spoons, bobbing up again, each in its world of thought.

"I'm thinking of getting off the grid," she said. "Leaving my job and just moving to the middle of nowhere."

He stopped chewing his french fry, stopped his hand midway to the plate. The coming end of the world was one thing, but the idea she might quit her job really alarmed him. She said she'd been thinking about it, indirectly, even unconsciously, not in a way she'd articulated to herself.

The moment ended, the chewing resumed.

"Why would you do that?"

She looked at him, this man who carried gods in his pockets. They were inside the floating particles of dozens of old conversations. Now and then over the years it seemed they'd switch positions, the wandering one and the one too bound to a sensible mind. She didn't know her position now. At least that was something.

"I've had a strange time."

"Since the cave."

"I don't know when it began. I just need it to end." If she described it to him he'd say that a strangeness had been visited upon her, and she would have to decide if she should tell him about the lost pregnancy. She supposed that the memory lapses, her vivid moments of déjà vu in the gallery, her fanciful notions of being a ghost, these could be made sense of as the mind's casting around for understanding after the body had sized things up and declined to bring a new life into the world. At the time, the loss hadn't devastated her but it did contain meaning, and in not pursuing this meaning, she'd left herself open to further losses.

A wind kicked up a tall dust devil and held it before them briefly before dashing it against the window. When it was gone he kept looking out to where it had appeared. "Some Apaches think that up in the Superstition Mountains there's a bottomless hole that connects to the lower world, and the winds that blow up into ours cause havoc and dust storms."

"I hope you're not planning to crawl down it," she said.

"It's what you're considering."

"Like father, like daughter."

"But I haven't quit my life. When I'm done at the lab I'm heading to Colorado to see old friends. There's an ancient dry lakebed up there with hundreds of extinct species perfectly preserved."

Extinction was all the rage now, he said. Funds were streaming in. His academic friends would put him up for a few days in a grand hotel. The oldest bones by day, the newest cocktails at sundown.

"Will you tell your friends about China?"

"They'll all know soon enough."

"What do they make of the new you? There can't be a lot of god seekers among them."

He smiled. "I seem to make some of them nervous."

"They must like that you still tickle the ivories now and then."

He described the Colorado lakebed. The ivories to be tickled there belonged to mastodons.

"*Mammut americanum*," she said.

"That's my girl. And giant ground sloths and *Castoroides* beavers the size of black bears." He described the creatures drinking in the shallow water when an earthquake liquefied the sand. They dropped a few feet, struggled. The quake ended and they were trapped, some with their heads above water, some below. "Whole families lost where they stood. I'm still amazed at such a finding but the terribleness of it stays longer in the throat than it used to."

The conversation was full of deathbeds. She wanted free of it but the time was theirs and they drew it along, outlasting the lunch crowd, through the end of Deena's shift, they kept talking, about lakes and monsters, ancient calendars and codices and number systems, and Celia realized, and knew her father realized, that they were each preparing the other for an ending. One would lose the other before long. How could they know such a thing? She saw the thought take hold in him. He looked away again, out the window.

"Here's an idea," she said. "This time that I'm taking off, what if I took it with you? What if you promised to stop flying around and I came to live with you for a while?"

He'd reject the offer. He'd find the setup custodial.

"I'd love you to live with me. But I won't stop the flying around. I'm going after things, Lia."

They'd reached an impasse. It was terrifying. When the dishes were cleared away, they finally fell silent, and Celia felt her state progressing toward the absurd. Had she already considered getting off the grid, or had learning of Koss's disappearance sparked the idea? There he was again, robbing her of something, a clean, sure gesture. All these disappearances promised some final perfection of irony.

"I have a car to return, a plane to catch. Thanks for the little god." She took her gift from the table and pocketed it.

"There are more of those handmade dolls now than there are mountain gorillas or finless porpoises."

They couldn't help themselves. Nowhere a safe parting line.

She got to her feet and he looked suddenly lost. He stood and they hugged. She turned and walked the length of the diner. Against a heaviness in her limbs she reduced all thought to pure motion. As she stepped through the door, a woman moved past her and a young man caught the door and held it for Celia, who nodded to him. They were eye to eye in a flash of recognition, though at the same time she knew they'd never met. She was in the parking lot, at her rented car, when she turned around and saw him looking in the reflection of the door, which he was holding at an angle to see her. Then he stepped inside and the next thing she knew she was on the highway.

In the distance the dust devils began to appear in numbers, four or five at a time. She drove past broken scrub, wire fences and cattle gates, short trees bent and swollen at the joints, an old silver car plugged dead in its ruts years ago. She tried to call Indrani for an update on Hartley but had entered a cold spot and the call wouldn't send. The highway ran on in cursive tarpatch. Cacti and creosote, an apron of burlap desert spread to the base of a low mountain.

Miles passed without a cell signal and in time the signs stopped rolling up. No distance to Santa Fe, no posted speed limits or highway number. Without the markers she crossed into the pure size and duration of the great west of things. A small dark cloud out ahead of a mass had assumed the shape of a black flint carving and then it stalled and seemed to penetrate the torso of the larger cloud. She'd seen it, a rudely tooled piece of rock, flat black stone, and could still sort of feel it in her thoughts, vivid, particular, and she wondered what the species had done to itself, what utility there was, in evolving the power to see likenesses. The persistent presence in mind of things that are not. She was coming around to the idea.

The road surface changed and a white noise set in. She drove into yellowing sky and the more distant mountains lost their shadows and then themselves were lost. She was either at the onset of something huge or already in its aftermath. What she felt wasn't fear but a whirling certainty. A high wall of approaching dust was drawing over all, a shuttering lid, closing the mountains, the plain. As she slowed and before the black road disappeared she saw or thought she saw the square cab of a pickup at some distance in the mirror but then the mirror was shut too. On the signal arm she found the lights, the wipers fore and aft, but nothing helped. She needed to move to the shoulder but what if the truck lost its line and didn't see her in time, there was no seeing anything now. She tried to stay in motion but could not and drifted over, trying to feel the edge of the road through the tires. She stopped. A headwind blew the dark to other darks of different intensities.

She looked for the truck to loom up and move by her but it wouldn't appear. Imaginary things stay in the mirror but real things come to pass. What was real would come to pass, all things and their kinds come to pass.

From nowhere a deer buck shot out of the murk and slammed itself into her hood. It fell, struggled up and fell again, its antlers cantilevered as if hung too far forward, got up and bounded off with one front leg flopping uselessly as the hail began with two clean pops and then set in full force all at once in a crushing sound filled with trace frequencies. The stones shot off her windshield and danced before her and when it seemed they couldn't fall any harder the wind reversed and the windshield cleared for a few seconds as if to let her read the ice denting the hood in a storm of notational symbols. And then there it was, the truck, square behind her, sitting more or less on her tail. The caution lights flashed—she'd forgotten to put hers on—and up high sat a figure in the seat, motionless, waiting.

She kept checking her gauges, she didn't know why. The hammering sky drove out all thought. Then a shock of sharp webbings on the glass and they were coming down like grapefruits and the whole windshield bent inward and separated and punched sheetform into the car. She felt the wind as she drew her legs up and threw herself over the seat onto the floor but the rear window was blooming constellations and now it shattered, the hail ricocheting off the back dash and bursting around her like cut-glass tumblers, and she couldn't find cover for her head. Beneath the passenger's seat a little plastic man, some kind of armored superhero, lay lost and perfectly protected. A blue, articulated arm. Then the strike. A stone hit the back of her head and she almost passed out but the pain broke clean through and she was taking more direct hits when the door opened and someone had her by the ankles. She struggled and kicked but this creature was hugging her knees now and drew her out. At her feet she saw not a head but a spade head with arms and a voice shouted at her, a flat spade for a head covering and the handle fixed in place along the spine, shouted to get under the car. She hit the ground and rolled even as she was pushed under the chassis. The legs ran back to the truck and she dropped her face to the asphalt and said three times over what the fuck.

She was lying half on the shoulder with the heat of the pavement bisecting her body even as everything in her field of vision turned glassy. The sound alone would kill her. She looked out at the truck tires as the hailstones came slanting now in spears and white fists and ice sprayed into her eyes. One of the truck's headlights burst and the bulb sprung and dangled impossibly from a filament that seemed hardwired to her chances. Then the hail stood vertical again and an outer sheet appeared surely defined in the air and moved off the vehicles and into the ditch and the desert ground until enough distance opened that the sound changed to muffled percussives and dull thuddings that returned Celia to herself and her differentiated pains.

Minutes later she was sitting next to a russet hound with welding goggles around its neck. There were bloody mappings on her palms, a knot on the back of her head. The torn fabric of her pant legs stuck to the cuts on her knees and shins. The driver's name was Catty or Hattie and she tried to retrieve Celia's things but the mangled car trunk wouldn't open. Now they were moving through a hard rain. Celia hadn't been able to say anything when asked for her name. Hattie said Celia was in shock but she needed to say how bad she was hurt.

"I'm Celia. Cut and bruised."

At the sound of her voice the dog turned his head and looked at her.

"That's Corban. He only gets to ride up here when the weather goes sideways."

The truck's windshield, more vertical than hers, was cracked but in place. Her rental was basically plastic. She couldn't remember the make and model, kingdom and domain, the very idea of kinds.

"Sideways."

"That's the worst I've ever seen. Look back there." She jabbed her thumb toward the truck bed. It was full of ice and orange sludge. A pitchfork and spade sat on top, the remnants of wicker baskets. "That used to be root vegetables, apples, and carrot tops. The horses'll miss their treats for a few days."

"Where are we going?"

"We're going to the hospital in town and then calling your car people and getting you a new car. I'll come back later with a crowbar and get your stuff. Where were you headed?"

"It just came out of nowhere."

"Everything does."

Then Hattie was talking about horses. Celia looked at her now. She was thin and narrow-featured, maybe in her forties, a woman pretending not to be shaken. She wore a green rayon shirt, jeans, work boots. She drove with her hands at eight twenty. They were all, her clothes and hands, wet and mud-stained. On the dash was a roll of duct tape and a knife, and Celia saw that the back window slid open and she put it together, how Hattie must have pulled the spade and the dog into the cab, but how she could have taped the spade to her back while inside this small space would not easily resolve in her sense of things.

"I don't need a hospital. Nobody's ever saved my life before. How is it we aren't dead?"

"Maybe we are. I was hoping in the next world I'd be smarter or prettier. I'm the same except my truck's banged up and smells of wet dog."

She kept talking. She ran a ranch for troubled girls. There was some kind of therapy involving the care of horses.

"The girls come from all over, mostly cities. They've only seen horses on TV. You know anything about horses?"

She'd read about equine immunostimulants from dendritic cells. Did that count?

"I think I'm scared of them."

"They feel the same way about us, most of them, until you spend time to make friends. You have to kind of earn away the fear."

The rain had let up but she only now noticed. She asked about the girls. Hattie said they were what you'd think. Abuse survivors, addicts, kids with kids they'd had to give away or would have to soon.

"One of them hadn't said a word for months when she came to me. Then I found her in the barn telling fibs to a mare."

The road was white with crushed ice that moved under them in floes and now Celia couldn't recall where she was or how she'd gotten there. Through the side window the scrub gave way to a tufted grass plain. They passed cattle lying in a field, some of them writhing, some dead. A calf stood under a tree from which it was unlikely ever to move. A truck door opened and a man stepped out with a rifle. Hattie saw it too. Her face lost its set.

"Lord. Where we find ourselves."

She saw Hattie look in the rearview and away. There'd been something about horses.

"Will the horses be okay?"

"This kind of thing is local. I'm still twenty miles from here. Not that there's ever been this kind of thing."

"And we're still alive."

"Well, I'm taking a clue from Corban. He looks alive and, see, he turns his head when I say his name so that's a good sign for me, and I'm talking to you. The sky gives you a beating like that, makes you feel twice as alive." She turned to Celia and smiled. There were grains of ice in her hair. "Feel it?"

When they reached the ranch Celia opened her door and Corban scrambled over her and fell out onto his chest and ran up to the house. It was three stories, wood and stone, dormered, with trees shading a porch. She got out and stood beside the truck. At the screen door a tall black teenage girl appeared and came out onto the porch and smiled as Corban wagged madly at her feet. Hattie asked her about the storm and the girl said they'd seen it in the distance was all.

"Jana, this is Celia. She'll need dinner and a bed."

Jana led her to a second-floor room with a view of a little river and handed her a towel, as if she'd been expected. She showered and cleaned the red stars on her hands and knees and a round-faced white girl came to the bathroom door with a green cotton dress and took Celia's clothes for washing. She said to call her May but it wasn't her real name because she was in hiding. No one knew where she was, except her older brother knew she was somewhere. She asked Celia who had sponsored her and she said no one, she was just a guest for the night, and May said that Hattie had told them it might be longer. Celia asked about a phone but May said the line had been dead for hours. There was no internet in the house, Hattie wouldn't have it, and no TV. The radio said the storms were still out there.

She found herself in the kitchen helping Hattie prepare a green chili. The two girls she'd met joined them and asked her questions about where she was from and what state Canada was in and what the hailstorm had been like and after a few minutes Celia couldn't talk anymore, felt weak, and had to go outside and sit on the porch. At some point a woman around her age came out and asked if she was all right. The woman sat on the porch steps, leaning back with her limbs slightly splayed, and stayed with her, saying nothing.

May brought Celia and the woman bowls of chili and they ate watching a skinny blonde girl lead a gray horse up from the river, both of them covered in mud, and stand across the yard brushing it and then lead it under an arch made of punctured garden hose so that a rain fell on them and then she led the horse into the barn and the woman with Celia said, "Those two are in love." May collected their bowls and returned a few minutes later with three schoolbooks and sat on the steps and began to read and murmur to herself. The books had cracked, worn spines, barely legible titles. *Introducing Biology. A World of Literature. History Now.* Then the skinny girl went into the house and came out with her dinner and sat with May and they read side by side. The skinny one had washed her hands but mud was caked along her bare slight arms.

Celia went up to her room and lay down and listened to the sounds in the house. She woke after midnight with a fist in her head and lay there eyes open in pain. Past the mounds formed by her feet under the sheets she watched the ruled score cast on the wall by the moon as a breeze moved the latched shutters and the slat lines shifted and fixed, shifted and fixed. In the furrowed light dimly hesitant on the wall were parade grounds, canalscapes, microchips, fork tines and barrel staves, ribs breaching a cave floor. The images fired briefly and died. A pattern held in the sequence of things never fully read or proved before the pattern changed. Some mechanism of perception could make forgetting and knowing the same. The thought made no sense, there was something to it. At least the headache located her. When had she last felt fully and surely composed? In time the pain eased and she sat up, stood. She put on the cotton dress.

In the dim glow of a horseshoe night-light plugged into a hallway outlet she found outside her door the plastic superhero that wasn't hers, her suitcase, computer bag, and smashed cellphone. She took the phone and made her way in the semidark along the silent hall. The doors she passed stood open and the rooms were dark and empty. Moonlight through the windows guided her down the stairs and into the main room. She took a chair near an open screened window and a cold woodstove with a yard light fixed in the door glass. She felt like the issue of a stranger's dream. The house seemed empty, as if no one had lived there for years, but down the hallway the nails of the dog clicked along the pine floor. She had never before so needed just to sit still.

She pressed a button and examined the display on her phone. She'd received a text from her father or Indrani that must have arrived on the road somewhere, what seemed a single, broken word caught in the phone's spidering glass, the crystal letters fragmented, busted back to cuneiform, refracted out of sense. There was no signal. She stared at the shattered characters, trying to believe they read "safe" or "found" and continued to stare until they weren't characters at all but little shards of need caught in a webbing, the need to say, to be said to, and she supposed she was the webbing, still in shock, and she allowed herself to believe that what could be known was formed by what could not be, that at times the otherworldly came hammering down as if to reshape the tired realities, exhausted of force. And she was the webbing that radiated like light shined on a cave wall, like glass in broken memory theaters, in burst ice, shattered windshield and head-lights. She was the webbing was river mud caked on the arm of a girl trying to memorize kingdom phylum class and sonnets, the dates of imperial centuries, the definitions and numbers not taking, thinking instead of her new friend May who was think-ing of her older brother watching the news, some foreign streets on fire and where was she, his sister hiding somewhere, closing the old schoolbooks and thinking of her friend who learned today only how a certain gray horse liked a certain firm brushstroke and stood foursquare thinking blood bone I am thinking back into the girl into Celia thinking once you break it all up, the old ways of seeing and saying, you can know anyone, be right inside it, the thing itself.

The nails clicked on but Corban didn't appear. She shut her eyes and the sound stopped. When she opened them someone sat across from her in the dark.

"You were dreaming."

At first she thought it was the woman who'd been with her on the porch, but then it wasn't.

"I don't remember."

"You were talking. Not in words."

So she talked in her sleep.

"What's that sound?" asked Celia.

"Generator. The power's gone. I woke and here you are."

"Where? Another place I'm not from."

"None of us is from here. Not a soul."

A breeze moved through the window. Outside the vapor lamp spun insects in a multiple helix, pressed a thin silver dust onto the yard. She used to know the word for the force that drew them to the light.

The woman said, "Phototaxis." Almost a whisper.

Celia turned back. The woman's eyes weren't visible but she was facing Celia and the window. There was nothing to see out there but the light.

"Yes. Phototaxis." Celia nodded. "I don't know your name." Now the woman nodded. "I'm Celia."

"I know."

The woman's motions were the same as her own. Even her posture, sitting back, one foot rafted slightly forward, a reflection.

"One of those hailstones hit my head. I should try to keep awake."

"I'll stay with you."

The woman told a story about the house and the area and a neighbor who lived alone, and Celia tried but could follow only the voice, not the story, which passed by in images. A great fire, a man near the edge of the river and walking at night in the fields under the stars. The story then broke open and covered crowds and cities, planes and handwritten pages and sisters, and in the woman's voice the only question wasn't whether the stories were half-true or dead true but whether they were truthfully told, and though Celia was aware she was dreaming again the things the woman spoke of carried a desperate loneliness that felt the more real when other notes emerged or a chord of them she hadn't heard before.

The next time she opened her eyes the woman was gone. There was no generator. The yard light was there with the moon. Through the window she heard a sound like a great branch snapping far away. She couldn't see into the days ahead. Her eyes closed and when she opened them she had only her name and a shifting on the wall and something moving in the yard that set off the horses and then it passed and all was quiet again.

ACKNOWLEDGMENTS

All gratitude to dear friends Hendrik and Debi Poinar, who find sequences and the stories in them. Here's to their codes and expressions, and their guiding the way to remote caves and the mouths of worlds long past and to come.

For their readings I'm indebted to Gil Adamson, Richard Helm, Ben Lerner, Michael Redhill, and Karen Solie. For great catches, Anne Horowitz, Heather Sangster, and Müge Turan. Thank you Susan, Rob, John, Sandra, Glenna. Thanks to my agent, Ellen Levine, for her wisdom and support.

Thank you, Don.

Thank you to my wonderful US editor, Meg Storey, the All Seer, and to Nanci McCloskey, Cheston Knapp, and the staff at Tin House, people of surpassing imagination. Thanks to Lynn Henry, Anita Chong, Ashley Dunn, and everyone at McClelland & Stewart/Penguin Random House Canada Limited, who saw the novel home in hard weather.

There is no deeper or more exacting a reader than Alexandra Rockingham. She was with me city to city, border to border, and made everything itself by making it better.

With great courage, Ellen Seligman edited this novel. There's no end to what needs saying, no way to begin saying it. She was a friend and I miss her.

© ALEXANDRA ROCKINGHAM

MICHAEL HELM is the author of the novels *Cities of Refuge*, a Rogers Writers' Trust Fiction Prize finalist, a Giller Prize nominee, and a *Globe and Mail* Best Book of the Year; *The Projectionist*, a finalist for the Giller Prize and the Trillium Book Award; and *In the Place of Last Things*, a finalist for the Rogers Writers' Trust Fiction Prize. His writings on fiction, poetry, and the visual arts have appeared in several North American magazines, including *Brick*, where he's an editor. He teaches at York University in Toronto and lives in semirural Ontario.